# OPERATION FIREBRAND: CRUSADE

## Let My People Go

JEFFERSON SCOTT

BARBOUR
PUBLISHING

# OPERATION FIREBRAND: CRUSADE

© 2003 by Jeff Gerke

ISBN 1-58660-676-X

Acquisitions and Editorial: Mike Nappa and Shannon Hill
Art Director: Robyn Martins
Cover: Lookout Design

Published by Barbour Publishing, Inc., P.O. Box 719, Uhrichsville, Ohio 44683,
www.barbourbooks.com

 Member of the
Evangelical Christian
Publishers Association

Printed in the United States of America.
5 4 3 2 1

*For those who suffer in the south of Sudan
and those who try to ease their suffering.*

*For the precious children everywhere
who have been abducted, terrorized, molested, and killed
and their families left behind.*

# ACKNOWLEDGMENTS

I'D LIKE to thank all the advisors and readers who helped with the formation of this book.

For their help with the nation of Sudan and the problems of slavery and slave redemption, I'd like to thank Jok Madut Jok, Jim Jacobson, Peter Hammond, Cal Bombay, Pat Bradley, and John Eibner.

For their military expertise, I must thank Steve Watkins, former Navy SEAL and author of *Meeting God Behind Enemy Lines,* and Chuck Holton, former Army Ranger and author of *A More Elite Soldier.*

For his medical corrections and ideas, I am once again indebted to Dr. Clark Gerhart, author of *Struggling: Finding Lasting Victory over Fleshly Bondage.*

Thanks to my readers: John Miller, Chris Gilbert, Jim Lund, John and Anne Gerke, Stu Ehr, Tim Kizziar, Kirk DouPonce, Robin Gerke, and Gordon Golden. Thanks to Renni Browne for her editorial feedback. Thanks also to Mark Littleton, my editor, for his excellent critical mind applied to this book.

Thanks also to my wife, Robin, for her comments, her prayers, and especially her encouragement to this too-fragile author she married. Thanks to my children for being proud of their daddy. Thanks to my Lord for allowing me to write novels.

# QUOTATIONS

HOPE is an orientation of the heart, an orientation of the spirit. It's the ability to begin something not just because it has a chance to succeed but because it's a good thing to do.

It's not the certainty that everything will turn out well but the absolute conviction that something is worth doing regardless of how it turns out.

VACLAV HAVEL, *Disturbing the Peace*

FEAR God in the matter of your slaves. Feed them with what you eat and clothe them with what you wear and do not give them work beyond their capacity. Those whom you like, retain, and those whom you dislike, sell. Do not cause pain to God's creation. He caused you to own them and had He so wished He would have caused them to own you.

MUHAMMAD

# CAST OF CHARACTERS

## THE REGULARS

THE FIREBRAND team is a squad of specialists who go into the world's hotspots to conduct covert missions of mercy in the name of Christ, armed only with nonlethal weaponry.

## TEAM FIREBRAND

* **Jason Kromer** Leader of the Firebrand team; former Navy SEAL sniper and point man

* **Rachel Levy** Firebrand's language specialist and con artist; drop-dead gorgeous and knows it; former agent for Israel's Mossad

* **Garth Fisher** Firebrand's explosives and escape-and-evasion specialist; former Green Beret; very tall, very muscular, and very bald

* **Lewis Griswold** Firebrand's computer and electronics expert (i.e., geek); youngest member of the team

* **Trieu Nguyen** Firebrand's sniper and doctor; former Olympic sharpshooter and biathlete for Vietnam and then USA; plays the cello

* **Chris Page** Firebrand's point man; former Marine Force Recon; crazed ornithologist; a model's good looks

## THE PROFESSOR AND MARY ANN. . .

* **Eloise Webster** The founder and financier of the Firebrand team; African-American billionaire CEO of defense contractor ABL Corp.

* **Doug "Chimp" Bigelow** Firebrand's operations man; stays behind to monitor the team when they go into the field; former Navy SEAL; paraplegic

* **Jamie Bigelow** Doug's wife and physical therapist

# AUTHOR'S NOTE

SOME OF the images in this book are extremely disturbing and grue-some. It is not my intent to shock or include violence for violence's sake. The reason I wrote it this way—indeed, the reason I've written this book at all—is that I feel I must, under God, draw attention to a hideous reality taking place in the south of Sudan.

What you are about to read is fiction, but only in the sense that it is a fiction-writer's depiction of something that is *reality* for too many innocent people, many of them our Christian brothers and sisters.

# PROLOGUE

THE SUN should rise differently if it is to be a day of death.

But it doesn't.

Anei woke when her brother, Mabior, slipped out of the tukul to milk the cows. It was still dark, but Anei could see her mother sitting up, nursing little Ajok. Her father, her *Wa,* was snoring softly

The air was cool and her mat was warm. But Anei was a Dinka girl approaching marriageable age, and she knew her place. She stood, pulled her red robe over one shoulder, and stepped out into the village.

Stars still punctured the black cloth sky, but milky orange light was already spilling across it from the east. The thatched roofs of the round tukuls grew distinct in her vision. The cows in the large pen to her right complained about the milking, and Anei heard grumpy boys doing their chores. Anei's nose delighted in the rich smell of the cattle byre in the morning. She picked up the water pot and headed for the well.

"Hello, Anei," a boy said behind her in Dinka.

Anei turned. "Oh, hello, Geng. Going to milk the cows?"

"No!" Geng's brow jutted, making his black face look more

15

sullen than usual. "I'm not a child anymore, Anei. This wet season I'll go to the cattle camp."

Anei smiled. "Already? Next you'll be thinking of taking your first wife."

They walked together silently. The village slowly roused itself around them. Smoke from cooking fires sweetened the moment for Anei.

"Anei," Geng said, stopping. "When I take a wife, will you. . . Ah. . . If I. . ." He faltered and looked at her nervously.

Anei clicked her teeth. "Perhaps, Geng."

The boy brightened. He let out a stifled whoop and took the water pot from her hands. "I will take you for my wife, Anei. I will!"

"I said *perhaps*, Geng, not *yes.*" They were walking again. "Do you have the bridewealth? It will cost you lots of cattle to marry me."

"Not yet, but I will by the time we're old enough. Anei, I. . .I think you are beautiful. I will have enough cows for you."

"Then we'll see." Anei took the pot from him. "Now, let a girl do her work."

Geng ran off toward the center of the village, his bare feet kicking up dust turned rosy in the morning light.

"Hello, sun," said Anei softly, approaching the line of girls waiting at the well. "What good luck you have brought me today."

She stopped, looking toward the edge of the village. Something was wrong. She hadn't heard anything, but she sensed she was in danger. Perhaps it was another lioness driven into the village by the war and famine? Perhaps an Antonov bomber at the edge of her hearing? She clutched her water pot.

A woman yelled, *"Jellabah! Jellabah!"*—the word for "Arab." Gunfire erupted around them. Anei saw horsemen break from the brush. Hundreds of horses, ridden by men in head-to-toe white robes and white cloth turbans, thundered toward the village. They shouted and fired their rifles as they came. Swords glinted in the morning sun.

"Wa!" Anei dropped the pot and sprinted toward her hut.

Behind her, the other girls followed; but already Anei could feel and hear horses' hooves coming from that direction, and she knew the girls would not escape.

Across the wide village she could see the horsemen descending on the outer huts, with men on foot following behind, guns or knives in their hands.

Fear gripped Anei's stomach. She felt horses overtaking her from behind, their harnesses jingling and their riders whipping them with cruel sticks. At the last moment she reached Acol Deng's tukul and ducked behind it.

Three riders pounded past her, followed by more than twenty others. Two noticed her and wheeled around, some horrible thought in their eyes. Anei pushed backward, hoping to find Acol's door.

A cry arose from the horsemen who had passed. They had reached the cattle pen and were driving the cattle out. The young boys who had been milking them shouted in fear and tried to run. Anei saw her brother, Mabior, and others of his age-set among the cattle, their curving horns slicing the air like knife blades, their bodies jostling the boys. Mabior looked terrified. The two horsemen who had spotted Anei left her and rushed toward the pen.

Anei coiled to sprint for her family's tukul but heard something crash in the cattle pen. The horsemen pulled down the stick fences. The cattle spilled out, their high, curved horns slashing furiously. She saw Mabior, without so much as a shout, go down beneath the herd.

*Mabior!*

She wanted to run to him, but what could she do?

Two other boys sprang away from the cattle, but the Arabs were ready for them. Men on horseback knocked them aside. Men on foot grabbed them. As Anei watched, the men held out the boys' arms and hacked them off.

The boys fell away, but the men held their gruesome trophies over their heads, showering everything with little boys' blood.

Anei almost fainted, but a crackling sound she knew broke

through to her. Acol's tukul was on fire. The thatch would quickly collapse within the mud walls, burning anything inside or around the hut.

Anei heard Acol screaming inside. She opened the door and found the old woman huddled against the wall, gaping at the roof. Anei pulled her outside. Outside to what?

The Arabs had set the cattle pen on fire, as well as most of the tukuls on the outskirts of the village. Men on horses and on foot—even men on camels and donkeys—thronged the dirt lanes, shooting and shouting and burning. Cattle screamed and fire roared, but above all the air was filled with the cries of Anei's friends and neighbors.

Anei could think only of getting home. She rushed away from Acol, heading toward the center of the village. But it seemed she couldn't take a step without seeing something she had to watch, something her eyes wouldn't let her miss.

In the distance to her right, she saw Abuk running away from the village, her two oldest children holding her robe, the baby in her arms. An Arab rode up behind her and struck her with his rifle. Abuk fell, and the man dropped off his horse and leaped onto her. She fought with him on the ground and her son, Yak, pulled at the Arab's arms. Anei could see the other two children wailing but couldn't hear them.

Finally the Arab backhanded Abuk and turned on Yak. He grabbed his rifle and struck the boy on the head. Then he shot Yak four times. Anei could see the boy's body bounce with every shot. The Arab grabbed Abuk's baby by the leg and cast her through the air as far as he could. She landed on the hard earth and didn't move. Abuk's other daughter lay shuddering in a ball, so the Arab left her alone. He tore at Abuk's robe and then lifted his own and lay over her.

Anei ran again, then paused beside an unburned tukul. Dinka women and children ran by in a pack, fleeing noise and fire like a flock of goats.

She turned back toward Acol's hut, which was now fully engulfed in flame. Three Arabs stood by. One held Acol. The others were holding two cattle boys by the arms. One of them was Mabior. He was limping and bleeding but still alive. With a shove, the men forced the boys and Acol into the fiery hut and held the door shut.

"Mabior! No! Mabior!"

She wanted to save her brother. But again she was paralyzed. If she ran out, the Arabs would throw her into the fire, too. But she had to do something. In her mind she ran to the hut, somehow invisible to the men, and pulled Mabior and the others to safety. But when the vision was over, she found she hadn't moved.

Now she did run, but in the other direction. Even as she went, even as their small voices silenced, their piteous screams echoed inside her soul.

Finally, she saw a hopeful sign. Fifteen Dinka men, the chief and his warriors, charged past her, raising the battle cry and brandishing their spears. The chief held his rifle.

They struck the Arab horsemen like a lightning bolt of black muscle and pride. White-robed Arabs fell from their horses, screeching in pain and surprise. Perhaps no one told them the Dinka might fight back. The chief fired his rifle and Jellabah fell. The warriors towered over the Arabs, more than a match for any opponent.

But then more Arabs rode up. And more still. They surrounded the Dinka, until the horses and the dust and the awful energy of the struggle blotted them from Anei's sight.

She ran.

Her tukul bobbed in her sight. So far it was untouched. She sprinted toward it, her vision blurred by tears. She tripped on something and fell. Gaining her feet, she saw what had tripped her.

A tiny leg. Some Dinka infant's perfectly formed left foot and knobby knee, dusty from playing on the ground. Was it her sister, Ajok's? Anei vomited, her stomach no longer able to absorb the images she was force-feeding it.

The sound of men arguing in Arabic drew her attention. It came from near her tukul. Two men—one in a jellabah and the other in the uniform of the Sudanese army—pulled at a woman as if she were a piece of meat. Anei saw that they were arguing over the most beautiful woman in the village: her mother.

She was naked and appeared half-asleep. She had blood on her face and her cheek looked swollen.

"Ma!"

Anei took two steps toward her mother but then was struck by something from behind. As she fell, her mind registered a horse's heavy hoof clops. Scarcely had she hit the ground, her right shoulder blade burning with pain, when a Jellabah dropped off his horse and tore at her red robe.

His turban came loose and unrolled around his head. His white robe was torn at the shoulder. His skin was as black as any Dinka's, but supposedly he was an Arab and therefore superior. He had a very narrow, ugly face. He mumbled in Arabic and smelled of horse droppings. He held Anei down with a forearm across her chest. With his other hand, he ripped away her robe and lifted his own. She couldn't scream. Only a whimper came out.

Then he fell off her, struck by someone else.

Anei scooted away, holding the shreds of her robe over her. The two men struggled on the ground. One was a Dinka.

"Wa!"

She had never seen her father so fierce. The Arab brandished a long knife, but her father knocked it aside and struck him in the face. The knife came up again, striking her father's leg and bringing out blood, but it only enraged him. He pounded the Arab's face until he stopped fighting back.

He stood off the Arab, but then fell to one knee, gripping the wound in his thigh. Anei ran to him. "Wa!"

"Anei!"

"Wa, why is this happening?"

His look was ferocious, his eyes like the eyes of the Arabs' horses.

"They are Baggara Arabs, Anei, riding with the military train." He gripped her shoulders. "You have to leave the village! Go! Find the SPLA! Bring the rebels here with their guns."

"No, Wa, I want—"

*"Go, Anei!* I can't protect you here. We will all be killed unless you can bring the SPLA with their guns!"

He shoved her toward the east edge of the village, where the thatch fires were already dying down.

"Go!"

As she watched, unable to move, he took the knife from the Arab's hand and limped toward the men raping her mother.

He fell upon them with such power that Anei was amazed. She saw the knife pierce one Arab's neck. The man dropped to the dirt, clutching his throat. His jellabah turned dark red.

The uniformed man rolled off her mother, his pants around his knees. Her father knocked him over, and they grappled for the knife. Her mother wasn't moving.

Suddenly the soldier had a small black gun in his hand. Her father stabbed with his knife just as the pistol went off.

They fell apart, both moaning, neither able to rise.

Her father's face settled to the side. His eyes locked onto hers.

*Go.*

She ran.

The whole village was in flames now, clogged by more men and horses than she had ever seen.

As she ran from concealment to concealment, she saw that the attack had changed. There was less fighting and more stealing. The screams had turned to groans, the gunshots to whiplashes. The Arabs were collecting what food and valuables the village had to offer.

When Anei reached the last tukul on the edge of the village, she scanned the dry steppe between her and the bush atop the ridge. Far on her left, the Arabs were gathering the horses and cattle.

They were also gathering the few Dinka women and children

who had been spared. Their wailing rose over the flames and the hooves. She didn't recognize any of the children from this distance, but she could tell they were mostly girls. The Arabs were forcing the women and older girls to carry away the spoils of their own village.

Geng's brooding face appeared in her mind. Had he been captured? More likely killed: decapitated or burned alive. But maybe he had escaped! Maybe he and others had gotten away into the bush. The thought filled her with energy.

She had to find the SPLA somehow. The Sudanese People's Liberation Army was her village's only hope. Nothing could save the village; but if she found them before the Arabs got away, her friends and family and neighbors wouldn't have to become slaves.

Her fear turned to fury. Somehow she would repay these "Arabs," these black-skinned Jellabah who raided peaceful villages.

And somehow one day she would do what she couldn't do today—what she *should've* done today—to save poor Mabior.

She bolted for the brush a hundred feet away. The heat of the fires receded. The clomping of the hooves, the shouts of greedy men, the tears of abruptly destitute women all dropped away behind her. Now she was Anei, avenger of her village, and nothing could stand in her way.

Except something did.

As she neared the brush, an Arab and four boys sprang out of hiding and grabbed her. She screamed and tore at them like a devil. She scratched a face, broke free, ran. But they caught her again. Again she flailed at them. Then the Arab raised the blunt end of his knife and struck her on the head.

\* \* \*

For the second time that day, Anei awoke.

This time, she was moving. Her neck was very sore and her head throbbed. She saw she was draped across the back of a horse, its haunches under her face and knees. Her arms and feet were tied under the horse's belly. Flies buzzed around her, and the horse's tail swished at them.

Behind her marched a line of horses and people—all connected by a rope. Most of the horses bore riders, but some had infants or food sacks lashed to them. She recognized the Dinka behind her. Women and girls from her village, all balancing valuables or supplies on their heads. She saw Abuk, looking dead but somehow walking. Her oldest daughter was tied to the rope ahead of her. No one cried.

Other horsemen rode beside them, herding all her people's cattle—the source of Dinka wealth and prestige and pride. . .and marriage. She saw one of the boys who had helped capture her. His face had two bloody scratches on it. Good.

She didn't recognize where they were. A line of dark green bushes behind them made her think they'd just crossed a river. But which one?

Unless she died or escaped, she was going to become a slave. How then could she avenge her village and her brother? And her mother, her father, and baby sister? She yanked her wrists, but the rope held her fast. The scratched boy rode close and lashed out with a green acacia stick. It stung her bare back like a burn.

Anei turned her face to the sky then. High above her, floating in a perfect blue pool, was the distant sun.

# PART I

# DOWN TIME

# CHAPTER 1

## DOWN UNDER

THE afternoon sunlight penetrated the lake water, turning it a milky blue and illuminating a school of bream like new quarters with fins.

Jason flipped his own fins leisurely to keep up with the palm-sized fish. He kept to the surface so he could breathe normally through his snorkel while he watched. Freshwater fish mingled with ocean life here, just as the freshwater from the rivers mixed with the saltwater from the estuary,

His back began to sting. It occurred to him that he'd forgotten to put on suntan lotion. He was going to pay for that.

Suddenly the bream flashed silver and vanished into the murkiness. Jason listened, but didn't hear anything unusual through the water. He imagined he could feel the rhythm of the sea. Just three miles to the south, the Indian Ocean merged with the Pacific and washed against Ninety Mile Beach.

Then an alarmingly large form glided into his vision. Teeth and dorsal fins. A gray nurse shark, jaws slightly parted. Jason stopped moving, but his heart rate doubled. The sleek beast was over ten feet long. If it wanted him, there was nothing Jason would be able to do to get away. It swept its unblinking eye over him before sliding away into the murk.

Jason shivered. He angled back toward the boat, looking again for interesting aquatic life. But in his mind all he saw was that round, black eye.

Unaccountably, the face of Damira floated into his memory. He saw her standing there in the rubble of Baikonur City in Kazakhstan, clutching a bottle of water, scared out of her wits. She'd been over-powered and helpless, too, like Jason had just been. Adrift in an ocean of ravenous sharks. She was so alone, so forsaken. So trauma-tized by angry men seeking to strike out against something weaker. In his mind's eye, he saw forty hungry faces lit by candles and the orange glow of a cheap space heater. Damira, Roza, Luda, Yelena, Natalya, Liliya. Orphans already. Twice orphaned by greed and anger and inhumanity.

And then his mind flowed easily to an image of Samantha Runnion, the five-year-old girl who had been abducted from in front of her home, probably sexually assaulted, and finally murdered—by a human predator. Samantha had had no ability to get away, either, though she'd done everything right—kicking and screaming for help. But the predator had had the advantage.

Of course he had the advantage. He wouldn't have attacked someone who could fight back. Sharks were cowards.

Jason submerged, kicking mightily toward the lake floor. Silt clouded around his hands when he reached the bottom. It was cold and greasy, and he imagined he could smell its stink through his mask.

The anger was waiting for him on the lake floor. He shoved him-self back up for air, but the anger was there, as well. He drew in warm, salty oxygen through his snorkel and opened himself to the flood of images.

Danielle van Dam. Seven years old. Taken from her bed. Murdered.

Casey Williamson. Five years old. Taken during a sleepover. Murdered.

Destiny Wright. Six years old. Taken during a sleepover. Murdered.

Jennifer Short. Nine years old. Taken from her home. Murdered.

Elizabeth Smart. Twelve years old. Taken from her bed at gunpoint.

Erica Pratt. Seven years old. Taken from her front yard.

How many of them had been sexually molested before being executed or rescued?

Then he thought of Andrea Yates, who had drowned her five children in the bathtub. He thought of Susan Smith, who had sent the car into the lake, her two boys still strapped in their car seats. He thought of the mass graves in Bosnia, filled with the bodies of little children. He thought of the Palestinian gunmen who walked into an Israeli household, looked a five-year-old girl in the face, and shot her.

And these were just the old ones. More recently, little girls and boys all over the world had been abducted or exploited, attacked or run down, dismembered or decapitated, drowned or smothered, burned or buried alive—and these weren't even in war zones. They were hurt by strangers or parents, those they trusted or those they'd never seen. Precious, innocent faces paraded before his eyes. The faces from CNN. Somebody had declared open season on little children.

Jason was too hot now, but it didn't have anything to do with the sun. He tore his mask off. The water chilled his face.

Not enough.

Twelve days after she was murdered, Samantha would've turned six.

He dove deeper, toward the cool depths, to where the light departed. His lungs burned, and the water squeezed his body like a pedophile's grip. And there he screamed.

He broke the surface, depleted. He floated on his back, breathing deeply and allowing himself to receive the sun's gentle warmth.

A sound like a goose call roused him. Soaring over the water, its head turning left and right, was what Chris had told him was a white-bellied sea eagle. Why God had made it sound like a goose was beyond him.

He swam toward their floating hotel. The houseboat was a beast. Eighty-seven feet long, eighteen feet wide. Room to sleep fifteen. A covered upper deck with six-person hot tub and patio furniture. Waterslide off the back. Jet ski ramp that raised and lowered like a drawbridge. Only the best for Eloise's babies.

The white and blue *Pride of Gippsland* lay at anchor in the calm waters of Lake Victoria, Australia. Beyond the houseboat was Rotamah Island, where the thick grove of eucalypts and melaleuca trees rose from the water. A pair of kangaroos drank leisurely at the shore.

Jason swam toward the houseboat, his mask and snorkel over his left arm. As he reached the metal ladder next to the waterslide, he heard the sound of someone turning a book page. He tossed his flippers and mask on deck and climbed aboard, then grabbed his towel and suntan lotion and took the steps to the upper deck.

Trieu lay on a chaise lounge in the shade, reading. She wore a navy blue one-piece bathing suit and a sheer white sarong. Jason had seen her in this suit every day for a week now, but he still needed to avert his eyes.

He sat in the chaise next to her. "What're you reading?"

"It's called *Devotional Classics.*" She turned her lovely Asian eyes on him and smiled. "It's a collection of short writings from the great Christian thinkers and mystics."

Jason tilted his head to read the cover. "Who's Richard Foster?"

"Oh! He's the most wonderful Christian writer. He chose the writings for the book. Have you ever heard of *Celebration of Discipline?*"

"Um, isn't that a parenting book?"

She tucked a strand of straight black hair behind her ear. "No. It's a famous book by Richard Foster, all about the disciplines of the Christian life. You need to read it, Jason. It will help you grow."

"Okay." He opened his bottle of suntan lotion and rubbed it on his shoulders.

Trieu watched him. "You're supposed to put that on *before* you go into the sun, Jason."

"Ha ha, thank you so much, Dr. Nguyen. Here," he said, handing her the bottle and turning his back to her, "make yourself useful."

She didn't move.

"Please?"

He heard her shut her book and squirt out some lotion. The touch of her warm hands spreading cold lotion on his back was. . . invigorating. He tried to think of Trieu's tender touch as if it were coming from a gnarly Russian masseuse.

"Trieu, can I ask you a serious question?"

She squeezed out more lotion. "I honestly don't know, Jason. Can you?"

He smirked at her jibe, then sighed deeply. "How do you deal with. . .bad things in the world?"

"I'm sorry?"

"I mean, bad things happen to all of us. That's not what I mean. I mean really bad things, like, you know, massive earthquakes that kill thousands of people or big plagues that break out and kill bunches of people. Or," he shut his eyes, "like when little girls get taken from their beds and sick men do horrible, *horrible* things to them and then kill them?"

Trieu's hands stopped. Neither of them spoke. Cicadas buzzed from the near shore in slow, rising and falling waves, like a sleeping giant. A mild lake breeze kept the bugs away.

Jason turned around. Trieu was staring into space. "Did I say something wrong?"

She smiled. "No." She handed the suntan lotion to him and sat back in her chaise. "It's just a profound question."

"I can see all their faces, you know? The children who have been. . .taken. Their cute little faces smiling in family photos or goofing off for the video camera." He leaned forward, his elbows on his knees. "And then they show the photo of the guy who did it, some paunchy, middle-aged pervert. And I think of that sweet baby, terrified by this lowlife, probably crying and feeling more alone than she's ever felt in her life. And this man, who's way too strong for her and way too fast for her, puts his filthy hands on her. And I just want to. . ."

Somehow he'd moved to the railing at the side of the houseboat.

"Just want to what?"

Tears jumped out of his eyes. "I want to tear his head off, that's what. I want to get there somehow. I want to find where they are and I want to—I want to take him out, Trieu. I want to save that sweet baby and. . ." He took a deep breath and turned to face Trieu. "I want to slice him open, Trieu. I want to use one of those two thousand ways to kill a man I learned as a SEAL."

She watched him carefully, unmoving.

He laughed miserably. "You know when I got out of the Teams, I swore I'd never kill another man as long as I lived. But, I don't know, Trieu. If I got locked in a room with the man who killed Samantha Runnion or one of these others, I honestly think I would kill him. I believe I would torture him and bleed him and terrify him and slowly dismember him. And I don't think I would hear the voice of God telling me to feel sorry about it for a week after, either."

They stared at each other in silence. Below, they heard footsteps and knocking around. Jason walked to his chair and sat down heavily.

Trieu took his hand. "Jason, this is. . .I mean, oh, my goodness. I'm still back at 'What are you reading?' Where did all of this come from?"

He chuckled and dried his eyes. "I have no clue. It's just been on my mind a lot lately. I think maybe it's been kind of slowly building, ever since Damira and the girls in Kazakhstan, you know?"

She squeezed his hand and let go. "You asked me how I deal with this kind of bad thing. I wonder if you're really asking another question."

"Like what?"

"Like 'How could God allow these innocent children to be taken?' "

Jason nodded. "Yeah, I guess. I mean, we teach kids that God's going to take care of them, and then this kind of thing happens. What are they supposed to think?" He stretched out on the chaise. "What am *I* supposed to think?"

"It's a very old question, Jason. Theologians call it *theodicy*, I believe: the justice of God. It's the ancient riddle: 'If God is all-knowing and all-loving and all-powerful and all-good, how can He tolerate such terrible evil?' "

He swallowed. "Well, how can He?"

"I don't know. But I think it has something to do with His love."

"His love? God lets little girls get sexually violated and killed because of His love? Girl, that's just crazy."

Trieu sighed. "Yes, Jason, I know it sounds wrong, but listen. God is a lot more upset by all this than you are, okay? Don't you think so? Don't you know He was there holding little Samantha's hand the whole time, that He was right there to welcome her into His arms the instant she died?"

A single tear escaped each of Trieu's eyes.

"Don't you know He's so sick of this world, Jason? That He wants to destroy the earth and bring judgment because of what people do to other people? But He holds off. And while He holds off, little girls keep dying."

Jason opened his hands. "This is what I'm saying. Why does He—"

"Why? I don't know why. But I know that you and I both owe our salvation to Him for holding off."

Jason blinked. "Come again?"

"Jason, God's been ready to wipe out the human race for a lot longer than you've been upset about pedophiles. It's only by His mercy that any of us are still here after so many centuries of evil. Now, what if His patience ran out, say, the day before you became a Christian? Did you ever think of that? One day He's going to pull the plug, Jason. He's going to draw a line in the sand and whoever's on the wrong side of that line is going to be in big trouble. One day He's going to say, 'That's enough!' What if that day had come the day before you became a Christian?"

"I. . .guess I'd be up a creek, wouldn't I?"

"Exactly. But He didn't. He stomached who knows how many injustices and innocents being killed just so that you and I would have the chance to come to Him."

Jason shook his head. "Wow. I never thought of it th—"

"And you and I sit here and wonder what's taking Him so long. We hear about terrible things and we throw our hands up and say, 'God, where were You? Why won't You hurry up and end all this?' But He still waits. Why? Because there are millions of people out there who might just come to Jesus if they were given only one more day. Just one more day to hear the Good News and come to Him."

She picked up her book. "So, yes, Jason, I think God allows bad things to happen—even though it makes Him sick to do it—out of a hope that someone's eternity will be changed. He does it out of love."

Jason watched her begin reading again. "Trieu, I didn't mean to. . .I mean, I think I've kind of upset you and I wasn't. . ."

She met his eyes. "I'm not upset, Jason. Not at you. It's one of those unanswerables. Even my answer only works partway. And it doesn't take any of the pain away." She wiped her cheeks dry. "If we get worked up, it's only because we hate it that we can't do anything about it. But guess what, Jason?"

"What?"

"Praise God, Jason, because you and I *do* have the chance to do something about it. Eloise has brought us together and put the tools in our hands to go out in God's power to try to save some of these innocents."

Jason felt a smile widening across his face. "Oh, yeah. That's right, that's exactly right! Oh, baby! Come on, Eloise, give us a call— I'm ready to go right now!"

He found himself standing again. Trieu was watching, a bemused look on her face. "What?"

She smiled gently. "You."

He sat back down. "What about me?"

"You have a great heart, Jason Kromer. A beautiful, passionate heart. It's one of the things—"

He waited. Then he lifted his eyebrows as a question.

Her eyes jumped to his and then off again. "It's one of the reasons *we all* love and follow you."

Jason watched her pretend to read her book. His smile deepened. "I like you, too, Trieu."

Heavy footsteps pounded up the forward stairs. A young man no more than twenty appeared, short brown hair kept tamed by enough hardened styling gel to turn a man to stone. He rotated his head to take in Jason and Trieu, then rotated it to the far shore. As he walked to the railing, he appeared to be lilting. His calves raised him to the balls of his feet with every step.

"Have you guys seen him?"

Jason leaned back in the chaise. "Seen who, Lewis?"

"Chunky! I told him to go right there to those kangaroos, but he hasn't shown up. I lost the connection with him about ten minutes ago. You guys, I'm really worried."

Jason crossed his legs at the ankles. "Well, where did you start him from?"

"Back there," Lewis said, thumbing toward the lakeward side of the boat.

"Where back there?" Jason asked. Trieu turned to her book.

Lewis squinted against the sun. "Right there behind you. I dropped him over the edge like an hour ago. I can't under—"

Jason sat up. "You did what?"

"Huh?"

"Lewis, you dropped a military prototype robot into the lake? What are you, crazy? That thing costs like a billion dollars!"

"Huh, hardly."

Trieu sat up. "Lewis, is it waterproof?"

"Supposed to be. Up to nine meters. That's what, ten yards? Is it deeper than that under us, Jason?"

"It's close to that right here. It could've slid on out to deeper water when it hit bottom."

Lewis stepped under the houseboat's roof. "Well, could you, like, go look for him, Jason?"

"Me? You're the one who dropped it in the lake, Lewis, not me. You go look for it. My stuff's on the aft deck. Man, I'm glad I'm not the one who's going to have to tell Eloise what happened to her spy toy."

"I'm sure he's fine, Jason. Trieu, he's going to be fine, isn't he?"

She shrugged. "I hope so, Lewis."

"Because he's supposed to be waterproof. And Chunky's smart. He's got better AI than half the guys I knew in high school. He'll. . . he'll show up." Lewis went back to the railing. "Come on, Chunky, show up."

Lewis's head swiveled a few degrees. "Do you guys hear that?"

Jason heard a high whine in the distance. "Somebody's coming."

"Do you think it's Chunky?"

"No, Lewis," Jason said with a smile. "I don't. Everybody strap in. The fun is about to arrive."

The whine increased, though it was still not loud. Laughter reverberated across the still lake louder than the whine.

"There they are," Lewis said, his eyes shielded against the sun.

A quarter of a mile away, two jet skis rounded the wooded shoreline and came into view. Each watercraft held two riders. They appeared to be racing. The engines made virtually no noise. The jet skis turned the water white and spewed tall fountains behind them like tails. The drivers swerved at each other, cutting each other off and hopping each other's wake.

Jason could make them out now. The blue and white jet ski was piloted by Doug "Chimp" Bigelow. His new bride, Jamie, held on for dear life. Garth piloted the silver watercraft. Because of his size, he made the three-person rig look like it was big enough for only one. Rachel clung to him so tightly she looked like part of his ski vest.

"I still can't believe how quiet they are," Lewis said. "I can hear Chimp trash talking Garth as clear as if they were sitting right here. Don't these things usually sound like formula one cars?"

"Yeah," Jason said. "It's the four-stroke. They're pretty quiet. But for the price we paid for them, they ought to fly and serve sushi."

"Jason," Trieu called from the shade, "don't you mean the price *Eloise* paid for them?"

Jason smiled. "Right."

The jet skis raced side by side, about a hundred feet from the houseboat and closing fast. Each driver nosed into the other's jet ski. Garth reached out a massive arm and grabbed for Bigelow's throttle. Jamie swatted Garth's arm. The jet ski started to tip. Everybody shouted at once.

Garth's hand zipped across Bigelow's lap and mashed the ignition button. The blue and white jet ski sank in the water, and Garth's silver one leapt away to victory.

He rounded the houseboat, one fist in the air and Rachel hooting in triumph, champion biker dude and biker babe of the high seas.

"Typical Green Beret stunt," Jason said, smiling in spite of himself. "Half-brilliant, half-brainless—all crazy."

Lewis hurried to the aft platform and lowered the jet ski ramp. Garth drove directly onto it.

"You guys!" Jamie called, as Bigelow brought their jet ski to the back of the boat. "That was so not fair."

"Yeah," Bigelow said, "is that how you treat a cripple, you big bully?"

Garth stood on the platform, ankle deep in water, and hoisted Rachel onto the deck as if she were a six year old. "Sorry, mate," he said to Bigelow, using his decent "Strine" accent. "Oy didn't mean to get on your quince there, squidhead. Fair dinkum!"

Bigelow idled behind the platform. "Whatever, dogface. Jamie, what do you say, want to go out again?"

"I don't think so, honey," she said, climbing off the jet ski onto the houseboat's metal ladder. "My tailbone's so sore I won't be sitting for a week. I think I'll dry off and go watch something on the big screen."

"Good on ya, sheila," Garth said. "No flies on that girl, eh, Jason?"

Jason exchanged a look with Trieu, who now stood next to him at the upper railing. "Um, I don't see any on her, no."

Lewis sank onto an ice chest. "What does 'fair dinkum' mean?"

Garth ruffled Lewis's gel-hardened hair. "It means 'honest,' mate."

"Somebody come with me," Bigelow said. His wide face was sunburned. Even his prominent ears looked red. "Jason, come on, dude. Race me."

"I don't think so, Chimp. Maybe later."

Garth and Jamie unzipped their ski vests and hung them on pegs. Garth's chest all but exploded out of the size XXL vest. Red lines streaked him where the vest had dug into his skin. The snake-woman-knife tattoo on his left deltoid danced when the muscle flexed.

Bigelow shaded his eyes against the sun. "What about you, Trieu? Want to take the other rig? I'll show you this amazing spot called Pelican Point."

"No, thank you, Doug," she said. "Perhaps another time."

"Oh, no!" Bigelow said. "I don't want to stop now. Soon as I get off the thing, I'm a crip again. Forget it. I'm staying out."

"Just be careful, honey," Jamie said. "I'm going in." She stepped through the sliding glass door to the air-conditioned lower deck.

Rachel zipped open her ski vest and peeled it off, revealing a hot pink bikini, the top of which almost kept her decent.

"Ow!" Garth said, shielding his eyes. "Rachel, girl, don't *do* that."

Rachel was a supermodel, no doubt about it. Jason really did want to avert his eyes. Fair dinkum.

Garth held a towel toward her, his face looking the other way. He looked like a junior camper trying to toss a twig onto the bonfire without getting singed. "Here. Take it, take it!"

Rachel ignored the towel and slowly climbed the stairs to the upper deck. "Oh, Doug, I don't think Jason will be joining you. He and Trieu are probably having too much fun together." She placed a hand on Jason's bare chest and pulled out a hair.

"Ouch!"

She slapped him playfully and walked to the hot tub for her wrap. "I'm just teasing, Jason. But you better put a shirt on before Trieu and I both go wild."

Jason looked from Rachel to Trieu to the others down below. "I. . . We. . . She was. . ."

"Look at him," Bigelow said. "He's going to come up with something good any month now."

"He's a ning-nong, all right," Garth said. "Kangaroos in the top paddock for sure."

Lewis lifted his palms. "What?"

Garth made the "crazy" sign by his head.

"Oh."

"What's that?" Trieu pointed to the near shore.

Jason looked. A small, tracked vehicle like a toy tank without a turret was emerging from the lake. Two appendages, looking like tracked arms, reached forward from the front of the vehicle. On the top platform, a metal neck swiveled left to right as if looking around.

"Lewis," Jason said, "I think we found Chunky."

"What!" Lewis stomped up the stairs and stared over the railing. "Chunky! I knew you'd be okay. Where were you, dude? I was worried sick."

Garth secured his jet ski and joined the others on the top deck. "Aces, mate. Glad you found the little ankle biter. You see, Bob's your uncle."

Jason, Trieu, and Rachel looked at Garth in bewilderment. "What?"

"It means, you bloomin' Yanks, that everything's okay."

Bigelow piloted his jet ski in a lazy turn to face the shore. "Hey, Lewis, you want I should get your toy and bring it back?"

"Sure, Doug, thanks."

"Hang on," Jason said, moving to the stairs. "I'll come with you."

"No, it's okay," Bigelow said, accelerating away from the house-boat. "I can do it."

Trieu hid her eyes. "No one tell Jamie."

The sun hung just above the treetops now. The air had begun to cool a bit. Mosquitoes whined about them in the air.

While everyone else was watching Bigelow, Jason turned back to Rachel. She was reclining on Trieu's chaise lounge, her perfect legs stretched out before her, one knee slightly up. Had he stumbled onto a swimsuit issue photo shoot?

"Rachel, girl, would you please cover up a little so I can talk to you?"

"What's the matter, Jason?" she asked, making no move to cover herself. "I thought you only had eyes for Trieu."

"Cut that out, okay? And put something on."

"Oh, all right." She arched her back, the vixen, and pulled a white garment from beneath her. It was a short sundress cover-up consisting mainly of gauze with big holes in it. It was something of an improvement. "All better?"

"A little," Jason said, coming to sit at the foot of her lounge chair. "Look, Rachel, I don't know what game you're playing, but I need you to cut it out. Now, I know you a little; and because of that, I'm certain that you know full well what effect your. . .*appearance* has on men. But could I humbly request that you calm it down?"

She appeared to pout. "Oh, Jason, don't lie to me. I know you like what you see."

"Stop it, Raych. Look, you're beautiful, no doubt about it. But is that all you want men to notice? Is that how you really want to carry yourself? You looked like a Playboy bimbo coming up those stairs just now. But you're so much more than that. You're incredibly smart and gifted and caring. You have beauty that goes way beyond skin deep."

Her expression softened. Her arched eyebrow dropped to its natural position.

"If you act like that, you're only going to attract men who are only after that," he said. "Don't you want someone who likes you for what's going to be left over in sixty years? If you catch a guy by your looks and nothing else, what's he going to do when those looks start to fade? He's going to find someone younger."

Rachel smiled slightly. "Do you know who you sound like?"

"Who, a nun?"

"No. You sound like my father." Her smile turned sad. "Well, I don't actually remember many talks like this. I don't know. Something about how it makes me feel when you talk like that."

Jason watched her. "Is it a good feeling?"

"Oh, yeah, Jason. It's a good feeling."

He sighed. "I won't tell you that I'm not attracted to you physically, Rachel. Because I am. But come on. I like to think I've got a little more depth than that. I want a woman who is kind and encouraging and smart—and godly. The woman I'm going to marry will be someone I can pray with, someone I can talk Bible with. And somebody to have fun with."

Rachel closed her cover-up across her chest. The look in her eyes was one he'd seen on only two other occasions. It was an unguarded look, as if she'd given him free access to peer into the most vulnerable corner of her soul. It was intense to the point of overpowering. But Jason held her gaze.

"Hey, Lewis," Garth said from where the others were looking over the railing. "Tell me again how a multimillion-dollar spy robot came to be called a fat kid's nickname?"

Lewis didn't take his eyes off Bigelow as he neared the lakeshore. "It's because the original version was called PackBot. PB, for short. Which is also peanut butter, which is also chunky."

Garth rubbed his bald head. "Oh. That was my next guess."

"The thing's nowhere close enough to the edge for him to reach it," Jason said, stepping to the railing. "How does that idiot think he's going to get it on the jet ski?"

"Oh, that's easy, Jason," Rachel said, coming to stand beside him. "He'll just get Chris to help him."

"Chris?" Lewis said. "I thought he was over at that bird island or whatever."

"I was," a man's voice called from down the shoreline. "Now I'm back."

Chris looked like an Australian park ranger. He wore a button-up short-sleeved bush shirt with wide, sensible pockets; matching Kakadu shorts; beige socks; high brown boots; and a dark brown kangaroo leather hat. But even these looked like the latest Oz fashions on Chris. Jason couldn't see the trademark blond curl on Chris's forehead, but he was sure it was there.

Chris trotted up the sand to the robot just as Bigelow neared the shore. "Give us both a ride, squiddy?"

"I could've done it myself, jarhead," Bigelow answered.

"I know you could have, Doug. But I'm glad I got back when I did. I wasn't looking forward to swimming across." He lifted the wagon-sized robot, washed the sand off in the lake, and climbed with it onto the jet ski. "Home, James."

Bigelow gunned the jet ski, nearly sending Chris and Chunky into the drink. He circled the houseboat full throttle, slicing the water at dangerously acute angles. Finally, with an artistic flourish of spray, he lurched up onto the jet ski ramp.

Chris handed the robot off to Lewis, who immediately scuttled inside with it. Then he looked down at his drenched clothes. "Yeah, I'm definitely glad I didn't have to swim."

Bigelow grinned. "Sorry, dude."

"Don't worry about it," Chris said, slapping his shoulder. "I know what it feels like to always have to prove something."

Bigelow looked at Chris, then up at Jason. He grimaced. "Push me off, would you? I'm going back out."

Chris shoved the jet ski backward, and Bigelow carved a white gash across Lake Victoria.

On the top deck, Jason opened an ice chest and served cold drinks to everyone. Mountain Dew for him, of course. Lesser liquids for the rest. He put on a comfortable blue T-shirt and pulled his chair over to the hot tub, where the others were putting their feet up.

"So, marine," Garth said to Chris, swirling a bottle of Sobe orange carrot elixir. "You see any yellow-spotted Ima Cuckoo birds while you were out?"

Chris finished a deep draught of bottled water. "Absolutely. Along with some bald-headed Ura Loser nuthatches." He winked at Rachel. "You guys, you've got to come check out Rotamah Island. There are over two hundred species there. I saw a great crested grebe, a family of emus, and a crimson rosella you'd have to see to believe. Rachel, sweetie, it's bright red on its chest and head and almost metallic blue on its wings, tail, and chin. You've got to let me take you to one of the hides so we can see it."

"Sounds nice, Chris," she said, looking at Jason. "We'll see."

The door to the lower deck banged open and Lewis leapt through. "Great news, you guys! Chunky's just fine! Totally waterproof. I knew it! And I figured out why I lost contact with him. I'd forgotten to turn on his extended range transponder. What a dork. But he's proven he's totally autonomous! Even though he'd lost contact with HQ, he stuck to the mission. He got a little lost under there, I think, but he kept to it and eventually figured it out. What a stud. Ooh, drink time, huh? You think Doug would mind if I had his last Virgil's Root Beer?"

Lewis opened a tall bottle and pulled up a chair next to Rachel. "Ah," he said, after a long swallow, "now that's smooth."

For awhile they didn't speak. Small waves lapped the houseboat's aluminum pontoons, making a hollow sound like raindrops in a barrel. The sounds of a game show emanated from the satellite TV on the lower deck. Chris cocked his ear toward the railing and appeared to stop breathing. A black bee buzzed Lewis's hair, its wings a low drone, before continuing to points beyond.

"Jason, mate," Garth said in Strine, tipping his chair back, "do we really have to go back tomorrow? Aw, don't answer that. I'd hate to have to chuck a wobbly. I'm much happier being a dole bludger, if you know what I mean."

"Um," Jason said, "no, I don't. But we do need to weigh anchor tomorrow, bright and early. You guys are getting soft out here. Got to get back to the Ponderosa so we can start shooting and running laps again."

Everyone groaned.

"I know, I know," Jason said. "But who knows how long it'll be before Big Mama wants to send us out again? Me, I'm guessing not long. This little vacation has been sweet, but I've got a ton of training we need to get to in the little time we do have."

"You mean we can't just keep drugging Lewis and tossing him out of airplanes?" Chris asked.

"No, I'm afraid not."

Lewis pointed at him. "That never happened."

"You're right, Lewis," Chris said. "My mistake."

"Ah, don't listen to him, Lewis," Garth said. "You believe what you want. You can't trust a marine to get anything right. Hey, did you guys know that in the army we called helicopters 'choppers,' and in the air force they call them 'whirlybirds,' and in the navy they call them 'helos'—but in the marines they just point up at the sky and say, 'Uh uh uh!' "

Everybody laughed but Chris.

"Oh, yeah?" Chris said, crushing his plastic water bottle. "Well, if you haven't heard that one, then I guess you haven't heard what happened when the soldier, the airman, the sailor, and the marine got to heaven. They had an argument about which service was the best, so they asked ol' St. Peter. Peter said he didn't know but he'd ask God the next chance he got. The next day, a white dove with an envelope in its beak flew up to the four guys. They read the letter: 'Dear soldiers, airmen, sailors, and marines: All branches of the United States military are truly honorable. You are all well trained and do your jobs exceedingly well. There is no service more honorable than the others. Signed, God, USMC, retired.' "

They laughed again.

Garth looked at Jason. "What are you laughing at, squiddy?"

"Come on, Jason," Rachel said. "Don't you have a good one on both of these bozos?"

"Actually," Jason said, "I'm not very good at jokes. The truth hurts more, anyway. I honestly felt sorry for the other branches."

"Ooh!" Lewis said, his eyebrows lifted.

"Not in a condescending way," Jason said. "But just because I loved the freedom and eliteness of the SEALs. Nobody came close to that."

Garth belched. "Hooah." Then he looked at the group. "I guess now I'll have to tell you about the SEAL who walked into the bar. Sorry, ladies. See, a SEAL walked into a bar. But the Green Beret saw it and ducked just in time."

This time everyone laughed except Lewis.

"He. . .walked *into* the bar, Lewis," Garth said slowly. "Hit him right on the head."

Lewis's eyes widened. Then he looked offended. "I knew that. I got it."

"Uh-huh."

The whine of Bigelow's jet ski bounced to them across the lake, then was gone again.

"Jason," Rachel said, "you really think Eloise would send us out so soon after Kazakhstan? It's only been three weeks."

Jason shrugged. "If I know Eloise, it's been all she could do just to let us have five days out here in the Outback, where it's nice and warm even in the middle of March. We'll be lucky if we're on the ground a week before we're going again."

Garth scraped his Sobe bottle cap against his orange goatee. "Yeah, I guess it's time we start making deposits into the Big Mama fund, instead of just withdrawals." He chuckled and looked out over the lake. "I think it's going to hit Bigelow the hardest, poor squid. It's got to be hard to go from jet ski to wheelchair."

"Yeah," Chris said, "but don't forget: He's married and the rest of us are just. . .losers. He does get a few advantages that we don't, eh, *mate?*"

An assortment of towels, shoes, and mosquito repellant bottles came hurtling at him.

Jamie walked onto the deck. Chris looked at her guiltily. "H–Hi, Jamie. Wow, don't you look nice today. I'm fine now, thanks. How are you?"

"What's wrong with you, Chris?" Jamie asked. "Trieu slip you a kindness pill?"

"That's right, sheila," Garth said. "Give the bloke what for."

"Yeah, okay," Jamie said. "Jason, telephone. I think it's Eloise."

Jason stood. "What'd I tell you guys?"

He followed Jamie into the wide living room belowdecks. The air was dry and chilly compared to outside. A plush couch sat across a glass coffee table from a recliner that Jason knew from experience was extremely relaxing. High stools stood at the kitchen buffet counter. Matching chairs were rolled up to the dining table on the beige carpet. Wooden cabinets, an expensive entertainment center, ceiling fans, and recessed lighting completed the room. It looked for all the world like a living room in a house.

Jamie was watching a rerun of *Match Game '76* on the plasma screen TV, so Jason went to the forward stateroom—Doug and Jamie Bigelow's room—to take the call. He sat on the queen-size bed and picked up the phone.

"Hello?"

There was a delay as his voice bounced through space and around the world and the other person's bounced back.

"Hello, Jason," a woman's deep voice said. "It's Eloise. Y'all having a good time out there?"

"We're having a great time, Eloise. Chris wants to permanently move to this bird island he's found. Lewis is playing with your expensive toys. Trieu's catching up on her reading. Rachel's been causing trouble, as usual, but I think we've come to an understanding. Garth and Doug about killed each other—and Jamie and Rachel—on the jet ski just a minute ago. And me. . .I think I'm doing fine. Thanks so much for sending us out here. Lake Victoria is beautiful, ma'am, and the ocean's just a stone's throw away. Next time you're coming with us, all right?"

Eloise chuckled, a sound rich with mischief and affection. "No, I don't think so, young man. I don't take kindly to swimming suits. But thank you for thinking of me."

"Well, Eloise, what can I do for you?"

When her voice reached him again, all the mirth had left it. "Something's happened, Jason. In Sudan. A slave raid. Massacre. Women and children taken or killed. Most of the men wiped out. I'll tell you more when you get here, but I want the Firebrand team to get over there quick as you can. Now, I know, I know, so don't bother telling me. I won't send you in too fast. I'll give you a little time to prepare because I want you coming home. But this one has really. . ." She paused. "I'll tell you more when you get here."

Jason sighed. "I understand. Do you want us to leave tonight?"

"No, you're coming back tomorrow anyway, so stick with that. I just wanted you to know that I've changed your tickets. You won't be flying into Utah; you'll be coming here to Akron."

"Copy. I mean, I understand. We'll see you soon."

"Jason," Eloise said, "be praying, son. I don't know what my Jesus has in store for us in Sudan, but I believe His Spirit's telling me it's going to be something big. You hear me, boy? Something bigger than all of us, understand?"

"Absolutely, ma'am. I'll be praying."

# CHAPTER 2

## SUDAN 101

"OH, YEAH. This is good coffee." Garth savored the aroma from his white Styrofoam cup. "Starbucks, eat your heart out."

The Firebrand team—Jason, Garth, Chris, Trieu, Rachel, and Lewis—plus Doug Bigelow in his wheelchair, loitered in the ABL Corporation headquarters reception area. They were dressed casually, in jeans and tennis shoes, waiting for their appointment with Eloise Webster on the top floor of the First National Tower.

The reception area was modern and stylish. White floors and walls, little nooks of thriving flora, abstract art, and expensive-looking chrome light fixtures. The receptionist's elevated counter was against the wall on the left of any visitor who pushed through the frosted glass entry door. A large wooden door, the portal to Eloise's suite, stood on the wall opposite the entryway. A column of small windows with black frames stood on either side of the doorway like sprocket holes.

"Man," Lewis said, helping himself from a domed pastry table in the waiting area, "these doughnuts are to die for. How can plain glazed doughnuts be this amazing?"

Chris looked up from his newspaper. "Lewis, dude, those are Krispy Kreme doughnuts."

Lewis managed to shrug at Chris and consume two-thirds of a doughnut at the same time. "Mmm?"

Rachel used a napkin to dab at Lewis's mouth. "They're famous, Lewis."

Lewis, his mouth still full, offered Rachel the other doughnut on his Styrofoam plate. "Hrr smm."

She looked at it with wide eyes, as if she'd just been shown the Hope Diamond but it was in a pool of boiling water. Her hand moved toward it. But it stopped, quivering.

"Uh, oh," Bigelow said, wheeling forward. "Moment of truth. Go for it, Rachel. Jason's going to make you run it off fifty times over, aren't you, Jason?"

"Oh, in the first day, easy."

The hand inched closer. Lewis swayed the plate tantalizingly before Rachel's eyes.

"Don't do it, Rachel," Trieu said, setting her fruit plate on the sofa cushion beside her. "It's not worth it."

"Do it, Rachel," Lewis said.

"Do not gaze at the wine when it is red, when it sparkles in the cup, Raych," Garth said. "In the end it bites like a snake and poisons like a viper!"

The hand began to shake.

"Do it."

"Don't do it."

"You want it."

"It's mostly air anyway, Rachel."

"Be strong."

An electronic tone sounded at the receptionist's desk behind them, and at the same moment the tall door clacked and swung open. Five large black women came into the reception area.

"Hey!"

Jason and the others turned to see why Lewis had cried out. The plate in his hand held only tiny flakes of glaze. Rachel stood with her eyes shut, apparently transported to a realm of endless bliss.

Bigelow nudged her arm. "Way to go, chick. But, hey, now that you won't be able to fit into anything in your closet, can Jamie have some of your clothes? I especially like the—"

That was how it was that Bigelow came to enjoy a Krispy Kreme doughnut of his own—after he removed the pieces from his ear, nose, and forehead.

"Ew."

Jason hugged the most elderly of the five women approaching them. "Good morning, Miss Dorothy. How are you today, young lady?"

The ladies giggled. Dorothy hooked her arm through Jason's and pulled him toward the glass door. "I'm taking this one home!"

Garth gathered two of the other ladies in his muscled arms. "How is the widows' prayer group today? Wilma, when you gonna fix that strawberry rhubarb pie you're always promising me?"

"Anytime, handsome man," Wilma said. "Just come on over."

"Tell us the truth now, ladies," Garth said conspiratorially. "Y'all do more than pray with Big Mama Eloise, don't you? Y'all are like the board of directors for our little playgroup, aren't you?"

The ladies fell silent. Jason noticed that his team members were all paying attention.

Finally Cheryl, one of the five, pulled her coat collar up. "We don't know nothing about that, you hunka man. Now step aside so some old women can get on with their business."

Garth winked, and they giggled all the way out the door.

Jason moved closer to Garth. "You really think they are? I hadn't made the connection."

"Absolutely."

The receptionist, a young Hispanic woman, called Jason over. "You and the others may go in now. I'll buzz you through."

\*   \*   \*

Eloise was on the phone at her designer desk when the seven of them entered her executive suite. She gave the "one minute" signal and motioned them toward the conference table.

The office could be divided into thirds—and each third would be larger than the typical CEO's office. Neutral blue carpet underlay the whole thing.

The third on their left had the largest conference table Jason had ever seen. It was a long racetrack oval of red wood and black lacquer edging. Nine black, very comfortable-looking executive chairs stood on each side of the table, and two more stood at the ends. Pop-up panels for video screens and data outlets were cleverly recessed in the tabletop. Floor-to-ceiling windows looked out over downtown Akron on two sides. It was a bright, clear morning. The other wall held a large, flat panel plasma video display.

Rachel walked to the window and looked down. The others sat or stood or studied the mounted photos of Eloise posing with various heads of state.

The middle third of the suite was Eloise's office proper. Eloise sat in her high-backed chair speaking into a black phone, dimples appearing on her chubby brown cheeks. She wore an ocean blue dress with matching jacket. It was bright and "African" and looked fantastic on her. Her fingernails were ocean blue, too. Eloise's desk was lozenge-shaped with matching cabinets and shelves beside it.

The final third of the suite kept the same color scheme as the rest—warm reds and black—but the furniture style gave it a different mood. Spindly Colonial chairs stood around small round tables with artistically bowed legs. It felt like a drawing room from *Pride and Prejudice.* But Jason knew there was a refrigerator with cold drinks on this side of the room, along with a bathroom, a door to an antechamber, and another plasma screen display. Lewis passed him, headed for the fridge.

Rachel stood beside the conference table, her cheek resting against the window. Jason came up beside her. "You okay?"

She didn't answer.

"Feeling bad about the doughnut?"

She harrumphed.

"I didn't think so," Jason said. "But I know lots of girls who would be puking it up in the bathroom right now. I just wondered."

"Jason?" She kept staring out across the brown Akron skyline. It was in the forties outside, but the sky was pure blue.

"Yeah, Rachel?"

"Do you ever feel, I don't know, out of control?"

He leaned against the window. "How do you mean?"

"I don't know. It's like I'm forgetting who I am. Or maybe that I never knew. You got me thinking about my father and how he used to like me just for me, and it's kind of messed me up. It's been so long since someone talked to me like that. And then now all this about trouble in Sudan caused by Muslim men. It's bringing up more about my dad. I'm just feeling a little off-balance.

"I have this dream sometimes. I'm chasing after this. . .thing. I never know what it is, but I guess I really want it because I'm always trying like crazy to catch it. Only I never can. It's always just out of reach and it's always leaving me. What do you think that means?"

Jason touched her shoulder. "I don't know, Raych. Maybe there's something you're afraid of losing? Maybe you're searching for something?"

She nodded slowly but kept staring out the window.

As Eloise talked on the phone, she drew out a remote control and pointed it at the wall by the conference table. The plasma screen came to life, and Jason joined the others in the cool, soft black chairs around the table. They made a *pshhhhht* sound when everyone sat on them, and everybody slowly sank half an inch.

"This is a BBC special report," the narrator said with a British accent. "Tonight: Sudan—War, Slavery, and Catastrophe."

In the thirty-minute segment, Jason and the others received a crash course on the largest nation in Africa. They learned about Sudan's successive governments and about the long history of slavery in the region. They learned about the civil war that broke out in 1955 between the Islamized northern two-thirds of the country and the "tribal" and Christian southern third when Sudan became independent from England. They learned about the rise of political Islam in Khartoum, the capital, and its increasingly Talibanesque fundamentalist bent. They learned about the eleven-year hiatus in the war that came about when the south was granted limited autonomy and self-governance and how the war began again when Khartoum disregarded their promises to the south.

Then they learned about the recent discovery of massive oil reserves in the southeast of the nation and how the north was conducting an eradication campaign against any southerners living within a hundred miles of the oil fields. Though Khartoum denied it, the BBC had ample evidence that the army and government-funded militias were systematically bombing and burning anyone and anything—schools and hospitals especially—too near the oil zones.

The report, which was evidently over a year old, mentioned the stalled peace talks between the warring parties, the rise of slave redemption efforts in the West, US and UN sanctions against Sudan for its treatment of civilians and for harboring terrorists, and the disastrous human cost of the war: more than two million killed by war or famine and almost five million displaced.

Eloise hung up and stood outside the circle, watching the video. Then she walked back to her desk and made another call.

The subdued voice of the BBC reporter concluded the report by mourning the death of hope for a solution in the south, while the camera showed children with bomb-amputated arms kicking a ball in a dusty village lane.

Jason swept his hands over the chilled, perfectly smooth surface of the table. "So, what do you think, guys?"

Chris blew air through his lips. "I think we're crazy to even be thinking about going there, but that's just my opinion."

"Oh, come on," Lewis said. "Chris, dude, look at those poor kids. We need to get over there and help them out. What are we waiting for?"

"And do what, Lewis?" Chris said. "If the UN can't solve this thing, what do you think we could do?"

"I agree with Chris," Garth said. "Maybe we just let these guys sort it out themselves."

Jason raised his eyebrows. "Interesting." He turned to Trieu and Rachel. "Ladies?"

Rachel just stared at the table.

"Jason," Trieu said, "did Eloise tell you what she wants us to do in Sudan? I mean, it's obvious that there is so much need there. But how can we six make a difference?"

Jason shrugged and swiveled to stare at Bigelow. "Chimp, you know more about this than me?"

"Sorry, Jace. I'm in the dark this time."

New theme music emanated from the speakers and the *60 Minutes II* intro graphics appeared on the screen. Jason looked over at Eloise, who nodded and pointed at the TV.

"Okay," Jason said. "I guess we watch some more telly."

Dan Rather introduced a segment on the slave trade in Sudan. The ten-minute report showed John Eibner of Christian Solidarity International handing over stacks of cash to black "Arabs" dressed in white robes and wearing white cloth as face masks. Then scores of black boys, girls, and women, who had been sitting in the shade of a large tree, were declared freed. Rather said that Eibner claimed to have freed more than sixty thousand slaves in Sudan.

The video shifted to a white woman and some schoolchildren. Barb Vogel and her fifth graders came on. The group became famous in the late nineties for raising money to redeem Sudanese slaves.

"But what has been done to these people and to these children may not be what it appears," Rather said. "One insider has come forward with claims that the scenes of mass redemptions seen around the world are a hoax."

Another man, Jim Jacobson, formerly with Eibner's group but later a detractor, was shown casting doubt on what was happening with the slave redemptions. "It's a show. It's a circus; it's a staged event," Jacobson said.

Then Jacobson told about a slave redemption trip he made to Sudan that was to change his mind forever about redemption. He arrived unexpectedly at the village where he was supposed to free the slaves. But no slaves were waiting for him. While Jacobson was told to go visit with the elders, his Sudanese contacts went through the village rounding up children who were playing.

"Instant slaves," Jacobson said. "I just wanted to cry."

Rather's serious face appeared on the screen. "Who is to be believed?"

The remainder of the segment offered further evidence of foul play in the slave redemptions of Sudan. It quoted UNICEF executive director, Cheryl Bellamy, who noted that paying for slaves only creates more slavery. The collection of seemingly shady practices and scamming left the viewer convinced that slave redemption was a very bad thing for Sudan and the Sudanese.

The screen went blank. Jason and the others stared at it, as if dazed. "Well?" he asked.

Garth shook his face and made a rubber-blubbery sound.

Jason smiled. "Anyone else?"

"So," Lewis said, his face the picture of consternation, "buying back slaves is bad?"

"That's what Dapper Dan Rather thinks, anyway," Bigelow said.

Rachel dropped her head onto the table.

Jason swung around in his chair. Eloise stood behind them, a pleasant but remote smile on her face. Jason got the feeling this was how she looked when she played poker. "Okay, ma'am," he said. "Want to clue us in? I think we're feeling a little lost."

Eloise took the seat at the head of the table. "I'm sorry about those phone calls, y'all. Just trying to get something together double quick." She sighed. "Okay: Sudan. You watched the videos, you know that the so-called Arabs of the north are at war with the so-called black Africans of the south. Rachel, what's the matter with you, girl? Sit up."

Rachel sat up. "Sorry. Just a little wiped out from the trip, I think."

"She's a wimp," Garth said. "Thirty-seven hours on an airplane and she thinks she's got the right to take it easy."

Jason smiled with the others. The team members were sitting in the seats closest to Eloise. To her right were Lewis, Trieu, Jason, and Chris. To her left were Bigelow, Garth, and Rachel. They all looked a bit beat.

"All right," Eloise said, "but try to pay attention. This is important. Now, while you all have been frolicking with the koalas and eating shrimp on the barbie, I've been getting myself up to speed on Sudan, and I'm telling you, it's a mess.

"Some people will tell you the civil war there is about race. They'll say the Arabs in the north don't like the black Africans in the south, so it's time for some ethnic cleansing. But I'm here to tell you that ain't it. Maybe there's a few true Arabs in the north, but most of those rascals is blacker than me. There ain't no genetic difference between the superior 'Arabs' of the north and the rest of their black brothers in the south.

"But here's the thing: The north has embraced Islam. You won't read this in any of those PC books on being a Muslim, but Islam is the most racist excuse for a religion you'll ever want to see. Muhammad was an Arab; and as far as Muslims are concerned, Islam is only for Arabs. Anyone else—"

"Arab *men,* you mean," Rachel said.

Everyone turned to her.

"You have something to share with the class, young lady?" Garth said.

Rachel looked only at Eloise. "Islam isn't just racist, it's sexist. You can be a full-blooded Arab and still be a fourth-class citizen—if you're a woman."

Eloise nodded slightly. "You're right, sugar. In Islam, there's Arab men," she held one hand high, "and then there's everybody else." She waved her other hand well lower.

"Here's what I'm driving at: If you want to have respect in Islam, you have to be Arab. But what do you do if you want respect from Arab Muslims but you're not Arab yourself?" She looked around the group.

"Ooh!" Garth shot his hand up.

"Yes, Mr. Fisher?"

"You convert to Christianity?"

"Wrong," Eloise said. "You invent an Arab ancestry. You come up with a hep story about how your great-great-great-great grandpappy on your father's side was a full-blooded Arab, straight from Medina, who married his black concubine and had lots of kids—all boys, of course—one of whom looked more African than Arab. That's the one who moved to Sudan; and that's how come you don't look any different from other black Africans, but you're really a true-blue Arab underneath your skin."

Jason nodded. "I wondered why those 'Arab' slave traders looked pretty much like the slaves they were selling."

"Exactly," Eloise said. "So, it's not a war about race or ethnic cleansing, since you can't tell anyone apart if you mix up their clothes. That's not to say that folks on both sides aren't racist or that some racial violence doesn't go on. I'm just saying that's not what the war's about." She fanned herself. "Hoo. Any of the rest of you want something cool to drink?"

They took a break while Jason and Chris brought sodas from the refrigerator.

"Muslims," Lewis said, popping open his Sprite. "Why are we always going up against Muslims?"

"Because," Chris said, "the wars of the twenty-first century are all going to be over religion. Didn't you know? The world's shrunk too much for people to just believe what they want to over in a corner. Mark my words, people: The world's going to be fighting about religion and race for the next hundred years."

"If the Lord tarries," Eloise said, opening her Diet Coke, "which I don't think He will do."

"You work in this business very long, kid," Garth said to Lewis, "and you won't only be fighting against Muslims. In Bosnia the 'Christians' were the bad guys." He turned to Rachel. "And aren't there a lot of Palestinian Christians?"

Rachel shrugged dismissively.

Eloise took a long drink from her Diet Coke. "All right, now. That's better. Where was I?"

Trieu set down her Diet Sprite can. "The war in Sudan is not about racism."

"Right," Eloise said. "Now, other folks will try to tell you that this war is a holy war between Muslims of the north and Christians and 'animists'—that's tribal religions to us slow types—of the south."

"I'd like to take a swipe at that one," Garth said in Strine. "That's wonky, too, am I right? Some yobbo's trying to come the raw prawn on you, I figure. Crikey! It's total waffle! Makes me want to chuck a burko. Know what I mean?"

Eloise looked at him with wide eyes while the others just snickered. She tilted her head toward Rachel. "Honey, you're the language expert. What'd Captain Kangaroo just say?"

Rachel set her Coke can on a cork coaster. "He said he doesn't think that explanation is viable, either."

"Umm-hmm." Eloise watched Garth suspiciously. "Well, you're right. Oh, don't get me wrong: Khartoum has declared jihad on the south and gives financial support to the family of anyone who dies fighting the non-Muslims. They make speeches about how it's every Muslim's duty to spread Islam by the sword. But it's not about that. Know how I know? Because there are Muslims in the south, and the north attacks them anyway.

"Still other folk will tell you that the civil war and the slavery is nothing but tribal feuds as old as the hills. They'll trot out some historian to talk about the bloody wars between the tribes, and they'll try to say that the war is nothing but that. But that's. . .waffle. . .too, because this warfare crosses tribal lines left and right. Khartoum fans the flames of tribalism if it helps them divide the rebels in the south or get Muslim tribes in the north to go attacking down south, but the war's not about that."

"All right, Eloise," Bigelow said, spinning his root beer in the can in his hand, "I'll bite. What *is* the real cause of this war?"

Eloise pointed the remote at the plasma screen and a relief map of Sudan appeared.

"It looks like a backwards comma," Lewis said.

Jason squinted at the screen. The country was wide at the top, with a flat northern border with Egypt, and did vaguely resemble a reverse comma—or a blunted fang.

Chris rolled his laser pointer to Eloise.

"Thank you, young man." She shone the red pinprick in a circle over the northern two-thirds of the nation. "Up here is all desert. About the only places it's green are along here, where the Nile River flows north toward Egypt. Down here at the very bottom of the country is equatorial rainforest."

Then she pointed out a region about three-quarters of the way down the map. "In here is semidesert. Which means it's desert with the occasional tree or stand of ugly grass. But in the wet season, which is our autumn, all the rivers feed into the Nile flood; and this whole area becomes a big swamp. Perfect for grazing cattle.

"This area is also the border between north and south. Up here, it's all Muslims. Down here, all animists and Christians. When the dry season comes and the swamp dries up—January to April—it's slave-raiding season. The army makes their big moves then, and the Muslim tribes just north of the swamp get on their horses and come on south to have themselves a good time."

Lewis raised his hand.

"Go on, Lewis."

"Ma'am," Lewis said, "I thought the video was saying that the whole slave thing was a scam."

"No, not all of it, Lewis," Eloise said. "Slaving is ancient history in this country. It's been part of their culture since they even had a culture. No one's doubting that slavery exists in Sudan—though Khartoum shouts itself blue saying there is none at all. The question is whether those massive slave redemption things we see on TV are legit. Some say yes, some say no.

"But I'm getting away from my main story, which is explaining what this war is all about." She picked up her remote control. "The magic key that unlocks the whole mystery is this. . . . Are you listening? Except for the bottom third of the country, Sudan is a wasteland.

"In the south there is rich soil for agriculture. In the north, only desert. In the south there is gold and other minerals. In the north, sand. In the south there is water and green grazing lands. In the north, nada. In the south there is gum arabic, which you and I have just enjoyed in our sody pop. In the south there are the headwaters of the Nile, which, as you can imagine, everybody downstream is very concerned about. In the south there are many defenseless, supposedly backward people who can legally be enslaved. You can't do that to your own people in the north.

"But the big ol' honkinest thing that the south has and the north wants," she said, "is oil. Black gold. Texas tea. Swimmin' pools and movie stars." She circled an area in the southeast of the country. "Chevron discovered huge deposits of it in here. And guess what? The north wanted it for themselves. So they came in and took it. They don't even refine it in the south. They pipe it all north."

She set the remote control down. "This oil thing is just a picture of what they're doing in every other way. The south has it, but the north wants it. So, what do you do if you're a fatcat elite in Khartoum and somebody weak has what you want? You take it. You roll out the tanks and the bombers, and you take the goods from the south and tote it all back north."

Rachel shook her head. "Typical."

"I'm sorry, Miss Levy?"

"It's classic Muslim behavior. They're raping the south just like they rape every woman they look at." She looked around the table, and her mouth opened in astonishment. "Oh, don't you all look at me like that. You don't know. A Muslim man gets four wives and as many concubines as he likes. But if that isn't enough, he can sleep with whatever woman he wants and call it a temporary marriage."

Rachel raised her hands as if frustrated at her doltish students. "It's obvious. Look, Muhammad was Captain Expediency, okay? He changed his policies and even his 'divine revelations' whenever it suited him. And the religion he created is just the same. Political expediency, sexual expediency, financial expediency—whatever. So long as the Muslim male gets what he wants. If Muhammad were president of Sudan today, you can bet he would be hearing a new revelation from Allah giving him divine permission to go into the south, steal the oil, and kill everybody who even stepped within a hundred miles of it, Muslim or not."

Rachel rocked back in her chair and shut her eyes. Everybody else exchanged surprised looks.

Chris stared at the table. "Okie dokie, Smokie."

Jason saw Garth affect a look of deep thought. "What is it, big guy?"

"Yeah. Hey, Raych, could we go back to the part about the four wives and all the concubines?" Garth said. "Because that sounded pretty good. I'm thinking about converting."

The laughter got them past the moment. Garth grabbed Rachel's cheeks in his massive hand and squeezed, saying "Pooky, pooky, poo" until she finally smiled. "Lighten up, girl."

Jason stole a glance at Eloise, who returned it seriously.

"Okay, settle down," Jason said. "Trieu, would you please take a shot at summarizing what Eloise is telling us?"

Trieu was sitting close to the table, her hands folded before her. "I believe Mrs. Webster is telling us that it is her conclusion that the power elite in the north of the country is conducting this civil war as a cover for what amounts to federally sanctioned burglary on a national scale."

Eloise laughed, a hard guffaw that didn't actually sound that amused. "That's it, girl. Burglary! Ha! That's what it is, all right. Breaking and entering and then walking off with the goods."

"But I don't get it," Lewis said. "Why doesn't the south just secede? Just write up a declaration of independence or whatever and be done with it? I mean, if they've got all the good stuff anyway, why do they just let it get taken out?"

"There's talk of secession," Eloise said. "Under the latest deal the folks in the south get to vote on that in just a couple of years. But they're not just lettin' anything get taken out, boy," Eloise said. "There's a war on, or maybe you missed it. The people in the south—most of them from the Dinka tribes, the most prevalent in the south—formed the SPLA, the Sudanese People's Liberation Army, back in 1983; and they've been fighting ever since. But their equipment is old, and anyway what are they going to do against tanks and MiG jets?"

"MiGs?" Bigelow asked. "Sudan has MiGs?"

"Yes, sir," Eloise said. "MiG-21 Fishbeds from China, MiG-29 Fulcrums from Russia. MiG-23 Floggers flying the Sudanese colors shot down a relief flight last week for chancing a trip into a no-fly zone. Turned 'em on civilians once or twice already, but they usually use their helicopter gunships on the villages."

Jason whistled softly. "Yikes."

"No kidding," Eloise said. "And American-made M-60A3 tanks, thank you very much. But to answer your question, Lewis, there is talk of the south of Sudan breaking off into its own country. The SPLA sometimes says that's what it's fighting for. Other times it says it's fighting for a unified Sudan. But secession would make a huge impact to all of north Africa. You've got to understand that not many people outside the south of Sudan want that to happen.

"You've got Egypt, who doesn't really want a rogue nation in charge of the headwaters of the Nile. You've got the oil companies, who already have a good deal going with the north and don't know what a new southern government might do. Who knows, they might want to keep the oil for themselves, perish the thought, and nobody wants that.

"You've even got the US of A with its hands in the pie. Did you know that eighty percent of the world's gum arabic comes from Sudan? The *south* of Sudan, I should say. Where would Coca-Cola and Pepsi and Minute Maid and even makeup companies be if the south seceded and decided not to play with the other children? Then of course you've got the north of Sudan, which doesn't want to lose its honey pot."

"Yeah," Chris said. "They might have to go work their fields or something."

"Heaven forbid!" Eloise said. "There is some belief that the oil reserves are the real reason the war is still going on. Not the reason for the war, but the reason it's become Africa's longest-running war. If you're in a civil war, see, it's okay to bomb your own people if they live too close to the oil fields. It's not very nice, and maybe you'll get some sanctions slapped up against you, but no one's going to invade your country to keep you from murdering your own people. If the south was to secede and the north kept on bombing and burning, then it would be an act of international war and somebody would send in troops.

"So Khartoum won't let the south split off. They'll do all they can to *depopulate* the south—through military actions against civilians, through slave raids, by encouraging old tribal hatreds, by preventing food and medicine from coming into the area, by displacing millions, by holy war, or by genocide. But they have no intention of letting the south get away."

"Big Mama?" Garth said.

"What is it, sugar?"

"Can I be excused? My brain hurts."

"No."

"Shoot."

"You think your brain hurts now, honey, wait'll you hear what we're going to talk about next." She stood. "You all take a break. I'll go get our special guest."

# CHAPTER 3

## RUMBEK

"HEY, boss?" Chris said to Jason. Only they remained at the conference table. The others were milling around or waiting for the bathroom.

"Yeah?"

"She still hasn't told us what she wants us to do in Sudan."

Jason nodded. "I noticed."

"Well, I know what I'd do there if I had me a crack team like us at my disposal."

"What would you do?"

"I'd take out the oil pipeline," Chris said, jabbing his fingers knifelike. "Think about it: A pipeline is impossible to guard. You're always going to have hundreds of miles of vulnerable pipe. A couple of well-placed satchel charges and no more crude, baby. When they fix it, you bomb it again."

Jason considered it. "I guess they'd send reprisals, but that's no more than what they're doing now."

The others began returning to the table.

"Are you guys talking about all the immunizations we're going to have to get if we do this?" Lewis asked. "Can't we just go back to Kazakhstan or somewhere where our shots are still good?"

"Nope," Jason said. "Chris is telling me what he'd do in Sudan if he had a commando squad at his beck and call."

"Oh, that's easy," Garth said, sitting again in the deflating chair. "I'd definitely teach the villagers how to fight or flee."

"Yeah!" Lewis said.

"Counterinsurgency, huh?" Jason asked.

Garth rubbed his bald head. "Absolutely."

"Well," Jason said, "who better to teach them than a Green Beret?"

"I wonder what spears and nets could do against tanks and jets, though," Trieu said, taking her chair.

"You don't always teach 'em to fight," Garth said. "You teach 'em how to use scouts. You give 'em a communications system that works for them. You teach 'em how to hide supplies and how to head for the hills when the dust flies. You teach 'em how to survive."

"Looks like they're doing a pretty good job of that themselves," Rachel said.

"So what about you, Rachel?" Chris said. "What would you do with a commando unit in Sudan?"

The group fell silent.

The side of Rachel's mouth twitched. "If I weren't a Christian, and if it weren't for the fact that we only use nonlethals, I think I'd slip into the slave raiders' camp the night before a raid and slit every one of their murdering, raping, child-molesting, expedient throats."

No one spoke.

"Girl," Garth said slowly, "you are really starting to scare me."

From the direction of the entry hall came the sound of the magnetic lock releasing and the heavy wooden door opening. A moment later, Eloise reentered the room.

Followed by the tallest, thinnest black man Jason had ever seen.

The young man had to be six-ten, at least; but his narrow shoulders, high forehead, and long neck made him look like he kept going up and never stopped. He wore a brown suit that was long enough but too wide in the shoulders, as if the tailor couldn't believe anyone who ordered a suit for that height could possibly have shoulders that narrow and so made it larger. He wore a gold tie and a white shirt.

"Babies," Eloise said, "I'd like you to meet Rumbek Koor."

Rumbek smiled shyly, his teeth shining like white neon against his black, black skin. "Good morning, how are you?" The words came out in two bunches, every R sounding like a D: *Goodmording, howahdoo?*

The team stood to greet him. Rachel and Eloise looked like kindergartners next to Rumbek. Only Garth rivaled him in height, but Rumbek took the prize. It was almost comical to watch him double over to shake Bigelow's hand. It looked like he was bending down to tie his shoe.

Eloise pulled out her chair at the head of the table. "Here you go, Rumbek."

The gangly young man sat, but he remained almost as tall as Eloise standing beside him. To Jason, Rumbek appeared to be about eighteen. He wondered quickly if the kid played roundball.

"As you may have guessed," Eloise said, walking beside the table, "Rumbek is from Sudan. He's a Dinka from the south part of the country. He's also a former slave." She sat in a vacant seat next to Rachel. "Rumbek, would you tell these people your story, please?"

Rumbek pulled gold-framed round glasses from his coat pocket and put them on. The simple change made him look more American to Jason. The young man's black hair stood an inch higher than the rest of his head, looking a bit like a furry cap. He cleared his throat.

"My name is Rumbek Koor. I am originally from Niendok village on the Lol River, in Bahr el-Ghazal province."

Eloise used the laser pointer to highlight the spot in southwestern Sudan.

"That land is all *Dinkaland,*" Rumbek said. "We always think of it that way, even when others come or take us from it. When I was five years old, I was hoeing my father's field when I heard the, ah, guns, you know? The voices of the guns. Many murahileen, many horses, coming in my village."

"A slave raid," Eloise said.

"I was frightened, so I hid in the—the forest. I could hear the horrible screaming of my people. I was in terror because my mother, you know, was there, and my sisters and brothers and friends. They burned our tukuls. All the tukuls they burned."

"Those are the round huts they live in," Eloise said. "Clay walls and thatched grass roofs."

"I wanted to hide until nighttime and then run away. But the murahileen found me. They beat me with sticks as thick as my leg. One man, Abdel Ibrahim, said he was my father now and I'd better follow him or he'd kill me. He made me march ten days, with some others from my village also in ropes, you know, to Abu Gabra."

"Abu Gabra is a village of the Baggara tribe," Eloise said. "The Baggara are Muslims. They are traditional enemies of the Dinka. Khartoum gives guns to them and says, 'Go kill Dinka.'"

Rumbek shifted in his chair. "I was Ibrahim's slave. I carried water and pounded grain. When I got older I tended the goats. I slept with the goats also!" He laughed.

The others chuckled politely.

"Usually they fed me uncooked sorghum. You know, the seeds, ah, the grain? Like a crow. I slept outside under a plastic sheet. They beat me every day. They also. . ." He paused, staring out the window into the bright morning. "Miriam was the worst wife. She did not like me. They all called me *abeed, abeed.*"

Everyone looked to Eloise. "That's the Arab word for *slave.* It's how they refer to any 'black African.' In other words, if you're black and you live in the south, you're just a slave waiting to happen."

"It is worse than dog or pig," Rumbek said. "I wished to become a dog, you know, to eat good food! Also they change my name to Abdullah and make me pray in the mosque and learn Arabic. My family was Christian! If I refuse, they beat me more and take away my plastic blanket.

"One day many years later, twelve years, you know, I decide to run away. Miriam broke, ah, broke the arm of other slave, Tabor, because she was angry at Ibrahim. I said, 'That's all! Now I would rather die than being a slave.'

"Two times Ibrahim catch me. He tie my legs to the–to the wall at night. Like a dog—but not eating so well! But I only waited. He say that if I, ah, one more time run away, he will kill me. But now I don't mind. I ran at night, and this one time I do not be found. I walk many days to Cairo. And," he lifted long fingers skyward, "I am here."

"Of course there's a little more to it than that," Eloise said. "He was in the hospital for weeks from his injuries and malnutrition and malaria. And he had to wait in Cairo almost a year to be officially declared a refugee. But it finally happened, and he ended up in Nebraska, where he got connected with an antislavery organization called iAbolish. Now he speaks to churches and groups and government officials, raising awareness about slavery in Sudan and elsewhere."

She beamed at Rumbek. "Thank you, my brother. Praise God you have come out of the valley of the shadow of death. And thank you for telling us your story."

Rumbek smiled again. "You are welcome."

Chris crossed the suite and brought Rumbek a bottle of water, which Rumbek opened and fairly drained on the spot.

"What I'd like to talk about now," Eloise said, "is slave redemption. I've brought Rumbek in because he's obviously intimately aware of the problem. But also he has been back to Sudan many times and seen the current situation. He's also interviewed dozens of refugees fresh out of the country. He's worked alongside slave redeemers like the ones you saw on the video, but he's also aware of the abuses, because he's seen them himself. Bottom line: He's a great resource for us."

She swiveled in her chair. "All right, who wants to go first?"

No one spoke.

Jason scratched his head irritably. "Um, ma'am, maybe it would help guide our questions if we knew what you were wanting us to do. I mean, I take it you want us to go over there and do a mission, right? Otherwise, why tell us any of this?"

Eloise smiled serenely. Dimples appeared in both cheeks. "Why, of course I want you all to go over there, Jason. I told you something had happened in Sudan. That's why I brought you here."

"Okay," Jason said, "but you haven't told us what has happened or what you want us to do about it."

"I want y'all to go over there," she said with intensity, "and I want you to redeem slaves. That's what I've been lining up on the phone." She stood up and began to circle the table. "As you heard, the dry season in Sudan and the slave season are one and the same. Right now, early March, we're just over halfway through this year's raiding season. End of April usually marks the rains and therefore the ending of the raids. Am I right, Rumbek?"

"You are correct," Rumbek said. "Unless the rains don't come until May. Sometimes the GOS and PDF come for one last raid in early May. Those are the worst. We pray for rains in April."

"What are the PDF and the other thing?" Lewis asked. "Not the PDF I know from computers, right? Portable Document Format."

"No, child," Eloise said. "The PDF in Sudan is the Popular Defense Force, which is a high falootin' way of talking about a rabble of Muslim militia groups armed, once again, by Khartoum and sicced on the south. The murahileen Rumbek referred to in his own story are the tribal militias of the Baggara and other groups. They usually ride on horseback and do much of the slave raiding. The PDF soldiers are recruited from the murahileen and aren't much different from them, except they have free reign in the whole south.

"The GOS Rumbek mentioned are the Government of Sudan regular military. GOS forces are the ones who usually engage the

SPLA in the formal civil war fighting. Everything else the PDF and murahileen do is just raping and pillaging, destabilizing the SPLA's support base, and depopulating the south.

"All these groups work together. Here's a good example. You see this railroad going right along here?" She pointed out the line that ran from Khartoum in the north all the way down to a city in the south called Wau. "This is the rail the so-called train of death travels.

"You see, GOS troops do hold a few cities in the south. These here, along the railroad. Wau is the southernmost city they hold. A few times every dry season, the military train makes its way south to supply the garrisons in these towns. But the SPLA has been so effective at destroying the tracks that the train doesn't choo-choo right along anymore. Now it comes at a walking pace. The GOS troops ride the train. The PDF ride their horses on either side of the track to protect the train. The murahileen ride even farther out from the train. These are the bad ones.

"In order to 'protect' the train, the murahileen, the PDF, and sometimes GOS troops conduct raids in any of the villages for fifty miles on either side of the railroad. These are the slave raids, the cattle raids, and the plain old terror raids. See, Khartoum doesn't pay the PDF, and they sure don't pay the murahileen. Their pay is whatever slaves and lucre they can collect for themselves on the trip. They take enough slaves to carry their loot, and they bring it all back to the train as it heads north again."

She slid her hand along the back of an empty chair. "That's not the only way the slave raids happen, but working with the train's travel is one of the main ones. And it shows how all the forces of the north work together to conquer the south."

"Eloise?"

"Yes, Trieu, what is it, honey?"

"You talked about helicopter gunships attacking civilians in Sudan. I remember reading about that before I had really paid attention to any of this. And the video talked about government forces bombing civilians to clear the oil land. Is that really happening? Do they really use military weapons against unarmed villagers?"

Eloise smiled grimly. "Rumbek?"

"That is true," Rumbek said. "I have seen it. When I was in Bahr el-Ghazal two years ago, the school in the village was, ah, bombed by the GOS. Antonov planes, you know? They roll the bombs out, uh, the back of the plane. Not very good at hitting anything. But they sometimes get lucky. That day, seven children and a teacher were killed when the bomb came. It was horrible. All I could hear was screaming. Very sad."

"Whoa," Lewis said.

Chris nodded. "Just like Iraq and the Kurds."

"Now," Eloise said, "before I send you over there to redeem any slaves, I want you to understand why it's such a hot potato issue. First, let me tell you how it started. Since these tribes really have been fighting on and off for thousands of years, swapping slaves and massacres, they've got a pretty good system for getting them back. They use—"

"Don't forget," Rachel said, leaning forward on the red table, "Muslims like to have slaves. Muhammad had slaves. The Koran assumes that Muslims will have slaves. So I think it's wrong, Eloise, to say that this war isn't about religion. Or maybe you're right, that it's all about greed, and religion is just the mask for it. But unless the Muslims of Sudan are ready to start tilling their own fields or watching their own flocks or cooking their own food, they need slaves." She appealed to Rumbek. "Am I right?"

He nodded vigorously. "Very true. My owners would not have been able to eat if slaves did not cook for them."

"All right now," Eloise said. "Anyhow, I was saying that the tribes have a system set up for retrieving slaves. They work through middlemen. You saw them on TV, the characters with the white getups and masks. These are Muslim men who, out of the goodness of their hearts and the fullness of their pockets, find out where certain slaves are, buy them back from the owners, and return them to wherever it is that the person paying the two cows each for the service happens to be. They were doing this for centuries.

"But then in the nineties, some Western Christian ministries heard about the slavery and wanted to help redeem slaves. It started small and in the right spirit. First a handful of slaves were redeemed with Western money. Then dozens. Then hundreds. The families were thrilled to get their loved ones back. They couldn't believe that white folk from far away would care about them enough to do it. During this time, the late nineties, is when that fifth-grade class in America got involved and it really hit the papers.

"I won't get into why the African-American community has been largely silent about the Sudan slave trade," Eloise said. "I don't understand it myself. I would think that we, especially those of us who love the Lord, would be leading the charge against slavery, wouldn't you? But with a few exceptions, we've acted like it wasn't happening. Some of it may have to do with some black folk being afraid of Louis Farrakhan, who says that Sudan is the model of a black Muslim nation and that slavery does not exist there. But that can't be all of it. I don't know and right now I don't care. I'm going to do what I can, and that's all a body can do."

She stared out over the Akron cityscape, a finger absently stroking her cheek.

"Anyway, back to redemption," she said. "Well, with all that Western money coming into Sudan and with human nature being what it is, it was only a matter of time before some sharp thinkers started coming up with ways to relieve the white man of his money. A whole industry sprang up around this craze to redeem slaves. Some of it was legit, some wasn't.

"You heard about some of the scams on the show. I don't think all of it is a scam. I think these redeemers do some good work. There are scores of stories about families being reunited by this outpouring of concern and currency from America and elsewhere.

"But I do think that most of it is a scam. When you've got that much money floating around a poor country and you don't speak the language and maybe there are some kickbacks happening, what's a dumb Westerner going to do? How does he know if the people on the dirt in front of him really do match the list of names in his hand? He has to take it on faith. Now, I believe God rewards good intentions, but I also believe that sometimes redeemers have gone their way with warm fuzzy consciences and empty pockets having 'redeemed' folks who never did need redeeming.

"And the sad thing is that these people aren't out of the frying pan just because they get redeemed. Let's say a young girl really is a slave and really does get returned to her family. What's to prevent her from being recaptured and needing to be redeemed all over again? People in the West think they're sending their fifty bucks and buying a new life for these people. In truth all they might be giving them is a new chance to be captured again.

"But I don't judge these people who give their money for that. No sir. Their hearts are in the right place. And if a redeemed slave runs the risk of being recaptured, I'm sure she and her family would say that's a risk they're willing to take. Temporary freedom with an option to turn permanent has got to be better than slavery with no options at all.

"And I haven't even talked about how this has created a slave economy, that we're trading in human lives, and that the presence of money for redemptions is the demand that the entrepreneurs in Sudan will be highly motivated to supply.

"So," she said, returning to her own chair, "where do I come down on slave redemption?" She pursed her lips. "I believe in it—with limits. We're going to do it, but we're going to do it differently. I think slavery in Sudan is real. I think slaves should be redeemed when they can be. I also think there is a high, high chance of getting duped, especially in the large-scale redemptions. But that doesn't mean all redemptions are wrong.

"I think the perfect scenario would be to work with the Dinka who want their family members back. You stand beside them when they talk to the middleman. You pay the middleman his deposit yourself, in their presence. Maybe you even go with the middleman to where the slave in question is being held. You take someone with you who speaks Arabic."

Everyone looked at Rachel.

"And you listen when he buys the slave back. Then you stand beside the parents and watch. If they say, 'Yes, that's our baby,' then you pay the middleman the rest of his money." She tapped blue fingernails on the conference table. "So you do redemptions, but you're sure you're not being duped."

Jason had a finger to his lips. "You want us to go do this kind of redemption, don't you?"

She chuckled. "Yes, sir, Mr. Bottom Line. That's what I want. It's next to impossible to get to these villages anyway. You almost have to be commandos just to get there. And we do happen to have someone who speaks Arabic. Rachel, you don't speak Dinka, too, do you?"

Rachel looked like she was feeling sick. "No, sorry. But I'm sure I could get some tapes, and maybe Rumbek could help me."

Jason watched Rumbek's reaction. Maybe he was imagining things, but it appeared his disposition improved with the mention of Rachel's idea.

Chris raised his hand. "I'm rusty, but when I was in Force Recon I learned Arabic. Maybe I could help out, too. But no Dinka, sorry."

"All right, good," Eloise said. "I've been on the phone for days now trying to line up a goodly number of slaves from this village who could be located and verified. Who knew it could be so hard? I need Doug Bigelow to come and be my logistics guru. You up to it, baby?"

Bigelow rolled his wheelchair back and forward. "You got it, Big Mama."

"All right. I'm thinking you all go back to your little clubhouse in the sticks and play army for awhile. I'll get this thing figured out and give you a call. You go redeem the slaves on the list I give you—

if and only if you have someone with you who can tell you for certain they're the right ones. Then you come home in four days. What do you say?"

Jason felt his forehead furrow. "That's it? Just the ones on the list? Just four days and we're out?"

"You want to stay longer?" Eloise asked. "Because I'm sure I could arrange it."

"No, I. . .I guess with all this talk of civil war and bombing civilians and all. . . . I don't know. Someone help me out. Doesn't it just feel like there's so much need here? Is our redeeming twenty slaves—who you said yourself might be recaptured the minute we leave—going to make any difference?"

"I totally agree," Lewis said. "Like, what's that going to do?"

Chris harrumphed. "And here I thought you were going to cut us loose to bomb an oil pipeline or something. It does seem kind of wrong somehow. Too small, I guess."

"Hey," Eloise said, "I'm only trying to think 'attainable objectives,' like Jason here is always trying to tell me. Babies, if I had my way, I'd set you free in Sudan for a year. You could just take your time and do whatever comes natural to them that shoot children and traffic in human slaves. But I also know that you six can't fight a war. Jason has finally taught me to think small, so I'm thinking small. You go in, save some slaves, and get out. Maybe you look around yourself real good when you go, so that next time we can come back and stay longer."

They sat in silence. The sun had risen over the city. Jason's stomach growled.

"Eloise," he said, "you never told us what happened in Sudan. You said something had happened that got you upset. What was it?"

The big woman sighed deeply. "You know that group Doctors Without Borders?"

*"Médecins Sans Frontières,"* Rachel said in perfect French.

"Right. Well, they were making a visit to an airstrip in Bahr el-Ghazal in an area that Khartoum had been holding as a no-fly zone until recently. Up walked this Dinka man with a bleeding and filthy leg wound. Turns out he was from the village of Akwer Nhom.

"He told the doctors that the murahileen had raided his village a few days before. They'd stolen or murdered or enslaved everything and everyone that wasn't nailed down—and burned everything that was. He said it was total chaos: children thrown into burning buildings, Muslims raping Dinka women right on the dirt, people hacked apart. He was knocked out and left for dead trying to save his wife. When he came to, the raiders were gone and his wife was dead; but the northward trail left by two hundred head of cattle, hundreds of horses, and a few bare feet wasn't hard to find.

"He knows his wife, son, and baby daughter were killed; but he believes his twelve-year-old little girl was taken for a slave, along with probably three or four dozen others from his village. He wants them back." Eloise pressed her fingertips together. "That's where we come in."

Jason was listening closely now. A little girl was in trouble. Abducted from her home. Terrorized. Suffering who knew what kind of fear and grief and loneliness. And abuse. All right, forget everything else: He was ready to go right now.

"I want you six to hie yourselves over to Sudan and meet with this man and the other survivors. And I want you to bring these people back to what's left of their home. I'll provide the money; don't you worry about that. You just go find this man's daughter and neighbors."

Garth nodded deeply. "When do we leave?"

"Just as soon as I can get it arranged," Eloise said. "Now, y'all sit tight. I need to take a walk with your team leader. Help yourselves to whatever's in the fridge. But don't overdo. We're off to Lanning's for lunch on me."

\* \* \*

"You think she's gonna blow?"

Jason smiled at Eloise's question. "Maybe, I don't know."

They stood in the spacious observation lounge overlooking ABL's *WarGames*-esque control room. Jason remembered this very circle of overstuffed furniture as the place where, just a few weeks ago, he had told Eloise and the others that he was not going to join their team—no way, no how. What a laugh.

"Do you know what's wrong with the girl?" Eloise asked. "She's always on about something, but she was downright unstable in there today. All that about slitting throats and words of poison on her lips for Muslim men. Thought I was gonna have to tan her hide right then and there."

"No idea," Jason said. "She started acting weird in Australia. Being kind of jealous of me and Trieu if she ever happened to spot us talking together. She snipped at the others, too, but it was usually reserved for me."

"Aren't you flattered? A beautiful woman like Rachel wants you all to herself. Sounds like every man's dream to me."

"No kidding. But this doesn't feel like a healthy thing, I'll tell you that much. We had a good talk down there, and I thought everything was settled. But where's all this anti-Islam stuff coming from?" he asked.

Eloise straightened her blue dress. "That she comes by honestly, or are you forgetting she's an Israeli Jew whose father was killed by Muslim terrorists?"

"Or how she was an assassin for the Mossad? You don't typically forget things like that about a girl." He played with a fraying tennis shoe. "I guess I'd be big-time bitter, too. It just surprised me, is all. Plus I thought she'd dealt with that since she became a Christian. Guess not."

"No, it surprised me, too." She pursed her lips. "I can't *not* send Rachel on this mission, Jason. Her Arabic may be the key to this whole thing."

"I know. I was thinking we'd keep that secret, you know? Not tell anyone that she speaks it. She's good at playing dumb when she wants to. That way we'll have a way of knowing if people are shooting straight with us, but without them knowing that we know."

"That's fine, Jason, you're the team leader. Strategy's up to you." She shook her head. "I'm just worried about her. I think she's about to come unglued. If so, sending her up against Muslims on a holy war is probably the worst thing I could do. But I don't see any way around it, do you?"

"Not unless you want us to hold off while she goes to counseling or something. Maybe we do this mission in a few months."

"Forget it," Eloise said. "I want these babies back before a month is out."

"All right, then," Jason said, standing. "Then I guess Rachel comes with us. Let's just pray she can hold it all together until we get back."

# CHAPTER 4

## A NICE DAY FOR A WALK

"HEAR that?"

Jason looked around the grassy Utah clearing. A mountain stream meandered between the forested hills on either side. Clouds were rolling in. "No, Chris, I don't hear anything."

"You don't hear that screeching?"

Jason lifted the Kevlar helmet away from his right ear. He did hear a screeching, like what you hear when you walk by the parakeet cage at the pet store. "What is it, you think? Suspension out on an enemy vehicle?"

"No," Chris said, as if that were a ridiculous guess. "It's piñon jays, dude, probably mobbing a snake."

Jason shook his head. "This *is* just training, Chris, but I want you to train like you'll fight."

"This *is* how I fight: ears always working." He shook his head. "Man, you have no respect for what nature can teach you."

"Okay, everybody," Jason said, "let's hold up."

Chris knelt in the grass, his eyes scanning the meadow ahead. He let go of his CAR-15 rifle, modified to shoot pepperballs and newly affixed with an underslung tear gas canister launcher, and the self-reeling harness sucked it close to his chest.

Jason glanced back at the others as they knelt or sat. Trieu was next behind Jason, her Dragunov SVD sniper rifle snug against her front. Next came Lewis, with his helmet's eye panel down, half virtual. Rachel knelt behind him, managing to make forest green camos look like they'd just been shown on a Parisian fashion runway. *You like her for things beyond her looks, remember?* Last was Garth, who sat facing the way they'd come. Jason saw an array of nasty surprises on the big man's load-bearing vest. All of them had the new weapon harness that allowed them to operate hands-free when necessary and yet still keep the gun close and ready.

"Okay," Jason said, "we're coming up on the spot our little flying banshee plane marked with the laser rangefinder. But, as you can all see, there's nothing there now."

As he spoke, heavy gray clouds slid in front of the sun, turning the sharp aspen tree shadows into a uniform dimness. A cooler breeze passed across Jason's face, and the green aspen leaves rattled. Thunder rumbled softly, like someone moving furniture in the next room.

"What a surprise," Lewis said. "Rain."

"What do you expect?" Rachel asked. "It's almost two o'clock."

"I know," Lewis said. "At least it's predictable."

"It's not a problem," Jason said. "We'll just have to be that much sharper."

"Besides," Garth said, not turning around, "God causes the rain to fall on the evil *and* the good."

Chris chuckled. "Uh, okay, buddy. Sure."

"I think what he's trying to say," Trieu said, "is that the enemy will be getting soaked in the miserable rain, too. If we are cunning, we can turn it into an advantage for us."

Fat raindrops began striking them, leaving quarter-sized dark green circles on their uniforms.

"Come on," Jason said, "let's move. I want to look for tracks at the spot the banshee marked before the rain smashes everything down."

They stood, and Chris stepped across the clearing, keeping the winding stream to his right and the line of aspens to his left. Jason came next, sweeping the right side of the clearing with his own CAR-15/tear gas launcher. Trieu came next, watching their left. Then Lewis, looking right; Rachel, looking left; and Garth, all but walking backwards.

"Lewis," Jason said into the squad radio microphone at his lips, "you see anything on the banshee?"

"Just a bunch of ning-nongs walking through a swamp," Lewis said. "I'm going to have to bring her down soon. The rain will cut her battery time down."

"Okay," Jason said, "but look up ahead first."

"Always."

"What was that thing it saw, anyway?" Rachel asked. "Do we even know what we're chasing?"

"It was a horse-drawn wagon," Jason said.

Rachel snickered. "So we're stalking Farmer John?"

"The idea," Jason said, "is for us to be able to track a mobile quarry. If Eloise has us going after slave raiders on their way from a raid, they'll be mobile, too. Chimp's just trying to train us in useful ways."

Garth chuckled. "Rachel's stalking Farmer John. Rachel's stalking Farmer John."

"You guys!" Lewis said. "I can't believe you're cutting up like this. Grow up, please. We're supposed to be simulating *war* here, not cowboys and Indians."

Chris saluted smartly. "Aye aye, Cap'n Crunch."

Jason flipped down his eyepiece. He used the three-button switchbox on his chest to cycle through the image sources on the tiny computer monitor. He switched from the banshee's camera feed to the gun cam menu to the GPS map. There, six green dots in a line approached and passed onto a tiny red dot.

"Okay, we're here," Jason said. "Hold up."

Jason searched the grass while Chris scouted forward and the others scanned the clearing. The rain fell in moving shower curtains across the field. Every color in the high-altitude valley became a hundred times more vibrant when wet. But it did cut down on visibility.

"I'm not finding any tracks," Jason said. "Lewis, you spot anything ahead?"

"Yeah! I got it. It's just around that corner where the hill slopes down. Come on, let's go!"

Lewis was on his feet and running ahead before Jason knew it. As Lewis neared Chris, he grabbed the kid roughly and pushed him back.

"Chris! The wagon's getting away."

Chris wasn't letting go. "No." His eyes passed over to Jason. "Come here."

His tone brought Jason forward quickly and cautiously. "This isn't another birdsong concert, is it?"

In answer, Chris knelt and pointed with the tip of his rifle.

Jason's eyes followed. The muzzle of Chris's gun lifted something long and thin that stretched across the path. "A tripwire?"

"What?" Lewis said, bending down. "Well, I'll be an orc chieftain. It *is* a tripwire."

"What do you know," Garth said, "the jarhead got it right. 'The steps of a good man are ordered by the Lord. Though he falls he shall not be utterly cast down.' "

"Huh?"

"It's Scripture, ya dumb marine."

Jason did a quick three-sixty survey. "We must be getting close to a stronghold or something. Great spotting, Chris." He stood. "Okay, everybody stay frosty."

Rachel hugged herself with one arm. "That won't be hard, boss."

Jason showed each team member exactly where the tripwire was as they stepped over it.

They moved more quickly now, trying to close the gap to the re-treating wagon. Lewis brought the banshee in for a landing. The radio-controlled rotorcraft—it always looked like a flying bubble gum machine to Jason—landed in Lewis's hand like a falcon. He folded the four rotor arms upward and stuck the little robot into his backpack.

Suddenly Chris stopped and dropped to one knee. The rest of the team dropped, too, and scanned the clearing and woods even more intensely. Chris brought his CAR-15 to ready position. Then he turned back to Jason and made hand signals. Two fingers pointed to his eyes—enemy spotted. Two fingers in the air—two enemies.

Jason crawled up to Chris's side, pulling out binoculars. He fol-lowed Chris's pointed finger and saw the two enemy soldiers—chubby white guys with plastic goggles and semiautomatic paintball guns. They shared a brown umbrella, looking exactly like any other soldier on guard duty in the rain.

Motion beyond the soldiers caught Jason's eye. He swerved the glasses to the left. "I see the wagon," he whispered into his helmet microphone. "Two horses, one driver, about five 'slaves' in the back, and ten guards walking beside it. But it's a good quarter mile ahead of us. Trieu, come up here."

When she was next to him, he pointed out the soldiers. "Think you can take them both out before they raise an alarm?"

She brought the Dragunov's scope to her eye. After a long moment, she pursed her lips. "Normally, yes. But with the rain and the gun powered down for training, I need to get another hundred feet closer."

"All right," Jason said. "Okay, guys, do you think you can move faster and be even more careful at the same time? I don't want to let that wagon out of my sight again."

They advanced across the slippery turf on their bellies. The rain had turned the field into a marsh. When Jason stepped into the three-foot-deep stream and out the other side, he could hardly tell the difference.

He checked the team's progress. Rachel had mud across her forehead and Lewis's left boot had gained a half pound of green turf that didn't want to let go. The others were similarly marked. A fine day for a walk.

Finally they were in range. The two men, now smoking cigarettes, were a hundred feet away. Jason brought the group, all prone, into a line on either side of Trieu while she prepared to take her shot. The smell of crushed mint rose from the grass.

"Everybody keep watching all around us," he said. "If one of those guys gives a shout in the thirteen seconds before he passes out, anyone around may come running to take a look."

Trieu flipped the safety off and peered through her scope.

Jason felt himself holding his breath. Not so very long ago he'd been the sniper for his squad in SEAL Team Three. This was the classic sniper moment: one hunter alone against the world, sitting in hiding, slowly squeezing the trigger on an unsuspecting target.

The Dragunov's exotic design heightened the thrill. The brown wooden stock had a large "window" in it, by design, to lower the weight and to allow the sniper to put his thumb through and hold it in a pistol grip. The barrel was very long and the silencer, a smooth cylinder the width of a Little League baseball bat, made it longer still. While most hunting rifles were bolt-action guns, the Dragunov autofed cartridges—in this case protein bullets that broke the skin and delivered a sedative but did no other damage—through a ten-round magazine. Trieu had wrapped the barrel in camouflage cloth and stuck moss around the muzzle. The whole thing was topped off by a 10X scope with a soft rubber eyepiece that Trieu held pressed against her right eye.

Jason watched the targets through the binoculars. Ideally, one guard would split off from the other, but neither seemed willing to leave the umbrella.

Beside him, Jason heard Trieu fire. The muzzle spit a spray of gas and made a high-pitched *pyew* sound like a Buck Rogers laser.

The man on the right jumped and held his thigh like he'd been gored by a goat. Jason could hear his *Ow!* over the drone of the rain.

The umbrella fell to the ground and the other man cursed. "What's the matter with you, Tom? Why'd you have to go and drop the—"

Trieu fired again.

The second man grunted and grabbed his gluteus maximus. "Ouch! Something bit me."

"Jerry," the first guy said, holding up a bloody finger, "I've been shot, dude."

That's when Jerry seemed to get it. "They're here!" He gripped his paintball gun and faced the clearing. "Tom, they're here." He backed toward the wooded hillside, where only now Jason could see camouflage tarps strung between the trees. "Hey!" Jerry shouted. "Hey, they're here! Everybody get out here now! They're using real bullets!"

Both men opened fire. They shot wildly, spraying the green and gray meadow with bright yellow paintballs. Voices and sounds of stumbling came from up the hillside behind the tarps.

"Tom," Jerry said, "fire over at that stump. I thought I saw. . .Tom?"

Tom collapsed on the soggy grass.

"Tom's dead!" Jerry shouted. "I'm out of here!"

Jerry turned to run up the hill just as four men came sliding down toward the action.

"Great," Jason said. "Okay, everybody come on line and let's take 'em down fast. The wagon's getting away."

Team Firebrand opened fire with pepperballs and tranquilizer darts. Chris and Jason fired tear gas canisters, which erupted into thin gray clouds. All five men still standing returned fire wildly, then coughed and wheezed, and finally fell.

"Hold fire," Jason said. He peered through the binoculars. The six enemy soldiers were either unconscious or still coughing their way to Lalaland. "Okay, they're all down. Great job, you guys. Perfect execution. Reload and let's get going before more bad guys come."

"Hey, Jason," Chris said, reloading his tear gas launcher. "I like this thing."

Jason smiled like a ten year old. "Me, too." He patted Trieu on the helmet. "Nice shootin', Tex."

She tucked a strand of black hair into her helmet. "Thank you."

"Take us there, Chris," Jason said, coming to a crouch. "Full throttle, baby."

They moved out at a three-quarters run, Chris on point and Garth bringing up the rear. Their boots splashed and slid, and the sky flashed white. They passed the sleeping soldiers and rounded the wooded arm of the hill.

Here the stream continued up the wide valley. Dark evergreen trees came almost to the floor of the clearing.

"There it is!" Lewis all but shouted.

The "slave wagon" jostled along a hundred yards away, moving toward an outcropping of twelve-foot-high boulders.

"Come on!" Jason said.

They went into a full run, still in their patrol line.

"Trieu," Jason said between breaths. "Can you take out the driver from here?"

"Maybe."

"Try," he said. "Keep them from getting behind the rocks. Everybody, swing around left to give her a clear shot."

Trieu dropped to a knee and brought her rifle up. Jason didn't wait to see if she fired. The soldiers around the slave wagon had noticed them.

But instead of opening fire as Jason expected, they shouted to the driver and ran for the cover of the boulders. The driver turned in his perch, looked over the field, and urged the two horses ahead. The "slaves" in the caged wagon fell to the floor and covered their heads. One of the guards suddenly clutched his leg and fell. Two others stopped to help him away. The team sprinted toward them.

Suddenly one of them shot a rocket into the air. At least that's what it looked like. Jason looked up at the white-yellow projectile climbing noisily toward the low clouds. It seemed unusually bright.

"Who shot a flare?"

Another flare shot up. This time Jason saw where it launched from: a shrub at the nearby creek bank.

"Tripwires! You guys, stop. We're setting off booby traps."

Before they could all slide to a stop, they'd set off two more alarms—noisemakers that whistled and popped like fiesta fireworks.

"Not good," Rachel muttered. "Not good, not good."

"Uh, Jason?" It was Trieu's voice over the radio.

"Not now, Trieu. We're in a little trouble here."

"Well, you're about to be in more. I'm hearing engines behind me. Motorcycles, I think."

"It's a trap!" Chris said, his eyes wide.

"All right," Jason said irritably. "Listen up. The objective's just ahead. We'll overtake it, take out the guards, free the slaves, and then get lost in the forest. We'll take the long way back to base." He gazed around at his team. They looked nervous but not panicked. "Okay?"

Garth nodded. "Bob's your uncle."

"Trieu, get into the trees and join us at the wagon if you can."

"Affirmative," she said. "Jason," her voice was punctuated by her footfalls, "I'm seeing at least ten motorcycles headed this way."

"Understood," Jason said, running beside Chris and Rachel. "I can hear them now."

As they ran, they set off more flares and sparklers.

"Don't worry about it!" Jason shouted. "Just go."

They reached the mossy boulders completely out of breath.

"Man, Lewis," Chris said, "wish your banshee was up."

"Want I should send her up?"

"No," Jason said. "No time. Chris, take a look. Everybody, get ready to rumble."

The motorcycles rounded the wooded slope where the soldiers had been knocked out. Jason counted at least fifteen mud-spewing dirtbikes, driven by men with helmets, goggles, and paintball guns slung over their shoulders. The tinny whine of the two-stroke engines was briefly muted by a thunderclap that resounded across the wide meadow. At least the air was cool enough to keep Jason's heat level manageable.

Chris poked his head and gun around the boulder. He looked, swung back, then looked again. He turned back to Jason and waved the team forward.

They resumed their patrol formation and came around the corner. The wagon was twenty yards ahead, recessed against the line of rocks on one side and a steep hill on the other. Jason couldn't see anyone near it.

"Let's move," he said.

They trotted forward.

"This is funky," Chris said softly. "Where is everybody? Something's—"

*POW-POWWW!*

Twin blasts of noise and light exploded on either side of them. Automatic noise limiters in Jason's helmet clamped down immediately, cutting off the sudden blare, but couldn't do anything about the surprise. Jason spotted soldiers emerging from the trees and rounding the wagon. They were shouting and firing paintball launchers. Splashes of yellow and red and blue began appearing on the grass like multicolored raindrops.

Chris dropped to one knee and fired at the attackers on full auto. "Ambush! Ambush!"

Jason saw the others beginning to come alongside Chris to shoot. "No! It's too narrow here. Peel. Australian peel! Like we practiced. Chris, go!"

Chris fired pepperballs nonstop until his magazine was empty. Ten men had white powder on their shirts and were in the mud coughing. Chris fired the tear gas canister and then ran back toward Garth at the end of the line.

That left Jason on point. As soon as Chris cleared his field of fire, Jason shot the tear gas canister toward men on their flanks. Then he emptied his own CAR-15 into the cloud. Finally, he pulled a smoke grenade from his vest and flung it down between him and the attackers.

He stood and ran past Lewis, who began firing on full auto, past Rachel, who looked scared but determined, and past Garth, who was prepping a pepper bomb surprise.

Following proper Australian peel procedure, Jason ran toward the last man in the line—Chris—who was supposed to be pointing them toward a way out. Chris was at the edge of the boulders, reloading quickly. Jason could hear the motorcycles very close now.

"Which way, Chris?"

Chris swung around to the right and pointed toward the nearest stand of heavy forest that wasn't swarming with bad guys—across thirty yards of open field. He whirled and aimed at something moving left to right at high speed. He fired, and Jason heard a motorcycle engine scream and die. Mud flew up and sprayed Chris in the chest and face.

Jason ran toward the woods. As he cleared the cover of the boulder, he saw what Chris was seeing: a horde of dirtbikes tearing up the turf. Several men had dismounted and were creeping forward, firing as they came. Chris ducked and fired another tear gas canister into the fray.

Reloading, Jason spotted Lewis running toward him at full speed, so he pointed the kid toward the forest, which was still twenty yards away. Lewis sprinted by and went all the way into the cover of the evergreens.

"Lewis," Jason said over the radio, "not so far. Come back out. Lewis!"

Rachel splashed toward him, zigging and zagging. "Where's Lewis?"

Jason was about to point the way when two Suzukis streaked toward him, paintball launchers in the riders' left hands.

He stood his ground and raised his over-and-under weapon. Purple paint splattered at his feet, but did not strike him, and pellets whizzed past his head. His aim was better. Two pepperballs impacted on each rider, just below the facemasks.

They dropped their paintball launchers and reached for their throats. The bikes got tangled and the riders went down in a slushy heap.

*BA-HOOM!*

Jason knew what it was before his eyes registered the billowing white cloud by the wagon: Garth's pepper-claymore special. A bitter disappointment to their pursuers.

Then Garth was lumbering toward him, his rifle looking like a toy against his massive chest. Jason saw Garth's eyes searching the field. He opened his hands to Jason. *Where are they?*

Jason looked. If anything, the rain was coming down harder now—a torrent. There was no sign of Lewis or Rachel.

"Lewis! Rachel!" Jason said into his mike. "Where are you guys?"

"Where are *you* guys?" Lewis said. "I'm up the hill like you said."

"Lewis! You're supposed to wait for the next person to pass you."

"Oops."

Rachel's voice broke through: "Anytime you guys want to get here, that'd be nice."

Jason crept toward the edge of the boulder. Chris and Garth were there, holding off the cyclists. Already there were signs of movement from the cloud by the wagon.

"Rachel," he said, "where are you?"

"I'm in the woods, too. I couldn't find Lewis so I just went forward twenty yards, like you taught us. But I was totally exposed, so I got to the trees. Sorry."

Jason put his knuckles to his temple. *Great job, Buckwheat. Now what?* "Just stay there, Rachel. Lewis, come back down and find either us or Rachel. We've got to regroup."

"Oh, man!" Lewis said.

"Do it," Jason said. Then he noticed something different on the battlefield. "Why is it so quiet?"

"Look at them," Chris said, pointing across the mud-tracked

clearing. "I think they're going to charge us."

Jason could just make out the motorcycles in a line. The engines must've been off or idling. "Or maybe they're coming on foot now so they can aim better."

"Either way," Garth said, "we don't want to be here."

"No kidding." Jason peered in the direction of the wagon. Men crept forward in twos and threes. "Trieu," he said into his microphone, "you still with us, girl?"

"I'm here, Jason. But I haven't been able to circle around to you. I've taken a paintball to the right leg. I guess that means I'm supposed to not move, right? Or am I dead?"

"Gee, Trieu," Lewis said, the sounds of footsteps behind his voice, "can't you, like, operate on yourself or something?"

"That's enough, Lewis," Jason said. To punctuate his order, he tossed another smoke grenade in the direction of the creepers. "We've got to move."

"Okay, boss," Chris said. "What'll it be?"

"I'm working on it!" Jason said.

He flipped his eyepiece down and cycled through the displays. On the map he saw three green dots bunched together, one dot a hundred yards southeast (Rachel), another way south but moving northeast (Lewis), and a sixth green one two hundred yards to the northwest (Trieu).

"Okay," he said. "Lewis, use your dot race map to find Rachel. Rachel, do you see him on the—"

His helmet speakers popped and his screen went blank.

"Oh, no." He smacked himself on the helmet. "Don't do this. Rachel, Lewis, Trieu—anybody hear me?"

Nothing.

Across the field, the riders revved their motorcycle engines in an eager roar. The smell of gasoline and carbon monoxide was hung over the field.

Jason tapped Chris and Garth on the shoulders. "Radios are out.

All our tech stuff is out."

"Now what?" Chris asked. "They're about to rush us."

Jason dropped to one knee. *Lord, help me figure this out.* His team was split up. Together they had a chance. Separated, they'd be taken out one by one. He, Chris, and Garth were extremely vulnerable where they were. It was a miracle they'd only taken one casualty so far. Their high-tech toys had failed them. He couldn't even communicate with the others.

"Any time, Jace," Garth said.

"Make a decision, Kromer," Chris said, "or I'll do it for you."

Jason stared at the wet grass. Trieu was wounded. She would slow the others down. The cruel calculus of war kicked in and advised him to leave her behind. The three of them could get to Rachel and Lewis and be a working unit again. But SEALs didn't leave people behind.

"Okay," he said, standing, "we go for—"

"There's Rachel!" Chris yelled.

Forty yards away, Rachel sped toward them in a crouched run.

Just then the motorcycles sprinted forward in a line. It sounded like a motocross race had begun. At the same moment the soldiers behind them screamed and charged, firing paint pellets.

Jason threw a smoke grenade toward them, and they slowed.

Acting on some cue, the motorcycles wheeled almost in a parade line and came right at Rachel.

She screamed.

"Rachel!" Chris shouted.

He and Garth ran toward her.

"Wait!" Jason called.

But they weren't coming back. They fired tear gas and pepperballs at the motorcyclists. Rachel stumbled back toward the woods.

Jason looked over his shoulder. The attackers on foot pierced the white smoke cloud. The other direction wasn't any better: Garth and Chris weren't going to make it. They would be enveloped by the dirtbike line and still not save Rachel. Paintballs splattered all around him.

His only opening was back toward the boulders and beyond, toward Trieu. The attackers would expect him to head for the woods, not the open field.

He fired his full magazine of pepperballs at the frontrunners and sprinted for the open.

The rain was stopping, and the dark gray clouds had given way to light gray ones quickly departing. Birds sang from the forest, oblivious to the human drama.

Behind him he heard shouting and engines and the clicking of paintball and pepperball launchers. Nearer, he heard slogging footfalls as his pursuers rounded the boulders. Jason zigzagged, thanking God for brutal conditioning and comfortable boots.

The ground began to climb. The trees didn't reach the bottom of the clearing here. Small boulders dotted the hillside like chocolate chips.

He heard shouts of victory far behind him from about thirty men. That probably wasn't a good sign. Then the motorcycles revved again, and he knew right where they were headed.

He saw movement in the trees ahead. He kept running. If it was the napping soldiers up for another sleeping pill, he'd try to oblige. If it was a deer or a bear, it would run. If it was a forest ranger, he'd smile and wave.

It was Trieu.

She knelt beside an aspen, her Dragunov raised and ready. Jason lowered his head and ran in a straight line. He knew he'd outdistance the runners over this last fifty-yard dash, but the motorcycles were another matter.

Trieu's muzzle spat gray gas.

Jason ran.

Dirtbikes whined.

Trieu fired quickly. Twice. Five times. Another very bad sign.

Paint exploded in primary colors all around him.

Trieu lowered her rifle to reload.

Jason ran up the hill. The aspens towered over him.

A spoked wheel entered his periphery vision.

Ten yards from Trieu, something struck him hard in the leg.

He kept running, knowing he was supposed to fall and play dead, but caught up in the moment. Two more impacts ended that notion right away. Blue paint splashed across his shoulder, and a yellow pellet struck him just below his helmet.

He went down to the turf just as four squealing Yamahas cut in front of him and finished off Trieu.

More motorcycles zoomed up, spraying mud everywhere. The riders raised their guns in victory and hooted like Apaches.

Jason sat up and wrapped his arms around his knees. "Game over, dude."

Trieu came and sat beside him. She looked like a piece of abstract art. "That didn't go too well." She reached over and removed a slab of mud from the front of his helmet. "Or is this how you'd planned it?"

A lime green four-wheel ATV rolled up from downstream. Doug Bigelow killed the engine and shook his head. "You guys are so toast."

Jason nodded stoically. "Yup."

A group of riders and walkers rounded the boulders in the near distance. Jason could see Garth towering over the others. Beside him came Chris and Rachel and Lewis, all looking like soggy rodeo clowns.

Bigelow produced a bullhorn and raised it to his mouth. "Thanks, everybody! You guys on bikes—great job. And thumbs up to our slaves and ambushers and guards. Everybody deserves Oscars. That's it for today. If you're on a bike, give somebody a ride back to the parking lot. Remember, showers and drinks at the lodge. Okay, you guys can go! Thanks again."

The "enemy force" cheered wildly. Then the motorcyclists hooked up with passengers, and the cycle gang left the field in a spray of mud and turf. The mountain meadow looked like it had been the site of an old-time hoedown.

Garth and the others reached Jason and Trieu and Bigelow. Lewis had his helmet off, revealing a blue paintball wound that had bled from his scalp into his shirt.

Bigelow laughed harshly. "You guys don't look so good."

They sat on the ground in a circle. Chris sneered. "Shut up."

"Wait a minute," Bigelow said, pulling out a digital camera. "I've got to get a picture of this."

"No!" Rachel said, covering her muddy face.

How could she be this dirty and this beautiful at the same time? She did have a pretty nasty case of bright yellow acne, but there were soaps for that. And Jason knew she did clean up real well.

"Okay," Lewis said, "I have to know. How did you make all the computers and radios go down without me knowing you were tampering with it?"

Bigelow took his photos and dropped the camera in a pouch at his waist. Jason noticed the straps holding his legs in place. "I'll tell you, Lewis," Bigelow said. "But first: Jason, do you want to talk about it here or get cleaned up first?"

"Definitely we get cleaned up first," Rachel said.

"All right," Bigelow said. "Rachel, honey, you want to ride in my lap? The rest of 'em have to walk."

"No thanks, Doug," Rachel said. "I don't think Jamie would approve."

"I'll ride," Lewis said.

"All right," Bigelow said, sounding disappointed. "Come on, then, geekazoid. Get on back. The rest of you, cheer up. The lodge can't be more than six miles away. Jason, why don't you have them run it?"

Chris lifted his rifle and started shooting pepperballs at the ATV.

Bigelow and Lewis sped away.

# CHAPTER 5

## LESSONS LEARNED

"BUTCH, dude, you need a pedicure."

The old bloodhound stopped clicking across the porch long enough to look at Lewis as if considering the comment. His long brown ears swayed, and the extra skin on his forehead lined in an appearance of worry. Then he sat on the wood planks and dove after an itch in his private regions.

Lewis shook his head and pulled up a rocking chair. "Stupid dog."

"Hey," Garth said, easing into a porch swing, "only I get to call him that. To you, he's *Mr. Stupid Dog*."

They were back at the lodge in their training facility, a Utah compound that had once been a white supremacists' camp. The lodge itself was a beautiful edifice, looking more like a posh ski lodge than a survivalist HQ.

It was raining again. Water streamed off the wooden roof in orderly lines. The Firebrand team—plus one hound dog and one man in a wheelchair—was congregating on the long wooden porch outside the lodge. Wooden planks on the floor, wooden posts to the roof, wooden pole railing at the porch's edge.

Jason sat on a polished railback chair and surveyed his team. They had cleaned up and changed into civilian clothes, warm ones, against the cool, wet air. Lewis sat in a rocker on Jason's far right. Next came Garth, Trieu, and Rachel—nursing a mug of hot chocolate—on the long swing. Chris sat at Jason's left on a wicker chair that had seen better days. Bigelow wheeled out onto the porch, a legal pad in his lap.

Butch crashed on the floor.

"Hey, Trieu," Garth said, "this rain is depressing. Why don't you go get your cello and cheer us up with a requiem or something."

Trieu smiled. "With an invitation like that, how could I refuse? But," she said, staring out at the deluge, "the humidity isn't good for it. I usually only play indoors."

"Oh," Garth said, "too bad."

"Okay," Jason said, "before Doug gets started, I'd like to lead us in prayer."

The team bowed their heads. Chris took off his Nike cap and smoothed his hair.

"Father, thanks for our training today. Thanks for keeping us humble. Lord, I also want to thank You that nobody got seriously hurt. And thanks for Doug being such a great trainer. Father, help us figure out what to do better next time. Use us, Lord. Amen."

Chris put his cap back on. Thunder rumbled distantly.

"Jason," Rachel said, "could you shut the flaps? I'm cold." She wore a simple gray sweatshirt that looked especially huggable. Her black hair was up in a cute ponytail. She held a steaming ceramic mug in her hands.

"Sure."

Jason and Chris unrolled the clear vinyl flaps between porch pillars. They snapped them down to the posts, creating instant walls.

Garth turned on the large heater at the corner of the porch. Fan-forced heat began to fill the enclosed space.

"All right, sports fans," Bigelow said, flipping back the first yellow page. "Who wants to go first? Let's start with the positives. What did you guys do right out there? Anyone? Anyone?"

No one answered. Jason shifted in his chair. Trieu looked like she was trying to figure out the last word in a crossword puzzle. Rain spattered quietly against the vinyl.

"Well, I'll give you one for free then," Bigelow said. "You guys moved very quickly to the objective. Having that banshee mark the wagon's spot on your maps was more effective than I thought it would be. You almost caught the bait before it could spring the trap. Good job." He checked something off on the pad. "What else?"

No answer. Butch got up and walked over to Garth's feet.

"Come here, stupid dog." Garth hefted the brown and black hound into his lap and rubbed the dog's belly. It was the large-scale version of a dachshund in anybody else's lap. "Don't let these prima donnas intimidate you."

Bigelow tapped his pencil. "You guys are too hard on yourselves. I'll give you another one. Great use of tear gas. Man, I'm glad we had them all sign papers, because we had a couple guys get hit by tear gas three different times. By the time they left, they felt like they'd watched John Wayne die in *The Sands of Iwo Jima.*"

"Oh, yeah," Garth said, sniffling. "I hate that part."

"He's so close to the top," Jason said, weepy. "They're all having a good laugh."

"And then *boom,*" Chris said, "out jumps a Jap who gives it to him right in the heart. No offense, Trieu."

Trieu scrunched her face up. "Why should I be offended? I'm Vietnamese, not Japanese."

"Well. . . ," Chris said. "You know. . ."

Everyone watched him.

"Give him enough rope," Garth said. "Somebody give the jarhead a little more rope."

"Anyway," Bigelow said, "great use of the tear gas. How'd you guys like the launchers?"

"Awesome," Jason said. "Really great. Wish there was a way to load more than one at a time, though."

Chris crossed his legs, apparently trying to pretend nothing had happened. "But the M203 grenade launchers these things are modeled on are single-shot breach loaders, too." He uncrossed his legs, the wicker chair squeaking in protest. "I love the launchers. All of us with CAR-15s should have them."

Jason nodded. "Agreed. Can you do that for us, Chimp?"

"Absolutely," Bigelow said. "Glad you liked my little invention. Stay tuned for more."

"Well, I've got some positives to talk about," Jason said.

Bigelow wheeled to face him. "I was hoping you would, team leader."

"First, I want to praise you all for your conditioning. We did a lot of running in the mud and water out there, in full gear and under stress. We were all out of breath, but nobody was sucking air or puking."

"Does that mean no more running?" Lewis asked. Then he raised his hands at Jason. "I know: fugedaboudit."

"Nice try," Jason said. "For the most part, we stayed cool under fire. Great job, you guys. It got crazy at the end, and we'll talk about that in a minute. But for ninety-eight percent of the time you guys kept your heads and remembered your training. That would be expected of a special forces team in such a situation; but for you guys who were never in the military, I think it's pretty amazing. Good job."

Jason caught pleased looks from Lewis and Trieu. Rachel's face flushed.

"Here's something else," he said. "All of our specialists performed their specialties with skill and precision. Trieu must've taken out twenty men with her little protein packets of love. And Garth's use of the pepperbomb to cover our retreat was escape and evasion at its best. Chris was awesome as point man, guiding us rightly and even finding the first tripwire. Lewis had the banshee up and at 'em perfectly, something that really helped us move so quickly. Outstanding job, you guys."

"What about me?" Rachel said. "Didn't I do a good job?"

"You did a great job," Jason said, meeting her eyes. "I didn't mention you because you didn't have a chance to practice your specialties, but I didn't mean you didn't turn in a solid performance. You shot well, you moved well, you kept position and followed orders. I know you got separated during the peel, but that wasn't your fault. It just—"

"No," Lewis said, "that was all me, baby. I went too far. You couldn't find me. Totally my fault, Rachel. Sorry."

Rachel gave Lewis that melt-your-innards smile she reserved for special occasions. "Oh, aren't you sweet, Lewis. It's all right."

"I've got one more positive," Jason said. "Our early assault on the guard outpost was executed perfectly. We came online together and fired with precision. Our pals Tom and Jerry—yuk, yuk—might limp for a couple days, but they'll live. With what Eloise was paying these guys, they can afford to go buy a dozen new pairs of paintball pants. So, great job. Even the Australian peel was working as planned except for one thing. It just shows we need to work on that more. All in all, I'm mostly pleased with how we dealt with our first overwhelming force situation."

Bigelow checked things off on his legal pad. "All right, now let's talk about the not-so-greats." He looked up. "Anyone? Anyone?"

Lewis raised his hand.

"Yes, Mr. Griswold?" Bigelow said.

"Can we do this after dinner?" Lewis asked. "I'm starved and that barbeque smell is driving me crazy!"

Jason smirked. Bigelow had brought Texas-style barbeque for the team, and the sweet aroma of it heating in the kitchen was making his own stomach complain.

"No," Bigelow said. "But since it's going to be ready in about twenty minutes, that'll encourage you guys to join in the discussion, won't it?"

Butch whined and wiggled out of Garth's lap. He trotted clumsily to the door to the lodge and pushed through toward the kitchen.

"Leave some for me, Butch," Garth said.

Bigelow tapped his pencil. "Trieu, you're always thinking. What was something you guys could've done better?"

Trieu tucked black hair behind her right ear. She was wearing a white cardigan sweater over a black T-shirt and faded blue jeans. "Well, since the whole team died, I think I'd have to say that we could've done better at staying alive. And staying together. If we'd been together instead of spread all around, I wonder if we could've fought our way out of the trap."

Everyone nodded. Jason rubbed a finger across the five o'clock whiskers on his chin.

"Okay, good," Bigelow said. "Teams do split up for various reasons, and I didn't see anything wrong with how you were split. But when the cow pies start flying, getting back together has to be a priority." He circled something on his pad. "Don't worry, I'm going to give you lots of opportunities to learn that one. Okay, what else? Garth?"

Alone among the team, Garth seemed unaffected by the cold. He was wearing flip-flops, ratty jeans with no knees, and a faded tie-dyed T-shirt with a purple and ice blue swirl. "I agree with Trieu. We should've tried harder to not be dead. I also think we pretty much stunk up the joint when it came to sniffing out an ambush. We should've known as soon as we found the first wire."

Bigelow laughed. "I have to say you guys did that just about perfectly wrong. I had no idea you'd fall right into the front of the trap like that. You don't know how many tripwires I had all through those woods. But I didn't need any of them! You find a tripwire, but you keep going. You set off multiple booby traps—that you have to know are going to bring bad guys—but you keep going. Jace, dude, what were you thinking?"

Jason looked down at his soft leather moccasins and the elastic cuffs of his bright green sweat pants. "Yeah, I know. I should've waved us off." He opened his hands and looked at Bigelow. "I knew about the guys coming up behind but not the guys waiting in ambush. I should've sniffed the trap, but I didn't. I was hoping we'd get there fast, take out the guards, and escape into the woods with the slaves." He shook his head. "I should've figured it out."

"We all should've," Chris said. "It was everybody's fault."

Garth nodded. "Hooah."

"It was a good setup," Bigelow said, "if I do say so myself. Even if you'd done everything right, I was going to get you. I wanted to see if you'd smell the trap, yeah, but I also wanted you to see what you'd do outnumbered five to one."

"It's the Kobayashi Maru."

Everyone looked at Lewis.

"The what?" Bigelow said.

"The Kobayashi Maru. Oh, come on. Don't you guys ever watch *Star Trek*? It's a simulation, a test they give at Star Fleet Academy."

"Oh, great," Chris said. "A message from Geekland."

"You guys are such dwrrls," Lewis said. "The Kobayashi Maru is an unwinnable test. It's designed so that there's no way to win it. Everybody fails."

"Except James T. Kirk."

Now everyone turned to look at Jason.

Chris groaned. "Not you, too."

"Yeah," Jason said, " 'fraid so." He lifted his right hand to Lewis in the Vulcan V. "Live long and prosper, Lewis."

"Right back atcha, big daddy," Lewis said, returning the sign.

"Kirk's the only one who ever beat the Kobayashi Maru," Jason said.

"Tell 'em how he did it," Lewis said.

"He cheated."

Lewis giggled. "He reprogrammed the simulation."

"O–kay. . . ," Bigelow said. "Any moment now we're going to get on with the debriefing so you guys can smack down some ribs and chicken, right?"

"All right, but I want to know one thing," Lewis said to Bigelow. "How did you cause the Land Warrior system to go down? I mean, I know that code and I know how the components work. We even lost our radios. So how'd you do it? The only thing that even could take 'em all out at once would be a. . ." His eyes got wide. "No. No way."

Rachel sat forward. "What?"

"Yeah," Bigelow said slowly, as if too humble to show his blue ribbon from the 4-H stock show. "I have my own EMP bombs."

Jason whistled softly.

"What's an EMP bomb?" Rachel asked.

Garth looked at Bigelow through narrowed eyes. "No, you don't either have EMP bombs, squid. Tell the truth."

Bigelow raised his right hand. "I cannot tell a lie."

Rachel reached over and knuckle punched Garth in the thigh. "What's an EMP bomb?"

"Ow!"

"Electromagnetic pulse," Lewis said. "They're released whenever you detonate a nuke, but the military's been working on portable EMP weapons for decades. They're murder on electronics. He must've had it somewhere on the battlefield. Or is it a dish on a truck somewhere?"

Bigelow rubbed his face. "It was on the slave wagon. Detonated by remote." He shrugged. "I had to try out my toy."

"Well, however he did it," Jason said, "it points up how quickly we've come to rely on technology. I admit, without my little green dots, I was lost. It was against my better judgment that we made the toys part of our standard loadout anyway. But that's over. From now on we're going back to the tried-and-true ways: hand signals and two-man fireteams."

"Whoa, whoa, there, Bessie," Bigelow said. "Not so fast, Jace. There's nothing wrong with Lewis's toys. Yes, you need to know how to conduct your mission if you lose the tech, but that doesn't mean you shouldn't use it if it gives you an advantage. Look, I'm thinking that you're probably not going to come up against too many EMP bombs in Sudan, okay? So just relax, will ya?"

Jason clenched his jaw but gave an almost nonexistent nod.

Bigelow consulted his yellow pad. "Okay, we're also going to get lots of practice on the Australian peel so you don't have a repeat. I'm not going to pick on Lewis here. He knows what he did. But if one person got it wrong, it just shows me that the concentration level in the whole team isn't high enough on this drill. So we're going to run it again and again and again." He slapped Jason's knee with his pad. "Right?"

Jason sighed and nodded. "Yeah, Chimp. That's right."

"All right," Bigelow said, "now let's talk about what happened at the end. Jason, want to take it here?"

"Yeah." Jason put his hands on his knees. "Chris, Garth, what happened? The three of us were at the boulders. And then what?"

"Then we saw Rachel running at us," Chris said.

Rachel set her mug on the boards. "I was trying to get back with the group, like Doug said."

"But then the dirtbike brigade charged," Chris said. "When they swung around and headed straight for her, and then she screamed. . ."

They all waited for him to finish. The vinyl panels had fogged up, but it was still raining heavily. Judging by the sounds, somewhere just beyond the porch a large puddle had formed. The heater had brought the temperature up, and team members were peeling off layers.

"I'll admit it if GQ won't," Garth said. "We freaked. Something about seeing little Rachel exposed like that in front of all those bikes." He shrugged. "We freaked."

Rachel reached her hand across Trieu to pat Garth's knee. "It was heroic."

"Plus," Chris said, "maybe there was a little. . .lack of. . ." He looked at Jason.

"You think I couldn't make the call, Chris?" Jason asked. "You think I was paralyzed by indecision?"

Chris considered it. "Yes."

"Yeah, squiddy," Garth said, "me, too. You choked."

Jason had the feeling Garth could tell him he was ugly and his mother wore army boots and somehow Jason wouldn't be offended. "Okay, maybe I took a little extra time to consider. But that—"

"You choked," Garth said. "It's okay."

"No, it's not," Chris said. "The leader can't afford to freeze up."

"Okay, maybe I did choke a little," Jason said. "I couldn't decide who to sacrifice, Trieu or Rachel."

"What about me?" Lewis said.

"Oh," Garth said, "sacrificing you was a no-brainer."

"Hey!"

Rachel looked offended. "You boys be nice to Lewis. He's a good boy."

"Yes, ma'am," Garth said.

Bigelow put his pad and pencil away. "You guys are laughing, but none of you had to make the call Jason had to make." He faced Jason. "Did you ever decide who to sacrifice?"

Jason stared at the floor. "Yeah. . .but I'd rather not say."

"Doesn't matter anyway," Bigelow said. "The point is that when the crucial moment came, command structure fell apart and everybody just acted on instinct." He opened his hands in a gesture of helplessness. "What're you gonna do? The exercise was designed to show you, not me, what you'll do when the pressure's really on. There's no blame to hand out here.

"But I will tell you one thing: You've got to stick to Jason's leadership. If you start thinking he's going to choke and you start wondering if maybe you know better, that's a great way to get everybody killed, understand? I know Jason Kromer. Given another two seconds, he would've made the tough call. You've got to trust him."

He rocked his wheelchair from side to side. "You know the place in the Bible where Jesus says, 'You trust in God, trust also in Me'? Well, Jason's no Jesus, but I think for you, you can extend Jesus' words one more step: 'You trust in God and you trust in Jesus—trust also in Jason.' Corny, I know, but it's gospel all the same. You've got to believe that Jason's going to make the right call."

Chris slid his foot across a wood plank. "And if he doesn't?"

Bigelow's gaze was fierce. "He will."

Jason cleared his throat and stood. "Okay, Chimp, thanks. Great work today. That was an amazing ambush you pulled on us."

"Hurray for Doug," Trieu said.

"Now," Jason said, "today's shown us we've got some things to work on, some lessons learned. We also have a lot to be proud of. Chimp and I will come up with all kinds of nasty ways to address both sides in the next few days. For now, let's go grab us some Texas-style barbeque."

They stood to go.

Garth high-fived Jason. "I knew you'd make the right call, chief!"

\* \* \*

Before grabbing a Styrofoam plate and getting in line, Jason snagged a long-necked bottle of another Texas specialty—Big Red, a soft drink like Coke but red and sparkly—and ran by the bunkroom he shared with Chris, Garth, and Lewis.

He removed the pile of laundry from his desk chair and set it on the bookshelf next to his recently awarded "One Jogging Shoe" award. Then he sat and checked E-mail on his computer. There was an encrypted message from Eloise.

*Dear Jason:*

*I hope these two weeks have been helpful to you and the team and that your bite-sized training thingamajig is working. How is Rachel doing with her Dinka language tapes?*

*I've been doing my thing on the phones and whatnot, and I think I'm ready for you all to start getting geared up for Sudan.*

*I'm attaching some articles for you to look at. I think they will be of some help to you as you plan. But here it is in a nutshell: I want you to go in posing as well diggers. You're part of a ministry—Plumbers Without Borders or something—that's coming in to give the folks in the south potable water. You might even let Garth dig a few real wells just for show.*

*But then you're to work with those Arab middlemen to get back everybody from Akwer Nhom. There's a copy of that list attached here, but you won't be able to read it, probably. You're to guard the money and to pay it when you're sure you've got the right people.*

*You leave just as soon as you're ready. (See travel plans doc attached.) But please not later than two weeks from right now. The mission shouldn't take you more than four days.*

*Love to my babies,*
*Eloise*

Jason sat back. He took a long swig from the icy Big Red and wondered what wonderful or terrible things this little E-mail was setting in motion.

# PART II

# SUDAN

# CHAPTER 6

## ANEI

*SOMEONE is coming for me. I believe it is my father, though I think he is dead. I saw him shot by the soldier as they fought in my village. But I still believe it is him. Because of the dreams.*

*This branch is good for firewood. It is thick as my arm and not too leafy. Ahmed will beat me again if it is too leafy. I could bring back two or even four more such branches. But I will not.*

*The sun is unfriendly. It scalds me now in the afternoon, but it leaves me to freeze with the goats and the other slaves at night when I need it most. I used to believe the sun was lucky, that it was the eye of God looking upon me to give good things. Now I know it is only the sun.*

*I am always hungry.*

*On the walk here, Abuk told me she saw my mother dead. She said she would be my mother instead. But that cannot be, now. I have lost two mothers in one week.*

*Fatma is here! If she sees me with only one branch, she will burn me with hot water like she did to poor Alek. The wives are worse than Ahmed and his five terrible sons together. If I go behind the goat pen. . .Yes! She did not see me. Have your stick, Ahmed.*

*I am Dinka, but I must live like Baggara to survive. In two weeks already I have learned this. My family is Christian, but I pretend to be Muslim to avoid the beatings. I had not been here one day before they gave me a Muslim name—Miriam, upon the sound of it I spit—and made me pray to Allah and learn Arabic. They do not let me speak Dinka at all. But we do anyway, the other slaves and me.*

*There is no one to teach me Christianity. I should have listened better to my father. He would know what to do. Christianity does not make you kill people.*

*I am Anei, Dinka, Christian.*

*They nailed Majok's knees together after he tried to escape. There were six other slaves here before me: three girls and three boys. When Majok died, Ahmed made the girls do his work, too.*

*My father can teach me about Christianity when he comes for me.*

*Now I will get water for the goats. Then I must hurry to feed the chickens so that Fatma will not be waiting for me to do the dishes. I never have rest. Baggara goats smell worse than Dinka goats.*

*I do not know where they took the others from my village. Abuk's daughter cried on the sixth day of our march north, so the murahileen shot her in the head. When Abuk cried, they raped her more than usual and then killed her, too. I saw it. They beat her until she vomited blood. Then they sliced her throat.*

*Alek and Ateng have both been circumcised. Fatma says a girl is not clean if she is not circumcised. She says you are an animal until it is done. I am very afraid. The Dinka do not circumcise their women. Ateng said it is very painful. She is terribly scarred. I am twelve. Already my body is changing. I know they will be coming for me!*

*I have to get away.*

*When Ahmed finishes beating me, he calls me Miriam and touches me where he should not. He speaks Arabic, but I know he is saying he will come for me as he does for Alek and Ateng. The other girl, Akiir, is already pregnant. She is fourteen.*

*His sons rape the girls every day when Ahmed is not around. We are not allowed to wear clothes. Ateng says Ahmed said he is afraid his sons will prefer boys over girls, so she is to teach them how to like sex with a woman.*

*Ahmed rapes the boy slaves when Fatma is sleeping.*

*Ateng says they have not raped me yet because they want to sell me for a higher price. I do not know why they don't touch me. Alek says Ahmed made her pregnant when she was only ten. The baby did not live.*

*I pray that my body will stop changing. I am frightened of the pain. Fatma beats me more now. First they will cut me so I can be "clean," then they will pollute me. No Dinka man will ever want me then. What will I be then?*

*Is this what life is supposed to be? Is God so angry that He allows us to live in this way? Every day now I curse the sun.*

*My father would tell me to love Ahmed and his terrible boys. Even Fatma. He would say the Lord Jesus would want me to pray for them. I. . .I cannot. I will not. I will pray for them, yes, but to suffer everything they have given out. I will pray for their house to catch fire and demons to possess their chickens and lay poison eggs.*

*For this I will be happy to be scolded by my father. When he comes for me.*

# CHAPTER 7

## THE FRIENDLY SKIES

"OH, STEWARDESS?"

Rachel turned away from the pilots in the cockpit and looked narrowly at Jason. "Are you talking to me?"

"I was wondering if you were going to be serving any snacks on this flight?"

She sauntered toward him. "Oh, a big strong man like you doesn't want poor little ol' me to get you a snack."

Jason wondered if she was going to change *snack* to *smack*. "I don't?"

"Un-uh, no," she said, caressing his cheek with the back of her hand. "Because a big strong man like you can *get it yourself.*"

The pilots laughed raucously. Rachel turned back to them and said something loud and fast in French. The two men laughed harder.

Garth stirred in his sleep. The bald giant, dressed in faded blue jeans and a laundry-worn Pepsi T-shirt, snoozed on the single seat side of the plane, his head on a miniature pillow.

Trieu, wearing sturdy olive walking shorts and matching vest over a white T-shirt, sat in the seat behind Garth, reading *Devotional Classics* and listening to something on her MP3 player.

Across the aisle from her sat Lewis, looking like a nerd in red tartan shorts and a beige T-shirt, showing off his portable DVD player to one of the two SPLA "handlers" that had boarded the plane with them at Lokichokio, Kenya. The young black man's wide-eyed expression when Lewis had turned on *Terminator 3* had been worth the price of admission in and of itself. He'd looked like he'd just seen a live *T. rex*. But now he was quizzing Lewis on how the thing worked.

Behind them sat Chris, dressed again like the Australian park ranger, and the other SPLA handler. Over the growl of the Cessna Caravan's single turboprop, Jason could faintly hear bits of their conversation. Chris pumped the guy for information about any battles he'd been in. The soldier's English was limited, but he was augmenting his story with hand motions and sound effects, and Chris was a persistent audience.

Behind the seats was their gear: boxes and bags designed to look as boring and no-these-are-not-really-full-of-military-equipment-ish as possible.

Rachel, wearing her short black shorts and white blouse unbuttoned three from the top, sat in the captain's chair, flying the plane. The pilot draped his arms around her from behind, "helping" her hold the yoke.

Jason turned to the window. Below him was the southern tip of the Sahara Desert, miles upon miles of packed tan dirt and dead grass the color of a lion's hide, interrupted by the occasional clump of low trees and bushes.

For the first few hours after they'd taken off at Lokichokio, the terrain below had been the hot green equatorial rainforest. But they'd long since left that behind on their trek northwest. Nothing now but dreary savannah. If this was the "rich" part of Sudan, Jason didn't want to see the poor part.

He kept his eye out for fast movers. Everybody in Lokichokio had assured him that they'd never seen the MiGs supposedly operated by the Sudanese military. But Jason had no doubt that if one were in the area, its pilot would find their illegal flight into a southern no-go area a tempting target.

Jason got up and stretched, something he had to do half bent over because the Caravan's white dome was only four and a half feet high. For this safari he'd chosen to wear an old pair of long brown corduroy pants, a beige denim shirt, and his desert combat boots. He made his way back to the cargo area. Two barrels of gasoline—*petrol,* they called it out here—sloshed quietly beside the door. Bahr el-Ghazal was five hundred miles from the Kenyan border. The pilots would need to refuel at the airstri—

Jason heard a sudden roar from the rear of the plane, like a tornado overtaking them. The pilots dumped Rachel onto the carpet and dove the plane. Jason was slammed into the cargo and then into a seatback. The petrol swished loudly and the engine roared. Garth tumbled out of his seat.

Jason pulled himself up by a blue armrest. "What's happening?"

Chris stared above them out the window. "Helicopters. Military."

The pilots pulled the plane level again.

Jason returned to his seat and peered out the window. Above them and heading away in formation were three attack helicopters—Russian-built Mi-24 Hinds. The gunships zoomed north.

"They buzzed us," Rachel said, sitting down beside Jason and buckling herself in. "Came up on both sides. I think Olivier wet his pants. After Jean-Claude figured out we weren't being rear-ended, he changed course, since they'd be legally justified in shooting this plane to splinters."

"I don't think so, Rachel," Lewis said.

"Lewis," she said, "this is a no-fly zone."

"Nah," Chris said. "They were just having fun with us. If they wanted us gone, we'd have been dust before we knew they were here."

"Plus," Lewis said, "Dau here tells me that TrackMark—you know, the guys we chartered the plane from—has some kind of kickback deal with Khartoum. TrackMark planes can go wherever they want."

Jason felt his eyes widen. "A deal with Khartoum? Are you sure?"

The SPLA soldier next to Chris, Akot Deng, started speaking very quickly and harshly in a language Jason did not recognize.

Finally Dau, the soldier next to Lewis, spoke, not making eye contact. "I am mistaken, Lewis. Sorry." *Soddy.*

"Oh," Lewis said, "now he says he was wrong."

"We can hear him, Lewis," Chris said.

"Never mind, Lewis, thanks," Jason said. He leaned his head back against the rest. Then he glanced at Rachel.

Her shirt was standing all but open. Though he'd seen more of her in that pink bikini, there was something gravitational about an unbuttoned shirt. He clenched his teeth and looked away.

He nudged her with his elbow. "Jean-Claude, huh?"

"That's his name."

"You were getting pretty friendly with them, weren't you?"

"Why, Jason Kromer, are you finally getting jealous of me?" She held his gaze with her deep brown eyes.

He puffed out a breath. "Why do you do that?"

"Do what?"

"Flirt with every man on the planet. I thought we'd talked about this."

She pulled the hem of her shorts lower. "I don't flirt with *every* man." Rachel turned back to the pilots, then leaned closer to Jason. "Look, when you were in the SEALs, you used a gun, right?"

"We used quite a f—"

"And your gun was your instrument, right? It was the thing you used to get your way and accomplish your objectives, am I right?"

"Yes."

"Okay, so shut up about how I use my body and my looks when we're on a mission. It's my *weapon*, don't you get it? It's what I use to get my way and accomplish my objectives. Yes, we had a nice talk and, believe me, I haven't forgotten it. But God gave me this set of features, and I know how to use them. So back off and let me do my specialty to help the team."

She leaned back in her seat, her head shaking like there were a thousand more words bouncing around that wanted a piece of Jason.

"I . . . ," Jason said. But then his mouth didn't say anything else.

She looked at him sharply. Then she turned away and seemed to deflate. When her eyes came back to his face, they had lost their fire. "Relax," she said, nodding toward the pilots. "They're harmless, okay? Just a couple of mercenaries looking for some action. Military action, if they can get it, but I'm sure they'd be happy with other kinds, too. If even half of the stories they told me are true, they're a couple of crazy Frenchmen."

Jason nodded.

Rachel leaned her head against his shoulder. "But don't worry. I won't act that way around you anymore."

"Good. I think."

He turned to watch the helicopter gunships vanish into the hot blue distance, hoping to never see them again.

They flew in silence for twenty minutes. Garth fell asleep again.

Then the copilot turned and spoke to Rachel in French.

She answered and turned to Jason. "They've spotted the airstrip, but they say it's too muddy to land. They want you to come take a look."

He unbuckled and stepped into the cockpit, a clean but cramped spot with a ceiling even lower than in the passenger area. He leaned between the two pilots.

"The airfield, she is there," the copilot said. "You see?"

Jason saw what looked like a short dirt road ahead of the airplane. It was distinguished from the rest of the packed earth around it because it was a few shades darker brown and no yellowed grass grew on it. They were moving over countryside that appeared greener than anything he'd seen since they'd left the rainforest. Perhaps a recent rain had given the flora a bit of false hope.

"You think it's too muddy to land?"

Jean-Claude, the pilot, shrugged dramatically. "Perhaps. We will circle once, d'accord? L'avion, she is thirsty, no? But we must land to refuel. Perhaps it will be the bumpy-ride, no? But this should not be the trouble for. . ." He winked at Jason. ". . .well diggers like you."

He and the copilot laughed heartily.

"Olivier," the pilot said, "have you ever seen well diggers such as this?"

"Mais non! With well diggers such as these, what must the American army look like, Jean-Claude?"

Jason kept a straight face. "I have no idea what you guys are talking about."

"But of course!" Jean-Claude said. "Now, tell me, Monsieur Well-Digger Man, where would you like unloaded these boxes of well-digging equipment?"

"Shame on you, Jean-Claude," Olivier said. "It must be somewhere dry so the 'well-digging equipment' is not too wet to shoot at the GOS army."

"But of course! I am forgetting."

Jason went back to his seat. "Funny guys, these friends of yours," he said to Rachel. "If they tell someone, like our pals in uniform on the plane here, what they think they've guessed, we could be in big trouble."

"Relax, Jason. They won't turn us in. They'd probably come with us if we asked them. Besides," she said, buckling his seat belt for him, "they like me."

As they circled the muddy airstrip, Jason spotted a black Land Rover waiting in the shade, along with several dark-skinned adults in clothing of various colors, styles, and degrees of coverage. "Welcome to Sudan," he muttered.

Mud flew in brown fans when they touched down, and Jason felt the plane wanting to spin to the left. But Jean-Claude handled it perfectly; and before the Caravan had fully stopped, Olivier had both doors open and was down the steps with the first can of petrol.

"Okay, let's go," Jason said. "Everybody remember who your buddy is."

"Boy," Garth said too loudly, "sure is a great day to *dig a well.*"

* * *

The heat hit Jason ten feet before he reached the door of the airplane. He'd mercifully forgotten it since Kenya, but it hadn't gone away. As he stepped down onto the dirt, the sun stood overhead. It pressed upon him steadily as if slowly driving him into the earth. He put on his "French foreign legion" hat with the two long flaps in the back and looked around.

He felt as if he'd emerged on an uninhabited planet. They had landed in a brutally flat dead place only differentiated from a desert by the wilted, thigh-high grass, the soupy mud, and the stand of low trees whose color was as close to brown as green could get. Aside from the team members stretching in the sun and the welcoming committee of dark black women and children, there didn't appear to be anyone on the whole continent. The glistening white Cessna looked like it belonged there about as much as a Starbucks.

Trieu held a hand over her eyes. "Oh, my."

Jason chuckled. "Exactly."

Akot and Dau pushed their way off the plane and headed straight for the uniformed man beside the Land Rover, which looked decidedly less sturdy close up. Akot tore into the driver with a verbal tirade. The driver answered casually in one-syllable replies. Meanwhile Dau sidled over to two young Dinka women sitting in the shade nearby and struck up a conversation.

"Careful with that!"

Jason turned toward Chris's voice. He relieved Jean-Claude of a large box marked "Surveying Equipment." Garth and Lewis hurried to help unload.

Jason headed over to the Land Rover. "Hey, Akot?"

Akot spun as if caught stealing office supplies. The driver, a round-faced man with mismatched green camos, looked at Jason but did not face him directly.

"There is a very big mistake," Akot said, striking the Land Rover with an open palm. "We radioed for large truck for you and your baggage. But Dhor say truck not working anymore. No more trucks today. So he bring this," he slammed the Land Rover's roof, "and porters. You ride in the truck. Porters bring your baggage."

Jason studied the women sitting in the shade. There were twelve of them, wearing everything from rag togas to linen dresses. A gaggle of naked boys up to about ten years old sat in the dirt staring wide-eyed at the white people.

"Uh, I don't think so. Akot, some of these boxes are fifty pounds or more."

"No," Akot said, "it's okay. Dau will carry biggest box."

Dau broke out of his conversation with the young women—who weren't looking too impressed, anyway—and began complaining to Akot. But Akot walked past him and addressed the twelve women. Their tired expressions didn't change. They stood slowly and walked over to where the white men were stacking the gear.

Jason felt someone watching him. He caught Dhor, the driver, scratching the whiskers on his round cheeks and regarding him thoughtfully.

When Jason looked back to the gear, most of it was on the heads of the women. The "Surveying Equipment" box rested on Dau's shoulder, but he didn't look too happy about it. If he only knew what he was carrying. . .

Jean-Claude called to Jason before pulling the last door shut on the Cessna. "Bonne chance, Monsieur Well-Digger Man. I hope you don't find this kind of plumbing too dangerous!" He blew a kiss to Rachel. "Au revoir, mademoiselle! Next time with Jean-Claude you stay, okay?"

The engine whined and the propeller began to spin. Jean-Claude shut the door. Within seconds the plane taxied toward the end of the airstrip.

Rachel and Trieu walked up to Jason. Together they looked at the women with their burdens.

"Are you really going to let them do this?" Rachel asked.

He shrugged. "When in Sudan, baby."

In the end, all six "well diggers," along with Dhor and Akot, climbed aboard the Land Rover. Akot, now equipped with one of the four assault rifles Dhor had in the backseat, rode on top with the spare tire. As the last naked boy followed the procession off the airstrip, the Cessna roared into the early afternoon heat.

Even if they didn't have to go at the rate of the walking women, the two-rut excuse for a road wouldn't have allowed them to travel any faster. They inched along a brown gash between high hedges of yellow grass that looked perfect for thatched roofs. All the way to the horizon on all sides it looked like a giant backyard that God had forgotten to water for about a hundred years.

Jason leaned forward from his third-row spot sandwiched between Chris and the right side of the vehicle. "Hey, Dhor, do you speak English?"

Dhor shook his head negligently. "Only when I have to."

Jason and Chris exchanged a look.

"Um, okay," Jason said. "Well, can you say where you're taking us?"

"SPLA checkpoint."

"Okay," Jason said. "Then can you take us to Akwer Nhom?"

Dhor's eyes snapped to Jason's in the rearview mirror. "You are going to Akwer Nhom? Why? There is nothing there."

"We know," Jason said easily. "That's why we are going there. We have. . .brought equipment that might help them get back on their feet."

Since there wasn't much danger of traffic, Dhor drove while staring at Jason in the mirror. "You are coming to dig a well in Akwer Nhom?"

Jason licked his lips. "Um. . .well. . ."

"Well digging requires much research," Trieu said from the front passenger seat. "You must find suitable underground water tables and uncontaminated water supply. Perhaps Akwer Nhom will offer appropriate conditions for a well, perhaps not."

Jason had to smile. *Oh, deftly done, Trieu. Not a lie, but not exactly the answer Dhor was after.*

"Look at them," Lewis said, looking out the back window at the porters strung out behind. "How can they balance that stuff on their heads like that?"

"I have no idea, Lewis," Jason said. "But I've got new respect for these women, I can tell you that much."

"What's that song they're singing?" Trieu said, tilting her head. "It sounds so familiar."

Rachel cocked her head. "Could be something they learned from a missionary."

"Hey, Dhor," Chris said, "we ran into some Sudanese military helicopters on our way here. Have you heard of any attacks today?"

Dhor noticed he'd veered off the road. He corrected and hit the gas briefly, jolting everyone. Jason heard Akot tumble on top, then yell at Dhor in a language he supposed was Dinka.

"Yes, one attack," Dhor said. "Out by the White Nile. OLS food drop site. Only ten killed this time."

"Wait a minute," Lewis said. "Are you saying military helicopters attacked a food drop site? Were your soldiers trying to take the food for themselves instead of leaving it for the people or something?"

"No," Dhor said calmly. "They attack the civilians. That is why they come."

"Dude," Lewis said, "what kind of government uses its military against people picking up food from an airdrop?"

"The sort of government that wants no one near its oil," Dhor said.

"But, I mean, does the UN know about this?" Lewis asked. "OLS— that's Operation Lifeline Sudan, right? Aren't they part of the UN?"

Dhor shrugged. "OLS tells Khartoum where they will do food

drops. It is the rule that the north has made. If OLS wants to drop the food, they must tell where and when. Then, two or three hours after food is dropped, when many people are getting the food, bombers or helicopters or tanks or murahileen come."

For a moment of bouncing travel, no one spoke. In his mind's eye, Jason saw dozens of families picking through bright orange containers—and three Hind gunships rising over a ridge and opening fire. How did those crews sleep at night?

Rachel growled. "Typical."

# CHAPTER 8

## ONE DAY SALE

AFTER another thirty minutes of travel, with an air conditioner that blew only hot air, they reached a stand of shrubs. A wooden sawhorse blocked the road, though Dhor could've easily gone around it. Jason noticed movement in the shade of the bushes. At least two men in green camos, armed with assault rifles. Beyond the bushes stood a line of trees. Perhaps there was a river here.

A barefoot man in desert fatigues and a tan beret stepped out of the shade. Akot was already talking to him in Dinka. The man moved the sawhorse out of the way and waved Dhor through. He peered shamelessly through the windows at the group.

Dhor pulled into the shade of the trees and killed the engine. Jason and the others piled out to help the women ease their burdens to the ground.

"Come," Akot said, jumping down from the Land Rover. "You speak to commander."

Jason turned to his team. They looked like white tourists who had wandered away from the bus. They all wore the long French foreign legion hats—except Chris, who had his dark brown kangaroo leather hat. They stood beside their boxes and bags.

"Lewis," Jason said, "work with your buddy Dau and find out how much we should pay these ladies for their work."

"Okay."

"Rachel, I'd like you to come with me to meet this commander. Remember," he said, leaning toward her, "you only speak English."

"What are you talking about?" Rachel said, suddenly possessed of a Scottish brogue. "Of course I only speak English. What do you take me for?"

Jason looked at her. "Aboot?"

Rachel arched a perfect eyebrow at him.

He shrugged. "Whatever. The rest of you guys stay with the stuff."

"Goodonya, his nibs," Garth said in Strine. "And if anyone wants to go biffo, we'll stick it to the bogan, won't we, mates?"

"Qué?" Lewis said. "No comprendo, señor."

Jason shook his head and followed Akot into the trees.

Ten thatched-roof tukuls stood on stilts along the bare earth beside a creek bed. Small black chickens pecked around. The air was cooler here beside the narrow stream. Armed men, some looking as young as fourteen, lazed in the shade of trees or underneath the raised tukuls. Some wore camouflage uniforms, watches, and boots. Others wore just a pair of shorts. But everybody carried a rifle or machine gun. And many of them had bottles that looked suspiciously like they contained a variety of alcoholic beverages. The reek of vomit and urine took hold whenever the breeze stilled.

As Jason and Rachel followed Akot, many of these extra-tall men stepped out to see, some having trouble balancing. Jason thought they were shocked to see their white skin. But then he noticed that no one was looking at him at all. He felt Rachel walking very closely beside him. By the time they reached a man lounging in the only chair visible in the camp, Jason felt like Britney Spears's bodyguard.

Akot saluted loudly and spoke to the commander in an African language. The commander turned around to face them.

He was shockingly young: maybe sixteen. He had long gangly legs crossed at the knee like he was watching television. His skinny black arms folded across his lap as he slouched in the handmade wood and thatch chair. He wore dark green pants and shirt, shiny combat boots, and a maroon beret. His AK-47 leaned against the tallest, broadest tree Jason had seen since landing.

When he stood, he was easily eight inches taller than Jason, yet probably weighed half as much. He smiled with prominent front teeth. "Greetings. I am Isaac Aguir. You are welcome in my camp."

"Thank you," Jason said. "Um, Stephen Wilcox, Global Vision, and this is Annamarie Bloom. The rest of—"

"A pleasure, Miss Bloom," Isaac said, tipping his beret. "You bring great beauty to our poor land."

"Thank you very much, Isaac," Rachel said, sticking to the brogue. "Aren't you a charmer, then?"

Jason gave her a double take.

Isaac lifted his chin and said something authoritatively to the crowd of men standing around. They began to disperse, reluctantly. It took a second command to send Akot away with the others.

"The rest of our team is over there," Jason said, pointing. "Thank you for sending a car to pick us up."

"It was no trouble." Isaac offered his chair to Rachel, and she sat. "Tell me, what brings you to my humble outpost?"

"We're here to see about digging a well in Akwer Nhom," Jason said.

"I see. A well." He folded his arms. "Why Akwer Nhom? Akwer Nhom had a well. Many villages do not. Dig one somewhere else instead."

Jason was working on a response, but nothing was coming to him.

Rachel took care of it. Her answer sounded like this: "That's a greit idea, Isaac. We'd laike to look all around the eeriah to see aboot

127

digging more wells on laiyter trips."

"It is amusing, Miss Bloom," Isaac said. "I would not have taken you for a European."

Jason lifted his finger and opened his mouth, but nothing came out. It didn't matter: Rachel was already speaking.

"Me dear mither was from Glasgow, Isaac, but me fayther was from Iran, you see. Then me dear da keeled over and me mum took me to the hoowse of her bairth, where I was raised by my maternal paereents. Ach, whits fur ye ye'll no gen bye eet."

Isaac looked at Jason, who could only blink and smile.

"Okay," Jason finally said. "Well, Isaac, now that that's settled, I was wondering if you could spare a couple trucks to get us and our baggage to Akwer Nhom."

Isaac stared stupidly at Rachel. Then he clasped his hands behind his back and turned to Jason. "You will have to wait."

"Wait for what?"

"The SRRA secretary. You must register with him. He will inspect your things."

*Uh-oh.*

"No problem," Rachel said. "Myself, I love looking at drill bits and shovels. Don't you, Isaac? Never get enough."

Jason kept his gaze steady. "When do you think this secretary will be by?"

Isaac shrugged. "Two days. Three."

*Wonderful.* "Now, Isaac—"

"Brawlie," Rachel said. "We canna compleen. That's no bad, conseederin. Two days would be joost raiet, in fact. We'll joost call Dr. Garang on the radio and tell him Isaac Aguir wanted us to wait here for tyoo days instead of sticking to the shhedule he sketched oot for us."

Isaac stopped moving. "You do not know Dr. Garang."

"Aye, we do. Don't we, Stephen?"

"John Garang," Jason said, nodding like an idiot, "the leader of your movement."

Isaac's lips closed over his teeth. "I know who he is!" A fly landed on his ear. He swiped at it violently. "You will wait with the others!"

Jason and Rachel walked away, trying to look nonchalant.

"What are you doing?" Jason asked quietly. "We can't call John Garang. And if we break out the radio, they will see everything else we—"

"Relax, Jason," she said, patting his arm. "You won't have to break out the radio. This is what I do, remember?"

"You lie like it was your native language."

"*Toda raba,* Jason," she said in Hebrew. "I will take that as a compliment."

Through the trees Jason saw Garth, Chris, Lewis, and Tricu sitting on the boxes. Beyond them the savannah baked and shimmered like the inside of a pellet stove.

He took Rachel's arm and stopped her. "This isn't a game we're playing here, Rachel. They all think you're from Scotland now. Can you keep that up the whole time we're here? What are you going to be next time, Swedish?"

"Ya, shoor."

Jason felt his blood pressure elevating. "Would you cut it out?"

"No, you cut it out." She kept her voice low and pretended to pull away from his grip. He let go and she shook her head. "No, grab me again. Look mad."

"I *am* mad."

"Just grab me, okay? And hold on if I struggle."

He grabbed her arm. "Rachel, I don't—"

"Just shut up," she said, speaking quietly but with an intensity in her eyes that held his attention. "Listen, I was conning my way into the PLO while you were still a babykiller, okay? I'm sorry you think less of me because I'm a good liar, but don't you try to say that I'm not being professional. This is part of me using what I have as an instrument."

She pulled against his grip but continued to whisper. "You think you're more serious about this mission because you're so grim all the time. You and Chris. But I haven't been this serious about a mission in five years. The accents and the fast talking—that's why I'm on this team, Jason. And I'm good at it, too. So just shut up and let me do the talking."

She struggled more. "Okay, now say something mean and push me away so the twenty guys watching us will think you're a big dominant male."

Jason finally noticed the men staring at him. "Um, you're crazy, woman! That's right. Crazy! Now get back to the others." He released her hand and pushed her toward the rest of the team.

He nodded roughly to two soldiers leaning against a tree. "Women." He left them and strutted toward the rest of his team.

Trieu stood with her arm around Rachel, apart from the men. When Jason rejoined the circle, the ladies moved closer.

Chris looked from Rachel to Jason. "What was that all about? I thought you were chewing my sweetie out for something, and then she says it was all an act."

Jason sat on a wood box. "I don't exactly know what it was, Chris. But I do think Rachel just saved our backsides about four times over in there."

Garth offered his hand and Rachel gave him five.

"We may be here awhile," Jason said, "but at least our cover isn't blown."

"Well," Lewis said, looking toward the soldiers, who had gone back to their naps and bottles, "what do we do now?"

"Now," Jason said, stretching out, "we wait."

\* \* \*

"Pass the Goldfish."

Jason handed the bag of cheddar snacks to Lewis, who poured out half its contents into his orange-tinged fingers.

Jason popped a Goldfish into his mouth. "And you guys thought this was going to be all hard work and danger."

"This is so typical," Chris said, the only one still standing. "The little gatekeeper wants to prove his power by making us wait. What a joke. Typical Third World bureaucracy."

"I don't know," Trieu said. "I encountered the same thing in America the last time I went to renew my driver's license."

"Ooh," Garth said, "good one."

Jason noticed a barefoot man in black shin-length pants and white button-up shirt approaching them from along the tree line. "Bottle up," Jason said. "Company."

The man walked directly to Rachel. "Pretty lady, please, please help me." He was not as tall as most of the soldiers—a mere six feet, three inches. His forehead was shaved to the top of his head. He smiled, drawing amiable lines on his handsome face.

Jason, Chris, and Garth interposed themselves between the man and Rachel.

"What kind of help do you need?" Jason said.

The man tried to get a glimpse of Rachel between the shoulders. "You are Americans coming to buy back slaves, yes? This is very good."

"No, sir," Chris said. "We are not here to redeem slaves. We are here to dig a well." He pointed to the boxes. "See?"

The smile didn't waver. "But you can be buying slaves back, even so." He thumped his chest. "James show you how. Come."

"We told you," Jason said, "we're not here to redeem slaves. Why don't you just move along?"

"Pretty lady," James said, standing on his toes, "there are seventeen slaves in next village. Waiting to be returning to their families. They are released and brought here, but last American redeemers, they run out of money. So they are still trapped. Cannot return to families."

"Aw, that's sad," Lewis said, standing and searching his pockets.

James turned to him. "Yes, very sad."

"So, what do you want us to do, James?" Jason asked. "Because we're not redeeming any slaves."

"I know. No redeeming. Only buying freedom of one child." He held out his hand to Lewis but kept talking to Jason. "Very great news. Slave masters say they tired of these slaves. Want to send them home. Charge only fifteen American dollar for each slave."

When Lewis didn't put any money in his hand, James let it drop. "You are agreeing to pay this price? I bring them here so you see their beautiful faces. You wait here."

"Forget it," Jason called after him. "We're not buying any."

"Of course. No buying. I bring them." James strode away.

Lewis put his hands on his hips. "Now what do you suppose that w—Yah!"

Jason turned and jumped, too. Dhor was standing right beside them. "Dhor, I thought you were sleeping."

"Only when I have to." Dhor was even shorter than James: no taller than six feet. And his slight pudginess differentiated him even more. He pursed his lips and his cheeks bulged. "You are being played a fool. That man has no slaves to redeem. If you had been unwise enough to give him money here, he would simply have vanished."

"You think he's taking off now?" Jason asked.

"No, he will certainly come with people he will say are slaves. Do not be surprised if they cry and carry on."

"But they won't really be slaves, will they?" Chris said.

Dhor smiled sadly. "We are all slaves to something."

Jason found himself nodding. "Why are you telling us this, Dhor?"

"Because I am a Christian man, sir, as perhaps some of you are. It is not easy in Sudan keeping Westerners and their money together. But sometimes I do what I can. You will find that for every dollar you have brought with you, there are ten slaves, five sick grandmothers, and two crates of medicine that will save a village if only you would pay transportation." He stepped back toward the Land Rover. "Beware, my friends. Here you will always be the enemy."

Jason noticed something happening in the trees. A tall man in a white tank top and khaki slacks had bent over double. He was retching.

Finally, he wiped his mouth on his tank top and made his way toward Jason's group.

"Got a new one coming in, gang."

The man hurried forward and, without introduction, sat down heavily on one of their boxes. He sat there breathing, swaying sometimes to his right. Jason and the others just watched him.

"You must all leave," the man finally said.

Jason looked at Garth, who was looking around as if expecting a cargo plane to taxi up at any moment. Jason shut his eyes and tried not to crack up.

"Um, sir," Jason said, "we'd like to stay, please."

The man was very dark. His was the blackest skin they'd seen yet. He had a full head of short black hair. He appeared to be about Garth's height and had long, muscular arms. He looked like an NBA forward ten years retired. He brought long fingers to his forehead and rubbed. "Visa, please."

Jason pulled from his pocket the travel visa Eloise had secured for them from the SPLA's cover group in Nairobi. "You're the SRRA secretary then?" he said, handing over the little booklet.

"Yes, yes." He studied the visa quickly, then began flipping pages as if looking for something that wasn't there. "This is no good."

"Excuse me?"

"Nairobi office always forgets to add petrol tax." He looked up at Jason. "You owe two hundred thousand Sudanese pounds, or you must go back to Kenya."

"Two hundred thousand?" Jason said, doing the math. "That's, what, two hundred American dollars? For a petrol tax, huh?"

The man launched into a bored discussion of the costs of overland travel in this part of Sudan. But Jason's attention was drawn by the eyes on him. It was Dhor, sitting in the driver's seat of the Land Rover, shaking his head slightly.

"No," Jason said, interrupting the secretary.

"No?"

"No, we will not pay. Your petrol tax is not real. Now stamp our visa or whatever you need to do and let us get on our way."

The man sputtered and might've leapt to his feet, but he stopped halfway and sat back down, his fingers pressing against his temples. "We will see. You will pay." He looked up. "But you must first convert your money to Sudanese pounds."

"What?" Jason said. "No, we don't have enough money to make it worthwhile. We think we're going to stick with American dollars for what we do have. We were told that would work fine."

"Not in Bahr el-Ghazal," the man said, sounding surly. "You will need Sudanese currency for your slave redemptions."

Jason chuckled. "We're not here for slave redemptions. Why does everybody think we are?"

"Because," the man said slowly, "that is only reason pink skins come to Sudan."

"Where would we do the currency exchange, anyway?" Chris asked. "Is there a Bank of Sudan branch around here somewhere?"

Lewis nodded. "I was thinking an ATM."

"Oh," Chris said, "much better choice."

The man turned and called into the forest. Two naked boys ran out clutching double brick-sized stacks of paper money bound with string. The secretary took it from them. "I do the exchange for you. Very favorable rate."

"I'll bet," Jason said. He looked at Dhor, who shook his head again. "But I'm afraid we're not going to take advantage of your service. Thanks, though."

"You need this currency to buy food, to buy slaves, to buy. . ." He leered at Rachel and Trieu. ". . .other pleasures."

Garth growled.

Jason stuck his hands in his pockets. "No, thanks."

The secretary handed the money to the boys, who scuttled back into the forest. He eased himself to his feet. "You will be wanting to use the Rover to get to. . . ?"

"To Akwer Nhom," Jason said. "Yes, we'd like to use the Land Rover, and maybe also a—"

"Then you pay seventy-five thousand Sudanese pounds."

Jason nodded slowly. "Seventy-five bucks, huh? That doesn't sound too bad." He looked at Dhor, who nodded once. "All right, it's a deal."

The secretary called for the boys again.

"Whoa, whoa," Jason said. "We don't need them."

"But you must pay in Su—"

"No, I must not. Here." He counted out seventy-five dollars into the man's hand. "Now can we have our truck, please, and maybe a trailer, and also my visa?"

"I suppose something could be arranged. But the trailer will cost you twenty-five more."

Jason paid it.

"Thank you," Chris said as the man walked away. "Pleasure doing business with you."

"Let's get some of this stuff in the Land Rover," Jason said. "And quick, before James comes back with a boatload of bargain bin slaves."

# CHAPTER 9

## AKWER NHOM

"OH, NO."

Jason looked out the Land Rover's window. "What, Trieu? More wild dogs?"

Trieu, sitting in the passenger seat up front, just shook her head and stared forward.

The Land Rover and its flatbed trailer—loaded with their gear, two bicycles, and Dau and Akot—crested a ridge and began descending into a shallow valley. On the floor of the valley lay the remains of what had once been a sizable village. Now it was just packed beige dirt and blackened circles of debris.

"Yikes," Jason whispered.

On second glance there were some signs of recovery. At least ten new huts stood bunched together at the far right of Jason's vision, close to some hardy trees. Freshly cut wood poles stood upright in the ground in two other spots, the framework for wattle and daub walls yet to come. Piles of fishing pole-width sticks stood beside the frames. At a third new dig, a completed thatch roof sat on the ground like a conical tiki hat, next to a heap of sturdy wall poles.

Tall black people, mostly adult men, labored in the sun or lazed in the shade of the huts. Dinka. They wore brown rags or only shorts. The few women wore Sunday school castoff dresses or simple robes with African print. A small number of children played in the dirt or chased the equally small number of goats.

Jason was struck by what he saw: tenacious people rebuilding their homes in defiance of sun, desert. . .and man.

None of the Firebrand team members spoke. The Land Rover crept slowly, almost respectfully, into the village like a hearse coming for a loved one.

The handful of children, wearing faded T-shirts or simple frocks or only beads, ran toward the vehicle. They were too thin. They all had very short hair or shaved heads. "Look at them," Lewis said, "they're all hurt."

"It's like a plague village or something," Chris said. "Look at that one in the white shorts—he keeps falling to one side. And that other one, dragging his leg."

"Oh!" Rachel said, her eyes tearing.

Filthy bandages covered some of the wounds. Some were missing hands and arms. One little girl was missing her right arm, and her left arm was wrapped with a crude rag bandage stained crimson-brown. She had a terrible gash in her chest, which oozed green and tan.

But none of that could quench their curiosity. They thronged the car and patted its sides, smiling blinding white teeth and singing a lively song at the tops of their voices.

Dhor pulled up next to a thatched roof lying on the ground. A man in a long blue robe stood from where he had been scraping out a circular trench in the dirt with a stick and faced the Land Rover and the children. Even from twenty yards away, Jason could see the man's grim expression, made more severe by ritual scars on his forehead.

"Okay," Jason said with a sigh, "everybody out."

The children backed away from Jason and the others as they stepped out. All singing abruptly ceased. The smallest child, a precious boy with a bloated belly and something like dried clay all over his head, began to cry. Then, when Garth got out and stood to his full height, the whole group shrieked and ran away.

"Way to go, boogie man," Chris said to Garth.

"Yeah," Garth said, watching the kids retreat, "I get that a lot."

By now the adults in the village had gathered. Jason counted eighteen adults and teenagers, and there had been around eight children. Judging from the number of black circles dotting the valley, this village had once been home to one or two hundred people.

Akot jumped off the trailer and issued orders. He sounded rude even to Jason, who didn't have a clue what the soldier was saying. The villagers hurried to the trailer and began offloading it. The Firebrand team moved to help. The SPLA soldiers, Akot and Dau, had a smoke.

Jason noticed several religious symbols in the village. Carved totem poles four feet high stood beside most of the huts. Some of the poles—with faces resembling lions, monkeys, or demonic beasts—lay on the ground, partially burned. A three-foot pyramid of stone stood in the center of the clearing, its top and sides adorned with dried fruit and flowers. A wave of supernatural fear swept across Jason's spirit. But he brought out the Sword of the Spirit, and his quietude was restored.

Trieu walked toward where the children were peeking at them. Jason heard her trying to coax them to come to her. Three boys peeked around the corner, looking as precious and "normal" as any black kid in urban America. One smiled toothlessly at Trieu; another bit his bottom lip thoughtfully; and the third just watched with wide eyes.

"Ow," Rachel said, putting down a box and holding her back. "Jason, could you come here?"

"What'd you do, Raych?"

"Nothing," she whispered. "Just wanted you to know that our friend Akot there has told them we're stupid Westerners and that we're not to be trusted."

Jason smirked. "Okay, girl, thanks. Good work." Then he took a step away and spoke loudly: "Just work through it, Miss Bloom. You'll be fine."

"Right," Rachel said—*raieet*. "Leave it to you to give me the best medical advice, Stephen."

As they unloaded the trailer, Jason noticed that almost all the adults had injuries, too. One man's bloody bandage had slid down to his elbow, revealing a gaping arm wound. A fist-sized chunk of his arm was missing, exposing the meat and bone underneath, as if a lion had taken a bite. A thick flap of flesh hung over the gap. The wound stank like a dead rat and had maggots crawling around inside. Jason began to doubt whether Trieu had brought enough supplies.

He walked to Dhor, who sat in the driver's seat, staring down the valley toward where the flat tan grassland met the hazy blue sky. "You headed back to the camp?" Jason asked.

"Yes."

"Yeah, we'll be fine. Maybe you could come check on us in two days? We don't have any way of getting in touch with you."

"Yes, you will have a fine way," Dhor said. "Akot and Dau, of course."

Jason looked at the two soldiers, who were now sitting in the shade of a completed hut. "I thought they were going back with you."

"No," Dhor said, laughing. "You must always have SPLA with you. It would not do for you to be getting lost in the desert."

"I suppose not," Jason said, watching as Akot and Dau passed a bottle back and forth. "Well, could you at least tell these people what we're here to do?"

"Ah," Dhor said, his eyes narrowed. "What *are* you here to do?"

Jason suddenly wished "Miss Bloom" were nearby. "We're here to dig a well."

"Of course you are." Dhor peered into Jason's eyes.

The moment prolonged. A fly swirled over Jason's nose. Sweat trickled between his shoulder blades. He met and held Dhor's gaze, though he blinked about ten times more often than usual.

"Yes," Dhor said at last, "I will tell them why you are here." He stepped up onto the empty trailer and spoke to the Dinka.

Jason made sure Rachel was listening. From time to time during Dhor's speech, the villagers peered at Jason or one of the other team members, their expressions inscrutable. Many of the men had the forehead scars he'd noticed before, but there was no common element between them. The designs seemed to be as individualized as the people who wore them.

Dhor hopped off the trailer. "There," he said, climbing in the cab, "I have told them." He started the Land Rover's engine. "I have left bicycles for Akot and Dau. Send one of them to Isaac Aguir's camp if you need something." He shut the door and poked his head through the window. "May the Lord bless your new well."

With a honk, Dhor pulled away. Jason stood with the rest of his team, watching him go.

Lewis scratched his arm. "Anyone else feel like we've just been marooned on the surface of Mars?"

The villagers stood around restlessly, swatting at flies. Some of them went back to their tasks. The children watched the white people, giggling and whispering. They were just like kids anywhere else, Jason thought. Except their mailing address was hell on earth.

Jason nudged Rachel. "What did Dhor tell them?"

"I didn't catch it all," she said, fanning herself with a paper plate from their snack. "He went a lot faster than Akot did, and I'm just learning Dinka, remember? But I did hear him say *well* and *water* and *dig*. So I guess that's good, right?"

He winked at her and then stepped over to Trieu, who was trying to open a crate marked "Medical Supplies."

"Do you realize this is the only box we brought that actually has in it what it says it has?" he asked.

"Jason," she said quietly, "these people need to be in a hospital.

Some of them are dying. It looks like they received some basic treatment early on, judging by the bandages I've seen on the children, but they need more. Their dressings need to be changed. Some of the wounds are infected. Some were never cleaned in the first place. It's obvious they are all undernourished. Most of the children have intestinal worms and at least two are showing early signs of malaria." She covered her eyes with a shuddering hand.

"Hey," Jason said, taking her hand and kneeling beside her, "you're here now. You can do something for them. You can't fix them all, but you can help them some. And maybe we can get the dynamic duo over there to bring Dhor back with the trailer and they can take a few of them to the nearest hospital, okay?"

She kept her eyes shut, but she nodded.

"But in the meantime," he said softly, "we need to get our 'handlers' off our case so we can crack open these crates and start doing what we came here for. Is there any way you could slip them something to knock 'em out? Or are we just going to have to tranq them?"

Trieu studied Akot and Dau. "If we wait awhile, they are likely to pass out on their own."

"I know," Jason said, "but we can't count on it. And I'm itching to get busy. Any way to expedite their journey into Neverland?"

"Why don't you just shoot them with pepper and the tranquilizers?"

"Because I don't want them seeing us being the *A-Team*, okay? When they woke up, they'd go tell Captain Babyface back there that he's got a bunch of American commandos loose in his territory. That's not exactly the way I was thinking this would go down."

She tucked a strand of hair behind her ear. "They would only say they saw commandos if they remembered seeing commandos."

Jason grinned. "Oh, you are devious. You're talking about Versed."

She smiled.

"Did you bring any?"

"Of course. I didn't know if we'd need to throw Lewis out the back of a plane again."

"You're sure they won't remember anything?"

"That's what Versed does, Jason. It causes amnesia, remember? But it's amnesic effect actually predates its administration, so they won't even remember being hit by the dart or seeing whoever shot them. Just remember to pick up your darts and leave the bottle next to them."

"Can you mix those little cocktails now?"

"Of course."

He pulled her head forward and kissed her on the forehead. "Beautiful. Let's do it."

By now the Dinka villagers had all gone back to their business. All except for a gangly boy in bright red swim trunks, who hopped merrily from box to box.

"Man," Garth said when Jason rejoined the group, "is anybody else hungry? I'm so hungry I could eat Lewis's hair gel." He pretended to gnaw on Lewis's head.

Lewis moved away, his hands on his hair protectively. "It's mousse, you big moose, but not chocolate."

"All right, you guys, listen up," Jason said, his back to the SPLA soldiers. "We're going to put our baby-sitters to sleep so we can get moving."

"You want I should put them in the sleeper?" Lewis said.

"No, we're going to use our guns," Jason said. "But I don't exactly want these village people to see us shooting at folks they think are good guys. That wouldn't help us, I'm thinking."

Chris slapped Jason's back. "Good thought."

"So we're going to have to do this real quiet-like."

"Hey," Lewis said, "are we stealth warriors, or what?" He struck a ninja pose.

"Look at him," Chris said. "Crouching Hacker, Hidden Dweeb."

"Okay," Jason said, "Garth, you and Chris break out two guns, but keep them hidden. If somebody comes up, act like you're pulling out pipes. When Trieu brings you the darts, we'll move."

Ten minutes later, everything was ready. Trieu walked to the far side of the village and began treating the children. Lewis and Rachel went with her. When the adults saw medical care being given, the wounded gravitated there, too.

Garth, Jason, and Chris stacked boxes and bags eight feet high in a makeshift sight block between the medical area and the shade where Akot and Dau were sitting, looking sullen. Their AK-47s were leaning against the hut at arm's reach.

"You move your baggage," Akot said, kicking dirt at them. "Move, move, move."

"Sure," Garth said, standing in front of Jason and Chris as they dug in a duffel bag. "We'll move it in just a second."

Jason felt the cool pistol grip of his modified Heckler Koch MP5 submachine gun inside the bag. He turned to Chris, kneeling beside him. "You ready?"

"Let's do it."

"You take Dau and I'll take Akot."

"Check."

"Remember," Jason said, "they'll have thirteen seconds before they're out."

"Gotcha, chief."

"Okay. . .go."

They pulled the guns out of the bag and stood on either side of Garth.

In that moment of surprise, as the soldiers' eyes flew open and their inebriated minds staggered from realization to assessment to action, Jason and Chris fired. The silenced MP5s made soft *pt pt* sounds, like pneumatic nailguns firing only air.

Dau slapped his shoulder as if he'd been stung by a wasp. Then he looked at them, still not comprehending.

Akot figured it out right away. He cried out and clutched his thigh. Then rage lit his face, and he reached for his rifle.

Garth heaved Akot away from the gun like a bouncer sorting out a drunken brawl.

Chris swept by Dau just as the young man turned to look for his own gun. Then Chris darted behind him to collect Akot's gun, too.

"Chris," Jason said, clapping his hands.

Chris tossed him his MP5 and trained an AK-47 on Dau and Akot, whom Garth deposited on the dirt nearby. He tossed the other assault rifle to Garth.

Jason plunged the MP5s back into the duffel bag. As Akot and Dau watched in confusion, Jason collected the AK-47s and leaned them back against the hut. He trotted over to the SPLA soldiers. "Good night, boys."

Dau was on the dirt before Jason finished his sentence. Akot had time to look down at his comrade before joining him in the world of dreams.

They carried the soldiers back to the shade of the hut and arranged them in good poses, heads slumped on chests. Chris poured the rest of the alcohol on their shirts and couched the bottle in Akot's slack hand. Garth and Jason picked up the darts.

"Get one of those bikes," Jason said. "I want to send a rider up to that village—what is it called? Oh, Mashar—to get this deal set up."

Suddenly, he felt someone watching. He spun around and saw the man in the blue robe, crouched over his circular trench, watching them. From the man's posture, Jason could tell he'd seen way too much.

"Uh, oh."

Jason walked slowly toward the man, his palms out and fingers splayed, trying to look as harmless as possible.

Behind him, he heard Chris ask Garth, "What's he doing?"

"That guy saw us," Garth said.

Chris blew through his lips. "Oy."

The scars in the man's forehead were deep but exquisitely done, Jason saw. Four furrows arched forward from the ears and came together in four perfect Vs between his eyebrows. For some reason it made Jason think of speed, like the ridges might slice the air for a sprinter. He was very thin, but broad shouldered and eight inches taller than Jason. He stood solemnly as Jason approached.

"Hello," Jason said. "Um, we didn't really shoot those guys, not with real bullets. They're just asleep."

The man wrinkled his brow, constricting the scars. He spoke in a deep voice, but Jason didn't know the words. He seemed a little agitated, but not afraid. He pointed toward the soldiers with the stick he'd used for digging.

Jason glanced back over his shoulder. Garth and Chris were beside him, trying hopelessly to look like tourists.

"Jason?"

Jason turned toward the voice. It was Rachel, wiping her hands on a bloody towel and trotting toward them. "What is it, *Miss Bloom?*"

"It doesn't matter," she said, now walking forward slowly. "They don't understand and they sure don't care." She dropped the towel on the dirt. "Would you like a little help here?"

Jason exhaled. "Please!"

She said something that immediately caught the man's attention. He began talking to her quickly and gesticulating with the stick. Rachel held her hands up and asked a question. The man responded, and then they both started speaking another language altogether.

Chris stepped up to Jason's shoulder. "Arabic."

After a long string of words from Rachel, the man groaned loudly and fell to his knees. He crawled toward her, speaking urgently through sudden tears.

Dinka came running. In seconds Rachel was surrounded by everyone in the village. Three boys ran over to Dau and Akot, then came shrieking back.

Rachel's voice rose above the ruckus. Jason watched her in awe. Here she was in what seemed to be the most godforsaken spot on earth speaking like a native to a band of people so different from her as to defy comparison. She was unbelievable.

Unless he missed his guess, she was telling them about the arrangements Eloise had made to get their children and family members back.

Jason watched them hugging and smiling and screaming with joy. And he started to think that maybe they weren't so different, after all.

"Good news," Rachel said, walking toward him after finishing her speech. "They understand what we're here for. They're okay about the SPLA guys. As you can see, they're excited about getting their loved ones back. And the guy in the blue that you were talking to is the man we were supposed to meet—he's Anei's father."

# CHAPTER 10

## WATER WITCHING

"HE WANTS you to look at the dirt here," Rachel said.

Jason followed the man's pointed finger to the twenty-by-twenty-foot square of newly smoothed dirt and ash. "What about it?"

Rachel spoke to the man—Anei's father, Lual Ngor—in Arabic. The rest of the Firebrand team stood around next to the Dinka tribesmen, looking like fans who'd won a dream field trip with the Harlem Globetrotters. Jason noticed that even the children stayed off the unpacked earth they were looking at. The sun was dropping in the sky. Around the village people burned cow dung to keep away mosquitoes and flies.

Rachel's voice changed as her talk with Lual became prolonged. She went from surprised to stricken to furious. When she turned to Jason, she didn't speak for awhile. Her eyes bulged; and when she breathed, her nostrils flared.

"He says it's the grave where they buried the villagers who were murdered. Including the chief and. . ." She looked at the gray dirt, her jaw muscles flexing. "Lual's wife, son, and youngest daughter. What was left of them, anyway. Scores of bodies—and body parts." She crossed her arms. "The Arab bodies they left for the hyenas."

Trieu moved to Rachel and placed an arm around her. Rachel remained rigid.

Lual pointed again at spots on the grave, speaking solemnly in Arabic.

"Do you see the anthills?" Rachel said, translating.

Jason noticed the dozen or so mounds of bright tan dirt dotting the gray surface like volcanoes on Io. He nodded at Lual.

"When the Muslims fly over our land," Rachel said, "this is how they see our villages."

Jason turned back to the grave. It did look like an aerial photograph. Scattered here and there were little colonies of pests just begging to be eradicated. Tiny figures toiled busily, trespassing on the land and spoiling the real estate value. What was needed was gasoline and a match.

Then he looked at the burned village around him.

Yikes.

Jason turned to his team. "Why don't you guys break our stuff out? I want to go just as soon as Lual's ready. Put just what we need in backpacks. Stash everything else. Let's keep the tourist look going, though. Garth and Chris, you guys figure out how to hide the silenced MP5s under your shirts. Everybody else gets the pepperball pistols. Trieu, you hold the money. Lewis, carry the seismograph thing so we can look like we're looking for water tables."

"You don't want me to pick up a forked stick and go divining?" Lewis asked.

"No," Jason said. "No water witching for now. Okay, let's move."

They headed over to the boxes near where Akot and Dau still slept. The children went with them, watching everything.

Jason caught Rachel's arm. "Are you going to be okay?"

"Are you kidding? We're going to take back what Muslim males stole—you bet I'm okay. But I wish we were snatching them back, not paying for them." Her eyes pressed into his. "The Muslim raiders get the slaves, the Muslim masters get paid for them, and the Muslim middleman gets his cut. We're telling them this is a good business to be in. I'd rather shoot them for what they've done than pay them. But maybe I'll get my chance." She looked up into his eyes and smiled. "Relax. I'm kidding."

"Hmph," Jason said. "Well, in the meantime, could you ask Lual when he can be ready to go? Mashar's eighteen klicks away. If we can get moving, we could be there about nine. If the guy on Akot's bike gets there and convinces the middleman to do the deal in the dark, we could be on our way back here before daybreak. Oh, and have the others tell Akot and Dau when they wake up that we're out looking for a good spot for the well."

"Aren't they going to figure it out when we come back here with all these redeemed slaves?" Rachel asked.

"Maybe, but then it'll be done and we'll be out of here. They're supposed to want their own people returned, so I can't see them complaining too hard, except maybe that they didn't get their usual kickback." He winked at her. "Go on, tell him."

Rachel conversed with Lual as Jason walked over to the boxes and got himself equipped.

"Look at this," Chris said, brandishing a slightly curved sword. "Has to be a Baggara blade. The Dinka don't use these."

Jason took it. It was balanced and heavy. In his mind's eye, he saw it hacking off the arms of the children standing around. He gave it back to Chris. "Where'd you get it?"

Chris pointed over his shoulder. "At the west edge of town. They've got a few more of these and some AK-47s. Looks like they took out eight or ten bad guys."

Jason slipped on a hunting vest with lots of pockets for secret goodies and strapped the peppergun pistol holster to his leg. "Hey, could you go get me one of those rifles? I'll carry it for show. No one will think an AK-47's the slightest bit unusual out here."

"Sure." Chris trotted off.

"You'll carry it for show," Lewis said, tinkering with his handheld seismographic instrument, "and for lions and pythons and rhinos."

Jason smiled. "Oh, my."

Rachel began packing her gear into a backpack. "Lual says he's ready now. I think some other men are coming with us. He wants to know if we'd like to eat some leaves before we go."

Jason straightened and looked around. The Dinka women tended cooking fires with big pots of water, into which they were dropping leaves and roots. He shut his eyes. How many times had he complained because his steak was too well done?

"Come on," Garth said, slapping him on the back. "Let's go do some good."

Chris returned with an assault rifle. "Here," he said, handing it to Jason. "It's Akot's. I figured there's a better chance of this one working than any of the others. I put one of the old guns next to Akot."

Jason hefted the AK-47. Its weight and the way it fit in his grip took his mind back to a hotel hallway in Kazakhstan where he almost unloaded one of these into some guys in turbans. He removed the thirty-round curved box magazine, checked the first bullet, replaced the magazine, and chambered a round, reveling in the sharp action of the lethal machinery. "Thanks, Chris."

Jason looked at his team. They wore their same clothes and hats from the plane, but had added hunting vests, belts, holsters, twenty-pound backpacks, and dark sunglasses to their ensembles. Chris and Garth had suspicious bulges under their vests. If these were tourists, he was Indiana Jones.

Still, it had to be better than wearing desert "salad suit" fatigues and Kevlar helmets. At least these costumes provided a veneer of deniability.

"All right, you gangsters," Jason said, "let's go. Chris, take point. Garth, watch our backs. Patrol formation, everybody."

As they moved toward the north edge of the village, Lual joined them. Rachel said something to him and Lual pointed into the trees.

"Uh-oh," she said.

"What?"

From the trees two Dinka men, an old man in a white T-shirt and frayed black shorts and a teenager in a ripped beige cloth that used to be a robe, drove four cows and about ten goats toward the trail north.

"Whoa, whoa," Jason said. "What's this? Raych, ask him—"

She was already talking to Lual. After an extended conversation, during which Lual and the other men seemed very surprised and kept looking at the Firebrand team like they'd suddenly transformed into wood elves, the men called over some boys to take the animals back to the village.

Rachel walked to Jason. Lual was with her. "They were bringing the livestock to trade for their people," she said. "It's everything they had left. It took a bit of convincing for them to believe we had enough money for it and that we wanted to use it for them."

With children running along beside them, their wounds covered with clean white bandages, the six Westerners and three Dinka left Akwer Nhom headed for points north. The shadows lengthened, and the sunlight turned a dreamy orange. Finally the last child turned back and the quest truly began.

"Man," Garth said, looking west, "I thought Montana was Big Sky Country. Would you look at that?"

The horizon was so flat and unobstructed that it truly did look like the edge of the world. The sun peeked out beneath a band of black clouds and above the black earth, creating a stripe of orange from north to south.

Jason whistled softly. "Yep, that's pretty barren." He walked in the middle of the pack, the AK-47 over his shoulder. Behind him, he heard Lual ask Rachel something, and Rachel answered. Whatever she said, the Dinka must've liked it because they *oohed* and *aahed* and seemed energized.

"What was that all about?"

She shifted her backpack. "They wanted to know why we would come all the way out here to do this, why we cared about them at all."

"What did you tell them?"

"I told them that the great sugarplum princess had put us all under a curse to obey her every absurd whim." She flicked his ear. "What do you think I told them? I told them that we love them because Jesus loves them."

Jason put his hand on the back of her neck. "Nicely done."

She grabbed his hand and pressed her cheek against it.

True, the sun was going down, but Jason felt a sudden surge of heat from somewhere.

"That's all you told them?" Chris asked, looking over his shoulder from the front of the line.

Rachel raised an eyebrow at him. "What do you mean, 'that's all'?"

"Tell the truth, girl," Garth said from behind. "What she really said, ladies and gentlemen, was that we came out here to kick some Muslim male derrière. And why? Because they are Muslim, male, and they have derrières! What other reason do we need?"

Lewis sniggered; and before long Chris, Garth, and Jason had joined him in juvenile cackling. The three Dinka men looked at them like they were the rudest boors to ever walk the earth.

"You boys leave her alone," Trieu said. "Rachel did the right thing. She planted a seed. What have you done that compares? Just watch, that seed could end up being the single most important thing we do on this trip."

"You're absolutely right, Trieu!" Garth said. But he said it with such conviction and sincerity that it set them to giggling all over again.

Rachel lifted her nose. "Laugh it up, fuzzball."

They tromped up the valley until it widened out into the endless hay-colored expanse of southern Sudan. The dying sun turned the clouds the color of orange and strawberry sherbet.

"Hey, Jason," Lewis said, "can we stop for dinner?"

"Let's get a few miles down the road first."

"Yeah," Garth said, "because there's a stand of really nice ferns up ahead. Mmm-mmm, them's good eatin'!"

\* \* \*

"Someone's coming!" Chris hissed.

The noise limiters in their helmets doubled as sound enhancers, in effect giving the Firebrand team superhuman hearing. The team scurried off the trail and pulled out their weapons. Rachel whispered to the Dinka and got them to hide, too, though there wasn't anything but a clump of five-foot-tall elephant grass to hide behind.

The Big Dipper, on the northern horizon, was almost invisible—not because it couldn't be seen but because the superabundance of stars around it made it lose its prominence. The Milky Way arched overhead like a white ribbon wrapped around a glass basketball. Just rising above the southern horizon was the Southern Cross.

Jason had his night vision goggles on. Through these lenses the world was green, like photos of the *Titanic* on the ocean floor. The thermal and infrared optics detected heat and displayed it as relative brightness. Jason's bright green arms stretched out across an expanse of dark green grass toward a number of bright green humans, some of whom were wearing black optics systems on their faces.

From the trail ahead appeared a bright green glob riding a rickety bicycle.

Jason recognized Akot's bike and the villager they'd sent ahead as a messenger. "It's okay," he said softly. "It's our guy."

Rachel whispered to Lual, and the three Dinka men stood and called out.

The rider's eyes doubled in size. He yelped and lost control of the bike, finishing with a magnificent face-plant in the grass.

"Ouch," Garth said. "That's gonna leave a mark."

Lual and the others hurried to the rider and calmed him down.

Trieu took her goggles off and used a hooded flashlight to check the man for injuries. Finally Rachel talked to the messenger.

"It's all arranged," she said to Jason. "They were getting antsy so they sent him back to find us."

"All right, good. We're only, what, about half a klick out? We can do this thing and get halfway back to town before sunup." Jason touched her shoulder. "Would you go through the drill with them one more time?"

"Why don't you tell me what to tell them so I'm sure I don't forget anything?"

"Okay, circle the wagons."

While Chris scanned the way ahead and Garth watched the path behind, Jason crouched with the others in the glow of the flashlight.

"First," Jason said, removing his goggles, "they have to remember not to let on that you understand a word of Arabic or Dinka. As far as anyone else is concerned, we're dumb Americans who only speak American."

Rachel turned to the four Dinka men and spoke in Arabic. They answered seriously, then laughed loudly. It was a sound at once familiar and exotic there on the plains of Sudan under constellations from both hemispheres.

"Okay," Rachel said, "they get it."

Jason nodded. "Next, make sure we're on the same page with our signals. We'll go through the slaves one by one. If the one we're on is from their village, they are to call her by name and hug her or shake her hand or whatever they do. If they see someone not from their village, they shake their heads no. If we have to have a conference about something, somebody has a coughing fit and the rest of us crowd around him to talk."

Rachel relayed the message. The men answered, their excitement level rising. Lual kept standing and crouching, standing and crouching.

She nodded at Jason. "They've got it."

Jason sighed. "Okay, people, let's go do this thing."

"Wait," Trieu said.

"What is it?"

"Can we pray first?" she asked.

"Sure," Jason said. He reached for Trieu's hand. The others joined. "Lewis, will you do the honors?"

"Me? Oh." Lewis was suddenly very interested in the hem of his vest. "I don't really. . ." He swallowed. "Oh, okay." He took Rachel and Lual's hands. "Dear God. . .um. . .help us to do this thing and be safe and everything, and get these people back to their homes and help us not get faked out or anything."

Lewis stopped talking. Around them, African crickets sang their lullaby. In the grass nearby, something small dashed from spot to spot. The air had been steadily cooling and was now probably under fifty.

Rachel translated the prayer for the Dinka, then fell silent.

Jason turned to Lewis. The young man's mouth was opening and closing. His forehead was squeezed with concentration or consternation. He hadn't let go of anyone's hand. Maybe he was waiting for someone else to take up the prayer. Jason was about to pray when Lewis spoke again.

"Dear God, You are the light of the world. You are the only hope for any of us. The only reason anybody should even have for their lives. I mean, without You this world is just a stupid, messed-up place. Dear God, I pray that You would show Yourself to these Dinka people in a way they've never seen. I know some of them have heard of You and stuff, but they're still mixing You with the old ways. Do some kind of miracle, dear God, to make them know You are the only real God there is." He breathed quickly, as if close to hyperventilating. "In Jesus' name, amen."

Jason looked at Rachel. Was she going to translate all of that? Surely she wouldn't.

She did.

"Wow, Lewis," Jason said as they were standing to go, "that was quite a prayer. Totally bold."

"Thanks."

"I hate putting God on the spot like that, though," Jason said. "I mean, now these guys are going to be expecting a miracle, and God may not be in the mood. Know what I mean?"

Lewis looked stricken. "Oh, no. I didn't think of that. You want me to unpray it? I could get them back and—"

"No, Lewis," Jason said, chuckling. "I think it's okay. What you did. . .I think it was great. I haven't been that bold in my prayers in a long time." He shoved Lewis playfully. "Who knows, maybe God gave you those words because He *is* in the mood to do some rockin' and rollin', huh?"

"Oh, wow. I sure hope so."

"All right, you guys," Jason said to the group, "let's go free some slaves."

# CHAPTER 11

## SWING LOW, SWEET CHARIOT

"WELL? Are they from your village?"

Jason watched Lual's face lose twenty years as he and the other three Dinka men saw the fifty-odd black-skinned people—young women and girls, mostly, but also some boys—sitting in the cattle pen staring into the torch-lit darkness or sleeping on the dirt. They cried out and rushed to greet them.

"I guess so."

Three Arab men, dressed head-to-toe in white jellabah robes, lowered their Chinese-made assault rifles and forced Lual and the others away from the slaves.

*No touching the merchandise, I guess.*

The captive Dinka quickly fell silent, either from fear of the Muslims or from lack of energy. As soon as Lual and the others stepped away, most of them sat down and went back to staring blankly.

The Firebrand team, their night vision gear stowed and their backpacks on the ground, sat under a nearby tree with Jason. Torches mounted on stakes surrounded the courtyard and the large tree. The rest of the village, Mashar, appeared to have been abandoned some time ago. The huts slanted over as if by wind, and nobody stepped outside to see what the ruckus was about.

Lual began pleading in Dinka with the women in the cattle pen. His distress was spiking for some reason.

Jason looked at Rachel for help and saw that she was silently weeping, a vein bulging on her forehead.

He heard a muffled voice beside him. It was the chief Muslim of the pack, the middleman, also swathed in white cloth like a kid trick-or-treating as a ghost. The man's turban was wound around his head like a bandage, with only a finger-wide eye slit.

Jason sat back down to powwow with him. "I'm sorry, what?"

"You pay now." When the man talked, the bottom of his eye slit bounced up and down.

"Not so fast," Jason said. "I want to have my Dinka friends look at them one by one. I'm not paying for anyone they don't know."

The middleman stayed quiet.

Jason motioned to the team. "When the Dinka positively identify these folks, my associates will bring them out one at a time to a separate area. How about here under the tree? You can have your men watching, too. Then, when we're through in the pen, I'll pay you for everyone under this tree."

"No." When the man shook his head, the eye slit spread enough for very black skin to show through. "Pay first."

"Sorry, Charlie," Jason said. "We'll be doing it my way or we'll be leaving. With our American dollars."

The middleman looked at the stack of bills Trieu displayed for him. Then he shook his head again. "All other ones pay first."

"Look, buddy," Jason said, "don't know if you've noticed, but you're kind of in a buyer's market here. You've paid for these slaves, right? You've bought them from their masters to get them here. Am I right?"

"Yes. Very difficult to get them all. Having to pay many more than before."

"No doubt. And the only way to make back what you've spent is for us to buy them from you. Right again?"

No answer.

"So you pretty much have to do whatever we say, don't you?"

The man didn't speak, didn't even appear to be moving. For a harrowing second, Jason thought the guy was going to freak and order his men to open fire. But then he nodded and stood. He spoke authoritatively to his men in Arabic. Jason wondered if he was announcing that he had just decided to change the rules and do it a new way.

The middleman turned back to Jason. "Yes, we now go. As you say, as you say."

"Good decision," Jason said. He turned to his team. "Rachel, please come with me. Bring our Dinka friends. The rest of you guys form a perimeter around this tree. Let me know if anybody tries any funny business."

"Check," Chris said.

"Jason," Trieu said softly as he passed her, "are you certain it is wise to be belligerent to this man? He is our only link to the people we have come to redeem."

Jason blew out a sigh. "Yeah, I know. Do I think it's wise? No clue, sister. I'm just winging it here."

The middleman led them toward the cattle pen. Rachel's tears had dried in clean streaks down her dusty face. Lual had gone zombielike. By comparison, the three other Dinka looked like kids crossing the parking lot to Toys R Us.

Jason whispered to Rachel. "What's wrong?"

"Lual's daughter isn't here."

He looked at the tall black man in his blue robe. Something about Lual's lost expression opened a window in Jason's mind through which streamed the anguish of not knowing where his child was.

And suddenly he was thinking about Samantha Runnion again.

He studied the middleman, now seeing him as part of a system that preyed on little girls. He wanted to rip his arms off.

But now it was time for something happier. As they went through the crowd in the pen, the Dinka men embraced each one and turned to Jason with a comment in the Dinka language, sometimes quite animated. It felt like a *Three Amigos* moment: "This is Carlos! We fought together the priests of this mission! This is Pedro! Together we defeated the Federales on the plains of Oaxaca!" Their stories usually ended with laughter and tears and more embraces.

The slaves' reactions were more subdued. One or two of the little girls managed a smile, but most simply endured the process, their eyes looking almost vacant.

Out of the fifty-seven people in the pen, the men from Akwer Nhom passed over only nine. To Jason, these didn't look any different from the rest—they were women and girls and a boy. One of the women held a baby to her breast. The baby's skin was much lighter than her mother's, and her hair was straight and fine. But they were apparently not from Akwer Nhom.

During the whole process, which took over an hour, Lual couldn't seem to rise above an expression of utter despair. And Rachel seemed locked in a tug-of-war between elation and anguish. She pretty much wept the whole time.

Finally the forty-eight who had been positively identified sat under the tree, surrounded by the torch-stakes, the Firebrand team, and the Muslims in their KKK sheets. Only the nine outsiders remained in the pen.

The middleman placed his fists on his hips and faced Jason. "Now you pay."

"Yes," Jason said, motioning Trieu over from where she'd been examining the slaves, "now I pay." He took the bills from Trieu. "Let's see now. What's the going rate for a human life these days?"

"One hundred dollars a head," the middleman said.

Chris coughed.

"Actually," Jason said, "I happen to know that you've agreed to an amount much less than that. Half that, to be exact. Fifty dollars each."

He heard his own words and couldn't quite believe them. It was atrocious to be measuring these lives in terms of dollars at all, but here he was *lowering* the price. Who was the one cheapening human life?

Still, he wasn't about to let this guy profit any more than possible from slaving.

"Price go up."

"No, price not go up. Remember: It's a buyer's market."

The middleman nodded. "But first must change American money to Sudanese pounds. Your money no good here."

Jason couldn't see the smile behind the mask, but he knew it was there. "No, that's not actually going to happen, either." He counted out the money and held it out to the man. "Forty-eight slaves is two thousand four hundred dollars. Take it or leave it."

He took it.

It was an insignificant event, over almost as soon as it began— one hand offering something and another hand accepting it. And yet in that trivial transaction, forty-eight humans moved from bondage to freedom.

The enormity of it struck Jason like a train. Here he was, surrounded by people who five seconds ago had been someone's property, sitting on the dirt with a traveling salesmen who hawked humans. What must it be like to be owned by someone? What must it do to you to be purchased like a cow? And what must it do to you to go the other direction in a single day, from freedom to utter bondage? The flickering village courtyard began to liquefy in his vision. The yellow torch flames became slaves, bound to the spot, writhing in a hell of someone else's making.

His eyes snapped back to the middleman. This punk, this criminal, hiding behind a mask, raking in cash for the crimes of his brothers—and very possibly his own. They called him a middleman, but really he was the "end man," collecting the final proceeds from a tidy little racket, one round of which began with a slave raid on an unsuspecting village of free people.

Jason wasn't ready to join Rachel in hating all Muslim men. But he would gladly give the rest of his wad of cash to take a shot at this one.

"Where are the others?" he asked, glancing at Lual.

"Others in the pen."

"No, the others on the list you were working from." Jason brought his copy from his pocket and showed it. "Where are the others from this list?"

The Muslim made the same elegantly dismissive gesture with his hand that Jason had seen Osama bin Laden make on tape. "Some not do well in captivity. They die. Others," he shrugged, "sold in Iran or Iraq."

"Lual," Jason said, "what is your daughter's name?"

"He not speaking English," the middleman said.

"Well, then you ask him."

The middleman spoke to Lual in Arabic. Jason watched Rachel for any sign of translation anomalies.

Lual lifted his chin and said two words, almost singing: "Anei Ngor."

Jason found it on the list. "There, what about Anei?"

The middleman produced his own copy of the list. It had Arabic scribbling next to every line. He pried his eye slit open as he scanned the page. "Ah! In Safaha village. Farm of Ahmed Ali Diab." He folded his list. "Ahmed not selling her. Going to make her his concubine."

"She's alive?" Jason said. "And here in Sudan? Where's Safaha?"

"Not far. In the north. Near Bahr el-Arab River. Thirty kilometers."

"This is great. Tell Lual she's alive and where she is."

Jason watched Lual's face as the middleman relayed the news. His head popped up, his eyes locked to the Arab's, and his forehead scars seemed to lift. Then he was on his feet, talking. He ran to the group of his neighbors and shouted something, and they shouted back with joy. For the first time Lual seemed loose and light. A smile broke onto his face like the moon coming out of a long eclipse.

He ran to Rachel and swept her up in a hug. Then he set her down and started speaking to her.

In Arabic.

*Oh, no.*

Rachel tried to look clueless. She scrunched her eyebrows and jutted her head forward. But Lual wasn't getting it. Jason didn't know what he was saying, but he was afraid it was something like, "Why aren't you talking to me now like you were just before we walked into town?"

He glanced at the middleman, who was watching carefully. Then the eyes slid over to Jason's and did not waver.

*So what if he knows she speaks Arabic?* he thought. *What does that prove?*

"He is very happy," the middleman said to Jason. "He is asking her for you to go with him to Safaha and use your guns to get his daughter back."

Jason laughed nervously. Peripherally, he saw Chris and Garth slide their hands into their vests. The other Muslims gripped their weapons with both hands. Every muscle in Jason's body felt bunched, like a leopard in the thatch.

"The others," the middleman said, pointing to the cattle pen. "You buy others, also."

Jason shook his head. "We don't know them. For all I know, they're your own family."

"No! They Dinka slaves from far villages. I get them out. You buy them. They go home."

Rachel went into a coughing fit. It sounded pretty bad. Jason didn't recognize it as the signal until she'd almost spit up a lung.

"Hang on a minute," he said to the middleman.

He pulled Rachel away from the tree and offered her the canteen from his backpack. Trieu came, too.

"She's a doctor," Chris said to anyone who might care.

Jason, Rachel, and Trieu huddled.

"Buy the slaves, Jason," Rachel said.

Jason looked at the nine in the pen. Their expressions were life-less, but their eyes were all on the freedmen under the tree. "Yeah, let's do it." He smiled. "I know what Eloise would say. She'd say, 'He has sent me to proclaim release to the captives and to set free those who are oppressed.' "

Trieu took his hand and Rachel's. " 'And to proclaim the favorable year of the Lord.' "

Jason redeemed them all.

# CHAPTER 12

## THERE AND BACK AGAIN

"PA GRAPE, Pa Grape, this is Larry-Boy. How copy? Over."

Jason went from a crouch to a full sit as he waited out the radio delay.

His team followed suit. The more than sixty Dinka they were escorting stood still or sat, but stayed in their long line.

The acacia trees they'd passed fifty yards back were still black with the night. But the sky behind them was peach and pink and purple, becoming dark blue and finally black. Birds and frogs and who knew what else welcomed the sun in a rich, hopeful chorus. The smell of dew and dirt and the cold damp ground beneath him made Jason feel connected to the earth, a tiny part of something majestic. Any more of this and he was going to break out into "Circle of Life."

He looked at his watch—5:48 A.M. Sudan time. That made it 10:48 the previous night in Akron.

"You think they're there yet?" Lewis asked, cradling the satellite radio with his legs.

"I hope so," Jason said. "We're running out of rest times. Akwer Nhom's not more than two miles ahead."

"Maybe you should try them again."

As Jason raised the black telephone to his ear, the speaker crackled. "Larry-Boy, this is Pa Grape. Copy fine. There you guys are!" It was Bigelow's voice. "Thought we'd never hear from you. What's your status? Over."

Jason grinned at Lewis. "Pa Grape, Larry-Boy. Status is positive. The whole veggie crew is here, safe and sound. We've also made our waltz up and down the produce aisle. All went very well. We've passed checkout fine and are just about to put the groceries away. Over."

He set the phone on his thigh next to his AK-47 while he waited for his voice to bounce across the globe. "Dude," Lewis said, "I totally can't believe we're using *Veggie Tales* as our protocol. I mean, grow up already."

"I know," Jason said. "Doug and Jamie have to hurry up and have babies so the rest of us can have an excuse for watching the show."

"Hey, Garth," Lewis said, placing the seismograph on the ground and pulling out the little PDA, "pick up that big rock and drop it on the ground."

"Lewis," Jason snapped.

"What? It'll be okay. I want to try this thing."

Garth picked up a rock the size of three bowling balls, held it over his head, and drove it into the ground.

"Whoa!" Lewis said, watching the dial on the car battery–sized yellow device. "Dude, you just caused a 2.2 earthquake. Do it again."

Bigelow's voice came through the speaker. "Copy, Larry-Boy. Great news! Ma Grape's about to do a jig, I think. Whoa, girl! Larry-Boy, will you be catching the next flight back to Bumblyburg? Over."

"Negative, Pa. There was one. . .baby carrot that the grocer didn't want to part with. As soon as we get these groceries put away, we're headed out to get her back." Jason took a breath. "But it will mean we will be going over into the Rumor Weed's land. How copy? Over."

After the delay, Bigelow answered. "Copy going into the weed patch, Larry-Boy. Ma Grape wants to know how deep you're going, how long you'll stay there, and if there are any, uh, pesticides where you're going. Over."

"Copy, Pa. With no surprises it should be a one-day trip up and a one-day trip back. Maybe another half day to wait for just the right moment to harvest. Over."

"Copy three days, Larry-Boy," Bigelow said. "Ah, Ma Grape wants to know if this trip is really necessary. Over."

Jason watched absently as an adult baboon trotted across their path, its pink face almost luminous in the cherry light of dawn. Lewis had put the seismograph away. "Tell her that a precious baby is going to become some *person's* concubine if we don't get her out. Over."

The delay seemed especially long this time. "Ah, copy, Larry-Boy. Ma Grape says 'Be careful.' Let us know when you're done. Out."

"Copy, Pa Grape. Out."

Jason handed the radio back to Lewis and stood. "Okay," he said to his team, "let's move. Last stretch until home."

As the group got moving, Jason noticed Lual at the back of the pack, glancing northward.

*   *   *

"We've got guests."

Chris had a thin sheen of sweat on his face when he trotted back up with his report, and his blond hair was dark and stringy in the back. A wet curl coiled on his forehead.

"Who is it?" Jason asked.

"Looks like SPLA soldiers," Chris said. "I counted eight in a desert paint jeep and our old Land Rover."

Jason turned to his African entourage sitting in the shade of the trees just beyond Akwer Nhom's limits. Rachel spoke earnestly to the four men and the eldest women, apparently trying to convince them that this stop was necessary for safety.

"Guess the SPLA's not exactly thrilled that we disappeared on them," Jason said. "Let's just hope they recognize an aunt or cousin in our group here and forget all about being mad."

The sky was bright blue now and the air was already hot. The optimistic chorus of dawn had segued into the enduring drone of day. From the valley floor wafted the smell of onions being sautéed for breakfast.

"Come on," Garth said, "let's get it over with. I need a nap."

Jason nodded. "All right. Rachel, tell them they can go now. We'll follow them in and deal with the SPLA."

At first the redeemed Dinka moved no faster than they had the whole walk. But as soon as they rounded the edge of the trees and saw their village, it was as if their souls reentered their bodies all at once. They ran screaming and laughing the rest of the way. The villagers at the bottom of the valley shouted back and ran to them.

The Firebrand team stood on the ridge watching. Jason put his arms around as many of them as he could. "That's what it's all about, isn't it?"

"Oh, yeah, baby," Lewis said. "Let's go get some more!"

"Not just yet," Trieu said, taking her pack down. "We all need to sleep."

As they descended the hillside toward the village, Jason pulled Rachel and Garth to his side. "You guys remember what countries you're supposedly from?"

"Crikey, mate," Garth said, "how could oy forget?"

Jason looked at Rachel expectantly.

"Aye-m froom the highlunds of souooth Texas, u'coorse."

By the time they reached the village proper, the party had already begun. The women ululated and danced, their arms held over their heads like the curved horns of their cattle. All the men who could do so leapt into the air in what appeared to be a contest to see who could jump the highest. Whoever thought white men could jump hadn't seen these Dinka. The children did everything they saw and some spontaneous silliness besides, even the bandaged ones. An old man plucked a lively tune on his lute, while two teens pounded the tar out of a drum big enough for a child to hide in.

Men who had stayed behind in the village rushed Jason and the others and swept them into huge embraces, speaking Dinka the whole time. Rachel squealed with laughter. She and Trieu raised their arms and joined in the dance. Garth and Lewis dropped their packs and boinged around like lunatics.

From the far end of the village, six of the SPLA soldiers climbed out of their vehicles, lowered their rifles, and approached. Jason felt Chris—and the AK-47 Jason carried—at his back as they neared. He recognized one as Isaac Aguir, the underage SPLA commander from the creek. Akot and Dau were there, too. A figure that looked very much like Dhor, their driver, stood behind them at the Land Rover.

"Hello, Isaac," Jason said.

But Isaac didn't answer. He glanced quickly at the man next to him, then stared at the ground.

This tall, thin man wore a tan uniform unlike any Jason had seen so far. It was not camouflage. It looked a little like the khakis sailors wore on a ship, except it was long-sleeved. He wore a tall helmet covered with tan cloth fraying at the seams. Tan earflaps with blue edging dropped well below his chin, making him look a bit like a basset puppy. In his teeth he clenched an ornate pipe with a curved protrusion on the end. Sturdy brown boots and a golden wristwatch rounded out the ensemble. He appeared to be in his twenties.

He stood still, puffing his pipe and looking from Jason to the dancers and back through eyes tinged pink. The soldiers around him stared only at Jason and Chris.

Finally the man took his pipe out and pointed at the villagers with it. "It will be very helpful," he said in English with a British accent, "this well you have dug."

Jason winced. "We hope so."

"Tell me, Mr. . . . ?"

"Stephen Wilcox," Jason said, extending his hand, "Global Vision."

The man didn't take Jason's hand. "Tell me, Mr. Wilcox, do you intend to dig any more such wells while you are our guests?"

"As a matter of fact, Mr. . . . ?" Jason said.

The pipe went back into the mouth. "I am General Deng, commander of the Third Division of the Sudanese People's Liberation Army."

Jason nodded. "As a matter of fact, General Deng, we don't intend to. . .dig any more wells—not of this size, anyway. There may be one more small one we want to think about. But that's all we have planned."

"And then you will leave?"

Deng was pretending to watch the revelers. The jumping contest was down to a young Dinka man and, of all people, Lewis.

"Yes, General Deng," Jason said. "And then we will leave."

The contest ended in victory for the Dinka. Lewis sat on the ground sucking air, but was soon mobbed with giggling children.

General Deng laughed brightly. His men laughed, then, too.

"Right," Deng said, turning to Jason. "In future, please do not go sneaking away from my men—no matter what opportunity they may give you."

Jason saw Akot's forehead wrinkle. Dau was trying to hide a smile.

"Of course," Jason said. "But we do still want to go after one more. . .well. Where we're going I don't think your men will be welcome. For that we will need to go alone. And then we will rejoin your men and request transportation—for which we will pay, of course—to the airstrip of your choice."

Deng chewed the pipe. "And if I refuse? If I cast you into the brig and confiscate your belongings?"

"Oh," Jason said with intensity, "don't do that. For one, our *organization* would not take kindly to unjust treatment. For another, your Dinka brethren might not take kindly to you stopping us from helping one of their own. They might even start to ask why you aren't trying to do this instead."

Deng was quickly in Jason's face—over it, really. "They will believe what I tell them to believe, Mr. Wilcox, when I tell them to believe it. And when I tell them to believe something else, they will."

Jason smelled sweet pipe tobacco, which was an aroma much to be preferred over the bouquet of a large, unwashed man in long sleeves in the middle of the desert.

Finally, Deng turned to go. His men followed, scattering goats and children as they went.

"I guess that means 'okay,' " Chris said.

All eight men climbed in and on the jeep and Land Rover. The drivers started the engines and, with a last wave from Dhor, drove out of the village into the shimmering morning.

The Dinka settled into conversation groups in the shade at the edge of the village. The team joined them under the trees, downing water and leaning against tree trunks.

"Hey, Lewis," Garth said, "way to go with that jumping contest. Who knew a white boy like you could catch the air like that?"

Lewis smiled. "Yeah, I know. I just started jumping around. Then they kept pointing at me and doing their hands like this: 'Jump, jump, jump.' So I kept jumping. My calves are going to be sore for a month."

"That's Lewis," Trieu said, glistening with sweat, "always bringing out the best in people—without the use of words."

"Oh, wow," Lewis said. "Thanks, Trieu."

"Aw, don't tell him that," Garth said. "He's still got to fit inside his helmet, you know."

The acacia trees above them provided little shade, but it was the best to be found for miles around. The team began staking out spots of shade to lie down in. Jason had intended to work out a schedule of watches while the others slept, but it occurred to him that if they weren't safe in the midst of people they had just rescued, they weren't going to be safe anywhere. The last thing he saw was Lual standing at the edge of the village, gazing north.

*Let us rest awhile, my friend. Then we'll set out to bring your little girl home.*

# CHAPTER 13

## CREEPY CRAWLERS

"IS IT HIM?"

Jason waited as Trieu looked through her sniper scope at the man approaching their position beside the big rubber tree. To Jason it looked like any of the hundreds of white-robed Baggara men they'd seen that day, and the fading sunlight didn't help. Jason and the rest of the team gripped their MP5s—now loaded with pepperballs—and CAR-15 rifles—loaded with Versed darts above and tear gas canisters below—ready for fight or flight.

The muzzle of Trieu's Dragunov SVD sniper rifle tracked slowly right as the man neared. The scope's optics painted her eye with blue light. Finally she smiled. "Yes, I can see the Vs on his forehead. It's Lual."

Garth slumped into the dirt with a moan. Lewis fluttered his lips.

Lual was tromping through thigh-high grass, looking around. From the cover of the tree's wide trunk, Chris whistled a series of short, high-pitched notes, and Lual's gaze snapped to the spot.

Chris smiled at Rachel. "Lesser kestrel. It's. . .like a falcon."

"Oh."

Lual hurried over to them.

Jason handed him a canteen when he reached the shade. To Rachel, he said, "Ask him which farm it is."

Rachel and Lual spoke in Arabic. Then she turned to Jason. "It's not this first one but the one just beyond it," she said, pointing northwest. "The slave he talked to said there were over thirty slaves on this farm here, but less than ten on the one where Anei is." She folded her arms and spoke softly, looking over the field. "This one man owns thirty human beings. Can you imagine it?"

Jason stroked the several days' of chin stubble. "That's a lot of enemy-held open ground to cover. I guess it's finally time to dress for success, gang. Break out the salad suits." He shook Lual's hand. "Good job. Rachel, tell him he did a good job. And tell him he can get out of his jellybean outfit whenever he wants."

Rachel spun around. "It's *jellabah,* Jason. Jellabah. What's so hard about that? And did you ever think it might get you farther if you tried saying *please* now and then?"

Jason stared at her. "Um. . .please?"

She growled and pulled Lual to the side, speaking in Arabic.

Lewis pulled his desert camos out of his backback. "What's got into her?"

"No idea," Jason said. "Maybe she's caught the scent of Muslim males and she won't be able to rest until she's hurt one. Let's just get on with it."

When they were ready to go, Lual gave them a look that made Jason chuckle. Though he'd watched them pull on their gear, the six creatures before him—wearing helmets with black wires down the back and strange devices on the front, carrying black assault weapons unlike anything he'd ever seen, and almost disappearing in the underbrush—must have looked otherworldly. The poor guy's eyes seemed to double in size every time Lewis unfolded another of the banshee's four appendages.

"Rachel," Jason said softly, "would you. . .please. . .tell Lual not to worry about how we look. He looks like he's having a problem."

"Huh," Lewis said. "Looks like he's going to wet himself is what you really mean."

"Stow it, Lewis," Jason said. "Get that baby aloft and let's go."

"Sir, yes, sir!"

Lewis handed the four-armed bubblegum machine to Chris, who held it above his head like he was reaching up to change a lightbulb. The model aircraft's black rotors gleamed in the sun's last light. Lewis pressed a button on the three-button "mouse" on his chest, and the rotors began to spin.

The sound began low and soft, like an electric shaver in the bathroom next door. Then, as all four rotors gained speed and joined their voices, the noise rose in pitch and volume. It kept increasing, until it seemed it would never max out.

Lual dropped to the ground and covered his head.

Lewis nodded, and Chris released the banshee with a little toss. The exotic craft rocked slightly, like a spinning top gaining its balance, and streaked into the sky, taking the sound with it.

Even so, it was several seconds before Lual dared a look. Rachel knelt beside him and spoke soothingly.

Jason flipped down the eyepiece on his helmet and called up the live video coming from the banshee's wireless camera. Through the slightly jerky movement, he could see miles and miles of endless savannah. The image grew fainter as the sun set, but he could still make out square farm fields and various clusters of buildings here and there. Large herds of cattle—Dinka cattle, perhaps—grazed in the fields. Farther north, toward a barely visible line of trees that Jason thought probably marked the Bahr el-Arab River, the buildings were more densely packed.

"You want her locked in hover?" Lewis asked.

"Yeah, but first try to give me a look at ol' Farmer Ahmed's place so we can be sure he's not having a barn dance or anything."

Two hundred feet above their heads, a silent black speck moved northwest and focused its monocle at the farm and home of Ahmed Ali Diab.

It was a squalid place, though probably middle-class by northern Sudanese standards—and a veritable Tara Plantation by southern Sudanese standards. A low, flat-roofed, mud-brick home stood at the center of a cluster of henhouses, goat pens, and assorted shacks and sheds. Goats and chickens poked about for food. On the south side of the farmhouse, Jason spotted a small black boy leading twenty-five or so cattle into a large corral.

*Done for the day,* Jason thought. But as soon as the image of this child coming home and being greeted by a warm meal entered his mind, he thought of the verse in which Jesus said that the slave had to first come in and serve the master his food before he could take any for himself. It was one thing to think of slaves in the remote, New Testament sense. It was something else entirely to think about them actually living that kind of life when, but for God's grace in assigning birthplaces, it could've been him.

"Okay, Lewis," he said softly into his microphone bar, "bring her back down. Soon as it gets dark, she's not much good to us out here."

"Roger, Roger," Lewis said.

Chris keyed his mike. "What's your vector, Victor?"

"Check your clearance, Clarence," Garth said.

Jason flipped his eye panel up and saw that Lual was standing again. Rachel was at his elbow. She looked like a child next to him. "Rachel, would you warn Lual that we're bringing the banshee down? But tell him we're going to put it away as soon as it gets here. Then we'll move out."

\* \* \*

"Whatcha got, Trieu?"

Once more they waited in concealment while they put eyes on

the target unawares. For a small team deep inside enemy territory, it seemed like a good way to operate.

Jason went prone beside Trieu and received the sniper rifle from her. "Trouble, I think," she said. "But not for us."

It was full night now. Strange stars occasionally pierced the high clouds. The temperature was dropping. The Firebrand team and Lual hid beside the lone acacia tree in the cow pasture. Safaha wasn't long on electric lights, certainly not here on the outskirts, so it was almost completely dark. Pinpricks of yellow candlelight marked the windows of neighboring homes.

But when Jason looked through Trieu's scope, the world was bright as day—albeit a monochrome green day. He saw green cattle huddled together in the pen. He didn't need any advanced gear to hear their incessant lowing. The few plants and bushes showed up as almost white. Then he saw humans: an adult black man and four black boys. Something about how they were moving caught his attention. He toggled the scope to maximum zoom.

His suspicion had been correct: The man was hitting one of the children. He held what appeared to be a broomstick and slammed it against the boy's shins and thighs—while two of the other small figures held the boy in place. Jason thought he could hear the snapping impacts and the victim's cries.

He wanted to charge in right then and end the beating. But the team wasn't ready. Ten more minutes and they'd be set. Ten more minutes and the horsemen that had ridden by a few moments ago would be that much farther away. And so he settled back down to watch a man and his helpers—Ahmed and his sons?—torture a small child.

A thought struck Jason like a meteorite: They couldn't rescue Anei and leave the rest here. There was the question of security—if they swept in and took Anei, there was a good chance that some of the other slaves would see and report them. Better to take the whole lot of them. But that wasn't his concern now, watching the boy fall to his hands and knees. How could he pluck one child out of this life and condemn the others to stay in it?

He looked around at the yellow dots from the farmhouses nearby. Was the plight of the slaves on those farms any better than here on Ahmed Ali Diab's. Were slaves—young children abducted from their homes—being beaten on those farms right now? In his mind he heard cracking bones and crying children; he saw swords hacking like cleavers separating hands and feet and arms and heads. The sounds and images overran his mind like slave raiders descending on a village.

Suddenly he felt the weight of the entire north of Sudan, of the slaves in every farm and household. Across his shoulders was the crushing burden of the abuse and sorrow and fear and hate. The religious and government system that allowed and promoted it smashed him into the dirt.

And all he wanted to do was put a stop to it.

But what could he do? What could even his whole team do against centuries of slavery and cruelty? They couldn't free every slave. They'd be lucky if they could get out of Safaha with the one slave they'd come to retrieve.

But surely they had to do something.

Jason brought the scope back to his eye. One of the helper boys ran from the cattle pen to where the adult was breaking his stick over the slave boy's back. The boy running up must've said something alarming, because the adult stopped in midswing and ran to the cattle pen. He stood up on the fence and hand-counted the cattle.

Jason swept the scope across the farmhouse. The boys holding the slave dropped him and ran toward the cattle pen. Another boy, a teenager, arrived from around the side of the house. He half-carried, half-dragged another figure—a nude pubescent girl. He dumped her on the dirt and ran to the cattle pen, too.

The girl lay on the ground a moment, looking stunned, then gathered herself up and ran to the goat pen. Jason tracked her movement. When she reached it, another girl met her and wrapped an arm around her protectively, pulling her into the shadows.

Back at the cattle pen, the boys were next to Ahmed, also hand-counting. As one, they dropped their hands and turned to Ahmed. Together they walked around to the far side of the cattle pen, where Jason could not see their legs or bodies. He could only see Ahmed's head.

A moment later, Ahmed's stick rose into view, then fell like an executioner's axe. It was clear to Jason that Ahmed was angrier than before.

A small black boy darted out from beyond the cattle pen, Ahmed's helpers in hot pursuit. The teenager caught the boy by the elbow and shoved him into the dirt. The other boys pounced on him, holding him down or kicking his body and head.

While they kept the child pinned, Ahmed walked past them toward the house. He walked up the steps, opened a door—where at least two adult female forms were clustered—and went inside. Ten seconds later, he reappeared. The women gave him a wide berth as he passed. In his right hand he held something long and straight. Something that glinted.

"He's got a sword," Jason said, whether aloud or to himself he didn't know. "We can't just sit here. For all we know he's going to wipe them all out right now."

The team clustered around him.

"What's happening?" Rachel asked.

"He's going after at least one of them with a sword," Jason said. "His sons are holding this poor kid down, and Ahmed's coming with a sword."

"We've got to go!" Lewis said.

"No!" Chris and Garth said together.

Garth grabbed Lewis by the backpack and sent him to the dirt. "We're too far away."

Lual pulled at Rachel, pleading something. She didn't answer.

"Let's approach," Chris said. "But quietly. If we get close enough before he does anything, we can act. But if we go sprinting over there and they see us, they can raise the alarm and we'd be up a creek."

"Yeah," Garth said, *"without* Lual's little girl."

"Okay, okay," Jason said, his hands held in front of him as if trying to contain something from exploding. "You're right. Let's move now. Chris, you and Lewis on the left. Trieu and me on the right. Garth and Rachel with Lual behind. Everybody remember the plan and wait for the signal."

Trieu took the sniper rifle again and stared through the scope. "Oh!"

Jason spun. "What? Did he kill him?"

"I can't tell. He didn't chop down. He seemed to be cutting. The others act like there's lots of blood. They're backing off. The child is rolling on the ground holding his face."

"That's it!" Jason said. "Go, go, go!"

Though they were in a hurry, they were also well trained. They crossed the hundred yards of darkness with stealth and skill.

Every few yards Jason switched between his night vision goggles and his helmet's eye panel to check their progress and unit cohesion. Using his own three-button mouse on his chest strap, he cycled through the views until he could see the topo map that showed their GPS-accurate locations as moving green dots. They were doing fine. The map showed the outlines of Ahmed's farm just twenty-five yards away from Chris, the nearest green blip.

"Hold up," Jason said over the squad radio. "Let's take a look around."

They stood at the edge of the knee-high grass. With them all lying facedown, they were only partially camouflaged. All someone would have to do would be to shine a flashlight on them and they'd be exposed—especially when they ventured into the barren area closer to the farm. But judging from the utter darkness and the lack of any signs of modernity, there didn't appear to be much chance of that happening anytime soon.

Jason didn't need Trieu's Dragunov to survey the situation from this close. Even if he didn't have enhanced vision gear, his nose told him he was on a farm. The stench of the cattle pen and goat shack assaulted his nose like smelling salts. The henhouse to his far right was quiet, but the cattle pen on his left and the goat pen on his near right stirred with the animals within. Straight before him was the flat-roofed farmhouse.

Ahmed and company had gone inside. It hadn't been more than ten minutes since the episode with the sword, so everybody was probably still awake. The boy whose blood had scattered them was nowhere to be seen, nor were any of the other slaves.

So far no dogs.

"What do you think, boss?" Chris whispered over the radio.

"I think we wait," Jason said. "We missed the party, so there's no need to rush. Let's wait an hour or so until the lights go out in the house."

"But what about the bleeding kid?" Lewis said.

"We'll have Trieu look at him, Lewis," Jason said. "But we have to be careful."

Jason heard Rachel talking to Lual in Arabic. He glanced over at the man. He was crouching in the grass, looking like a sprinter in the blocks. What must it be like to be so close to his daughter and be made to wait?

Had Anei been the one being carried by Ahmed's teenage son? Had he been doing to her what it looked like he'd been doing?

He swung his goggles over to the goat pen. He thought he could hear soft voices. Maybe even a snatch or two of singing? He spotted a farm cat staring at him. The large male stood at the side of the house, under the stairs, watching him with God's own night vision gear.

"Hey, Jason," Lewis said, "can I eat while we're waiting? I'm starved."

"Yes. Just keep it quiet."

They took turns eating and drinking in silence. After thirty minutes, the light through the windows dropped away, a candle at a time.

"You guys," Jason said ten minutes later, "I've been thinking about something."

"Oh, great," Chris said. "Here it comes."

"Should we, I don't know, maybe take all the slaves on this farm? Not just Anei."

"What?" Garth said incredulously. "And take them away from all this?"

"It's just that I can't imagine leaving them here, now that we've seen what we've seen."

"About time," Lewis said. "This guy's a maniac. Make him do his own work."

The team voiced general agreement.

"But he won't, you know," Rachel said.

"Won't what?"

"Do his own work. You think you're solving anything by taking these poor slaves away from him? You think it'll make him see the error of his ways and he'll give up slaving forever? Forget it. He'll just buy new ones—and once again the demand for slaves will go up and once again the raiders will come to another village, and the whole stupid thing will start over again."

"Well, what do you suggest?" Lewis asked. "Isn't it—"

"I'd suggest we steal a nuke and set it off in Khartoum," Rachel said evenly, as if she'd been thinking about it for days. "Except that would kill all the Dinka that had been displaced there. Or I'd suggest going back in time and offing Muhammad in his crib, if I had the means to do it."

"Whoa," Lewis said. "Terminator Girl."

"Okay, look, Raych," Jason said. "Unless you've come up with a nuclear weapon or a time machine in the last ten minutes, I'm guessing those options are out of the question. But I'm with you on the idea. We can't solve this whole thing, but we *can* do some small good thing here, which, as someone once told me, is better than doing nothing at all. I say we nab every slave on this farm and skedaddle. Who's with me?"

"Right behind you, boss," Lewis said.

"Can we handle six?" Trieu asked.

"One each," Chris said, "plus someone left over."

Jason nodded. "We've got at least two boys injured up there, so let's revise the plan. Chris and Lewis take the left side of the farmhouse as we planned. Trieu and I take the right. Garth and Rachel work with Lual to find not just Anei but all of them and get them out. We'll peel off as we have to, to carry anyone out. Chris and Lewis take off next, then Trieu and me. I'll leave last. Questions?"

They shook their heads and checked their gear one last time.

"Rachel?" Jason asked, looking at her glowing face in his goggles.

She smiled grimly. "Let's go hurt a Muslim male."

# CHAPTER 14

## For Samantha

"Three. . .two. . .one. . .mark."

With Jason's emotionless word, the operation began.

While Lewis and Trieu trained their rifles on the door of the house, Chris and Jason stepped forward in a commando crouch—bent double but weapons shouldered.

Chris reached the corner of the cattle pen and checked around the side. A heifer spooked and blundered into her neighbor but didn't make any noise louder than the ones the other cows were already making. "Clear."

Jason reached the fence beside the goat pen and checked his direction. He could hear the goats vocalizing and shuffling in the dirt. He peered under the goat shack's roof with his night vision gear and saw two small people sitting on the floor. But no bad guys with guns. "Clear."

Lewis and Trieu trotted forward, rifles forward, while Jason and

Chris covered the doorway. Lewis passed behind Chris, springing slightly with those foreshortened Achilles tendons, and moved five steps toward the shack beyond the cattle pen, then knelt. Trieu did the same toward the goat shack.

"The area is covered," Jason whispered. "Go to phase two."

Jason glanced over his shoulder and saw Rachel, Garth, and Lual approaching. Garth had Lual, who was essentially blind without night vision gear, at his side. When he stopped behind Jason, he pulled Lual into a squat.

At a nod from Jason, the three of them passed him and knelt behind Trieu.

Goats in the pen sensed something and brayed nervously, pressing against each other to get away from the threat.

Garth and Rachel swung around, ready to add their guns to the welcoming party for anyone coming through the door. But no one appeared.

Jason heard Rachel whispering. A quick glance showed Lual slowly moving beyond Trieu toward the goat shack.

"Anei?" he called in a loud whisper. "Anei Ngor?"

There was no reply. Indeed, the silence from that direction seemed to deepen.

Lual whispered in Dinka, all the time easing toward the goat shack.

Jason's attention jumped back to the house. Had he heard something? Someone moving inside?

From his right, he heard a child's voice. "Wa?" A beautiful but filthy Dinka girl, perhaps twelve or thirteen, with cornrow braids along her scalp and a rag robe tied over one shoulder, stepped tentatively out from under the goat shack roof. "Wa?"

"Anei!" Lual spread his arms and ran to her. He swept her into his embrace and spun her around and around until they collapsed on the dirt. Jason couldn't see that smile explode on Lual's face, but he felt it inside himself all the same. They were laughing and crying—and beginning to forget all about stealth. Trieu and Rachel and Garth shushed them.

Rachel approached Lual and whispered in Arabic. Lual conferred with Anei, who appeared to be having trouble concentrating. But soon she led Lual and Rachel and Garth into the goat pen.

Garth came out a moment later escorting a teenage girl who walked with a limp. They passed behind Jason and headed for the taller grass.

Rachel stopped beside Jason, with Lual and Anei in tow. "Ahmed has the other girl in the house," she said. "The boys sleep over there in the cattle shack. There are three. Anei says they took the boy Ahmed cut there, but she doesn't know if he's alive or not."

Jason nodded. "Can you take them over there so they can tell the boys it's okay?"

"Yeah," Rachel said, "but there's one more thing. Anei says that Ahmed or one of his sons may be coming out with the other girl. Ahmed's wives won't let them have their fun with the slaves inside the house, so they could come out at any moment." She pursed her lips. "I hope they do. I'd like to shoot him myself—and no way do I want to leave just one slave here if we can help it. They'd kill her, because they'd be so mad at losing the others."

Jason nodded, and Rachel led Lual and Anei toward the cattle pen.

The longer the mission took, the more nervous Jason got. How long before somebody made a mistake? How long before the barnyard got so loud as to be suspicious? Was that a match-strike in that side window?

Through the helmet's sound amplifiers, Jason heard someone moan. It sounded like Rachel. "What's going on?" he asked.

"Oh! Oh, sweet baby!" Rachel cried. "Oh, no. Trieu, Trieu, come quick! Oh, oh, no."

Trieu, still crouching next to Jason, looked at him, and he nodded.

As Trieu crossed quietly to the cattle shack, Jason heard Lewis's voice.

"Oh," Lewis said, as if aghast. "Oh, no, that can't—that's too—"

Lual stepped out carrying a child's body. Trieu was right beside him, holding a cloth to the boy's face. Lewis followed, carrying another boy. Anei came last, pulling a third boy, who seemed reluctant to leave. He kept looking at the farmhouse door in terror and pulling against Anei.

"Chris," Jason said, "get them out."

"Check."

Then Lual was at Jason's side, lowering the boy he carried.

"No," Jason said, "take him that way, with the others."

Trieu lifted the cloth. "He wants you to look."

Jason looked.

The little boy's nose was gone. Hacked off. Along with most of his upper lip. The bone of the upper jaw and the open hole of his nasal cavity were revealed. Flaps of skin stuck wetly to the spot. The skull around the base of the nose was exposed. It looked like a skeleton staring out from behind the flesh of a living child. The boy's wounds weren't bleeding much anymore, and he was either unconscious or dead.

Trieu covered the wound again with her blood-soaked cloth. "Apparently he lost a cow."

Jason shook his head. Lual and Trieu took the boy out the way the others had gone.

He waited until they were gone, then backed away, his muzzle still aimed at the farmhouse door. Just as he was about to turn and run, the door opened and someone holding a candle stepped out.

He froze. This could be bad. If the slaves were discovered missing this early, things could go south in a hurry. As the figure came down the steps, Jason noticed that there were two people, one obviously pulling the other. His first guess was that it was the teenage boy coming out with the slave girl to finish what he'd begun earlier.

Jason had pepperballs and tear gas, but no memory-erasing tranquilizers. He cupped his hand over his microphone. "I need somebody with tranqs."

When the figure stepped out from the shadow of the house, Jason finally got a good look.

It was Ahmed. He was pulling the third slave girl, still nude from before. Ahmed shoved her to the dirt, set the candle on the step, and loosened his knifebelt to lift his robe. The girl lay on the ground as if stunned, looking too battered to resist or even protest.

Something happened to Jason then. The weight that had crashed upon him before now drove him into the mat again. In that instant the whole inhuman system that created a market for human lives and then broke all rules to supply that market, the whole culture that thrived and sustained itself by stealing children and delivering them to torment, the whole religious empire that said this was not only allowed but good, suddenly coalesced into the body of Ahmed Ali Diab.

That thought was chased by an even more powerful one, as if letting a dog out released a ferocious grizzly bear, too. In this moment, the man before him in the dark courtyard was not only the embodiment of the machinery that had locked the people of south Sudan into misery, he was the proxy for the men who had abducted and murdered Samantha Runnion and the others. Standing before Jason—his robes up, beginning to kneel over this defenseless girl—was the personification of every sexual predator that had ever preyed upon little girls.

Instantly Jason was back to the waters of Australia, feeling the chill of the shark as it passed, jaws slightly parted, unblinking black eye sliding across him in search of easy prey.

A blitz of faces overwhelmed his memory: Danielle van Dam, Casey Williamson, Destiny Wright, Elizabeth Smart, Erica Pratt, Jennifer Short. Little Samantha, who should've had her sixth birthday.

And suddenly he was on his feet. Walking toward Ahmed.

Ahmed spoke gruffly to the girl, who finally tried to resist. She put her hands on his shoulders and tried to roll away. Ahmed punched her in the shoulder blade, bringing a tiny yelp from the girl.

He rolled her around to her back.

Jason slipped his pack onto the ground. Tore off his helmet. Unslung his gun harness. Dropped it.

"Hey, Ahmed," he said, "I've got what you're looking for right here."

Ahmed turned at the sound, angry at first and then alarmed. He was about to shout when Jason's fist intersected with his mouth.

Jason was on him like a maniac. The right to the face was followed by a left to the gut. Ahmed doubled over, and Jason brought up the hardest uppercut he'd ever thrown. Ahmed's head snapped back, and he tumbled onto his backside. Jason's follow-through sent him sprawling.

The girl watched in disbelief. She didn't run or even try to cover up.

A distant voice called to Jason—was it from his discarded helmet or only in his head?—begging him to back off. But anger and agony surged the louder.

Ahmed came to his elbows and gathered his feet under him. At the same moment, he reached for his belt and the knife dangling there.

"Oh, no, you don't." Jason launched a flying roundhouse kick that connected with Ahmed's left ear and rolled him over. The knife went flying.

Jason wasn't through. He left his feet and focused all his weight into the point of his knee, which he buried just under Ahmed's right shoulder blade. Ribs cracked and Ahmed whimpered.

It was a glorious sound to Jason's ears, a sound Ahmed had extracted from others, including the girl who only now was crawling toward the goat shack, but had probably never made himself. Jason wanted him to go on making that sound.

He grabbed Ahmed by the puff of wiry hair with his left hand and drove his right into the side of his face.

Jason heard himself cussing. Language he hadn't used in years surged into his mouth like it had never left him. The part of him that felt ashamed of his words and actions was far away right now.

Still holding Ahmed's hair, Jason delivered more punches to the right side of his head, each one with a name attached.

"This is for Danielle." *Whap!*

"This is for Destiny." *Whap!*

"This is for Casey." *Whap!*

"This is for Elizabeth." *Whap!*

"This is for Erica." *Whap!*

"This is for Jennifer." *Whap!*

Ahmed's cheek crunched mushily under the last punch. His blood mixed with the blood from Jason's knuckles.

Jason stood up. "This is for Anei." He kicked him in the broken ribs.

"This is for every other child who's ever been abducted and afraid of garbage like you." *Kick!*

"This is for that girl you just tried to rape." *Kick!*

"This," Jason said, falling elbow-first on Ahmed's other shoulder blade, "is for that boy who just lost his nose."

He backed ten feet away and pawed the dirt like a bull. "And this, you piece of trash, is for Samantha Runnion." He ran forward, Ahmed's head in his sights, his gait timed so that his right boot would send Ahmed's head into orbit. Ahmed looked up at him, his bloody mouth working numbly. Jason brought his leg back and then forward—

And was knocked on his side. He hit the ground hard, someone large on top of him.

Jason lifted his legs and sent the man flopping to the side, only then realizing who it was. "Garth?"

Chris was in front of him, MP5 leveled at Jason's chest. "I've shot you before, cowboy. Don't make me do it again."

"What?" Jason looked around. Garth pulled him to his feet. Lewis and Trieu were twenty feet away, their rifles trained on the front door. Rachel was in the goat shed, leading the girl away. On the ground beside him, Ahmed hardly moved.

Jason stood as if dazed. Garth led him away. Distantly he heard Chris give Trieu an order that sounded logical.

Trieu fired her rifle at Ahmed, then ran toward him out of Jason's field of vision.

Something told him he was going to feel really bad about this very soon. But right now all he could think of was Ahmed's whimper and how just maybe Samantha Runnion was resting a little easier in her grave.

\* \* \*

"Are you completely nuts?" Chris stared at Jason through night vision goggles. "We're trying to get out of here, and you're beating up the locals? What were you planning next? Maybe breaking and entering? Why not go in and help yourself to the fridge and maybe some of the guy's wives? I can't believe you, Kromer. You're a total psycho, man."

Jason couldn't argue. He sat against the rubber tree shaking his head and flexing his right hand. At least the last slave girl had been rescued.

"Here," Chris said, dumping Jason's pack and helmet and gun into his lap. "You'll need these if you ever decide to be part of the program again."

"All right, Chris," Rachel said, kneeling beside Jason. "Give it a rest."

Jason put his helmet on and lowered the night vision goggles so he could see. Beside him under the tree crouched the Firebrand team and the Dinka children. Trieu worked on the boy's nose. Jason smelled disinfectant. Anei was curled in her father's lap.

He turned to Rachel, also in her goggles. "I was going to kill him."

She reached out and caressed his cheek. "I know. I had a big speech made up about you not doing stupid things to endanger yourself unnecessarily. I don't actually want to lose you, remember? But then it hit me that I wish I'd thought of doing what you did, and all of a sudden the speech sounded a little hypocritical. Still, don't do stupid things, okay?" She brought his hand up to kiss it, but saw the bloody mess of his knuckles. "Hang on, let me get something to treat that."

Jason scooted over to Trieu. "Is he alive?"

She nodded. "It's a miracle, although I'm not sure he will appreciate it when he recovers." She caressed his forehead. "His name is Jok."

Trieu's face showed concern, but none of the revulsion or panic he felt chasing each other around in his mind. Once, long ago, he had thought it would be a bad idea to have any women along for these missions. Not today.

She lifted her dark eyes to him. "You had this coming, didn't you?"

"Which?"

She jutted her chin toward the farm. "What you did there. This goes back to your question to me in Australia, about people who hurt little girls."

Jason smiled sadly. "Yeah, I guess you're right. It's been about to blow up for a long time. Guess it just found the right opportunity."

She tucked a strand of hair behind her ear. "A great heart, Jason. Like I told you. A great heart."

He sighed and shook his head. Maybe it was the shock of Jok's injury or the smell of the alcohol, but Jason's mind was returning. "Okay. I'm really sorry about that back there. I think I just kind of. . . lost it. I'm not even sure about everything I did."

"You beat the snot out of Ahmed Ali Diab," Lewis said, in such a stunned voice that the rest of the team almost laughed.

Jason sighed. "Right. Well, anyway, I'm sorry. But I think I'm back now. Trieu, can Jok travel?"

"I'm not leaving him *here,*" she said.

"What about the other boy?"

"I've got him," Garth said, lifting the boy who had been Ahmed's target before they'd discovered a cow missing.

"Lewis," Jason said, "let's you and me and Rachel split up Garth's pack."

"Yes, sir."

In five minutes Trieu had Jason's knuckles bandaged and the team was headed south, their plucked firebrands safely in hand.

# CHAPTER 15

## FUNNY YOU SHOULD ASK

"THE BROTH has real beef in it."

Rachel looked from Jason to Lual, who was beaming.

Jason took a sip from his wooden bowl and savored the beefy tang. "Tell him it's delicious."

She did.

They were back in Akwer Nhom, dressed in their well-drilling costumes again, sitting by a large fire just beyond the new tukuls. The children they'd brought back with Anei weren't from this village, but it didn't matter. The ones who knew their parents were dead would be adopted by the villagers. The ones who might have relatives elsewhere would be taken there soon. But now it was party time.

It was the evening of the day they'd returned to the village. The celebration they'd left a few days ago seemed to have never ended. This time they'd sacrificed one of their remaining cattle to thank the Firebrand team.

Suddenly Jason felt a push from behind. His bowl dumped onto the dirt. He staggered forward and turned around. Garth and Chris stood behind him.

"What is this, guys?"

Garth grabbed him by the hunting vest and lifted him off the ground. Jason wondered if he was about to become another one of Lewis's seismography tests. He saw Rachel and Trieu and Lewis coming forward in alarm. Garth carried him behind the nearest tukul and then dumped him on the ground. At least a 2.2 on the Richter scale.

"Garth!" Rachel said, running now. "What are you doing?"

Garth came forward to grab him again. Jason knocked his hands away and crawled backward.

"Get his arms," Garth said to Chris.

"Cut it out, you guys," Jason said.

He could hurt them and get away, he knew. But he didn't need to do that. Did he? On the other hand, they might be able to hurt him, too, especially the two of them together. Chris tackled him, and Jason let himself be taken to the packed dirt. Maybe if he gave up it would be over quickly. Chris locked his arms across Jason's chest from behind.

Garth sat on Jason's legs, then grabbed him by the shirt and leaned his buccaneer face close. "Now you listen to me, squidhead. Me and you and jarhead are gonna have us a little summit, got it?"

Rachel tugged at Garth's arm, with predictable effect. Lewis lunged at Chris, who swept a leg out and sent him to the ground. Trieu just watched. A few of the Dinka children had come to see the show.

Jason nodded into Garth's very near face. "Got it."

"I don't know if you remember it, because you're a squiddy, which is close to a marine—no offense, Chris—but after your stunt in Baikanour, you agreed not to run off on your own anymore. We gave you the one black shoe award, remember?"

"Yeah."

Garth's massive jaw worked left to right as if about to crush a golf ball in his teeth. "Now I know what you were thinking when you laid the smack on that puke, and don't try to tell me it didn't feel good. Can't say the idea didn't cross my mind a couple thousand times. And you were saving that girl. But—are you listening to me?" He whacked Jason on the side of the head. "Are you listening now? Do I have your complete and utter attention, squiddy?"

"I'm listening."

"Now I like to have fun and tell a joke now and then," Garth said, "but right now I am stinkin' serious. I'm going to say this nice and slow so you can get it: You cannot be Rambo. Understand? Repeat after me: 'I cannot be Rambo.' "

"I can't be Rambo," Jason muttered.

"I can't *hear* yoooo."

"I can't be Rambo."

"Chris," Garth said, "punch him in the gut next time he says it. See if you can't get that diaphragm working. Say it again, squiddy, nice and loud."

"I cannot be Rambo!"

"Again!"

"I cannot be Rambo!"

Garth's mitts were on Jason's face forcing his mouth open like he meant to give him a pill. "Will you run off like that again?"

He moved Jason's mouth open and shut and spoke for him: "No, I won't."

"Good. Will you stay with the team?"

"Yes, I will."

"That's what I like to hear. Will you carry out personal vendettas that endanger the lives of your team, no matter how good it feels to do so?"

"No, I will not."

"And will you use more force than what's necessary to stop a bad guy from doing a bad thing?"

"No, I will not."

"Excellent! That's a good squidhead." He let loose of Jason's face but grabbed him around the back of the neck and pulled him forward. "Because I will not follow a loose cannon. Do you hear me? No matter how good your intentions are. Controlled force, my brother. If my CO did on an op what you just did, I'd be in for a transfer so fast your head would spin. Trouble is, there's no place for me to transfer to now, is there? So it's *you* who would be doing the leaving, understand me? Shape up and march right, soldier, or your team ain't gonna be your team anymore. Am I making myself clear?"

Jason looked at the rest of his team—for now it was his team, anyway. They stood in a semicircle watching him, arms folded.

"Yeah," he said. Then he looked at the ground. "Yeah, I hear you."

"Don't let him loose yet," Chris said to Garth. "I want a piece of him, too." He pulled Jason's forehead back against his chest. "Kromer, there's no reason I couldn't command this team. Before Eloise found you, I *was* going to be team leader. There are those who wonder if that wouldn't have been a better idea. So listen to me: You screw up one more time, and I'm taking over, got it? Shoulda been me, anyway."

Jason looked up at him. "I hear you."

Chris loosened his grip.

Jason sighed and looked again at the others. "I'm sorry I flew off like that, you guys. I just. . .lost it. But you're right, Garth. If somebody in my platoon had done that, they'd be out of here so fast it wouldn't be funny. I–I won't do it again." *I hope.*

Garth looked around at the others. "What do you say, people? Is he forgiven, or do we bury him neck deep and pour honey on his head?"

"Ooh," Lewis said, "definitely the honey."

Garth stood and helped Jason to his feet.

"Man," Jason said, slapping hands with Garth and Chris, "is that how you talked to your superior officers in the army?"

"Sure. Isn't that how you do it in the navy?"

"No," Jason said, grabbing Garth's wrist, "this is."

He kicked the legs out from under him, and the big man went to the ground, but he pulled Jason down with him. Then Chris jumped into the fray, followed by Lewis.

Rachel and Trieu watched the four of them wrestling on the ground.

"Welcome to Romper Room," Rachel said.

Ten minutes later the scuffle was over and they went back to the party. Lewis went after the high jump title again. Garth took a turn on the big skin drum. Trieu sat on a log by the fire, looking wiped out but relaxed. Rachel played with the children, learning more of the Dinka language. Chris went to learn how to carve a throwing spear from some of the elders.

Hyenas yipped somewhere in the night; but by the crackling orange fire, there was no fear. Moths danced among the sparks.

The remorse that Jason had eluded during their long trek back ambushed him here, thanks partially to the pounding he'd just received. Curiously, the thing that grieved him most was not that he had almost killed an unarmed man in pure rage. For that he wondered if there hadn't been just an atom of righteous indignation mixed with his own. What really bothered him was that he'd cussed. He'd thought all of that garbage had been cleaned out. Apparently not.

Someone touched his shoulder. It was Anei. She began speaking to him in Dinka. Little emotion registered in her voice or expression, but the words kept coming, as if someone were squeezing them out of her.

Jason looked to Rachel, clustered with the children thirty feet away. She must've caught a look of desperation in his eyes because she came over to him.

Lual knelt beside his daughter. At a pause in Anei's monologue, he turned to Jason and began translating into Arabic, and Rachel translated what he said into English. "She says Ahmed was going to take her as his woman in two more nights," Rachel said. "He was supposed to wait for this old woman to come and circumcise her, but there was some holdup—praise God—and he got tired of waiting.

He'd gotten bored with his wives, concubines, and the other slave girls, apparently. Pig. I guess there's nothing like an innocent little virgin girl for a. . .person. . .like him."

"Um, Raych," Jason said, "how much of this did Anei say and how much of it is your embellishment?"

Rachel turned to Lual and spoke, and he nodded to Anei, who began speaking to Jason again.

"She says the Christian God told her in dreams that her Wa, her daddy, would come for her. She says she didn't believe it because she thought she'd seen her father killed in the raid. But now she says she believes that the Christian God must be stronger than the other gods."

Jason noticed belatedly that the music had stopped and several of the villagers were standing around the fire staring at him.

"Whoa."

Three of the village elders, including one of the men who had gone to Mashar to redeem the slaves—he appeared to be their chief elder—began conferring audibly behind the fire. Lual went to them, and they spoke intensely for several minutes.

The Firebrand team gathered around Jason. Anei looked at him shyly and finally offered her hand. Jason took it and put a brotherly arm around the girl's thin shoulders. A woman dropped a thick branch onto the fire, sending up a swarm of orange sparks.

The elders seemed to arrive at a decision. They rounded the fire and stood before the team. Jason stood up. The men's faces were nearly invisible with the fire behind them, but their heads glowed with orange nimbuses.

The chief elder said something with conviction and an air of ceremony. A buzz passed through the rest of the Dinka. He walked to Lewis and brought him forward.

"But I don't want to be a human sacrifice!"

"Relax, Lewis," Rachel said. "I'm pretty sure you're safe."

"Pretty sure?"

"Oh, sure," Garth said, "you just thought that was beef in the stew. Ever see *Soylent Green?*"

Lewis whimpered.

The chief placed both hands on Lewis's shoulders. It looked like an NBA star telling a talented high school player to keep at it so that maybe one day. . . He spoke earnestly and forcefully to Lewis, as if giving him a lifetime's worth of advice in one sitting. Lewis relaxed as the moment extended. He stared into the chief's eyes.

A chill ran down Jason's arms. Whatever was happening, it was a far cry from a typical night out with the team. He looked hard at the tableau, willing it onto the emulsion of his memory.

The chief stopped speaking. He dropped his hands from Lewis's shoulders. Lewis wiped tears from his cheeks. The elders walked to the far side of the fire and rolled the large drum to them. Two of the elders began beating out an austere rhythm.

Lual spoke to Rachel in Arabic. She asked a question, sounding amazed. Lual answered, gesturing to Lewis. Finally Rachel nodded. Lual called Anei to him, and they walked to the other side of the fire.

"Lewis," Rachel said, walking back to the team, "you're never going to forget this."

"No kidding," he said, still wiping his eyes.

The Dinka began to chant. Only the men danced this time. The rest of the team crowded in to hear Rachel.

"I don't think this is something Eloise ever envisioned when she launched this group," she said.

"Cough it up, Raych," Chris said.

Rachel surveyed the team conspiratorially, like she had the most delicious morsel of gossip ever spread by mouth or mail. "The whole village wants to convert to Christianity—and they want Lewis to tell them how."

Lewis's eyes bugged out. "Say *what?*"

Rachel nodded. "The chief remembered that on the way up to Mashar, you'd prayed that God would do a miracle to show that He was the only real God. Remember?"

"Oops."

Garth grabbed Lewis by the neck. "What do you mean, 'Oops'? The whole tribe wants to convert, Lewis. That's not *Oops,* that's power evangelism, baby." He gave Lewis a noogy.

"What was the miracle?" Chris asked.

Rachel swept her hand toward the eighty-odd Dinka dancing and chanting in the firelight. "Do you remember what this place looked like when we got here? There were, what, fifteen people here. They were so depressed they couldn't stand up. Now look at them. All that, plus Lewis's prayer, plus Anei's dreams—it's plenty evidence for them. The way they see it, *their* gods didn't protect them from this situation, and *their* gods didn't send people from the ends of the earth to get their families back. So they're ready to jump ship."

"Also," Trieu said, "several of the villagers were Christians already, I believe."

"That's right," Rachel said. "But they couldn't make any headway with the others. *And* these people have seen enough of the Muslim god for ten lifetimes. Yeah, they're ready for a change."

Jason rubbed his face. "I don't know, maybe I'm a doubting Thomas or something. But I just keep worrying about their faith. I mean, if they're ready to swap gods because something bad happened, are they going to swap back the first time God doesn't prevent another raid? And how can the whole village convert? Whatever happened to individual faith? The whole thing just feels wrong."

Garth groaned. "Don't worry about it, Jason. Are you going to stand in the way of these people coming to Christ? Just chill and let God take care of it."

"Huh," Lewis said, "easy for you to say. You don't have to tell these people how to become Christians. Rachel, I don't have a clue what to say."

"You'll do fine," Trieu said. "We'll help you."

"Hey," Garth said, "maybe we can get Big Mama to get some tapes sent out or some literature printed up or something. Do they have the Bible in Dinka?"

"They do," Rachel said, "but most of them can't read their own language."

"Someone could read it to them, though," Chris said, looking at Lewis.

"And the *Jesus* film has been dubbed in Dinka, too," Rachel said. "Maybe we could get that out here."

"Cool," Lewis said. "Okay, I don't feel so bad."

Chris grabbed Lewis's arm. "Well, what are you waiting for?"

"What, you want me to do it now?"

"If we're leaving tomorrow, you'd better get busy."

Jason touched them both on the shoulder. "Hang on, hang on. Let's talk about this."

The drumming stopped and the Dinka sat close to the fire. More and more eyes were turned toward the Firebrand team.

"Rachel," Jason said, "please tell them Brother Lewis will be with them in a minute, after we talk."

After Rachel delivered the message, Jason pulled his team together in a huddle on the ground.

"Okay, look," he said, "we've done what we came here to do and more. Our supplies are starting to run thin—three more days without rationing. This evangelism thing is a great surprise, and I think we can give them a good start into Christianity. But really it's time for us to go." He looked at each of them, gauging their expressions. "Right?"

Trieu held a finger horizontally across her lips. Lewis looked over at the Dinka. Chris stared into the fire. Rachel folded her arms. Garth appeared to have fallen asleep.

From the nearest tukul came the sound of a child moaning.

"Jok is coming out of the sedative," Trieu said, standing. "If we go, perhaps we could transport him to a hospital? The other boy will recover on his own."

Jason looked at her. "Is there more you could do here if you had more time?"

"Of course. But I have the feeling there would always be more. At some point you either have to stay permanently or just leave some things undone." She smiled at Jason. "Excuse me."

When Trieu was gone, Rachel arched an eyebrow at Jason. "I saw that."

"What?"

"You want to stay, don't you?" she asked.

Jason shrugged. "I don't know. Maybe. Seems like there's a lot left to do here. But it's not my call. What do you guys think? Should we ask for more time or should we just get on back to the ranch?"

Chris scratched his scalp. "What did you have in mind to do if we stayed?"

"Yeah," Garth said, "and how much longer were you talking about? I don't mind eating everything in Lewis's pack, but I'm not exactly hungry for leaves and grass."

"Stay outta my pack," Lewis said.

"I don't know," Jason said. "That's why I'm bringing it to you. Back in Akron we all had ideas about what we'd do in Sudan if we had a team like us at our disposal. As I recall, Chris was going to take out the oil pipeline, Rachel was all for slitting some slave raiders' throats, and Garth was talking up counterinsurgency."

Jason lifted his hands. "So now here we are. We've seen the system at work, up close and personal. Thanks to Eloise and Rumbek, we know what's behind it all—the power elites in the north stealing everything from the people in the south, remember? Are we just going to redeem a few slaves and leave?

"I mean, look: There are plenty of people who will say that what we did actually contributed to the success of the system, since we paid cash for illegally abducted slaves, thus rewarding the slave takers and creating a need for more slaves. If we really wanted to set things right, we'd go find every slave and every cow and every barrel of oil that's been stolen out of the south and steal it all back."

The team looked at him in dismay. Lewis's hairline rotated

backwards his eyebrows rose so high. Even Rachel looked stunned. Then Garth snickered, and the rest of them followed suit.

"Yeah, right," Chris said.

Lewis wobbled his head as if snapping out of a daydream. "Whoa. I mean, how could you even do that?"

"You can't," Rachel said.

Trieu approached their huddle. "Can't what?"

"Jason wants to save the world," Garth said.

She sat down and looked at Jason. "Oh, I already knew that."

"Yeah," Lewis said, "but he wants to do it one goat at a time."

"And don't forget those poor barrels of oil," Chris said.

Trieu looked at them strangely. "Barrels of oil?"

"Never mind," Jason said. "How's Jok?"

"As well as could be expected under the circumstances." She tilted her head. "So how are you going to save the world?"

"By staying longer," Chris said.

"Okay," Jason said, holding up his hands in surrender, "it was a stupid idea. Sorry. Let's just go home."

"I gotta admit, though," Garth said, looking toward the Dinka, "it would be a shame not to at least teach them to set up a scouting system to watch for raids. I mean, all they'd need is a few hours' warning to get somewhere safe or send a runner to the SPLA. You can't exactly hide hundreds of horses in the open desert."

"Oh, man," Chris said, digging the dirt with his heel, "wouldn't you love to run into one of those raiding parties and give 'em a nice little surprise?"

Lewis's head popped up. "We could totally be like *The Seven Samurai,* you guys."

"The seven what?" Chris said.

"*Seven Samurai.* Or *The Magnificent Seven,* same difference. Hello, anybody ever watch classic movies but me? Even *The Three Amigos* works."

"Spit it out, junior," Garth said.

"You know, the seven hired heroes who come in and get a town all fired up to finally stand up to the big bad guy who's always bullying them around? That's us."

Garth harrumphed. "Actually, kid, it's probably smarter to teach them how to run than how to fight. But I like your thinking."

"And the longer we stayed," Lewis said, "the longer we'd have to be sure they got started right with Jesus and didn't, you know, combine Him with a lizard god or something."

Jason turned to Rachel, whose dark eyes glinted in the fire's glow. She noticed his stare and returned it. Was she thinking about hurting Muslim males? Or getting back to perfumed bathwater? Or something else entirely?

"I can't believe you guys are really thinking about this," she said. "We're not set up to fight a war, we six. And nothing we could do would end this thing, anyway. So what's the point? We could end up getting hurt or killed—and what would we have to show for it?"

"Pshaw, girl," Garth said. "Isn't this the woman who wanted to kill Muhammad in his Pampers? What's got into you now?"

"I'm just saying that we ought to thank God we've made it so far and get on home." She clenched her jaw. "Or we should commit to staying here until the job is done or we're all dead, whichever comes first. I don't see how anything less helps anybody."

Jason straightened his legs. "Okay, look. Let's vote. Either we leave tomorrow or we stay at least awhile. Who votes for leave tomorrow?"

"No, I don't want to do it that way," Lewis said. "Too much peer pressure. Can we have a secret ballot?"

Chris whacked him upside the head. "No."

"Why don't we call Eloise," Trieu said, "and let her decide?"

"Good idea," Jason said. "Maybe she can have us party in Nairobi for a few weeks while she flies in some more gear and maybe the *Jesus* film stuff. Then we come back." He stood. "Okay, guys, thanks. Lewis, get me set up on the sat phone and then you and the others go do your Mars Hill thing."

"My what?"

Trieu dusted off her pants. "He means your sermon."

"Oh."

\* \* \*

"Come again, Larry-Boy? You want to do *what?* Over."

Jason had to chuckle at Bigelow's tone. "Pa Grape, this is Larry-Boy. We'd like Ma Grape to advise whether we should come on home tomorrow or extend our stay in the produce aisle. Over."

As his words winged their way to early afternoon Akron, Jason tuned in to Lewis's oratory.

Lewis stood beside the fire so the Dinka could see his face. Rachel stood in front of him on his left, beside Lual. Trieu, Garth, and Chris stood behind Lewis, chiming in occasionally.

A typical round went like this: The five Firebrand members would confer about what to say, then Lewis would say it loudly to the uncomprehending crowd. Rachel would repeat it quietly in Arabic to Lual, who would proclaim it at full volume in Dinka, at which point the villagers would respond with a phrase Jason had taken to mean something along the lines of "We're down with that, baby."

They had started at Genesis 1:1 and had just about made it through Solomon's tragic lapse into idolatry and madness. It had been Trieu's suggestion to survey the Old Testament before coming to Jesus. The idea was to show the absolute hopelessness of men to satisfy a holy God, thereby creating a hunger for the One who did it for them.

"Hopeless! Hopeless!" Lewis cried. "Everything is worthlessness and striving after wind! What is the point of wisdom? What is the point of wealth? What is even the point of godliness? I have searched out work and laziness, wealth and poverty, pleasure and pain, and all I find is emptiness! Somebody show me what meaning there is to this life!"

Jason whistled softly. The kid wasn't half bad.

Bigelow's voice crackled in the speaker. "Larry-Boy, this is Pa Grape. Ma Grape wants to know what you think you could do by staying longer. And she wants to know how long you might stay. Over."

"Copy, Pa Grape. We don't have to stay—we're just asking for counsel. We've bagged everything we came here to shop for and then some. Junior Asparagus is right now preaching Jesus to a whole vegetable salad, and it looks like they're all going to convert. So maybe some follow-up personnel or media might be provided for them. Maybe we could stay to facilitate that. And certainly there are many more baby carrots being held in Rumor Weed territory.

"And then there's the issue of the Rumor Weed itself, the whole system that makes harvesters come down here looking for easy pickings. The whole infrastructure you taught us about back there in Bumblyburg. We couldn't take down the whole thing, of course, but we might be able to spray Weed-Be-Gone on a few shoots. The thing is, Pa Grape, we'd need more supplies. If we're going to stay even another week, much less more than that, we'd need more goodies.

"We haven't decided one way or another. All of us can see reasons to stay, I think, and all of us can see reasons to go. There's so much evil here, Pa Grape, but there's also so much good hiding away. It's like we're at the raw edge of life here or something, and both supernatural good and supernatural evil are more. . .unmasked. Have I freaked you out, Pa Grape? Over."

Over by the fire, Lewis had gotten to the prophets. "All of us like sheep have gone astray. But God has caused the iniquity of us all to fall on Him. He was pierced for our transgressions and crushed for our sins. And by His scourging we are healed."

The delay seemed especially long this time. The translation had time to travel all the way through to Lual and for the Dinka to voice their reply—full of emotion—before Bigelow's voice returned.

"Uh, copy your request, Larry-Boy. No, we're not freaked out over here. In fact. . .well, I don't really know how to tell you this, Larry-Boy, except to just tell you."

Yet even with that lead-up there was an extended pause. Jason plugged one ear and pressed the handset hard against the other.

"You see, Larry-Boy, it seems that Ma Grape has been. . .well, she's been kind of expecting this call for awhile now. Maybe even hoping for it. She said she had a premonition it would come to this, and, well, she's kind of prepared for it."

Jason heard Bigelow take a large breath.

"Larry-Boy, the stuff you need is already there. It's sitting at the airport you flew in from, the airport in the neighboring, um, aisle. The whole time I was working on the logistics of getting you guys there, Ma Grape had me also working on getting a ton of gear forward positioned, just in case you guys got it in your heads to stay longer. I—just a minute."

Jason heard Bigelow cover the microphone. He pictured the operations room back at ABL headquarters with Bigelow sitting in his commander's chair watching the satellite feed and, now, talking to Eloise Webster, who was no doubt hovering beside him. He could almost smell her sweet perfume.

"Larry-Boy, Ma Grape wants me to say that she's not trying to influence your decision whether to stay or leave. But if you did decide to stay, we just happen to have about a month's worth of very yummy things for you to play with. It can all be there tomorrow if you say the word. Funny you should ask, huh? Over."

"Yeah, Pa Grape," Jason said, "very funny. Let me talk to the guys and get back with you. But something tells me you just made the idea of staying a whole lot more attractive. Out."

As Jason put the radio away, Lewis's voice pierced the dark night.

"But the angel said to them, 'Don't be afraid. Because guess what: I bring you good news of great joy for all people. Today in the city of David there has been born for you a Savior, who is Christ the Lord!' "

As Jason walked toward the bonfire, he heard Trieu speak to Lewis and Rachel. "I finally figured out what song those women were singing back by the airfield. I think these people might know it, too, and anyway it's appropriate."

Lewis opened his hands. "Go for it, chick."

Trieu stepped in front of the others and faced the Dinka. The fire lit them all in a steady orange glow. Then she began to sing.

"O come let us adore Him, O come let us adore Him. . ."

Her voice was simple, unadorned, yet it rose strong and pure like moonlight over Africa. The Dinka began nodding and looking at each other incredulously. Then they joined in—though the words were different, the tune was identical.

> *O come let us adore Him*
> *Christ the Lord.*
>
> *For He alone is worthy*
> *For He alone is worthy*
> *For He alone is worthy*
> *Christ the Lord.*

# PART III

# CRUSADE

# CHAPTER 16

## BEGIN THE BEGUINE

"CHUNKY!"

Lewis slid the crate lid onto the trailer bed and plunged his arms into the box. He lifted out the autonomous tracked PackBot he'd baptized in the Gippsland Lakes. Then he seemed to remember where he was. He glanced at Dhor, standing by the Land Rover that the trailer was attached to, and smiled nervously. "Would you believe I use it for my seismic readings?"

Dhor rolled his eyes.

They were at a different airstrip this time. This one was just a sliver of dirt on a low, barren hill. No trees for shade and navigation. Eight Chinese-made trucks and half-tracks, burned spoils of war, sat rusting around the perimeter of the airstrip. It was a rare cloudy morning; and though the sun's direct rays were hidden, the gray dome made the whole world feel like a butterfly hothouse at the zoo.

A TrackMark Cessna Caravan stood at one end of the strip.

Olivier rolled a barrel of petrol to the rear of the white turboprop plane. Jean-Claude and the Firebrand team unloaded cargo onto the packed brown earth.

Dhor and two SPLA soldiers lounged by the Land Rover and its trailer. Dhor stood in the open driver's door, smoking a cigarette. The other two, teenagers no older than sixteen, played cards in the backseat.

Jean-Claude rode a four-wheeler ATV down the cargo ramp, spitting out a gleeful string of French expletives as he drove it. Garth rode the next one down, smiling like a kid on a playground, and coasted up beside Jean-Claude. Rachel drove the third one, Chris gripping her waist from behind. The desert tan ATVs looked like they could carry three people, pack five hundred pounds of gear, and pull a fifth wheel trailer besides.

Jason and Trieu walked down the cargo ramp carrying large duffel bags.

"*Excusez moi,* Monsieur Well-Digger Man," Jean-Claude said to Jason, "but I must ask why you are needing these *bonne et belle* machines? Not for well digging, I think."

Jason deposited his bag on the trailer behind the Land Rover. "Well, you know, Jean-Claude, the longer we stayed here, the more we realized what a vacation paradise it really is. So we ordered these babies to go four-wheeling around. You ought to stay and give it a try."

"*C'est trop triste,* we cannot," he said, admiring the ATV. "Perhaps next time."

Jason helped Trieu lower the bag to the trailer. "Suit yourself."

"Can we load Jok now?" Trieu asked.

"Yeah."

Jason opened the Land Rover's rear door as Chris and Garth started their ATVs. They were astonishingly quiet, almost like the purr of the jet skis they'd played with in Australia. Jean-Claude fiddled with the controls until his four-wheeler turned on, too. Rachel climbed on the back of Chris's and Lewis jumped on with Garth, and the three ATVs zoomed almost silently up the airstrip, throwing up dirt that probably hadn't moved in a decade.

Jason and Trieu shared a smile.

Jok slept on the pallet in the back of the Land Rover. Jason and Trieu carried him to the Cessna.

Olivier watched the ATVs weave between the burned hulks on the hill. He laughed. *"Magnifique!"* Then he turned and helped get Jok secured aboard the plane.

When the cargo door was shut and Olivier had cranked up the single engine, the ATVs finally came in to roost. Amidst much hooting and carrying on, Jean-Claude embraced his fellow riders, dipped Rachel and gave her a massive kiss, and trotted to the plane and up the passenger ladder. Moments later the white airplane roared down the runway and into the African haze.

And suddenly the Firebrand team was truly *in Africa* again. Alone. Stranded. Accompanied by a pack of ten giraffes in the distance and a trio of rebel soldiers armed with assault rifles.

But this time there was a difference. This time they weren't merely equipped to redeem some slaves and leave. This time they were outfitted to take the battle to the enemy.

\* \* \*

"Thank the Maker. This oil bath is going to feel so good."

Everyone looked at Lewis.

"This what?" Chris said.

Lewis entered the shaded tukul, slung the wet towel off his shoulder, and sat on an overturned crate. "Never mind. It's from a movie you guys have probably never heard of." He pulled out a comb and worked it through his dripping hair. "I'm just saying that the solar shower is, like, the best thing Eloise sent in her care package."

"Un-uh," Rachel said, chewing slowly. "The chocolate bars are the best things."

Jason felt his smooth face. "I liked the razors and toothbrushes.

I feel presentable again."

Rachel raised perfect eyebrows at him. "Uh rike it," she said around the chocolate.

The team had showered, shaved, brushed, and otherwise helped themselves to the amenities sent in with their new supplies. They were in an unused tukul in Akwer Nhom, sitting in a circle on the opened boxes their stuff had come in. They wore shorts, T-shirts, tennis shoes, and floppy hats. Dhor had long since left, taking the trailer and the two young soldiers with him, either trusting the team now or giving up hope of containing them.

"All right," Jason said, unfolding a large map, "let's get down to business."

Garth sang, "To defeat the Hun."

"Do what?" Chris said.

"I got it," Lewis said. "It's from another movie, Chris. You wouldn't understand." To Garth he sang, "Did they send me daughters when I asked for sons?"

They slapped hands.

"Okiedokie," Jason said. "If the concert is over, maybe we can talk about what we're going to do next. Trieu, we have any company?"

Trieu lifted the desert-camouflaged Kevlar helmet from her lap and placed it on her head. She flipped the eye panel down. "Nothing on Chunky's camera." She switched to another view. "And nothing unusual on the banshee. Only our little hut here and Lewis's robot endlessly circling around it. The Dinka are going about their business in the village. Besides that, there is only grass and trees as far as the camera can see."

"Okay, good," Jason said. "Lewis, your PackBot will send an alarm if anyone approaches, right?"

"Did Chunky warn you when I came back from my shower?"

"That's what that beeping was?" Chris said. "I thought all our helmets were getting a cell phone call."

"All right," Jason said. "Let's look at the map."

The durable paper map was bigger even than the floor space between the crates. The team grabbed edges and held it in their laps to look at it.

"Now that's what I call a map," Chris said.

"And it's just one-eighth of south Sudan," Jason said. "I've got seven more just like it for the south and about twenty for the north, if we need them. In a minute we can put our helmets on and take a look at the newest sat photo provided by Chimp and the Icarus satellite."

He picked up a narrow stick and used it as a pointer. "We're here, in Akwer Nhom. Isaac's little oasis is off east right. . .here, by the creek. Near as I can figure, the airstrip we were at this morning is a good thirty miles south, somewhere in here." He circled a white area on the map. "And the strip we landed at last week is here, east of Isaac's camp." He traced a line from Akwer Nhom to the north edge of the map. "This is the path we followed to get to Mashar, which is here. Safaha is off the map north. That's pretty much everywhere we've gone since we've been here."

Jason pulled another map out and unfolded it on top of the first one. This map was not as big as the other, but it showed all of Sudan. Again he pointed with the stick at a spot in the middle southwest of the country. "Akwer Nhom." He pointed to a city in the central north. "Khartoum." He traced a straight black line on the map going south-southwest out of Khartoum. "The railroad. Starts way up in Egypt, comes through Khartoum, then hits Al Fula, Aweil, and ends in Wau, here in the south."

"Where's the oil pipeline?" Chris asked.

Jason pointed at Khartoum again and followed a green line south-southeast to a spot roughly east of Akwer Nhom, but on the other side of the country. "Begins here in the Nuba Mountains."

Trieu ran her finger over the map. "This is where they've been bombing civilians to clear the oil fields?"

Jason nodded. "Yeah." He set the stick down. "You guys, we haven't really talked about what we're trying to do here yet. When we found out all this stuff was sitting in Lokichokio, we pretty much just decided we wanted it. But does that mean you want to stay? And for how long? And to do what? More than racing around on four-wheelers, I hope."

Garth looked up from rubbing his scalp. "There's *more?*"

"Yes, bonehead, there's more," Jason said. "Keep in mind that the Baggara aren't the only enemies here. They're not even the main enemies, because they wouldn't be so successful against the Dinka if the whole government weren't arming and encouraging them. If we're going to make life difficult for anybody in the north, let's not forget that ultimately the black hats here are the power elites in the north."

"Who are," Chris said, glancing at Rachel and nodding his head as if the statement were self-evident, "Muslim males."

"All right," Jason said, "knock it off and tell me what you're thinking."

They were silent for several minutes. The sounds of Chunky's servos and the banshee's rotors merged with the locusts' buzz pulsating in the early afternoon.

Finally Trieu lifted her chin. "I think. . ." She swallowed. "I think that we should extend our stay. Now that we are resupplied and have basically everything we could wish for, I—"

"Except for my computer games," Lewis said.

"And microwaves," Garth said.

Rachel smiled. "And bubble bath."

Trieu looked at Chris and Jason. "Anyone else?"

"I'm thinking," Chris said.

Jason smirked and shook his head.

"Now that we have basically everything we could wish for *on a mission,*" Trieu said, "I think we should use it. The need is certainly great. Since we're already here and have the means to help, perhaps we should. *If* we have a clear idea of what our goal is *and* a time limit beyond which we will not go."

Again they sat in silence.

At length Chris leaned forward and examined the map of Sudan.

"With the ATVs and all the gas Bigelow sent, we've got the mobility to pretty much cover the whole country if we wanted to."

"Those things are great," Garth said. "We used 'em in Afghanistan. The snipers especially loved 'em. You park it in the bushes, sneak up and take your shot, then climb back on and away you go. They're lots of fun to ride at night with low-light gear on." He pointed a thumb over his shoulder. "And the noise traps on the ones we have are even better than on the ones we had there."

"So what's our goal here?" Lewis asked. "Snatching more slaves off farms? Hijacking planes and bombing the north for a change? Ooh, we could go to Khartoum and take out the president!"

"Cool it, *Pastor* Lewis," Jason said. "We're not assassinating anyone, even if we had the weapons to do it."

"Oh, but we do," Garth said, rummaging in a box outside the circle. He pulled up a green canvas backpack.

Jason whistled in awe.

"What's in there?" Lewis asked.

"This, my civilian friend, is known as a satchel charge. And this," Garth said, pulling out a black sock from the pack and opening it, revealing a glob of tan putty, "is C-4."

Lewis leaned back from it. "Oh."

"Each satchel charge has ten of these two-pound clumps," Garth said. "That's twenty pounds of C-4, enough to make a very big bang. Our boy Bigelow also packed det cord, blasting caps, M-60 fuse igniters, and lots of other goodies. If we wanted to take somebody out—oh, yeah, we could do it. He also packed some more exotic explosives: nonlethals. Fun for the whole family."

"Okay, Garth," Rachel said, not taking her eyes off the C-4, "we like what you brought for show-and-tell. Could you. . .put it all away now, please?"

"Sure, Rachel, I—oh, no!"

Garth fumbled with the putty and it flew out of his hands. Rachel screamed and fell backwards off the crate.

When there was no explosion—and when raucous male laughter filled the hut—she peeked up. Her hair hung over her face and she'd scraped her elbow. "That wasn't funny."

Garth put the satchel charge away, and Trieu offered Rachel a small first-aid kit.

Jason brushed dirt off Rachel's back. "C-4 is completely stable, Raych. It won't go off without a detonator."

"Now you tell me."

Chris looked at the map of Sudan. "I keep thinking about what Dhor said on the way out to the airstrip this morning. Remember, Garth?"

"You mean about the Train o' Death being due this way any time?"

"No, about how some of the SPLA factions are working for Khartoum now. I mean, how do we know Isaac and Dhor and the others won't turn us over to the bad guys? I caught an SPLA kid looking in one of the bags—who knows what he saw? I don't even trust these Dinka. Sure, they like us now, but how do we know one of them wouldn't sell us out for a bowl of stew? Then there's Francois and Pierre, or whatever their names are. Jason, we are not exactly among friends here."

Jason nodded. "Yeah, good point. I remember something else Dhor said. He said that we would always be the enemy here." He sighed. "Okay, look, what about this? Let's pray. How about we spend a good ten minutes in silent prayer now and then another twenty minutes praying together? We seek God for what He'd have us do."

"What a concept," Garth said.

"Then we do whatever seems right at the end of that time."

Trieu nodded. "But what about duration? How long will we stay here?"

"We'll stay until it becomes clear that it's time to go," Jason said. "We'll trust God to guide us. What do you say?"

"I say it sounds good," Lewis said, "as long as I can have one of those candy bars."

An electronic beeping sounded, seemingly from all around them.

"It's Chunky," Lewis said, jumping up to look for his helmet.

Trieu beat everyone else to it. "It's some of the Dinka," she said, looking into her eye panel. "Three. Lual and Anei, I think, and someone else. Looks like they want to talk."

Rachel hurried to the wooden door. Jason followed.

The day was still cloudy, but the clouds were high and stretched thin like cellophane. It was hot and shadeless. The Dinka carted sticks and thatch and river mud to the village area at the bottom of the low valley, where men were building conical roofs, erecting pole frames, or shlopping mud against the frames to create clay walls.

Lual, Anei, and the chief elder stood twenty feet away from the team's tukul, looking nervously between the little rolling robot on the ground and the little flying robot in the air.

"Huh," Jason whispered to Rachel, "you'd think they'd never seen robots before. Where are we—the middle of Africa or something?"

Rachel gave him a look that said *Morons, go home.*

Even so, her eyes had an effect on him. Despite the look she gave him, he could still glimpse that private place in her heart that she'd shown him on the houseboat. She had definitely changed recently. She seemed calmer, more at peace. She hadn't made a threat on baby Muhammad in days now. Maybe she'd found her balance again.

Rachel opened her arms and walked toward Anei, speaking a greeting in Dinka. Anei smiled like an innocent young girl who had never seen horrors or experienced cruelty and ran to Rachel's embrace.

Jason greeted Lual and the chief according to the Dinka tradition. They clasped hands like a Western handshake, but they shook vigorously and for much longer. "Madhe," Jason said, meaning *hello.* "Cibak?" *How are you?*

Though he'd done it dozens of times in dozens of languages as a Navy SEAL, the thrill of communicating to someone of another culture never quite left Jason. Especially when it was a Christian brother he was talking to. He realized that, on a significant level, he probably had more in common with these African tribesmen with ritual scars on their foreheads than he did with 75 percent of American men. Bizarre.

Rachel and Lual spoke in Arabic. Jason watched them both to try to get some sense of what they were saying. The chief spoke passionately to Rachel, and Lual translated. To Jason their body language indicated the two men were not in agreement about something. Then Anei spoke, and Rachel knelt beside her while Lual translated.

After the Dinka stopped speaking, Rachel didn't move. The silence extended to almost a full minute, during which Rachel held her knees to her chest and rocked back and forth absently. Finally she turned to Jason, a complex expression on her face—a mixture of worry and joy and grief.

"Well, it's. . ." She folded her arms and stroked her upper lip. "The good news is they're getting the Christianity thing really well. *Really* well. Weak faith is not one of their problems."

"What'd they say? They want to march up to Khartoum and witness to the president or something?"

She smiled. "Almost. Actually, there're two things. They're both right. They're both bold. But I don't have a clue how they fit together. Neither do they."

"Oh, boy."

"No kidding." She sighed heavily, then chuckled. "The first thing is they want us to defeat the GOS army."

Jason felt his eyes bulge. "Us? They want us six to go defeat the entire government of Sudan military? With our pop-guns?"

"Oh, yeah. The way they figure it, the Christian God is stronger than the Muslim God, right? So it shouldn't be any problem. We shouldn't even need guns. In their minds, Christians are invincible. We ought to be able to go up against tanks and fighter jets and whatever else and just mow 'em down with the breath of righteousness or something."

An image came to Jason's mind from the movie version of Tolkien's *Fellowship of the Ring*. He saw Sauron wading through hordes of his enemies, swinging his mighty sword and sending scores of warriors flying with every stroke. Sure, no problem.

"You're sure that's the good news?" he asked.

"Oh, it gets better. They also want us to take care of the Baggara, the PDF, various troublesome insects, and, if we're not too busy, wipe out malaria."

"Wonderful."

An incredulous smile dawned on Rachel's face. "Well, we can't say they aren't taking Christianity seriously, can we?"

"No, but I think we need to get Pastor Lewis back out here to straighten some things out. I mean, God *could* wipe out malaria, but I don't see Him doing it. Is it going to crush their faith if He doesn't? And how are we supposed to take out the GOS military, even if we wanted to?"

"Well, more good news there," Rachel said. She nodded toward the Dinka, who were still standing there, watching. "They've volunteered to help."

"Oh, great. Can you please tell them that being a Christian doesn't make them Superman? I mean, it's great that they want to fight back instead of just take it. We'll get Garth to teach them how to use those radios Eloise sent to set up a security scouting system. But we don't want them charging tanks with their little throwing spears."

Rachel grabbed his arm. "There's one more thing." She leaned close. "They're having their first theological debate. The chief and most of the others are excited about following what they think is this SuperGod who will make them unstoppable against their enemies. It's like they've been stepped on for so long, and now that they've got some hope, they want to do some serious squashing of their own. But the other group, led by Lual and just a few of the others, has latched onto the Sermon on the Mount. One part specifically." She looked squarely into Jason's eyes. "They want to pray for their enemies."

Jason blinked. "Yeah? That's good, isn't it?"

"Sure. But I mean they *really* want to pray for them. Radical prayer. They're asking God to forgive the Baggara! The ones who came here and murdered their families and chopped off arms and burned children and old women! They're asking Him to do good to them, Jason, to bless them incredibly. They're asking—"

Finally Jason noticed that Rachel's eyes had gone glossy.

She looked into space. When she spoke, her voice wavered. "Anei is pleading with God to. . .to forgive Ahmed, the one who bought her like we buy a frozen pizza, the one who was going to rape her just a couple days ago! She's asking for a chance to tell him about Jesus." Suddenly Rachel was crying.

Jason pulled her to his shoulder and stroked her hair.

Her words came out between sobs. "She wants. . .him to be. . .to be in heaven with her." The anguish broke free and she cried deeply, heaving painfully in his arms.

He held her close, for once not thinking about his attraction to her, just comforting a hurting friend. Over her head he saw the three Dinka looking confused.

Rachel's words were muffled by Jason's chest. "I've never, ever, ever, *ever* prayed for the people who killed my father. I'd never pray that. I don't want them in heaven, Jason, I don't! I want them to fry in the hottest hell there is." She lifted her head. Her face was a mess. "If I had a chance to tell that man about Jesus or hand him one of Garth's bombs, I know what I'd do."

The sobs returned, and she dove into his shoulder. She screamed into his shirt, shouting expletives, proving that Jason wasn't the only one with some garbage left inside. "Die! Die and roast and writhe, you awful, horrible worm! If God offers second chances in hell, I pray you never get yours! You hear me, God? No second chances for him or anyone like him. Burn and die, you filthy pigs! I hate you! I hate you! I hate you forever!"

By now the rest of the team had gathered outside the tukul.

"What is going on?" Garth said, for once sounding truly alarmed.

"What'd you do to her?" Chris asked.

Jason put his chin on top of Rachel's head. "She's okay."

But she pushed off and ran away toward the other end of the village. Trieu went after her.

"Great," Jason said, staring at the Dinka, who were still waiting for an answer. "Now what?"

"Want I should preach again?" Lewis asked.

"No," Jason said. "Save it."

Trieu caught up with Rachel and guided her toward a log to sit.

"Come on," Jason said. "Let's go back inside and pray. She'll be all right." He shook his head. "More than ever we need to hear God's voice."

# CHAPTER 17

## JUST ANOTHER RAID

*WE ARE accursed.*

Mahmoud wasn't one to believe the superstitious ranting of the rabble he paid to come with him on these trips, but now it seemed less and less unreasonable.

He pulled his jellabah over his head. Now that they were so close to the Dinka village they planned to raid, it was prudent to cover up. The bright orange and yellow tassels on his horse's mane and around its neck dangled in the hot breeze. The bells on its collar jingled praise to Allah with every step south.

His twenty hired men rode behind him. Only Kalil, carrying the Sudanese flag as they boldly invaded southern territory, preceded Mahmoud. Another man would not trust such men at his back, but Mahmoud looked to Allah and his prophet to protect him.

Twenty-one horsemen would not normally be enough for a slave raid. But the village less than a kilometer ahead was so small it was on no map. Besides, he had raided this one before.

A commotion broke out behind him. Mahmoud stopped and looked back. "What is it?"

Two riders from the back of the pack spurred their horses to gallop, squealing and looking over their shoulders.

"Jinn!" one of them shouted. "Jinn!"

The others took up the call, and soon Mahmoud stood at the rear of his group and his own horse wanted to join the stampede.

Mahmoud reined him in mercilessly. Then he spun on the riders. "What did you see?"

It was Ali and Qasim, among the youngest riders with him this time. Ali was his third wife's brother, so he had to at least pretend to treat him with honor.

"Ali, you saw a spirit?"

Ali, like his sister, was not slim. But his skin was truly brown, not black, and his hair was like an Arab's. "N–no, brother. But we saw. . ." His eyes grew wide, and he shook his head and said no more.

Mahmoud turned to Qasim. He was no relation to him—and had an even less likely connection to Arab ancestry than Mahmoud himself. "Tell me what has you scared like a craven Jew," Mahmoud said, "or you may not keep any spoil from this raid."

Qasim looked up defiantly. "We heard something beyond the elephant grass. Something big."

The others muttered and glanced from face to face.

"It is the jinn who has been following us!" a rider said.

"The spirit of one of those we have killed!" another said, shifting in his saddle. "That is why it only found us when we crossed into the south! It will kill us!"

"This morning my water skin was missing," Ali said. "It was not on my saddle."

"And my rifle and sword," Qasim said. "They were missing as well."

"Ah," Mahmoud said, disgusted. "You are all women. There is nothing following us. You have misplaced your things, and you wish to cover your carelessness with this talk of jinn. We are not cursed! I will show you."

He kicked his horse toward the large stand of green, three-meter-high elephant grass they'd only just passed. He shouted as he went. "Come out, jinn! Come out and slay me!"

Nothing came out. He rode around the razor-sharp grass, shouting and calling. Finally he returned to his riders, who were breathing more easily now.

"You see?" he said. "There is nothing. Now, let us go to this village and gain what profit Allah may allow. If you die, you are a martyr. If you live, you are rich."

Mahmoud forced his horse through them and took the lead south. The others gathered behind him, riding as silently as their hooffalls and harness bells would allow.

*We are not accursed,* Mahmoud thought, shaking his head. Still, there had been a moment in his brave foray around the elephant grass when he'd felt a tingling of doubt.

This morning his rifle had gone missing, too.

Ever since that transaction with the strange Americans from Akwer Nhom, things had been going wrong for Mahmoud. Profits had fallen. He normally sold his slaves for 60,000 Sudanese pounds each, but had only been able to get 45,000 apiece on that deal. And the price he'd had to pay to buy them back had risen to almost 27,000 each. After the 50,000 pounds a head from the Americans, that left him with a total profit of only 68,000 pounds a head!

Those were not the kind of profits he'd gotten into this business to make. He had wives and concubines and children to support, after all, not to mention overhead for this band of cowards and their horses and gear. Maybe he should be like the other middlemen and deal in cattle, too, instead of specializing only in slaves.

If there was a curse, it was those Americans.

Mahmoud heard a tinny sound at the extreme of his hearing. It seemed to be coming from all around, yet it was so faint that he hadn't noticed it before. A part of his brain told him he'd been hearing it for some time. He scoffed. His men would think it was a malicious spirit.

"Ali!" someone behind him cried. "Where is Ali?"

Mahmoud spun his horse around. "What do you mean? Where is he?"

Ali was nowhere to be seen.

"Look!" a rider shouted, pointing toward an acacia tree thirty meters of horse-belly-high yellow grass away.

A brown horse with bright red tassels galloped, riderless, toward the open savannah.

"It is Ali's!" Qasim said.

The riders huddled together, jerking their heads to the front and back and side.

Mahmoud heard the horse's bells tinkling. Or was it something else? He looked up. The sun was directly above them. Was that a black dot hiding in it? A two-meter shadow swept over him. Perhaps it was only a vulture.

"It is nothing!" he said, surprised that his voice did not quaver. "Ali is relieving himself, and his horse got away. We will let him find his own way, or we will meet him on our return. When he sees your good fortune, he will learn to be more careful." He glanced again into the sun, then pointed his horse south. "Come, there is nothing to fear. Let your greed calm you. And remember, it is your duty as Muslims to attack the Dinka. Or have you forgotten we are on jihad?"

That seemed to steel them.

Mahmoud lifted his sword high. "Come, unconquerable men of Allah! We ride to glory or paradise!"

\* \* \*

The village was empty. Not deserted, just empty. Smoke rose from cooking fires. Water pots stood about, mostly full. Cooking utensils and farm implements lay around just as they would have been if the villagers had been there.

The village was nestled on the north bank of the Lol River, next to the wide rubber trees that lined its sides. To the north there was only endless thatch and the strand of trees and elephant grass that Mahmoud's group had used to conceal their approach.

Some of Mahmoud's men rode around the five tukuls shrieking and shooting into the air. But most of them sat uneasily in their saddles, their horses skittish and unsure.

"The jinn has taken them!" Qasim shouted.

"Silence," Mahmoud hissed. "Stop that talk. The rest of you, stop firing! Let me listen."

The guns silenced just in time for them to hear a man's scream somewhere in the trees beside the river. An alligator slithered into the water downstream and, overhead, birds of prey took flight.

"Kalil!" a rider shouted. "Where are Kalil and Ammar?"

"And where are the others?" Qasim said, looking around. "We are only fifteen now! Something is hunting us, Mahmoud! Something is hunting *us.*"

"Quiet!" Mahmoud yelled. "Stay calm." He shut his eyes and uttered a rare spontaneous supplication to Allah. "They must have seen us coming. They must've known." His head rose suddenly. "They must've had help."

It was like poor Ahmed Ali Diab! He had been beaten to within a millimeter of his life, or so the men from Safaha had said. They told him the slaves had risen up against him at night and escaped, though Ahmed was said to have no memory of anything. *Allah, be merciful.*

It made perfect sense to Mahmoud now. The Americans! He had told the Americans in Mashar that Ahmed Ali Diab from Safaha had refused to sell back the girl slave from Akwer Nhom. Not refused, actually—just asked more for her than Mahmoud would've been able to recoup. And then Ahmed had been assaulted and his slaves taken!

Mahmoud studied the trees and the tall grass. Where were they? It had to be them. He'd *known* there was something strange about them.

What had that idiot Dinka said? He'd said that the Americans should go with him to Safaha and *use their guns* to get his daughter back.

Mahmoud backed his horse away from the river. Were they American mercenaries? Or worse, American military? If they were, maybe it was no jinn picking off his riders one at a time.

They truly were accursed!

"Fly!" he shouted, standing in his saddle. "Fly back to your homes! American military is here!"

His men looked at him stupidly, their horses sidestepping clumsily.

"Americans?" Qasim said.

"Look!" a rider shouted, pointing at the river.

They all watched the brown waters as the Sudanese flag floated by.

"Hurry," Mahmoud said. "We must—"

Something struck him. It felt like a rock on his back. As he leaned over, almost falling out of his saddle, a shower of rocks impacted his men, the ground, the horses. The village thundered with horses stamping heavily and men crying out and falling to the ground. White powder exploded in small puffs. One of his men fired his rifle, striking the rider next to him in the leg.

Then Mahmoud was coughing. His eyes were watering and his throat began to close. He tried to fall out of his saddle but his foot was caught. His horse spun around, screeching in panic. All around him his men fell, choking.

Through bleary eyes, Mahmoud saw what he'd expected and feared: American soldiers stepping out of the trees and rising out of the grass. His horse froze when it saw them. Mahmoud clung to its side, willing the Americans not to see him.

The soldiers wore desert camouflage of a sort neither the SPLA nor even the GOS army gave its men. They wore oversized helmets with fearsome black patches over their eyes and black snakes draped down their backs. They advanced rapidly, shooting strangely silent weapons at his men where they crawled on the dirt, coughing. Mahmoud saw powder on his men's faces and chests.

Then the Dinka from the village were there. They erupted out of the riverbank and the grass, shouting savagely and rushing forward with spears. Mahmoud had never seen such fierceness in a Dinka's eyes. It was not the look of frightened cattle he had always seen before. If the American military was now siding with the Dinka, all was lost!

Hands grabbed his jellabah. Dinka hands pillaging *him!* He gave up hiding and rose in his saddle, striking at the startled Dinka with his fist and feet.

The Americans saw him instantly and swerved their weapons toward him, but the Dinka were in the way and he held himself low.

Even so he locked eyes with one of them—the one who was their leader. They were the same ones from Mashar. Someone north had to be told about them.

He kicked his horse forward and Dinka fell away. Rocks and spears and those hissing bullets flew all around him as he fled.

Another rock struck him on the head just as he was nearing cover. Powder enveloped his face and he almost blacked out. But he clung to his horse and galloped away.

# CHAPTER 18

## HI, JACK!

RAHMAN pushed the throttle all the way forward. The twin engines above and behind him roared throatily, and the Antonov AN-32 surged down the asphalt.

The old plane wanted to fishtail, like always, but far less on this smooth runway than on the gravel strips he'd been trained on. The metal fuselage rattled and banged. In the copilot's seat, Mazin shouted the Koranic passage he favored for takeoffs.

Rahman laughed at him as he eased the yoke back and the twenty-five-year-old plane left the earth. The rattling abated instantly; and Turk, kneeling in the back, resumed his morning prayers.

"You are getting fat, Mazin," Rahman said as he banked left. "I thought we would reach the end of the runway the nice Canadians built us before we reached takeoff speed."

In truth, Mazin was frail and thin, with delicate features and long eyelashes. When he wore a robe and turban on his off days, instead of the Sudanese Air Force uniform he wore now, he might pass for a woman—something the other flyers reminded him of on a weekly basis. But he was in the military, and he did fly a deadly Antonov AN-32 bomber to rain death on the enemy, so there was honor in that.

Turk, their bombardier, was just as black as Rahman and Mazin and just as wiry; but with his thick mustache and ugly face, nobody accused him of effeminacy.

So why did the plane feel heavier?

Rahman shrugged, leveling off the twenty-three-meter-long plane at five thousand feet. Maybe the boys had loaded more bombs than normal. That would make sense since they *were* hitting a school, a hospital, and a food drop site on this run. But they usually made a point to tell Rahman about the extra weight before takeoff. Come to think of it, he hadn't seen the bomb loaders this morning. Or any of the regular airfield staff, for that matter.

He shrugged again. They would lose reward from Allah for shirking their duties. No one could say that of Rahman.

It was a bright blue morning in south Sudan. The acacia trees dotted the green-brown grassland below at regular intervals, like soldiers doing calisthenics. The plane left the Greater Nile Petroleum Operating Company complex behind and followed a northerly heading toward the school. The faint smell of petrol lingered in the airy fuselage. The only time that reek would go away entirely would be when Turk pushed aside the rear curtain and opened the ramp to roll out the bombs.

Mazin unbuckled his seat harness and stood.

"Where are you going?" Rahman asked.

"Turk brought his literature."

"Ho," Rahman said. "You mean he brought his photos of naked women. I am ashamed of you both. Good Muslims do not gaze at such wickedness."

"I'll bring you one of the magazines."

"Good."

Mazin squeezed between the blue seats. "Turk, where are the magazines?"

"Mazin," Rahman called after him. "Your parachute is unbuckled."

"Ah," Mazin said, reaching down to buckle the harness between his legs. "Are you saying we'll need them today, Rahman?"

"If it is the will of Allah," Rahman said. "And if the Dinka and Nuer have traded their spears for shoulder-launched missiles!"

Turk and Mazin laughed with him.

"Or if the SPLA is there," Mazin said.

The laughter died.

"Look!" Rahman said, banking the plane in an arc to the left. "Run, little rabbits, run."

They passed near a Nuer village in the Nuba mountain region. Scores of black figures scurried about the village clearing, hopping for safety like fleas on a dog.

Rahman nosed the plane down, accelerating toward the grass huts and panicked villagers, relishing the increasing engine noise to the exact degree those below were fearing it.

At two thousand feet, he pulled out of his dive, laughing. "Today we let you live," he said, staring out the window. "Tomorrow is in the hands of Allah."

Turk watched from a window in the back. He laughed and knocked on the glass, then rejoined Mazin where he sat on the plane's metal floor looking at magazines.

The fuselage was a white tunnel four meters wide, narrower and shorter at the back. Twelve gray bombs—cylindrical but with tailfins to make them fall correctly—lay on the floor in three rows, ready to be kicked off the back ramp and onto the heads of the *abeed*. A brown canvas curtain screened the ramp off from the fuselage. Another canvas curtain, now open, separated the fuselage from the cockpit.

Rahman pressed the rudder pedal left, then right, then left, as if swinging the plane's hips. He drummed his fingers on the wheel in an energetic syncopation as he climbed back up to five thousand feet.

"My Muslim brothers," he said, "does no one wish to talk? I feel I could sing today! Think of it, my friends: We have the best job in all of Sudan. Every morning we get to fly airplanes. That alone is better than most of our brethren throughout Islam. But for us it is better still. The very sound of our passing sends unbelievers scurrying to their holes like dung beetles. The sound of our engines strikes the fear of Allah into their hearts. We are like the martyrs whose courage shook the Great Satan when they plunged their planes into the American decadence and sent so many to judgment.

"But it is not only fear we bring. We also bring the fires of wrath— the sword of Muhammad!—upon those who will not believe. We serve Allah in the great jihad to make the Word of God supreme and to bring men to His religion. And do not forget: We also serve our nation. Sudan can never be whole so long as it is torn by civil war, so long as any refuse to bow to sharia law. We serve the unity of Sudan."

He looked over his shoulder at his crewmen. "Best of all, we are paid well to do all of this. Now, where is my magazine?"

Mazin tossed him a pornographic magazine, and for twenty minutes they flew in silence.

Finally Rahman shut his magazine and sat up. "Mazin, we are coming up on the school."

Mazin groaned but stomped to the cockpit and strapped himself in his seat.

"The curtain," Rahman said.

Groaning again, Mazin unstrapped himself, closed the cockpit curtain, and sat back down. "You and your thin skin. Why don't you just bring a sweater?"

"Perhaps I should wear a woman's pink sweater, like you?"

The two white buildings of the Episcopal school were clearly visible a mile ahead. They weren't much more than cinderblock cubes, sitting there beside a spreading hardwood tree. Even from this altitude, Rahman could see the holes in the walls from previous bombings. But Christians were like warts—no matter what you did to cut them off or burn them out, they always came back.

"Open the ramp, Turk," Rahman shouted over his shoulder.

Moments later he heard the ramp drop open and felt the frigid air sweep under the curtain and around his legs. At least the smell of gasoline was gone. But he would've preferred to stay warm. The wind howled from the rear of the plane.

"Allah is great!" Mazin shouted over the din. "They are having classes. We will send many to judgment today!"

When they were in position, Rahman reached over his left shoulder and pressed a button that lit the green light at the back ramp. He dropped airspeed to keep them over the target as long as possible.

Below, infidel children scattered in a futile attempt to save themselves. Rahman smiled. The Sudanese Air Force did not have the precision munitions the Americans had, but the supposedly random flight of Rahman's bombs had many times hit those who had thought they were a safe distance away. Allah guided even errant bombs to those his will had selected for punishment.

They reached the end of their first bombing run. Rahman had not felt the Antonov's back end kick up like it always did when a bomb rolled off the ramp, nor had he heard or seen any explosions below. He turned to Mazin. "Did Turk drop his bombs?"

"Turk lives to drop his bombs," Mazin said confidently. Even so, he unstrapped himself and pushed the curtain aside. "I'll go check. Come around for another run."

"Close the curtain!"

Mazin didn't hear or couldn't be bothered to do anything about it. Rahman had to close the curtain himself, holding the bomber in a right bank with his knee as he did so.

A moment later he felt the plane's rear jump.

"Not yet, Turk! I'm not over the target."

He looked through Mazin's window as he banked. But instead of the smoke and fire of an explosion on the ground, he saw a gray circle inflate in midair.

A parachute.

The chute rocked side to side, but all Rahman could see beneath it was a pair of black military boots.

"Mazin? Turk? Who jumped? Who is the defector?"

Rahman leveled off. They were in position for their bombing run. He pressed the button over his shoulder again.

The rear of the plane sprang up, like the end of a diving board. Surely this was Turk kicking out two bombs at once.

Another parachute opened beneath him.

"*What?* You clumsy idiots!" He unbuckled himself from his seat. "I don't have automatic pilot, you know!" He held the yoke with a boot and lunged back to sweep the curtain aside.

And stared into the muzzle of a gun.

Held by the largest white man Rahman had ever seen. He was bent at the waist, but his shoulder blades brushed the dome of the plane. He wore a tan and brown camouflage uniform, like the Americans had worn in Iraq. His large face and angular jaw—and that orange goat beard and mustache—would've made Rahman afraid even if there had been no gun.

Rahman released the yoke with his foot. Instantly the plane nosed down and to the left. He fell into his seat and reached for the pistol at his waist, fighting to keep his balance as the plane listed.

He found his pistol grip and trigger, yanked, and fired all in one motion.

Except his arm didn't move. The big man shoved his elbow forward, so the bullet shot out the bottom of his holster and into the instrument panel.

Rahman felt the plane level off even as he realized another uniformed figure had slipped into Mazin's torn seat and grabbed the copilot's yoke.

The big man leaned over him, and Rahman knew he was short for this life. A giant hand gripped his right forearm and moved it as if he were moving the arm of a starving Dinka child at a UN clinic.

The man pulled the pistol out of Rahman's holster and tossed it toward the back of the plane.

Rahman watched it go. The morning sunlight flooded the Antonov's fuselage through the open ramp. The pistol clattered over the bombs, still lying in their rows, and bounced into space.

Suddenly he knew what had happened to Mazin and Turk.

"Please," he said, "don't throw me out. If I come down here, these natives, they will kill me! Please, have mercy! Or did you kill them and then throw them out? O Allah, be merciful!"

The big man watched him warily, but made no reply. Of course! If he was American, he wouldn't speak Arabic, would he? Rahman sank to his knees before the soldier. What injustice to be unable even to plead for his life.

"Get up and fly the plane."

Rahman looked up from the black metal floor, where the pornographic magazines were being whipped by the wind, and stared at the big man. Had such a weak voice come from this man? And in Arabic?

"Get back in your chair and fly this plane."

No, it wasn't him; it was the one in Mazin's chair. Rahman looked. A woman! A white woman, no less, like the women in the magazines. And more beautiful than them, even dressed in desert camouflage and wearing an oversized helmet.

"You speak Arabic?" he asked, realizing how stupid he sounded.

"I can keep us from crashing," she said, looking at him with a sneer, "but I can't land. You do it."

Rahman sat back in his chair, wondering when they were going to shoot him and throw him to his death. "Land? Why would I land?"

"Because if you don't," she said, blinking eyelashes longer than Mazin's, "my large companion will tear out your eyeballs and force them down your throat."

Rahman looked at the man, who bared his teeth.

"It is your best chance of living to see another day," the woman said. "If you comply, we will guide you to an airstrip almost to the border with the north. You may be able to reach a village friendly to the GOS military." She shrugged. "Or if you prefer, we can simply toss you out with your friends. I'm fairly sure the Nuer aren't cannibals anymore."

Rahman shivered in spite of himself. The adrenaline was wearing off. "And if I simply crash the plane?"

"Then you will have died for less than nothing."

"Allah will reward any—"

"Unless those girly magazines back there blew onto your plane by themselves, Allah won't be rewarding you with anything. Your evil deeds are way ahead of your good deeds, wouldn't you agree?" She shook her head sadly. "If I were you, I would wait for that meeting until I had racked up a few more wholesome acts of obedience to Allah's command. Perhaps when you get home, you should begin planning a pilgrimage to Mecca."

Rahman sat in his seat, facing forward. He placed his hands on the wheel and turned north, images of Mazin and Turk being eaten by cannibals flooding his mind.

Fifty minutes later, his captors indicated a landing strip ahead. Small vehicles like four-wheeled motorcycles were parked on the runway. Soldiers in the same tan uniforms drove the vehicles off, clearing the way.

"You will kill me when we land," Rahman said, descending.

The woman returned from where she'd tossed Turk's magazines out the ramp, then closed it up. "No, we will release you."

Rahman eased back on the throttle. "You will use this airplane to drop bombs on my people."

"No," she said, "but it's not a bad idea. It wouldn't hurt them to feel a little of the fear and pain you have been inflicting, would it?"

They were five hundred meters from the dirt airstrip. Rahman could see at least three other soldiers, all armed, on the ground.

"Are you Americans?" he asked.

She strapped herself into Mazin's seat. The big man disappeared into the back. "What makes you think so? I've only spoken Arabic."

"Ho, but he hasn't spoken at all."

"Maybe he only speaks Russian."

Rahman kept the nose up and pointed at the far end of the strip. "I have a slave at home, you know."

"Good for you," she said. "Bet you feel like a big man, don't you?"

Rahman smiled. "I will beat him when I return. Perhaps I will kill him. He is mine, you know. I own him."

She didn't answer.

"You Americans are all the same," he said. "In your decadent world, you forget what life is truly like. You must come to the Sahara to learn it. To kill. To own. To master. It is to be a man."

"No," she said, looking at him coolly. "That is to be a swine. Or perhaps you would like us to come to your home to remind your wives and children what life is truly like?"

Rahman cut back on the throttle even more. The engines stalled, and the Antonov dropped to the dirt in a perfect three-point landing. He braked to a stop and killed the engines. He turned to the woman to deliver a stunning reply.

But got shot instead.

It hadn't sounded like a gunshot at all. Maybe it was a silenced weapon. Or some poisonous dart. But it stung him just the same, in his right shoulder. The woman looked at him haughtily—beguilingly—over the strange-looking rifle.

"You said you would not shoot me."

"No, I said we wouldn't kill you."

His mind began to cloud. He was aware of light as the big man opened the side door. Other white faces appeared at his window and inside the plane.

*Allah, be merciful.*

He woke up at night, lying at the base of shrubs atop a sand dune. He sat up and rubbed his forehead. Warm sand sprinkled his uniform and face. His right shoulder was sore. A plastic water bottle sat at his feet, full.

How did he get here? He remembered the hijacking and the American soldiers—and poor Mazir and Turk. But nothing more. Had they rolled him off the back ramp of his Antonov? No, he wasn't wearing his parachute.

He took a moment to orient himself by the stars. And then he headed for home.

# CHAPTER 19

## TEXAS TEA

KHALEEL ibn Idris didn't know what to think. The rolling contraption before him was unlike anything he'd ever seen.

Its body was small and rectangular, about the size and shape of one of the computers on the desks of the Greater Nile Petroleum Operating Company employees. Not that Khaleel would ever rate his own computer, of course. The thing had tiny treads, like on the GOS tanks that had rolled through to clear these oil fields of undesirables. A metal arm rose from the horizontal bed of the little machine. Rotating at the top of that arm was an instrument package not unlike those on the probes Khaleel sometimes sent inside the pipeline for maintenance.

"What is it, Khaleel?" Amir asked, walking beside Khaleel and the machine.

Amir was the night guard at the pumping station, though from the way he wore his powder blue jumpsuit—soiled and unzipped—you'd think he, not Khaleel, was the systems mechanic. It didn't matter, though: Amir's skin was light and his nose was narrow—there was undeniable Arab blood in him. He would get a sparkling white desktop computer long before Khaleel ever did.

"Do you think it is from another planet?" Amir asked, his eyes open wide. "I read a science fiction story once—Allah forgive my indulgence—about two civilizations from other worlds. They both arrive on earth at the same time. One is good and one is evil, or so we're led to think. But really they're working togeth—" He did a double take at Khaleel and stopped himself. "Well," he said peevishly, "the nights are long here. I have to do something to stay awake, don't I?"

"Amir, I don't know what this thing is. But maybe you should run and get your gun, yes?"

Amir felt his waist and cursed. "I'll be back."

This late at night there were only Khaleel and Amir on the whole five-hectare plant. Powerful floodlights on ten-meter poles turned night to day over the multicolored grid of massive pipes and pumping machinery. The white-yellow light was tinged brown from the millions of moths swirling beneath the bulbs like pilgrims around the Kaaba. The main power generators chugged normally within their green metal cases. Every minute, millions of liters of crude oil passed through these red or blue pipes on its way north.

The little machine continued to roll toward the master pipe. It was twenty meters away, moving slower than a bathing hippo, but it was still a threat in Khaleel's mind.

Amir ran up, his keys ringing heavily on his thick leather holster. He held his pistol holster down with one hand and with the other kept his walkie-talkie from bouncing out of its pocket.

"Why did they stop guarding this place with soldiers?" Amir asked, fumbling with his belt. "We need them now."

"For what? A child's sled with an old sewing machine motor on it? Listen to it," Khaleel said, gesturing to the little machine. "Can you not hear the rabbits inside?"

"I still wish—"

"Amir, when this land was being cleared, they needed soldiers here. When the SPLA came to attack, they needed soldiers here. But now that the Canadians took their Talisman Oil away, only China and India and Malaysia remain. Their citizens do not demonstrate for human rights abuses, as Canada's did. Now our military can bomb and burn as they please. There hasn't been so much as a trespasser here for two years. The soldiers have been moved to where they are needed."

"So you think the rumor is true?" Amir said. "You think the SPLA has agreed to leave us alone in exchange for some of the profits?"

Khaleel stared at the device rolling along before him. "I don't know what to think."

"I think it is from another planet. The aliens in the story had devices such as this." Amir jogged in front of the rolling machine and sat in the dirt. "Watch, Khaleel."

The contraption continued rolling toward Amir, the camera and instruments on its metal arm level with his head, until it bumped into his boot. Then it stopped. The camera assembly pointed down at Amir's leg.

"Look at it, Khaleel. It is like my youngest child trying to see what she stubbed her toe on."

Khaleel stared into the gloom beyond their illuminated compound. It was no use; his eyes could not penetrate it. "Stop playing, Amir. I don't know what kind of toy this is, but I'm no longer in the mood to play. Whoever sent us this may still be around, watching what we do with it. Come, stand up. Let us take it beyond the fence and drop a rock on it."

"But I want to keep it," Amir said, tapping the machine with his toe. "My wives can use it to carry the babies from—"

The instrument head rose and seemed to lock into place staring straight ahead. Light began flashing from several lenses on all sides of the instrument package. The flashing was so fast, it almost disappeared into a continuous beam; but there was a barely detectable strobing, like what Khaleel sometimes saw when he glanced at the edges of one of those beautiful computer monitors.

The earth suddenly seemed to rotate off its axis. Khaleel found himself on the ground, smelling dirt and spilled oil. "What is happening?" He looked across the compound and saw it bulge and shimmer and distort. He tried to sit, but his equilibrium was gone. He fell back down to the packed dirt just as the contents of his stomach came up.

As if from a far distance, he heard Amir retching, too, and the receding sound of gears and servos from the little machine.

Between bouts of nausea, Khaleel watched the intruder roll toward the central pipe. Though he felt worse when he looked toward the light, he couldn't help himself. He watched as another metal arm began to unfold and rise from the body of the machine. This one was more like a true arm, complete with an elbow, a rotating wrist, and two fingers.

There was something in that metal hand. As the little toy came under the shadow cast by the sweep of the three-meter-wide blue pipe, the arm extended to its full reach, looking like a child trying to give someone a cookie.

Khaleel heard a metallic *cu-CLANG*. Then the machine began backing away from the pipe. It turned around and the arm folded away. As it approached, the vertigo returned full force, and he and Amir heaved dryly. The contraption rolled much faster this time. Had Khaleel been able to stand, he would've had to trot to keep up with it.

At the edge of the light, the machine stopped. The camera head rotated back toward Khaleel and Amir, though the strobing did not cease. A woman's voice came from speakers somewhere on the little frame. "Move away from the pumps," the voice said in Arabic. "In twenty seconds an explosive device will detonate."

The camera rotated away, and the machine zoomed into the darkness. Mercifully, the strobing disappeared with it.

Though he felt like he'd been bedridden for a week, Khaleel found he could stand. Amir pushed himself to his knees and drew his pistol. He fired three shots toward the machine.

"What are you doing?" Khaleel said, pulling Amir to his feet. "Get away from here!"

Together they lumbered toward the manager's office in the control room. Before they reached the back side of it, the bomb went off.

The flash came first—a pulse of piercing white—followed by an invisible hand that walloped them in the side and hurled them the rest of the way behind the building. *Pch-TOOM!*

The floodlights died before Khaleel and Amir hit the ground. Windows shattered, spraying deadly shards across their bodies. Shrapnel thudded to the earth and rained over rooftops. An ominous sound, like something huge falling and bouncing once, reached their half-deafened ears—and with it came the sound of liquid spattering upon itself.

Sirens blared and red emergency lights rotated on posts and panels across the compound, giving it a psychedelic light that made Khaleel feel sick again. Though he was stunned, he did know a bomb had exploded, probably rupturing the main pipe. He left Amir sitting on the ground like an old man and ran inside the manager's office to the control panels.

His footsteps echoed eerily on the slick floor as he made his way past the rows of now-dark computer monitors and reached the wide blue wall of gauges, wheels, and buttons. The wide observation window over the control panel had been blown out completely. Through it he felt the cool night air and heard the oil spilling—but not gushing. Control lights were on here, as was the panel itself. Emergency generators made sure of that.

A few checks verified what he'd hoped would be true: The pipeline had shut itself down automatically. Sensors all along the many kilometers to Khartoum and Port Sudan instantly detected any line ruptures, thus preventing devastating spillage in case of accident or sabotage.

Khaleel found a flashlight and headed out to the compound.

A wide pool of crude oil seeped out onto the dirt here. It was bad—

probably a thousand liters—but hardly a catastrophe. It stank like rotten eggs. An entire section of the fifteen-centimeter-thick main pipe had split apart at a seam and lay on the ground now like a broken arm.

Amir shuffled up behind him. "What. . .what happened?"

"It's a strange place to set a bomb, don't you think?" Khaleel asked, sweeping the flashlight beam toward where the little machine had gone. "Why bomb the pipe when the pumps would've been so much more damaging? And why come here at all?" He shone the light toward the far side of the compound, where stacks of spare pipe were stored. "We'll have this fixed tomorrow. Why not do it a hundred kilometers away?"

Amir coughed wetly. "You're worried about where they put the bomb? Khaleel, we've been attacked! We could've died. You sound like you wish they'd done a better job of it."

Khaleel shook his head. "What was that contraption, I wonder? And who sent it? The SPLA never had such a thing." He sighed. "I'll go inside and make sure everything is turned off. Amir," he said, gripping the guard by the arm, "get on your radio and get the soldiers back here."

*   *   *

It ended up taking two days to repair the severed main pipe. There was no way Khaleel ibn Idris could be allowed to retain his post after allowing such a debacle. He was barely allowed to retain his life. But after a month in the ghost house north of Khartoum, he would be begging for death. Sadiq Hafeez, nephew to a railway official in the north, took Khaleel's place. Amir, being of more noble blood, was transferred to the postal service.

Sadiq stood before the blue control panel, surrounded by representatives from all four partners of the Greater Nile Petroleum Operating Company—over twenty men, all wearing bright yellow hardhats for the benefit of the photographer.

"Allah is great," Sadiq said.

The officials mumbled their response, with only the representatives from the Malaysian petroleum company answering with vigor.

"Today we praise Allah," Sadiq said, "for by his power we have overcome the forces of evil and are now ready to resume glorious transportation of the crude oil he has so graciously given into our hands."

After the interpreters finished their translations, there was polite applause for Sadiq's words. The photographer snapped a photo.

"Thanks to the great wisdom and foresight of our partnership, there is enough oil stored in Port Sudan to allow exports to continue unabated. We will quickly refill those supplies in case such a thing should ever happen again.

"Now, if you will all watch through the window here, you will see this historic moment unfold." Sadiq turned to the control panel and pressed a button. A *whoop-whoop-whoop* warning siren sounded, loud even through the new glass window. "Gentlemen," Sadiq said, his hand poised over an oversized red button, "I give you the return of Sudan's national petroleum industry!" He mashed the button.

Lights all across the wide display flashed green.

And then immediately flashed red. An ominous *click* sounded somewhere deep inside the control panel.

The photographer took another picture.

Sadiq pressed the big button again and again. The lights stayed red. He turned around to the dignitaries. "Ah, it appears we will have to have our ceremony later, gentlemen. Something is obviously—"

Two filthy workmen burst into the room. They headed straight to Sadiq, speaking urgently and holding a radio toward him.

The interpreters dutifully translated every word.

Sadiq suddenly found himself alone in the room. He started to chase the executives down, but paused to speak into the large walkie-talkie. "Where is this other rupture?" He listened, looking at the readings on the control panel. "No, there must be something wrong with your instruments."

Nevertheless, he sprinted out of the control room and hopped inside the car last in line for the airstrip. Even from there he could see the executives' helicopters revving on the helipads. He managed to attach himself to the delegation from Petronas, the Malaysian partners, and secured a ride in their helicopter.

Ten minutes later, the four helicopters were loitering over the south Sudanese terrain. Though it was buried a meter beneath the surface, the ruthlessly straight path of the pipeline was visible stretching to the north horizon.

Fifty meters below them, pipeline workers stood beside a black blemish in the almost white stripe of the pipeline. A crater, not unlike those Sadiq had seen in many of the villages in a seventy-kilometer radius around the oil fields, marred the barren grassland. He could see the exposed and ruptured pipe from here.

Sadiq tugged at his ear. Two strikes to the pipeline at once! It was beyond comprehension. The SPLA had never been so coordinated. He remembered that Khaleel had written in his exit report something about the foolishness of the saboteurs to strike the pipeline in so visible and easily accessible a location.

Not so foolish, perhaps. The repairs had taken two days, almost exhausting the extra barrels stockpiled in Port Sudan. Now they'd discovered this rupture—which would take another three days to repair since they'd have to get trucks and cranes out here. Five days would certainly disrupt exports. And be noticed at the highest levels.

Sadiq wondered if he'd be seeing Khaleel in one of the horrifying ghost houses up north sometime very soon. Detainment in those torture pits was worse than death.

He was composing his good-bye letter to his wives and concubines and children when the Malaysian executives began speaking in angry and distressed tones.

"What has happened?" Sadiq asked in Arabic.

The helicopter tilted forward and the engine roared. The ground streaked by as they sped north along the pipeline.

The Petronas interpreter, an elderly Asian man with thick white hair and eyes that did not align, shouted to Sadiq over the noise: "They have discovered more ruptures."

Sadiq looked at him incredulously. "Impossible."

Before the helicopters ran low on fuel and had to turn back, they had found seven craters. Seven ruptures to the carotid artery of Sudanese self-sufficiency. It was beyond imagining. How many weeks would it take to repair this? How many more ruptures were there? Perhaps they went all the way to Khartoum at ten-kilometer intervals. The entire nation would suffer for this attack.

Sadiq felt a tightness behind his sternum. "Ask them if we can land at one of the sites on the way back," he said to the interpreter.

On the ground, Sadiq felt decidedly unsafe. This very spot had been violated by someone who hated him and all he stood for. This brutal puncture wound in the earth, this circular hole now awash with stinking black sludge and dirt and grass, was an assault on him as much as it was an attack on Sudan.

"Come," the interpreter called. "We must go."

Sadiq bent over something black lying on the ground beside a spray of light-colored dirt. It was a set of metal fins. He had seen such things before. He looked at the sky. Surely not. The Antonovs were not so precise.

Sadiq headed back to the helicopter, his find in his hands. Khartoum would want to know that Sudan's precious pipeline had been sabotaged by its own bombs.

# CHAPTER 20

## A PASSING BREEZE

*THE DINKA women get away with it—why can't I?*

Hana Idris stomped across the dirt breezeway, scattering the chickens that moved fast enough, kicking the ones that didn't. The air was still cold, but it did nothing to soothe Hana. Not even the pink and peach sunrise bathing the sky in pastels could reach her. She passed out of the breezeway and walked toward the well.

Hana, go check the baby.

Hana, go beat that slave.

Hana, go buy a rooster.

Hana, take your clothes off and pleasure me.

Not that she heard *that* one too often.

She threw icy water against her face, embracing the shock as representative of her life.

Third and fourth wives—especially fourth wives—lived little better than the Dinka slaves they supposedly ruled. Hana was last in line for clothing behind the other wives. She was last in line for food. Her children would be last in line, too, if she could ever have any. Himayat gave her his seed less than once a month, despite the Koran's admonition not to take a new wife if you couldn't take care of her properly.

She bathed her arms and neck, wishing that today would be the day he would be with her. The conditions were perfect. If only Allah had willed that Hana had been beautiful.

The Dinka women had a way of getting what they wanted, Hana knew. Third and fourth wives among them could not be so easily neglected.

Speaking of the Dinka, where were they all this morning? "Abeed?" she called, using the word for *black person* or *slave*. What was the difference?

No one answered.

Hana dried herself off and finally looked at the sunrise, smelling the sweet earth and listening to the restive movement of so many horses in the corral around back. Tonight Himayat would ride with the rest of the Baggara on a slave raid. Afterwards the slave pen would be bursting—and Himayat, as host, would have his pick of the bunch. With her fate, he would find five more women to impregnate before her. Last in line even behind slaves!

It had to be today, before he left. She would try it, that Dinka manipulation that worked so well for their women. Hana had beaten it out of enough of the girls to know it was an actual Dinka tradition.

She just wasn't sure it would work. Dinka men might believe that their women could be possessed by an evil spirit, but she didn't know if Himayat would. She was counting on one memory, hoping it reflected Himayat's beliefs.

A neighbor a few years back had been especially cruel to his second wife. Finally she had died at his hands. But every night after her death, he was visited by a strange blue light. Every night the blue light would appear in his bedroom, haunting him, cursing him, driving him mad. His crops perished. His livestock sickened. His cows did not calve. Finally he sold his farm and moved away west.

Hana remembered how Himayat had behaved during that time. He'd told Hessa, his first wife, that he'd actually seen the blue light once himself.

So there was hope.

The Dinka women, third and fourth wives, willingly opened themselves to demonic possession using intricate incantations that Hana had memorized. When the candles had burned low and a breeze passed by, the demon would enter and seize control.

The demon in the possessed woman would speak in a strange voice and make all kinds of demands on the master of the house, insisting that the woman be treated better—or else the household would suffer untold punishments from the supernatural realm. The demands usually consisted of more preference given to the woman, more attention from the husband, better care for her children—and gifts of jewelry and fine clothing. All to appease the "demon."

Hana thought that would just about do it. Assuming, of course, that it was all show and that she wouldn't be permanently possessed. But at this point, she was actually willing to consider paying that price if it would improve her lot.

She cocked her ear. Something had changed. The sounds echoing off the farmhouse walls were louder. The horses were spooked. A breeze passed by.

Hana felt her arms stipple with gooseflesh. Was it the demon?

*I'm not ready. I haven't opened myself to you yet. See? No candles. No incantation. Please wait.*

Then she saw the beautiful horses. Despite a life around Baggara horses, the sight of them in full gallop never ceased to thrill her. So powerful, so sure. Even in a group, each individual horse was mighty. Could she ever be like that?

She suddenly realized these magnificent horses were running free. And unless there was another herd of wild horses that just happened to be passing through Sudan, these were the horses belonging to the men who had gathered to go on their slave raid.

Hana screamed. She screamed and screamed and screamed, needing no demon to bring strange sounds from her mouth. When she found her words, her voice truly did sound like someone else's: "The horses! Come fast, come fast! The horses are running away!"

Men staggered out of the house, holding their heads against the effects of last night's drinking. The horses were off Himayat's land now. The air was full of the dust of their passing.

*The slaves. Get the slaves to run after the horses.*

Hana threaded her way through shouting men and rounded the farmhouse to the foul-smelling open-air pen where the excess Dinka were held for sale. Behind her, the whole house had awakened in alarm. She had done that much. Himayat should reward her, but he probably wouldn't.

She stopped, blinking and shaking her head as if trying to remember something from a dream.

The slave pen was empty.

The barred door and chain lay on the ground meters away from the cage. A sick feeling welled up inside her.

*The other slaves are gone, too. I know it.*

She ran toward the men in front of the house. Himayat wound his turban as he ran after the horses, now lost behind a shroud of brown dust pierced by horizontal shafts of yellow sunlight.

As the frontrunners reached the edge of Himayat's property, huge clouds of white smoke exploded around them. Hana saw them flinch and fall before the *wom-wom-TOOM* sounds reached her.

Himayat and the others skidded to a stop. Some turned and raced toward the house.

Hana ran to her husband, hoping to be the first to give him comfort. When she arrived at his side, her eyes were tearing. She thought it must be from the fear. Ahead, she saw the other men on the ground. They seemed to have all caught head colds at the same moment. They coughed and wheezed and rolled on the ground.

A gust of warm air passed Hana, rippling her robe and whirling the dust and smoke. Suddenly she had a clear view over the sand.

She saw the horses a kilometer or more away. Beautiful creatures running free, as they should. Perhaps it was a trick of the sun or her bleary eyes, but she thought she saw black people running beside the horses. Strangest of all, she saw small, wheeled vehicles, motorcycles or tiny cars, speeding behind the horses and freed slaves.

*Was that a rider? Was he waving?*

*No, it must be a trick of a demon.*

The dust swirled again, and the horses were gone.

\* \* \*

Brigadier General Nizzar ibn Abdallah stared at the map table in the crisis room. His advisory staff and senior field commanders stood around the rectangular table in the dim room, their faces lit from underneath by the lone overhead beam bouncing off the white map of Sudan.

Nizzar struck his palms on the table's raised frame, making the plastic markers on the map leap and fall. "Can none of you tell me what is happening in our own *country?*"

The men mumbled excuses or shifted blame or simply stared at the red incident markers dotting the south of Sudan like a pox. The three on the left were Nizzar's advisors. Worthless idiots, politicians picked by the president as favors to influential families or factions. Two of them weren't even Arab, no matter what names they called themselves by. But the field commanders, on his right, had been handpicked by Nizzar himself. They were battle-tested and savvy—and actual Arabs.

He looked at these three now. "How many new attacks have there been?"

Jabir, Fawz, and Sulayman studied the map and their notes.

"There have been twelve major incidents in the last three weeks, General," Fawz said. "But some of those, such as the pipeline ruptures or the sabotaged aircraft, consist of multiple attacks each."

Nizzar cursed—an action that shocked the politicians almost into unconsciousness. "How many attacks total?"

Jabir started counting on his fingers. "The pipeline was struck in ten places—using our own bombs. Eleven if you count the one at the pumping station. We have had fifteen Antonovs sabotaged: tires slashed, hoses sliced, avionics gutted. Will you count the flight crews who all seem to suffer blackouts just before these attacks? If so, there were more than twenty of them. Is someone writing this down? Do you count each spare aircraft tire that was slashed in the warehouse? Over thirty."

"Don't forget the hijacking," Sulayman said, pointing to a red incident marker in the southeast. "The pilot and his crew, twelve bombs, and an entire Antonov!"

Fawz looked up from a sheet of paper. "Do you want to include the indirect evidence of attacks, too? The garrison in Aweil that gathered for their Wednesday night of—" he glanced at the politicians— "*educational* videos about the life of the prophet."

The field commanders sniggered and elbowed one another.

"But instead of. . .what they were hoping to see," Fawz said, "a sacrilegious film played—*Jesus of Nazareth.*"

The politicians looked aghast.

"Or the children at the Koranic school in Wau," Jabir said, "who picked up their wood plaques to learn their Koran but found instead the deviant Jewish writing that Isaac, not Ishmael, was God's chosen one. Or the faithful who gathered at the mosque in Aweil and found that every copy of the holy Koran had been replaced with the New Testament in Arabic! Of course they were burned immediately. But the damage was done."

Harith Warraq, a stocky black politician on Nizzar's left, raised his hand. "If I may, General?"

"Why, of course," Nizzar said. "If I didn't want your counsel, I wouldn't have invited you to this meeting."

"Certainly," Harith said. "Unlike others who whisper to us duplicitously, I do believe that you desire our presence and advice and that it has nothing to do with our president, Allah preserve him, and his threat to replace you and all of your commanders if you do not allow us to come to such meetings."

Nizzar ground his teeth and made himself nod.

"You see," Harith said, "war is not altogether a military affair. If you do not take into consideration the political and econom—"

"You said you had something to offer, Mr. Warraq," Nizzar said. "Will you be getting to it soon?"

Harith took a deep breath and looked upward, as if preparing to say something profound. "I believe this," he gestured to the map table, "is beyond counting, General. How many slaves have been unlawfully stolen from Muslim owners in these three weeks? How many cattle? How many horses—the livelihood of the Baggara people? How many Muslims have been directly or indirectly attacked by this assault on Sudan's sovereignty? Can they be numbered? The loss of oil income alone will impact tens of millions of Sudanese. And if our exalted military forces," he said with only a hint of sarcasm, "cannot protect the pipeline from now on, Sudan will be further destabilized." He leaned forward into the pool of light. "It might even fall."

He brought out a sheet of paper. "I believe the Americans are behind this. It is not a novel idea, I know. The Americans are weak and too often bow to popular pressure or wealthy interest groups. Praise Allah such things do not occur in Sudan. Unfair as it is, Sudan has the reputation in the West of being a barbaric and backward nation, especially in regard to human rights, of which we all know we are truly champions. However, there have been too many mentions in all these incident reports of American or European soldiers on our soil for it to be coincidence."

Sulayman nodded gravely. "The SPLA are tenacious fighters, but never have they even attempted anything on this scale. There is a fearlessness to these attacks, an audacity. And it is having an effect in the field. The garrisons in Wau and Aweil report that some Dinka are actually fighting back."

Nizzar rubbed a hand through his short hair. "Fighting back? You mean the Dinka in the SPLA?"

"No, sir," Sulayman said, "the Dinka in the slave camps in Wau and in the markets in Aweil. They have a new confidence. I even begin to fear for the safety of the supply train. It left Aweil yesterday and hasn't been heard from yet."

Nizzar groaned derisively. "The train? You're worried about the military supply train with two hundred soldiers and seven hundred mounted PDF and murahileen? Sulayman, a horsefly can't come within a kilometer of that train without being spotted, shot, and hung. What makes you think any soldiers—even Americans—would be so foolish? It would take a whole brigade of troops to attack that train. Or are you suggesting that the Americans have hidden that many men in south Sudan?"

Nizzar surveyed the six men. They weren't looking too convinced. In truth, an attacker wouldn't need a brigade of soldiers. Just one laser-guided bomb could take out the train. He turned to the politicians. "We have spoken to the Americans?"

Harith nodded. "Secretary Rifa'ah has heard the American ambassador's assurances that they have no military forces in our country. He says his president would not risk the warming relations between our two countries. Rifa'ah is seeking similar assurances from the British, Germans, French, Australians, Norwegians, and many more."

Fawz harrumphed. "The 'warming relations'? Was that before or after he placed us on the list of nations sponsoring terrorism?" He lifted his chin. "I think he is a liar."

Nizzar examined the map again. His nation stretched out before him south to north. Most of the new attacks had happened along the wide horizontal boundary between the south and the north.

The south. What a travesty. He'd been a young man in those few years of peace between the civil wars. Even then the south couldn't govern itself. This war was a sad necessity to bring the south back into the care of wiser men who could guide it well. Secession would be a disaster for them. This new wave of attacks only gave them false confidence that they could join the fellowship of nations.

"We must find these Americans," he said to the men on his right. "Whoever these soldiers are and wherever they are from, they are here illegally and their presence is an act of war. Mobilize your forces. The president expects us to stop these attacks, and stop them we will. Draw up plans before the day is through. It is to be a major offensive. Include every asset of our military in your thinking. Do not forget the capabilities of the MiGs.

"Jabir, let the word out that there is money available for anyone who can tell us where these soldiers are. Talk to the soldiers and pilots and tribesmen. Someone knows something. These men have struck over too broad an area for no one to have seen anything. The money will bring them out, and it will shake them out of their amnesia. Allegiances in Sudan are always flexible, gentlemen, and it is for times like these that I am glad of it."

He gripped the map table's frame. "If we have to burn a two-hundred-kilometer strip across the belly of Sudan to flush out these Americans, this is what we will do."

# CHAPTER 21

## OPERATION: TURNABOUT

THE DEATH train.

Two engines. Twenty train cars. Seven hundred soldiers. Five hundred horses. The whole procession moved at walking speed toward the bridge that traversed the canyon. On the other side was southern Sudan.

Sudanese soldiers in uniform lazed atop the boxcars, their rifles across their laps. Others sat in the boxcars, legs dangling out the open sliding doors, cigarettes in their mouths. On both sides of the train, the mounted militiamen rode. These wore all manner of robe and turban, but the majority were in white jellabahs. Swords and rifles dangled in their saddles. Belts of ammunition crisscrossed their chests like Mexican banditos.

It was the hottest day of the dry season so far. Even the relatively lush growth along the canyon rim looked brown and browbeaten today. It was as if the sun had found its match in the shimmering yellow sands stretching out to all horizons and decided to best its reflection by bearing down more, only to have that bounce back to it, and so redouble its heat in revenge. Shriveled skeletons of grass and brush crumpled further beneath the merciless battle.

Still the train inched south.

Jason Kromer lowered his binoculars and turned to the Firebrand team. "Okay, guys, speak up. Are we absolutely sure we want to do this?"

Three men and two women, dressed to kill in desert fatigues and high-tech gear, looked at him and nodded. "Absolutely."

They were on the other side of the canyon from the train, a hundred yards from the near end of the bridge. The bridge was a towering wooden beast that stretched almost as long as the train that was about to cross it. With its sturdy crosshatch construction and peeling white paint it looked like an old-style wooden rollercoaster. The canyon wasn't more than three hundred feet deep, but the sides were sheer and rocky on both rims. A green ribbon of water sparkled beneath them.

A line of rust-colored boulders rimmed the cliff's edge on their side. Half a dozen towering mahogany trees stood beside their end of the bridge like sixty-foot passengers waiting to board.

"All right," Jason said, blowing out a sigh, "then let's do it right. Lewis, what does banshee see?"

Lewis had his eye panel down. He looked extremely young under the wide Kevlar helmet. "The train's stopped. Looks like they're pulling out ramps or something. Yeah, it's ramps from the boxcars. The horse guys are all getting off and leading their horses up the ramps. Oh, man, this is going to take forever."

Chris slid down from his vantage point between two boulders. He'd browned to a perfect tan in his time in Sudan, the stud. He was going to get back to Utah and look like he'd spent a month in Hawaii, not Africa. He brushed dirt from the orange-tinted lenses of his binoculars. "Once again our Dinka intelligence network is on the money."

Garth was sitting on the ground against the nearest of the three

ATVs, his legs stretched out in front of him, crossed at the ankles. He looked up into the blue sky, shielding his eyes against the sun. His orange goatee matched the hue in the boulders beside them. "Hey, you guys, there's our friends again."

Jason looked. Ten vultures circled overhead.

Lewis laughed. "Those guys follow us everywhere. Jace, you really think it's the same ten every time?"

"Nah."

"Sure," Chris said. "Those are *Trigonoceps occipitalis*—white-headed vultures. Quite possibly the ugliest birds in the avian kingdom. But they're no dummies. Plus, they're endangered. There aren't many of them in Sudan at all. I bet it is the same group."

"We're your friends," Garth sang. "We're your friends to the bitter end."

The rest of them sang the echo: "The bitter end."

"When you're alone. . ." Garth sang.

"When you're alone."

"*Oo* comes around. . . ?"

"All right, all right," Jason said. "Knock it off, you guys. We can sing through the whole movie later. Lewis, keep your eye on the train."

"Sir, yes, sir."

"I don't know," Garth said, still watching the vultures. "I wonder if they know something we don't know." He looked down. "Like maybe Miss Rachel's going to get crazy again and this time really give the vultures something to sink their beaks into. She's come close before. What about it, Raych, that fount of Muslim hatred ever run dry?"

Jason watched Rachel's reaction. She crouched beside Trieu, keeping watch across the canyon, her MP5 submachine gun at the ready. She slid backwards off the boulder and faced them. "How do you know the vultures aren't here for us?" she asked Garth, the eyebrows barely lifting. "Sooner or later, our luck's going to run out." She climbed back up next to Trieu.

"Oh, don't say that," Chris said. "You'll jinx us."

"Jinx?" Jason said. "You're not superstitious, are you, Chris? Christianity beats jinxes, or hadn't you heard?"

"Hey, don't mess with him," Garth said, affecting a shaky voice. "Chris keeps sending me these chain letters on E-mail. I haven't failed to pass even one of them on. No way."

"Yeah," Lewis said. "No kidding."

"I'm just waiting for that million bucks they keep promising," Garth said, his hands shivering. "But at least I can rest easy knowing my loved ones are safe because *I sent the chain letters to everyone I know!*"

Jason chuckled in spite of himself. He'd spent a month with Garth, and the guy could still make him laugh. That was a sure sign of something, but Jason didn't know what.

"What are they doing, Lewis?" he asked.

"Still loading. Dude, that's a lot of horses. I don't think they can get 'em all on in one trip."

"Doesn't matter for our purposes," Jason said. "Chris, hop up there and keep watch, will ya? I need to talk to Trieu."

They traded places.

Trieu's Dragunov would look exotic anywhere, it seemed to Jason. The stock with the scenic window through it and the wooden pistol grip were just too much. Even without the funky gel bullets and night-vision scope, the thing looked alien.

Strands of black hair sneaked out of Trieu's helmet and poked toward her Asian eyes like plastic pointers. While Rachel made her salad suit look like the height of Parisian fashion, Trieu made hers look like the most reasonable thing for the lovely girl next door to be wearing around the house. As always, her gaze was calm and pleasant, as if—wonder of wonders—her heart truly did contain love, joy, peace, patience, kindness, and the rest.

"What about it, doc?" Jason asked. "Anything we need to keep in mind?"

She pursed her lips. "Just remember to stay out of sight if they start shooting."

Garth nodded thoughtfully. "Ooh, good one, Trieu. Important safety tip, thanks."

"And try not to shoot if you don't have to," she said. "We don't want people falling asleep on top of these rail cars or coughing so hard they fall off the train and. . ." She made an over-and-down motion with her finger.

"No," Chris said, "we definitely don't want that."

"Uh, Jason," Lewis said, sounding nervous. "I think they're about ready to roll. They're taking the ramps away, and I don't see any more horses."

All six members of Team Firebrand bellied up to the boulders and watched, using scopes or binoculars or squinty eyes. The train belched black smoke and crept toward the bridge.

"Okay," Jason said. "This is it."

"What's the latest from upstairs?" Garth asked.

"Bigelow says yesterday's Icarus satellite imagery shows the Sudanese military really moving out from everywhere," Jason said. "Not just from the north but also from the garrison towns down south. He says it looks like something big is going down."

"Well," Trieu said, "you said you wanted a clear sign about when it was time for us to leave."

"No kidding," Jason said, checking the train's progress through his binoculars. "But Chimp thinks we've still got a day or two before we're in trouble."

"That's great," Garth said. "Thanks for the update from Bumblyburg. But that wasn't actually the 'upstairs' I was asking about."

"Oh," Jason said. "Then what did you mean?"

Garth pointed up. When Jason still wasn't getting it, Garth put his palms together in a posture of prayer.

"Oh," Jason said. "Oh, that. Well, it's all green from Him as far as I know. Why don't you do us a prayer this time, Garth? But make it quick."

"God," Garth said, his eyes snapping shut, "please help us all live through another crazy op. And help nobody fall and be crushed to bits on the cruel and jagged rocks below. Amen."

Jason examined him suspiciously. "The cruel and jagged rocks? Is there a hidden camera around here somewhere?"

Garth winked and stood. "Come on, my biker babe," he said to Rachel. "Let's go find a better seat for the show."

They climbed on the front ATV and eased away toward the trees beside the near end of the bridge.

Jason helped Chris lift the big solar-powered speaker into a concealed nest between three boulders. He plugged the microphone in and handed it to Chris. "You sure you're up to this? I thought your Arabic was rusty."

"It's cool, chief," Chris said, draping the microphone cable away from him like it was amateur night. "After all these chances to work on it, it's come right back to me. Too bad all I've learned here are Arab cuss words. Seems like that's all we ever hear from the people we've been visiting. Ever notice that?"

"I'll take your word for it."

"Besides," Chris said, nudging Jason with his elbow, "it gave me an excuse to have lots of intimate, extended, private lessons with Rachel. Ooh-la-la."

Rachel's voice struck them all through their helmet speakers. "I heard that, scumbag."

Chris gave an aw-shucks look and snapped his fingers.

Jason smiled wryly. "Come on, Trieu, let us go find a better spot, too. Show's about to begin."

They jumped on their ATV, and Jason turned on its whisper-quiet engine. Trieu's arms wrapped around his waist. He tried to think of it as an act of simple necessity that came with carrying a passenger on one of these things; but when Trieu or Rachel held him like this, it didn't feel the same as when it was Lewis on the back. He didn't drive quite as fast as he otherwise might've.

"Lewis," Jason said, "come on down from there. You can watch the fun through banshee's cameras."

"Okay, boss," Lewis said, sliding down.

"And if this thing goes bad," Jason said, "you guys leave every-thing behind. Just get on your scooter and get to the rendezvous point, got it?"

"Leave my baby?" Lewis said, watching the pinprick of black high over the train.

"Don't worry," Jason said, "I'm almost certain we won't all get shot, captured, and sold into slavery on this op."

Lewis looked at him beneath sunken eyebrows. "You're real funny."

"Hey, Jason," Chris said, rolling the microphone in his hand. "This thing we've been doing, this *crusade* of yours—it's been good, buddy. It's felt right, you know. And. . .it's been fun, too. I think I'm understanding a little bit of what you felt when you beat the crud out of that slaver."

Jason gave him a thumbs-up. "I know what you mean." He gunned the ATV. "Break a leg, superstar."

"Don't worry about me. Just a minute ago I sighted my first-ever lilac-breasted roller. I'm set for life now."

Jason and Trieu rolled away down the ridgeline toward the mahogany trees at the end of the bridge, moving slowly enough to keep a dust cloud from rising.

Across the canyon, the train's first engine, a sleek gray beast with Arabic lettering in bright red paint below the engineers' side win-dows, rolled onto the bridge. The sound of the train, which until now had been distant and muted, exploded into their hearing like—well, like a freight train—its powerful diesel roar magnified by the rock walls.

The near side of the bridge was in shadow. The ground where the tracks exited it was raised five feet above the level of the canyon rim. The row of rust-colored boulders intersected with the mound and then picked up again on the other side. Garth's ATV was parked in the trees, facing away. He and Rachel were crouched against the embankment, their weapons held ready. A detonator keypad sat on the ground against the row of boulders, its plastic lid standing open like a tiny laptop computer.

Beyond the canyon in all directions lay the endless savannah. The sky overhead felt enormous here, with nothing on the ground to block the view of it. How the dark green acacia trees could grow in this desert was anyone's guess. A few clouds floated across the sky, their shadows roving the plain to tease the land with moments of respite from the relentless sun. The heat was heavy on their shoulders.

Jason noticed Rachel watching him. He smiled.

An obstruction blocked the tracks. The engineers wouldn't be able to see it, hidden as it was in the shadows, until they got more than halfway across the bridge. And then, because of the branches and downed trees obscuring it, they'd have to actually walk up close to see that it was an old Chinese military transport truck.

Jason crossed the tracks behind the truck, then parked the four-wheeler by a bush. He and Trieu trotted to the boulders lining the rim and took a look at the train from this side.

Both engines and the first four cars were on the bridge now. The train was coming slowly, but at twice the speed it had to go when traveling with its horde of guards walking beside it. The first three cars were fuel and water cars. Beginning at the fourth, soldiers and robed men sat on top of the cattle cars or swung their legs out of the open boxcars.

"Hey, chief?" It was Garth's voice in Jason's helmet speaker.

"Yeah?"

"Are we a hundred percent sure this is a good idea?"

"Uh, that's a negative. That's what I asked you guys before and you all said yes."

"I know, but we could still call it off," Garth said. "We hop on our hawgs and skedaddle while they're messing with the truck. They'd never know we'd been here."

"Yeah, Jason," Lewis said. "There's a lot of bad guys on that train."

Jason sighed. "I know it. You guys, you can't change your vote now. Look, we're right at the end of the dry season. If we do this op right, we cut off the last slave raids of the year. How many hundreds of lives will we save? Yeah, the north can rebuild the bridge and come back, but maybe we give these Dinka families one or two years without the attacks that come with this train. They haven't had a two-year break since 1981."

"Plus," Chris said, "if this train doesn't get through, the north can't resupply their garrison towns in the south, and the SPLA might be able to take them. This one op could actually swing the balance of the war."

"I don't know," Trieu said. "I'm with Garth. This sounds like something a regular military team ought to be doing. Not us. But," she said, looking up at Jason, "I'll do whatever our leader decides."

"Rachel," Lewis said, "what do you think?"

For a moment Rachel didn't answer. Jason couldn't see her across the tracks. He wondered if she were rolling her eyes at Trieu's last remark. "I think," she said at last, "that we'd better shut up and pay attention. They're halfway here."

The train was fully committed now. A smoky cloud fell away from the train into the valley, black fumes from the train mixed with brown dust shaken off the bridge. Jason spotted a man staring forward in the engine's windshield. Another man stuck his head outside the engine window and peered forward. He could hear the railcars clanging against their linkages and the horses braying in their travel containers. So far the train was not slowing. Because he was looking for it, Jason could also see the banshee circling high above the engines.

"Look, you guys," he said into his helmet microphone. "This may be our last op here. Our time's run out. I don't know if we're the best-equipped team to do this or even if this is such a great idea. But I do know that if we're ever going to be stupid enough to accept seven-hundred-to-six odds, right now—while their superior numbers are negated by the bridge—is the only time to do it. So unless there are any last-minute words from God, I say we do this thing and get out. Besides, you guys all voted that we do this. Look, by this time tomorrow we can be in Kenya, headed home. Okay?"

He got affirmative replies from all five.

"All right," Jason said. "Then we're going for it. No more recounts. Team Firebrand, commence Operation: Turnabout."

The train began to slow. The first engine was only thirty yards from the end of the track now. Wheels squealed and hydraulic brakes hissed, until the beast finally halted ten feet from the obstacle on the tracks. The front of the blunt-nosed engine stood right at the raised earth beside Jason and Trieu. Half a dozen metal hoses dangled on either side of the jutting hitch assembly like a stringy mustache. The locomotive sounded like an eighteen-wheeler idling at a gas station.

"Engineer getting out," Lewis's voice informed them. "Garth and Rachel's side."

A thin black man wearing GOS army pants and a dirty white T-shirt opened a narrow door in the control compartment and walked on the platform next to the engine cowling. His head was shaved, and he held a stubby cigarette in his lips. He stopped at the ladder at the front of the engine to look back and wave. Then he waved again with a larger motion. Finally he made an "Aw, forget it" motion with his hand and turned back toward the thing across the tracks.

As he turned, twin clouds of white powder erupted on his chest and enveloped his head. Jason heard Garth's pepperball CAR-15, a sound like two wooden rulers slapping together. The man flinched and grasped his chest. Jason saw the cigarette go flying before the guy collapsed out of sight behind the raised earth. He could hear him coughing and wheezing. He also heard the *pffft* of Rachel's silenced MP5 delivering the Versed.

Jason realized he was holding his breath. He let it out and drew in another, full of diesel exhaust and tinged with oleoresin capsicum—pepper powder. For three eternal minutes, nothing happened. A meerkat scampered atop the boulder nearest the train. It sat up on its haunches, its front legs resting on its protruding belly. It bent over and sneezed, then hopped adroitly from boulder to boulder, away from the bridge. *Good idea, Timon.*

"Another guy's getting out," Lewis said. "Jason and Trieu's side."

A second engineer stomped out of the narrow door on the other side of the locomotive. This man was older and thicker than the first. He wore a full GOS army uniform, down to the polished black boots. His heavy brows bunched like biceps on his forehead, and his eyes shone whitely on his dark face.

He spoke irritably in Arabic. It sounded to Jason like he was calling for the other guy, perhaps suspecting he'd run off to the nearest Coke machine. He was eight feet from Jason when he left the ladder and stepped onto the track. He raised his hands in a gesture of frustration, looking side to side for his companion.

He looked right at Jason.

Surprise registered in his face, followed by incomprehension, chased hard by fear and alarm. He opened his mouth to shout a warning.

And took in a lungful of pepper powder instead.

He didn't crumple as the other engineer had. He stepped back once, coughing, but showed no sign of falling. Jason smacked another three pepperballs into the man's chest, and Trieu plugged him with her Dragunov, dialed-down to its lowest setting.

He recoiled when the gelatin bullet struck him in the thigh, but still he did not fall. Coughing and hunched over, he lumbered toward Jason like a creature from the crypt.

This was not exactly how it was supposed to go. Jason backed away from the man, keeping Trieu behind him. Jason hit him with another round of pepper for good measure. They could keep backing up, waiting for the thirteen seconds it took for the sedative to render the man unconscious, but they were running out of shade and might already be visible to soldiers from the train.

The engineer appeared to remember something. He reached toward his right ankle, where Jason saw a leather sheath and a bone-handled knife.

*Okay, that's enough.*

Jason raised the butt of his CAR-15 and pummeled the man in his right shoulder. He fell backward from the impact, his feet lifting in the air. Jason swept both legs aside with his rifle and fell on the man's ribs with his left knee. He lifted his fist over the man's face.

"Jason. . ." It was Trieu. She elongated the pronunciation of his name, as if trying to rouse him from sleep.

The engineer wasn't struggling. His eyes were not as wide as they'd been a few seconds before.

"I'm okay, Trieu," Jason said, breathing quickly. "I promise. This time I'm okay."

Finally the man drifted off to dreams of large women.

Jason and Trieu dragged him back to the tracks. Then Jason and Garth carried him to the driving compartment and laid him next to the other guy.

When they were back in position on either side of the tracks, Jason keyed his microphone. "We're set, Chris. The engineers are out. Go to work, Hollywood."

Suddenly Chris's voice coursed through the hot canyon like water from a busted dam. He spoke forcefully, like a policeman over a bullhorn. He was speaking in Arabic, but the tone said, "The building is surrounded. Come out with your hands up. This is your last warning."

Rachel's voice whispered in their helmets. "He said, 'Attention, attention. The train will not be allowed to proceed.'"

Jason flipped his eye panel down and used the buttons on his load-bearing vest to cycle through the views until he found the video feed from the banshee's camera.

He could see the entire bridge in the bug-eye view. It looked like a toy train left in the Arizona sun—except for the tiny figures of men moving atop it with anxious speed.

Chris's voice echoed over the canyon.

"Do not attempt to leave the train," Rachel said, translating. "Or our troops will have no choice but to open fire on you."

Now the whole length of the train was swarming as if someone had kicked a fallen log infested with ants.

*Oh, great. What have we done?*

Chris's voice still sounded commanding, but his pitch had gone up half an octave.

"Do not leave the—"

Rachel's translation was cut off by the sound of automatic weapons fire coming from the train.

"Get down!" Jason shouted. "Everybody down!"

The noise-canceling earphones in Jason's helmet protected his ears against the cacophony of seven hundred angry men firing hundreds of pounds of lead, the sound redoubled by the canyon walls. In terms of pure noise and lethal capacity—not to mention long odds—it ranked up there with almost anything he'd encountered as a SEAL.

His training and discipline kept him snuggled up behind the row of boulders. That and the knowledge that the enemy was firing blind. Still, though, the truck blocking the tracks was taking a pounding. It tinked and crashed and thudded until it was rocking side to side.

The firing stopped. When Jason's helmet allowed the noise through again, the echo of the gunfire was still ricocheting around the canyon. He heard Sudanese commanders shouting at their men. On his eye panel, he could see a dozen soldiers advancing on top of the train, crouching low and holding their assault rifles before them. Other soldiers were climbing up between cars. Many more gun barrels pointed out of every boxcar, sweeping nervously from canyon rim to canyon rim.

"Okay," Jason said, readying a flashbang grenade, "bad guys coming up the train. Let 'em have it with the fireworks. On three: one, two, *three.*"

He and Garth hefted their grenades as far up the train as they could.

While those were still in the air, Chris played over the speakers the sound effects tape Eloise had sent for just such an occasion. Sounds of rifles, tanks, rockets, grenades, artillery, and team-fired heavy machine guns blasted the canyon like sonic dynamite. It sounded like an entire battalion letting loose with everything they had.

The flashbangs exploded in the midst of it, sending men to their faces.

All six members of the Firebrand team fired pepperballs and tranquilizer darts, directing their fire away from those on the edges of the train and concentrating instead on those in boxcars or on the center of the rooftops. Garth, Jason, and Chris fired tear gas canisters from their CAR-15s. Men fell screaming and coughing—but did not fall off the train.

The noise and smoke and the sight of their comrades falling in battle sent the Sudanese scurrying for cover. They disappeared off the roof and inside boxcars as quickly as they had appeared.

The sound of firing stopped.

Chris's voice blared across the valley once more. His voice sounded more relaxed, like how the elephant tagger sounds *after* the big guy is sleeping on the savannah.

"Now you know that we are serious," Rachel translated. "Now that you see the soldiers where they lie. They are not dead. Some are sleeping while their bodies process the poisons we have used on our weapons. When they awaken, they will be docile and mute. Others of you were struck by a mysterious white powder. By inhaling it, you have rendered yourselves impotent. But please, come out again so we may see you. We fear we have not reached each one of you with our chemicals. Show yourselves so that we can turn you all into good little obedient men who do not pollute the world with children.

"You are no doubt wondering who we are. Is it the SPLA? you wonder. Is it the Americans or the British or the Norwegians? Is it the UN? We say only that we are friends of anyone who fights slavery, oppression, and the murder of civilians. We are on a crusade against injustice. A jihad against anyone who drops bombs on schools and hospitals. We are the ones who have been defeating your military and bombing your pipeline.

"You have come south to rape and pillage and steal. You have come here to plunder cattle and enslave free people and enjoy an adventure of violence in which you thought you would not be challenged and could not be harmed. But today you are in for a surprise. Today you will know what it is like to have done to you what you have done to others."

As Chris continued to speak and Rachel continued to translate, Lewis's voice broke through. "Three men crawling up car number four's rooftop, Trieu's side."

Jason and Trieu looked. Three soldiers in dark brown and tan desert camouflage inched forward on their bellies, their AK-47s held before them. They were about fifty yards away.

"Got 'em," Jason said. "Trieu?"

She wedged herself between two boulders and brought the Dragunov to her shoulder. She flipped the rifle off safety and took patient aim through the scope.

*Pyew.*

Again it sounded like a laser gun to Jason. The puff of gas dispersed instantly after leaving the muzzle.

The front man of the three clutched his side and groaned. He pulled his hand out and saw it covered with blood. Jason could hear his cries over Chris's oration.

Trieu fired again, and the second man rolled onto his back, holding his right shoulder.

The third soldier froze, flattened on the rooftop. He called to the others just as they both fell unconscious. Jason saw him begin to inch backward.

Trieu shot him anyway.

He managed to climb between two cars and get pulled inside a boxcar before passing out in the arms of other soldiers.

Jason patted Trieu on the shoulder and helped her back down behind the boulders. His mind returned to Rachel's translation.

"Some of you we will kill outright," Chris was saying. "Others will not receive such mercy. We will come through and cut off arms, hands, feet, fingers, and noses—just as you have done to others. Just as you were hoping to do today.

"The rest of you we will take as our slaves. First you will bury your comrades, collecting their severed body parts as you go. Then you will carry our plunder to our homes, where we will beat you, torture you, starve you, humiliate you, and use you for our perverse pleasures. Our women will spit on you. Our children will cut and burn you. When we tire of you, we will either sell you to those who treat you even less humanely or we will simply murder you to teach our children how to kill.

"A few lucky ones we will take for chemical reconditioning. We will train you to join our ranks and lead us in the fight against your own people. You will teach us the secrets of your tribes and villages so that you may more completely betray your heritage. If you are fortunate, you will even take part in murdering your own family members."

Jason put his hand over his microphone and leaned to Trieu. "He's really laying it on thick, isn't he? I think Rachel was coaching him in more than just how to say what he was going to say."

"Jason," Lewis said.

"Yeah, you got more?"

"Five more, Garth's side."

"Okay."

Jason nodded to Trieu, who ran at a crouch behind the truck and out of Jason's sight. He switched his eye panel to Trieu's gun cam. It was bouncing around as if in an earthquake. Then it settled and the train came into view.

He saw several soldiers, more like ten than five, leaving their boxcar and walking on the narrow ridge of bridge that extended beyond the girth of the train. They were staying as low as they could, and they had their rifles slung across their backs. But there was just one problem.

They were going the other way. They weren't trying to advance on the team's position, they were trying to retreat.

Jason switched to the banshee's camera and saw an exodus beginning. The formerly bold military and militia were slinking away north, leaving their fallen fellows behind.

Chris's voice hounded them as they fled. "With you in our slave pits, we will return to your homes and take your wives and concubines and daughters for our own pleasure. Imagine what we will do to them. Every last thing you have done to your slaves—who were mothers and wives and sisters and daughters of free men. These things and more we will do to your little ones.

"We will breed you out of them. We will raise up generations of children who do not remember you, who have no trace of your way of life, your language, your culture, your religion. You will be blotted out.

"Then, when we have tired of your wives and daughters, we will herd them into great buildings that used to be your own, and we will bomb them from our planes. We will bomb them until they try to run away, and then we will machine gun them or chop them to pieces with the swords you once used against the Dinka and Nuer. Finally, we will set the building aflame, and we will laugh as they cry for mercy."

*Yikes, Chris. That's probably enough.*

Jason checked the banshee's display. Probably a hundred men had reached the far side of the bridge. At least twice as many more were headed that way, many becoming bolder in flight, running atop the train cars without so much as ducking. But Jason could see others getting bolder, too: uniformed soldiers in the desert camouflage. Clumps of them crouched in boxcars or poked their heads and weapons up between cars.

Over Chris's speech and the idling engines, Jason could hear the horses again, stomping and neighing. There was another sound, too. Distant but disturbing. Like maybe the sound of reinforcements.

Rachel relayed Chris's words. "How does it feel to be afraid and powerless? How does it feel to go from the hunter to the hunted? Remember this feeling the next time you think about coming to south Sudan. Remember this feeling if you cowards manage to ever see your families again. Before we blow this bridge to the canyon floor, we wish to leave you with a final thought: Treat other people the way you want to be treated."

Chris's voice came through the squad radio. "Okay, I'm done. Let's blow this thing and go home."

"Okay, Chris," Jason said. "Great job, jarhead. Lewis, we all clear for a rush to the engine?"

"All clear, boss."

"Okay, Garth and Ra—"

A deep-throated rush like a space shuttle launching—coupled with a high-pitched screaming a hundred times more intense than the banshee's—split the air above the canyon.

"MiGs!" Chris shouted.

Two swept-wing, double-tail MiG-29 Fulcrums streaked over the canyon in formation. Jason ducked by instinct.

"That's it," Jason said, "we're out of here. Garth, you and Rachel get that train in reverse. Go, go, go!"

Jason saw Garth's head and heard Rachel's footsteps on the far side of the earth mound.

"I'm bringing banshee home," Lewis said.

"Fine," Jason said. "Trieu, stay here and cover this side of the train. I'll cover the other side. If they want to rush us now, I don't care if they fall. The situation has just officially changed."

The MiGs eased out of their steep banking turns and bore down on the valley and the bridge.

Jason arrived at Garth and Rachel's station. A brown lizard skittered over the edge when he fell against the rocks. The tracks were clear all the way back. Garth's detonator sat on a rock in the shade.

He heard clanks and grinds from the engine compartment. Then the diesel engines revved and hydraulic brakes hissed. The nose of the engine began retreating from the south side of the bridge.

"Coming by for their look-see," Chris said.

The MiGs arched over the bridge in a slow left turn, banked for the pilots to assess the situation.

"Anybody got their SAM missiles handy?" Lewis asked.

"Shucks," Garth said, following Rachel off the tracks and back down to Jason. "Left 'em in my other pants."

The train was gaining speed as it backed across the bridge, but it was still at only a walking pace.

Garth picked up his detonator, then looked at the MiGs. "Guess somebody had a radio, huh?"

"Yeah," Chris said, "and the planes must've already been up to get here so fast."

Jason watched the jets turning for another run. "Anybody willing to believe they were on a recon mission when they took off and so don't have any weapons on board?"

Garth and Rachel looked at him as if he were crazy.

"That's what I thought," he said. "Garth, did you put the train on slow rewind or what?"

"I put it on full! It's going to back all the way to Egypt on full speed, okay? But the thing doesn't exactly go from zero to sixty in five seconds."

Jason heard an odd staccato puttering from the direction of the MiGs. He had to see the plume of dirt erupting and barreling toward him before he figured it out. "Strafing run! Take cover!"

They dove for the boulders, squirming underneath as far as they could go.

A double line of impacts shredded the ground ten yards beside them like someone yanking a zipper. A shadow swept over them like the angel of death, complete with unearthly shriek. Clods of dirt and rock pelted them heavily.

"Oh, man!" Lewis said over the radio. "I did not sign on for this!"

"So much for the unarmed theory," Rachel said, her eyes flaring at Jason.

"It was a blind shot," Jason said. "They don't know where we are, so they're just strafing to make sure. They think there's a bunch of us, remember?"

Trieu ran up to them. She and Rachel hugged.

"Maybe now would be a good time to get out of here?" Chris said.

"No," Jason said. "The worst thing we can do is become a target they can aim at. We're safer here."

*"Safer?"*

Jason couldn't see Lewis's eyes, but he could imagine their size. He looked at the bridge. The train was two-thirds of the way off now and picking up speed. The MiGs were beginning their turn.

"On the other hand," he said, looking up, "the only place they can't see is in these trees. If I'm them, I drop a bomb right here on my next pass."

"Our bikes!" Rachel shouted, darting toward the ATV. Garth and Trieu ran to theirs, too. The MiGs were leveling out of their turn and pointing right at them.

"Chris," Jason shouted, running toward the bikes, "you guys get away now!"

Garth had Trieu on his four-wheeler, so Jason fell on with Rachel. They shot away from the bridge as the sound of the jets shut his helmet speakers down. A whistling penetrated anyway, just as the two ATVs left the shadow of the last trees at fifty miles an hour.

He felt the shockwave before anything else. It slammed his body into Rachel's and propelled the bike forward as if hit by God's driving iron. The ATV's engine whined at the extra speed.

Then came the heat from the blast. It seared through his back. It felt like his pack was melting.

Rachel hit a large clump of dead grass and fought for control, as dirt and wood and metal rained down upon them. She hit the brakes and brought their speed down, sliding too abruptly at the end and sending them tumbling to the turf.

Jason looked back at the trees in time to see the yellow fireball vanishing into black smoke under the clouds. Burning trees fell to the ground, lighting others.

"Blow the bridge, Garth!" he yelled. "Blow it, blow it!"

Jason couldn't see the other ATVs. He didn't even know if his radio was working. Overhead, the MiGs could be heard but not seen. Had they spotted the four-wheelers? Were they coming back?

He reached for Rachel's arm. She was bleeding from scratches on her wrist and neck, but seemed all right otherwise. They started working on righting the ATV.

Then he heard an agonizing creak behind him like a hundred sailing ships moaning in a hurricane. It was followed by a pair of low thumps that seemed to come from somewhere else up the canyon.

He felt a moment of vertigo then. He could see the bridge through the burning trees, but it seemed that the world was moving while the bridge stood perfectly still. Then the bridge simply wasn't there anymore. There was the wide canyon, shimmering in the flame, but only open air between the sides. A sound like the World Trade Center towers falling burst into his ears—a prolonged snapping, colliding sound of endless collapse. A Mount St. Helens of dust erupted from the canyon, spewing billowed clouds of dust thousands of feet skyward and swallowing up the MiGs.

Jason found himself standing beside Rachel. He put his arm around her and pulled her close. They stood there mutely, listening to the sound of the bridge settling on the canyon floor and watching bits of debris fluttering through the air.

Soon he became aware of additional sounds—the other two ATVs. The rest of the team rode up next to Jason and Rachel's overturned ATV and got off.

"Oh, my," Trieu said, looking toward the canyon. "Did we do that?"

"Afraid so, sweetheart," Garth said.

Chris took his helmet off. "I still can't believe nobody fell off the bridge."

"Hey," Garth said, "that's what we prayed for, isn't it?"

Jason looked at them. "So you think the train was all the way off when the bridge went?"

"Absolutely," Garth said, "or we'd have heard a lot bigger crash than that."

"A bigger crash?" Rachel asked.

Garth nodded. "Much."

"You guys," Jason said, "we totally lied to those people. All that stuff about us going to their homes and taking their families into slavery and everything. Does anybody else have a problem with that?"

"No," Rachel said, "we didn't lie to them."

"We didn't?"

"No, Chris did."

They chuckled.

Chris pursed his lips. "Thanks a lot, Raych."

"Besides," Rachel said, "I remember something Dietrich Bonhoeffer said about people who hid the Jews from the Nazis. He said that truth is not owed to those for whom truth is used for harm. We don't owe truth to the enemy."

"Hmm." Jason said. "Hmm."

"Still," Garth said, " 'Lying lips are an abomination to the Lord, but those who deal faithfully are His delight.' "

"Well," Chris said, looking up at the pillar of dust above them, "what's done is done."

"Hmm."

"Man," Lewis said, "if anybody ever figures out who did this, Eloise is going to have to pay a lot of money."

They laughed more easily.

"Is that all you think about?" Chris asked. "The bottom line?"

"No," Lewis said. "I think about getting in trouble, and I know that I don't have the cash to pay for that bridge and that pipeline and everything else. If they catch us, they'll go after the one with money."

"If they catch us," Garth said, "we've got a lot more to worry about than that."

"Speaking of which," Jason said, looking at the brown-tinted sky, "let's get out of the open before those MiGs get their air intakes cleared and decide to come back."

Trieu quickly field-dressed Rachel's wounds, and the others got the third ATV righted and cleaned up. The handlebars were bent out of alignment, but Garth fixed it with a single yank. The sound of jet engines faded and the bridge's death throes ended.

As they rode back toward Akwer Nhom aboard their silent ATVs, the only sound Jason heard was of some African bird singing brightly in the tall grass.

"Hey, Chris," he said. "What's that bird?"

"That, my friend, is the Big Mama Eloise bird calling her chicks back to the nest."

PART IV

# BACKLASH

# CHAPTER 22

## ALL GOOD THINGS. . .

"LOOKS LIKE your boys are doing their job."

Jason directed Garth's attention to two Dinka preteens sitting in the shade of an acacia tree, speaking on a small two-way radio.

"Of course they are," Garth said, sliding the ATV to a stop. "I trained them, didn't I?" He led the other two four-wheelers over to the boys.

The oldest boy, Geng, was around twelve. He had a mostly clean bandage over the stump of his left wrist. But his eyes were clear, and he smiled like an NFL fan when Garth came near. The younger boy was Geng's cousin, Bwoy. He was eight and looked frail. Both boys had been rescued from slavery during the Firebrand team's crusade.

"Madhe," Garth said to them. "Cibak?" Then he turned to Rachel for help. "Ask them if anything's happened here in Akwer Nhom since we've been gone. Please."

Rachel talked to them and then reported that they'd been hearing strange mechanical sounds from the southeast, and twice they'd seen fighter jets flying overhead.

"Okay," Jason said, standing beside Garth and Rachel, "have them radio the village that we're here. We'll just sit tight for a second to let Trieu have time to clean those cuts better, Rachel, and for me to check in with Bigelow."

The team dismounted and moved into the shade. Trieu broke out her medical kit and started treating Rachel's wounds in earnest. It was past lunchtime, so food and drink packets soon appeared. Garth passed Fritos to Geng and Bwoy. The day was as hot as the morning had promised, but a bank of dark clouds roiling at the horizon gave some faint hope of rain.

Lewis cranked up the satellite radio and passed the handset to Jason. "Dude, I am *so* ready to be out of here. Do you think we could be on a plane today?"

"No, probably not today, Lewis. Maybe tomorrow." Jason lifted the handset to his face. "Pa Grape, Pa Grape, this is Larry-Boy. How copy? Over." He slid his desert camo sleeve up to check his watch. It was 1:20 P.M. That made it 6:20 in the morning back in Ohio. He sat with his back against the narrow acacia trunk. "This is probably going to take awhile. I'm sure Chimp's nowhere close to—"

"Larry-Boy, this is Pa Grape. Don't you guys answer your phone? I've been trying to call you for three hours. You're in trouble. Repeat, you are in trouble, Larry-Boy. Bad guys beginning to close on your position from the northwest, northeast, and southeast. Icarus shows three brigade-strength elements closing in. You've got to get out of there now. How copy? Over."

Jason blew out a sigh. "Copy, Pa Grape. Copy three brigade-strength units closing on our position." He said it loudly, grabbing each of his team members with his eyes and tone.

They stopped what they were doing and knelt around him, grabbing their packs and darting their gaze across the barren grassland and clouding sky.

"So much for having learned to smell out an ambush," Chris said.

"Pa Grape," Jason said, "where does it look like they're headed? To the bridge we blew or to our current GPS coordinates? Over."

During the transmission delay, Jason turned up the radio's volume so everyone could hear Bigelow's reply through the handset.

"Larry-Boy, Pa Grape. Difficult to know exactly. The images are three hours old. But if I were a betting man, I'd say they were headed to a conversion point right over that little village you've been using as your hometown. Over."

"Copy, Pa Grape. Stand by."

Lewis's eyes were wide. "The army's coming to Akwer Nhom? How'd they know we were there?"

Chris scanned the horizon. "We've been ratted out, boys."

"What?"

"But how?"

"It can't be that."

"No one knows we're here."

"What else would they want with this village?"

"Nobody would do that."

"Those poor people!"

"It had to be that middleman," Chris said. "Remember we saw him making that other raid? He recognized us, I know it. And he would remember we were from Akwer Nhom because that's what we said when we redeemed those first slaves from him. Then he got away without a shot of Versed. I *knew* we should've gone after him."

Jason chopped his hand through the air. "Okay, knock it off. Who cares how it happened? The thing we have to worry about is how to get out of here before they can tighten the noose. Chimp says they're coming from the northwest, northeast, and southeast. I say we grab as much of our gear as we can carry on the four-wheelers and hightail it southwest. We cross into the Central African Republic and get a flight out from there. Feedback?"

"But what about the people in the village?" Lewis asked. "We have got to warn them."

"Of course." Jason said. "Garth's boys can radio a warning." He lifted the handset. "Pa Grape, this is Larry-Boy. We're thinking of grabbing our stuff and heading southwest to the nearest national border. How does that look from there? Over."

When he lowered the handset to wait out the delay, Jason saw Chris speaking in Arabic to the Dinka boys and the boys making the call. *That's strange. Why is Chris doing the translating?* "You guys, where's—"

"Larry-Boy, Pa Grape. Copy your plan of escape. It looks good from here, but the situation is fluid. Be aware that there are air elements in the area, as well. Fast and slow movers. Stick to cover when you can. Call when you get to a rear area, and we'll vector a transport to get you out. Also be advised that Icarus is picking up rebel forces on the move, too. Too early to tell what they're up to, but be careful no matter who you run into on the way out. Over."

"Copy, Pa Grape," Jason said. "You and Ma keep us in your prayers, all right? Larry-Boy out."

He gave the handset back to Lewis and stood. "Okay, let's move."

No one answered. They were all staring across the savannah.

Jason looked. Through a brown dust cloud a hundred yards away, he could see a figure in desert fatigues on an ATV retreating at top speed. He looked around at the group. The only one missing was Rachel.

"Where's she going?" Lewis said.

"She's headed toward the village," Garth said.

Chris ran to his ATV. "We've got to go after her. That's the only place she *can't* be."

"Wait," Jason said. He grabbed Trieu's sniper rifle from where it leaned against the tree. He swept it up and brought it to his shoulder, aiming toward Rachel.

"What are you doing?" Chris asked.

"Trying to save her life." He found her in the scope, but had no time to adjust for wind. He fired but couldn't tell if he'd hit. He fired again.

Trieu was suddenly at his shoulder. "Let me dial it up to full."

She reached for the power regulator on the barrel.

"Here," Jason said, handing the gun to her. "It's your gun. You take the shot."

Trieu lifted the rifle and leaned back in the biathlete's peculiar swayback posture. She seemed to take way too long to aim. Rachel was almost two hundred yards away now. Could a gelatin bullet fly so far?

Trieu fired. Then again and again. Eight times in quick succession. She lowered the rifle.

"Did you get her?"

Trieu brought the gun up again and looked through the scope. "We'll know in thirteen seconds."

The rest of the team stood in a line beside them, looking through binoculars or under a shading hand. They counted down from thirteen.

When they got to zero, Jason was watching through his light-enhancing binoculars. "She's still going."

"Then get on," Chris said from the ATV. "Let's go get her back."

They ran to the tree and grabbed helmets and packs and guns. Lewis jumped on with Chris, and Garth and Trieu climbed on the other one.

"Chris," Jason said, settling behind Lewis, "tell the boys to get to the village's rendezvous point."

Chris relayed the message and the boys nodded. Garth and Chris got the two ATVs pointed the direction Rachel had fled.

Just in time to see four M-60A3 main battle tanks streaking into view.

Plumes of dust rose behind the treads as the armored beasts executed a left turn in formation and accelerated toward the village. The roar of their treads and engines traveled quite clearly across the plain.

"Oh, no," Jason said. The same helplessness he'd felt in the MiG attack gripped his stomach now. All he could do was stare into disaster. "Oh, Rachel."

\* \* \*

*Anei will not live in bondage. Not again.*

Rachel clamped onto the thought like a dog pulling on a rope. Or maybe the rope was pulling her.

It had seized her mind the moment she'd heard that the Sudanese army was converging on Akwer Nhom. On Anei. While the others struggled with what to do and how it had happened, she had eased toward the ATV. There was no struggle in *her* mind. Just a purified conviction of that which she must ensure became truth.

Twice she'd heard something whizzing by her head as she'd ridden away, and once she'd felt something impact her backpack. She'd looked over her shoulder but had seen nothing besides dust. It clogged her nostrils and threatened to make her sneeze.

Seconds later she'd looked again and seen four tan nightmares kicking up a sandstorm of their own. If they opened fire, she would most likely die. But so far they had only pursued her, and now she had outdistanced them handily. The gun harness kept her MP5 held snug across her chest.

Her four-wheeler left the ground briefly when she rounded the trees and crested the ridge of the low valley beside Akwer Nhom. She landed heavily and braked, pleased to see the villagers streaming southward down the valley with their belongings and their retrieved cattle. Garth's warning couldn't have come more than ten minutes before, and here they were already vacating the village. He'd trained them well.

The Dinka cried out when she burst over the ridge toward them, but then they recognized her and kept going. Rachel spotted Lual and Anei toward the rear of the group and drove to them. The tall man was carrying a baby goat in one hand, and he held his daughter's hand in the other. Anei jumped up and down and called Rachel's name, but there was no smile.

"Lual," Rachel said in Arabic, "get her on here with me. You get on back. I'll take you to the hideout."

"But the goat!"

"Forget the stupid goat. There are tanks coming, Lual! Tanks. Giant guns on wheels." She grabbed Anei and pulled her into her lap, though the girl clung to her father. "Get on!"

A crashing came from the forest the way Rachel had come. The other Dinka gasped.

"Run!" Rachel shouted to them. "Get to safety now!"

Lual climbed on—goat and all—and Rachel tore off down the valley.

The tanks crested the ridge to her left, their underbellies lifting into the air, then slamming down with a creaking groan.

Rachel gunned the engine. She crossed the valley floor at a tangent to the tanks' approach. Her heart skipped with every large-bore barrel she passed in front of. The goat bleated and scrabbled against her side and backpack to be released. Anei held her arms locked against the center of the handlebars, alternating between whimpering and squealing in fear. Lual held on to both Anei and Rachel from behind.

She zigzagged down the valley, her whole being clenched for the first gout of flame and dirt to explode beneath her. But still it did not come.

Then she saw why.

Fifty white-robed murahileen on horseback spilled into the valley seventy yards in front of her, blocking her escape—and the escape of the Dinka coming behind. Driving the fox into the guns.

She veered right up the slope toward the trees along the ridge. The murahileen charged toward her.

The ATV bled off speed alarmingly as it struggled to carry its extra weight up the sandy slope. The nearest horses were twenty yards away when Rachel finally topped the rise.

The riders shrieked like American Indians and charged with rifle and scimitar. Anei screamed. Five yards now.

Lual threw the young goat into the legs of the nearest horse, and it tumbled, sending the rider to the ground hard.

Rachel grabbed her MP5 with one hand and inoculated the nearest seven riders.

She accelerated away through the trees. Branches and vines slapped across her helmet and tore at her pants. Sweat slicked her grip on the accelerator, but she squeezed it harder still. Her throat was as dry as the Sahara.

Movement ahead caught her eye, and she swerved left, heading toward the open savannah beyond the trees. She was in a zone now, reacting without thinking.

She broke out of the trees—and despaired.

Hundreds of infantry formed an unbroken line forty yards in front of her. Behind them came more tanks, armored personnel carriers, and armored reconnaissance vehicles. Hundreds of horses. When they saw her, the infantry broke into a bayonet charge.

She spun around and plunged back into the trees.

Anei had gone rigid and silent in front of her. Lual only hung on. Some part of her mind whispered to her that no one had fired at her yet. Strange.

Horses pounded the dirt on her right as she sped back toward the valley floor, their hoofbeats thumping in her ears like African drums. They came in a line, aiming to envelop her lines of advance or retreat.

Instead of turning left as they'd expect, Rachel swerved right and charged straight at the middle horse, a towering white steed.

The horse's eyes bulged and its forelegs locked. Dirt and rocks flew up, almost throwing the rider off forward.

Rachel passed through their line and gunned the four-wheeler for the valley, the horsemen spinning and again walloping the ground behind.

She shot across the ridge and down into a village aflame. She allowed herself frenzied glances as she looked for escape. The valley was full of uniformed soldiers and Baggara in jellabah robes. Several Dinka—but certainly not all the villagers—were huddled on the ground, guarded by GOS soldiers. The rebuilt tukuls were engulfed in orange fire, making the horses uneasy. At least eight M-60A3 tanks idled in the valley or bulldozed burning tukuls.

Before she even reached the bottom of the slope, hands grappled for her. Men on foot ran at her from all sides. She emptied her MP5 into the crowd and charged forward. If she could reach the other side of the valley and pass through their line again, maybe she could rejoin the team and escape.

The motor bogged down as more and more hands grasped the ATV's frame. Rachel kicked and swerved and swatted at arms. Men shouted and yelped.

She felt Lual lifted off the back. No time for remorse. The lighter load gave her a surge of speed, which she used to run down the soldier in front of her.

*Anei will* not *live in bondage. Not again.*

With a vicious swing of her submachine gun, she broke free of everyone's grasp. A way opened up before her straight to the ridge of escape. She swiveled the accelerator as far as it would go, and the ATV leapt forward.

She topped the ridge, elated.

And ran into the main enemy force.

Two hundred men stood arrayed in ranks before her, backed by tanks and trucks and horsemen.

"No!"

She swerved the handlebars.

But men were already upon her.

Anei went into captivity again. And Rachel went with her.

# CHAPTER 23

## GAMBIT

APPARENTLY many of the Dinka had gotten away. There were only forty sitting here in the shade with Rachel—and there wasn't a Dinka cow to be seen. She hadn't heard any shooting during that whole attack. If the soldiers had been here to slaughter these people, why had forty been allowed to live? Maybe the others had gotten to the hideout Garth had helped them prepare. She could only hope.

Rachel looked at Anei, sitting in her father's lap against a tree trunk. He was watching the soldiers guarding them and seemed poised to jump, but Anei only stared into nothingness.

*I'm sorry, sweet baby. I'm so sorry.*

The soldiers had finally tired of pawing through Rachel's backpack. The computer must've been damaged in the tussle because they couldn't seem to make anything work on her helmet's eye panel. Or maybe they just didn't know how to work it. If they'd been able to call up the position of every member of the Firebrand team. . . They

294

played with the night vision goggles, too; but without the computer's power supply to operate them, they fizzled as a party toy.

There seemed no limit to their fascination with her submachine gun and its curious ammunition—darts pulled from sleeping soldiers. Had they heard a report from the soldiers on the train? Did they think the darts would make them docile and mute? The officers examining them were down the slope from Rachel, standing amid a circle of the Firebrand team's gear that they'd had stashed here in Akwer Nhom. She was glad Lewis wasn't here to see them handling Chunky so roughly. They'd given up on it when it didn't work as a cart to roll down hills on.

But the piece of equipment that captivated them the most was her ATV. They all wanted to take it for a spin. Even if they'd worn no insignias on their uniforms, Rachel would've been able to figure out their hierarchy by who got to ride the thing. When one officer—a thick-bodied black man with a red beret—climbed out of his tank and proceeded to ride the four-wheeler for fifteen unchallenged minutes, she figured he was the top dog.

In the hour since her capture, units had continued to arrive in the valley. Now the whole area was like a used car lot for surplus military vehicles. Overhead she'd seen at least three flights of MiGs and a couple of Antonovs like the one she and Garth had hijacked. And she'd heard a suspicious *whump-whump-whump* from the distance, but hadn't seen what made it. A command tent and six other white tents had been raised beside the smoldering village.

The Dinka—men, women, and children—waited morosely, seemingly resigned to their fate. Only Lual had any fire in his eyes. When he looked at her, she felt her own embers glow red. But Rachel was certain that unless something radical happened very soon, these soldiers would find a way to smother even Lual's brave candle.

*O Lord, I don't care about me. You know that. I know I'll be on this earth until You say You want me with You. But please don't let this thing happen to Anei and her daddy. Please, if they are to be sold into slavery again, please let them catch some disease and die right away. They know You, Abba. Much better to be with You than here. . .with them. Glad You're in control, Lord. Amen.*

Three jeeps, all with their tops down, appeared at the far side of the valley, descending the same road Rachel and the Firebrand team had traveled a hundred years before. Riding in these jeeps were more truly Arab men than Rachel had yet seen in all of Sudan. The afternoon sunlight glistened off brass insignia on the collars of their dark green uniforms. The officer on the ATV got off and saluted.

Five of the newcomers spoke with the red-bereted tanker and three other officers from the invasion force. They were shown Rachel's equipment and all the gear the team had left behind. Red Beret gestured to the ATV like a game show model. Then he pointed up the hillside, and all nine men turned to look at Rachel.

As they walked up the hillside toward her, Rachel decided it was time for something radical to happen.

Soldiers shooed the other Dinka back as the officers arrayed themselves in a semicircle around where Rachel sat on the ground. They looked like a men's choral ensemble about to perform.

The man in the center had more bronze clusters on the collar of his uniform, so Rachel determined he must be the leader. Like the men flanking him, but unlike the lower-ranking officers, he appeared to be fully Arab. His skin was positively milky compared to the others; and his elegant eyebrows, finely chiseled jaw, and long nose set him apart further. He wore a wide, green officer's hat with black plastic bill and yellow brocade. A manicured wisp of a mustache darkened his upper lip.

"At last we meet the Americans!" he said in English.

Rachel bunched her eyebrows. She answered in Arabic: "Excuse me? I don't understand."

"No need to pretend with us, woman," he said, sticking to English. "We know all about you and the others with you. Where are they, by the way, your five friends? I don't see them here."

Rachel tilted her head as he spoke. Then she shook her head and shrugged with a look that said *I don't know what this wacko is saying, but. . .whatever.*

Red Beret stepped forward and kicked her in the leg. "Answer the colonel!" he said in Arabic.

"Leave her alone, you imbecile," the colonel said.

Rachel stood and brushed off her pants. "Before you release me," she said in Arabic, "I will want that man's name for my report. His highness is keenly interested in the treatment of prisoners. I'm afraid he has little tolerance for those who violate Koranic principles in such matters."

Now it was the colonel's turn to look confused. He lowered his eyelids to look at her, as if contemplating a possibly forged painting. He straightened and adjusted the pistol holster on his hip. "It is no matter," he said in English. "The Americans we do not capture we will simply kill. It is enough that we have you."

"And what is *your* name?" Rachel asked in Arabic. "His highness will want to know of the mental instability of one of Sudan's high-ranking officers."

From the looks they turned on her, she knew she would've received a barrage of kicks if the colonel had not banned it already. Just as had happened on the ATV, her mind switched into a mode of automatic answers and instinctive reactions. She knew enough by now to trust it.

"My name is of no concern to you," the colonel answered in Arabic. "Come," he said, turning toward the valley floor, "maintain your charade if you wish. When we reach Khartoum, you will tell us everything you know."

The men around her chortled harshly.

"I have noted your threat, Colonel, and I will not forget. However, I accept your offer to transport me to Khartoum. Indeed, that is my destination." She gestured to Lual and Anei with an open hand. "You will transport these two Dinka, as well. They will ride with me so that I may observe how your men treat them."

Lual and Anei looked at her in terror. She winked, but it didn't seem to lessen their anxiety.

Behind her the officers shuffled uneasily in the dirt. She loved this part, instilling uncertainty in her enemies. It was already a victory that the conversation had switched completely to Arabic.

"You wish us to take two Dinka north to Khartoum?" the colonel asked. "Why?"

"So they can come with me back to Riyadh, of course. These two are eyewitnesses to the brutalities visited on a free people by Muslims in Sudan. I will deliver my report to his majesty by myself, if I must; but hearing from those who have lived it is so much more effective, don't you think?"

The colonel regarded her steadily. "Riyadh? You are reporting to the crown prince of Saudi Arabia? I do not think so." Then he shrugged. "Why not bring them? Bring as many Dinka as you wish. There are millions of them in Khartoum already. Though I do not think you will find their situation there an improvement over here."

"Yes," Rachel said, pulling Lual and Anei to their feet, "the fabled ghettos of Khartoum. I understand that even those who convert to Islam are treated disrespectfully. What an affront to Allah and his prophet! While you are discarding the brotherhood of Muslims, why not throw out the Koran, as well?" She led Lual and Anei forward by the hand. "A trip to Khartoum is just what's needed."

But the colonel didn't step down the slope. "Stop this nonsense! You are a lying woman! Your uniform is American, your weapon is American, even the womanish supplies in your pack are American. Your helmet is unlike anything any Muslim army gives their troops. All of this equipment is what American soldiers carry. And this. . . vehicle—American, American, American." He jabbed the air toward her with a finger. "Cease this charade, or I will allow every one of my men to have their way with you."

Rachel raised an eyebrow. "Such language. I am shocked! And you call yourself a Muslim! Why do you choose to see only the Great Satan when you look at this advanced equipment? Do you concede to the corrupt West all scientific advancement? Do you have so little faith in Islam, the faith that developed modern mathematics and pioneered medicine, astronomy, and chemistry? For *shame*, Colonel, for shame.

"But please, do carry through with your threat, Colonel. When I do not report in tomorrow morning, the inquiries will begin. It is worth torture and even a martyr's death to expose the wickedness of this nation's military. Surely the sword of Allah will fall swiftly upon your necks!" She dropped Lual and Anei's hands and stood brazenly before him. "Take me if you can, Colonel. Defeat my 'womanish' protests and have your way with me. With such a crowd I'll easily be able to get four Muslim men to testify in sharia court that you raped me. If you are to die for your crimes and cause the death of your men, you should at least have the first taste."

The officers stood as if electrified. Rachel sensed soldiers coming up on all sides, but no one spoke. She heard Anei whimper and Lual pulling her away. Behind the officers, men pointed and came running. Adrenaline struck her system like a bus.

*You've finally done it now, Rachel Levy.*

She held her chin high, her eyes belittling the colonel and her lip half-lifted in a sneer.

*Might as well play it all the way.*

The colonel's eyes remained locked on hers fiercely, but his body language told another story. His muscles relaxed, the hand that had risen to jab her dropped, and he shifted his weight to the far leg. Then his eyes disengaged from hers and flicked to those standing around.

"The crown prince of Saudi Arabia has no authority here," he said, sounding almost certain.

She dropped her mouth open. "No authority? The guardian of Mecca, the protector of the most holy Kaaba, the ruler of the center of Islam has no authority here? Ha! He has authority throughout the Muslim world, which will soon extend over the entire earth.

"But even if you are so cavalier in your disregard for the curator of the birthplace of the prophet, the Arab League is not. When they hear my report about the contempt for Muslim conduct in Sudan, they will accuse your president of moral and religious laxity. They will issue a fatwa against Sudan, calling on all righteous Muslims to rise up in holy anger against the slide toward decadence that is the cancer of Islam.

"And they will rise, Colonel. There are still true Muslims in Sudan. Perhaps even in this very place. They will cast your president and his wicked regime down and replace him with a man of holy fear who will rule Sudan according to the mercy and love of almighty Allah. And when that day comes, it would be wise for you and your irreligious men to be far from here."

"How are they irreligious?" Red Beret asked. "You have seen men at midday prayers. You have heard them reciting the Koran. None of your precious abeed were killed today."

"Oh, yes," Rachel said, turning her imperious glare toward him, "I have seen much. I have seen you riding that vehicle through those very midday prayers."

Red Beret flinched and looked quickly at the colonel. Then he stepped backward.

"And your men," Rachel said, "yes, some of them prayed. But without ablutions! They made no effort to make wudu so as to come before Allah ritually clean. They knelt in filth and did not put on their cleanest clothes. Some even prayed shirtless—blaspheming Allah by coming before him uncovered! Oh, yes, I have seen.

"And I have heard. Colonel, your men have a pathetic grasp of the Koran. Their recitations were beyond recognition. How do you expect Allah to bless you with victory with prayers such as these? And more: I have heard your men singing. Singing! Coarse and lewd *drinking songs*. You will be fortunate to escape with only the loss of your hands and feet."

One of the officers beside the colonel touched him on the arm.

"If I may, Colonel. Young woman, perhaps you saw some of the men not praying because not every soldier in the army is Muslim. We have—"

"So! You admit it?" Rachel said. She turned her eyes back on the colonel. "I suspected as much but dared not put it in the report so as to save you from the shame. The idea that you would send unbelievers and pagans out with your firebrands of Allah is beyond shocking. Why is there no mullah here, Colonel? What have you been doing in your barracks all this time that these men have not bowed the knee to Allah? Tell me, what marching drill or brute work is more important than converting men to Islam?"

The officers were actually leaning away from her as she spoke. Behind them, she saw men putting on shirts and tucking in uniforms. Several Korans were suddenly in evidence.

The colonel folded his arms petulantly. "If you are on some mission from Saudi Arabia, why were you traveling in these clothes and with American soldiers?"

"They were not Americans," she said, rolling her eyes. "Again you assume that something superior must originate in the West. I am beginning to wonder, Colonel, about your loyalties. Is there perhaps some secret longing for the decadence of America in your heart?"

"There is no such thing! I crave only the Koran."

"Ah," Rachel said, nodding. "It is good to hear you at least try to sound devout."

"You have not answered my question," he said. "We have intelligence that you not only traveled with. . .those people who may or may not be Americans. . .but also paid in *American dollars* to redeem the slaves of this village and to conduct military actions against the sovereign nation of Sudan."

The officers' expressions were bolder now. Perhaps they thought they'd scored a point.

"I have already told you why I need these Dinka," Rachel said as if lecturing the slowest kid in the class. "If you cannot retain simple facts in conversation, then you are certainly unfit for command. As for what

I wear, whom I travel with, or how I conduct the affairs of his highness the prince, it is none of your concern." She put her hands on her hips. "Now, as it looks as though you won't be raping me after all, I suggest you put me and my companions aboard a transport for Khartoum this very hour."

The colonel and his officers stared at Rachel. Rachel stared back defiantly.

Inside, she was quaking. She risked the thought that she had just played her last scene. Had she really told this man to rape her? Had she actually *dared* him to—in front of men who would lose respect for him if he allowed a woman to speak to him so? She'd always known that one day she'd make a gamble too big. She'd wondered where the limit of her audacity was, where it crossed from daring to stupidity. Today might be the day she found out.

Finally the colonel grunted. "You," he said to Rachel, "will wait here. Guards!"

He turned and led the officers down toward the command tent. Three soldiers, looking much cleaner than they had half an hour ago, politely motioned for her to walk to where the Dinka sat in the shade.

As she was going, she heard Red Beret protesting to the colonel. "But I swear to you that is what the informant said. He said there were six Americans and that they'd come here to redeem slaves and fight us! He did lead us to the right village. I tell you, the woman is lying!"

Rachel heard someone else ask him a question but couldn't make out the words.

Red Beret's reply reached her loud and clear, though. "How can I find him today?" He looked around the shallow valley crowded with GOS tanks and troops. "He'll be with his SPLA friends to hide his treachery. With all of us here like this, do you expect a man like Dhor to simply drive his Land Rover right up?"

# CHAPTER 24

## Both Bound and Free

*Beware, my friends. Here you will always be the enemy.*

Dhor's words ricocheted inside Rachel's mind like a bullet in a rock canyon. It was good that she was sitting already or she would've fallen.

She was dimly aware of the Dinka villagers seated around her. The soldiers who had gathered for the excitement had gone back to their business, which appeared to mostly consist of sitting around and smoking.

Rachel held her face in her hands. It was *Dhor* who had betrayed them and tipped the army off as to where to find them? The kind-faced rebel soldier who had helped them see through the false slave scam? The driver who had first brought them to Akwer Nhom?

The Christian?

All along she'd thought it had been that Muslim middleman. Who else could it have been? Not once had she suspected betrayal by a fellow Christian. Not here, not with so much at stake. Not when they had come here in the name of Christ.

She felt nauseated. Was it Dhor's excellent English that had caused her to assume his absolute trustworthiness? Was it his round face and gentle eyes? Was it the fact that he'd protected them from a con artist? He certainly hadn't had to do that.

Never assume! She'd taught herself that, or so she'd thought.

Oh, Dhor. How much he'd seen! He'd been there when the TrackMark plane had brought in more supplies. He'd been there when General Deng had caught them returning with the redeemed slaves. Over the weeks they'd seen him at least one other time. He'd known or seen enough to get them all in trouble—and was certainly smart enough to have figured out the rest.

Rachel thought of a Michael Card song about Judas's betrayal of Jesus. Only a friend can betray, he wrote, because the same action by an enemy is simply an attack. Someone has to have your trust before he can betray it.

She knew, of course, why she had so quickly given Dhor a place of confidence in her mind. It called to her incessantly like a persistent child tapping her shoulder. But she didn't want to admit it. Because it spoke of a kind of prejudice she liked to believe she was incapable of.

Or maybe it spoke to an area of sin she didn't want to let God deal with just yet.

What could have motivated Dhor to betray them? Was he a mole for Khartoum? Had he been constantly feeding information about the SPLA to the north and thus prolonging the war? Or was this his first act of treachery? He certainly had valuable information, something the north would gladly make him a rich man to discover. All it would've taken was a sick child who needed expensive medicine or great gambling debt—or regular, old-fashioned greed—to make a man, even a Christian, sell them out. Was it the almighty dollar that Dhor served?

She remembered something else he had said: "We are all slaves to something."

Could she add Christian men to her list of people she hated?

The thought struck her as simultaneously hilarious and horrific. Christians had failed her before; why did it feel so brutal this time? Maybe she should just add all men to that list.

But even as she thought it, she shot the idea down. It wasn't men she hated, nor Christian men. Nor even. . .

No, she wasn't ready to go there yet.

It wasn't the men; it was the sin. Maybe Michael Card would use that line in a song one day.

She remembered what Garth had said back in Akron about how in Bosnia it had been the Christians who were the aggressors, who had committed every kind of atrocity against the Muslim civilians.

But it didn't excuse what Dhor had done. She could imagine him skulking away through the night, meeting some cloaked figure by the light of a hooded lamp, receiving a bag full of money. Thirty pieces of silver, perhaps.

While she could easily assign her anger to him, it was really the greed and deceitfulness that she truly despised. And the last time she checked, the market on greed and deceitfulness had not been cornered by Christian men. Nor men in general.

Nor Muslim men.

There. It was said.

Rachel felt a disquieting shift inside her now that she'd finally allowed the thought to be voiced. Something very old and very familiar detached itself from the roof of her abdomen where for decades it had both comforted and poisoned her.

The person who had hurt her the most on this trip was not a Muslim, but a Christian. It was not the middleman who traded in human lives nor the Baggara who sliced throats for fun nor the Antonov pilot who bombed civilians. But a brother in Christ.

Those other men, the Muslims, were not less guilty because they had not committed this particular crime. She knew they would've done it in a minute if they'd had the chance. But they had not done this one. Of this one sin, this one time, they were innocent. In a manner of speaking, in respect to this sin, they were more righteous than Dhor, the Christian.

A Muslim more righteous than a Christian.

Betrayed not by a Muslim but by a Christian.

It was as if two doors stood open before her. If she went through the one on the left, she would simply redouble her hatred. She would consider all men—all people—guilty and treacherous until proven otherwise. That old growth could reattach itself to her gut, and she could go right on squeezing out hate like paste from a tube.

The other door was much scarier. On the other side there was delight and sun, but the price of entry was too high. To go that way, she had to lay aside her suit of armor, the Kevlar heart she'd developed to keep out the piercing ache of death and loss and grief.

And suddenly she was back to that amazing morning in Tiberias. It was a school holiday, and the Sea of Galilee sparkled with all the joy and hope of a five-year-old Jewish girl's eyes. She remembered the salty breeze that always smelled like warmth to her and the fishy reek of the docks.

She saw again in her mind the Palestinian man charging across the street toward her father's hotel, his body wrapped in bright white robes. Even as a young girl, she felt his behavior strange. She remembered running across the green lawn toward the lobby doors. Her daddy would let her have a pastry if she got there before they cleared away breakfast. Also she wanted to see if the man would run up the stairs or wait for the elevator.

It hadn't sounded like a bomb at first. She heard the explosion and the breaking glass, just as she'd heard in the Tel Aviv market the year before when she was there with Mommy. Everybody knew bombs were not allowed in hotels. Hannah the waitress must've dropped her tray again.

It wasn't until the people had run outside—limping, bleeding, screaming—that she'd known something was wrong. Black smoke and the shriek of alarms chased them out.

No one paid attention to her, so she simply ran inside.

Several people lay on the ground as if tossed there. Blood covered the shiny floor in pools of shocking red. The man in the white robes was in the middle of them. His body was missing some parts. Who had hurt him so terribly, and why?

The elevators opened and people ran out. The doors to the restaurant and the pool and the stairs were open, too, as people kept running out, screaming.

She spotted her daddy lying on the floor. She went to him and knelt down. His eyes were wide open. Such beautiful eyes, like the soft leather chairs in the lounge. Eyes that made her feel protected and pretty and strong. He had nasty cuts on his neck and chest and tiny nicks like chicken pecks all over his face and arms.

"Daddy, you'd better get up. There's a big mess. And can you please turn off the alarm! It's hurting my ears."

Policemen arrived then. They shouted louder than the alarm and ran around very angry. Daddy would never allow people to behave like that in his hotel, even policemen.

"Daddy, could you tell them to be more polite? They will scare the guests."

Later, people told her she'd sat there talking to her father's corpse for twenty minutes before someone had finally thought to take her outside. It wasn't until she was going to bed that night—without her daddy's kiss—that she finally understood he was gone.

"He's with Abraham now," her mother had said.

"Abraham Yakov? Does Daddy need a newspaper?"

"No, darling Rachel. Your father is dead. He is gone. We will not see him ever again, except in the hereafter if it is allowed by the Most High."

She remembered crying. "But he said he was going to take me on the boat with the tourists!"

Such are the thoughts of a five-year-old girl. It wasn't long afterward that she realized it meant much more than a broken promise that her father was gone. But the one thing she learned from it all, the one new truth she gained about the universe, was that a Muslim man had taken her daddy away.

Sometimes she wondered what she would've been like if she'd not lost her father that day. If he were still alive, how would she be different? Surely she would not have killed, as she had with the Mossad. Surely she would not be so filled with hate that her vision blurred. Surely she would not use the arousing effect she had on men to deceive and destroy.

But what about the good things? Would she ever have seen as much of the world as she had, had the suicide bomber gone somewhere else that bright morning? Would she have ever served in Paris at the Israeli consulate? Would she have ever come to Christ?

Certainly she would not be in Sudan having done so much good for a cruelly oppressed people.

Like Anei.

Rachel looked at the young girl now. She was singing softly with her father and a circle of other Dinka. Lual stroked Anei's cornrow braids with his massive hand.

As He had done with Joseph in Egypt, God had worked in Rachel's life to take what was meant for evil and use it for great good, the saving of many lives. Her father's death had been the worst kind of tragedy. And yet here she was, heaping good onto the cosmic scales. Measured in human lives, the work she had done with the Firebrand team represented much more good than the evil that had been done to her.

It was a frightening thought. Had she finally overcome that evil with good? What would it mean for her to let go of that anger? Wouldn't she be betraying her father?

She would never *thank* God for that Muslim suicide bomber and the evil he had committed, and it wouldn't be God's way to ask that of her. All He asked was thankfulness *in the midst* of every situation—not thankfulness *for* every situation. But maybe. . .today. . .finally. . .she could switch off the hate.

"Rachel?"

It was Anei, touching her on the shoulder.

"Yes, little gazelle?" Rachel answered in Dinka.

"Will you pray with us?"

Rachel looked at the circle of villagers sitting on the dirt, some without limbs, their clothes in tatters—but saw only tranquil eyes and furtive smiles. Her spirit lunged toward them, yearning to join their circle like a drop of mercury merging with the rest.

"Of course."

Anei sat in her lap. Lual sat on her left. Four more Dinka completed the circle: the chief, two old women, and a teenage boy with only a left arm.

"Are we praying for deliverance?" she asked. "Or for a miracle?"

"Yes," the chief said through Lual's interpretation. "We have seen Christ God do many miracles. We will ask Him for another today—a miracle of deliverance. But we pray for something else, too."

The chief didn't finish the thought. He stared instead at Lual, a glimmer of a smile forming on his lips.

Lual's smile shone like the sun on chrome. "We pray for our enemies."

And then, without waiting for the thunderclap that had struck inside Rachel's heart to fade away, he took her hand and shut his eyes.

"Christ, God of Lual, God of Akwer Nhom Dinka, hear this prayer. You are mightiest of gods. Show everyone here today Your greatness. Shake the earth apart and set us free. But if You don't want to do that, then shake the hearts of these our enemies. Break away the brush hiding their eyes so they can see how much better You are than Allah. Give them the great calmness and laughter You have given us. So that we will all shout to You together and there will be no more war. Jesus is the powerful name we say this in. Amen."

"Amen!" the others answered.

The chief prayed next, but Rachel didn't hear. She had her own business to attend to.

*O Father. Mightiest of gods. Jesus, I. . .I think I'm ready for You to do some work in me. There's that one room in my heart that I've never given You the key to. But You just couldn't leave it alone, could You? You kept knocking. I'm actually amazed You didn't give up on me.*

Tears slipped out of her eyes and dropped with a *ptt* to her camouflage pants.

*I can't do it, Lord. I can't let go. How can You ask me to pray for that man? He murdered my father!*

A verse popped into her mind: *"Whatever you bind on earth will be bound in heaven, and whatever you loose on earth will be loosed in heaven."*

*I don't care, Lord. I don't even know what that means. But if it means my hatred here can bind that man to hell for eternity, then. . .*

She couldn't say it. Strange.

*I don't know, Father. I guess I do want to get right about this.*

She sighed.

*Okay, let's do it. Lord, help me out here. I. . .I want to ask You to forgive the man who murdered my father.*

She stopped. Had she actually prayed that?

*And I want to ask You to forgive me for being furious at him for so long. I know that's not Your will. But me? I can't. . .I can't forgive him. No, not yet. I don't even want to. I don't want to release him and his kind from that penalty. But. . .he's dead, isn't he? I guess the only one bound here is me.*

She sighed again.

*Okay. Father, I miss my daddy so much. But I know I have to let him go, too. Jesus, could You make me want to forgive that man and those like him?*

Even as she prayed it, she felt her heart sloughing off its plate armor. It chilled her, but invigorated her, too. Feeling as though this moment might never come again, she rushed the next part through.

*I forgive him, Lord. By Your power, I forgive that man. And I want*

*You to forgive him, too. Please, Lord. I don't know how I'm saying this, but I mean it. Release that man, Father. Loose him, whatever that means. I release him, too. And forgive Dhor, Father, for his sin. Forgive these men here for their sin and bring them to You so that we can. . . shout to You together and there will be no more war.*

She started laughing in her crying. She felt ludicrous, like two people inside a horse costume trying to go different ways. Because even as she sat under armed guard in the middle of an enemy military camp, surrounded by natives destined for utter slavery, in a land of bitter bondage. . .

She was free.

The Dinka in the circle were watching her with kind eyes. Lual's big hand stroked her hair now. She collapsed against his chest, crying out years of bitterness as if lancing a cyst.

"Is it my turn to pray?" she finally asked.

Lual translated her question into Dinka, and the others laughed heartily. The old women were weeping and smiling. How long had she been sitting there blubbering? It didn't matter to them. They loved her in Christ.

Rachel hugged Anei to her chest and closed her eyes to pray with the group.

That was when the tank exploded.

# CHAPTER 25

## SURPRISE

RACHEL turned to look down into the valley floor. One of the tanks parked beside the smoking ruins of the village was on fire. A crewman, his clothes aflame, crawled screaming out of the turret and fell all the way to the ground.

Across the wide valley, the soldiers and horsemen simply watched. Perhaps they thought, as Rachel did, that there had been some kind of weapons malfunction.

When three rockets streaming gray smoke shot up the valley and struck two more tanks and one of the jeeps, that theory pretty much evaporated.

"Attack!" the men shouted. "We're under attack!"

"To the tanks!"

"Where's my unit?"

"Get out of my way!"

Machine guns opened up at both the north and south ends of the valley, their lethal voices ripping the relative calm. Bullets struck tanks and tents and men. Man and beast cried out in fear. The soldiers dove for cover and began firing back, but at what, Rachel couldn't see. More explosions and heavy weapons' fire came from beyond the trees on both sides of the valley.

The men guarding the Dinka captives ran for cover. Only one of the three even looked back at them. But a bullet struck the tree trunk beside him, and he ran away.

"Come on!" Rachel said to the Dinka. "Now's our chance." She hauled Anei and Lual to their feet. To the chief, she said: "Get your people to the hideout. Go!"

The forty villagers cowered like kittens against the noise and fire of the gunfight below.

The scars on Lual's forehead rose. "What is happening?"

"Who cares?" Rachel said, pulling the chief to his feet. "The enemy of my enemy is my friend, okay?" She looked at the others. "Get up! Follow the chief. Run now or become slaves forever."

The chief and Lual called to them with authority. Finally they stood and started moving south down the treeline.

Anei looked back. "Rachel, come!"

"Just a minute, Anei. Keep your father safe, okay? Get him out of here."

Anei smiled—a preview of strength and beauty from the woman she would become—and tugged at her father's hand.

Rachel scanned the valley. Men in assorted camouflage uniforms or blue jeans and T-shirts swarmed into the valley from the north edge. As the tank crews ran to their machines, the invaders screamed and grappled with them hand-to-hand. The tanks that had crews were blocked in by those that didn't. One turret was swiveling toward the north, and at least two other men fired the machine guns mounted atop their tanks' turrets.

Men on both sides were dying rapidly, and for the moment Rachel was forgotten. At the bottom of the slope she stood on, in a spot completely exposed to fire from both sides, she spied her helmet and gun in a pile beside Chunky and her ATV. Could she get to Chunky and activate its buca effect—that flashing—that made everybody sick? As she watched, the ATV's rear left wheel took a hit and was instantly flat. It would be the height of foolishness to run down the slope to try to collect that gear.

She ran down the slope.

A pair of MiG-29s shrieked up the valley, bombs and missiles under their wings. The next pass wouldn't be simply noisy.

She left the cover of the trees just as a rocket-propelled grenade leapt from the south end of the valley and detonated inside the command tent.

Rachel tumbled as shrapnel and debris pelted the ground all around her. But even as she fell, she kept herself rolling toward her goal. As she came to her knees, sand pouring off her, she saw more rebel troops running up the valley from the south. They might be on her side, but they wouldn't know that until they examined her body if she wasn't careful.

She lunged-crawled-ran the final ten yards to her gear and dove to the ground behind the dubious protection of the ATV.

A tank driver crunched his steel beast into gear, and it accelerated south, the massive treads passing less than twelve feet from her, its body-mounted machine gun firing continuously and its main gun swiveling for a shot.

Rachel jammed her helmet on first, glad for once of its tight fit and noise dampers. Still lying on the ground, she strapped her backpack on next. She threw the MP5's self-retracting strap across her back and reached for Lewis's PackBot.

"Leave it."

Had somebody said that to her or was it the voice of God? She looked around.

The tank fired. The flame and smoke it spit out its deadly snout rocked the metal monster backward and thumped the ground like a seismic event. When the boom faded on this end, less gunfire came from the other end.

Rachel lifted the little robot into her lap. How was she going to carry this who knew how far?

"Put it down, Rachel. Leave it."

This time she heard where the voice was coming from. She looked up the slope she'd just run down. And looked right into Jason's eyes.

Such beautiful eyes. Eyes like the moors of Scotland in a rainstorm. Eyes that made her feel protected and pretty and strong.

To her right, she heard the MiGs returning. Then came a whistling sound she remembered from the bridge.

\* \* \*

"Hit the deck!" Jason shouted.

He dove beside a tree trunk and went fetal on his side, hoping the rest of his team would have the good sense to follow suit.

The flash was what he encountered first this time. Even with his eyes squeezed shut, it turned the darkness behind his eyelids a pasty pink. The shockwave ran him over like a freight train flattening a penny. He heard the *kk* part of the explosion—the intake before the outburst—but the noise limiters clamped down, and he heard the *WHAM* as through a dozen buckshot comforters.

When the main hail of debris had landed, Jason dared a look into the valley. The trees at the north end were mostly gone. What remained, trees or otherwise, lay burning on the ground. A lot of SPLA troops had just died.

Down the slope below him, Rachel stirred. She rose to her knees and looked from Chunky to him.

"Come on, Rachel! Get up here."

On his right, Garth and Chris broke down the hill to Rachel's side.
*Aw, nuts. Here we go again.*

Jason got up and ran after them, providing rearguard as they pulled Rachel up the slope. As he backed upward, two more M-60s extricated themselves from the gridlock and began driving directly toward him.

"Let's go!" he shouted.

"We're here!" Chris shouted back. "Come on."

He turned and ran the rest of the way up.

Back amid the trees, Jason saw that Lewis had the robot in his arms. "Lewis! Leave it! Let's go."

"I'm not leaving him!"

A barrage of explosions behind him sent Jason to the ground for cover. But to his great relief, he didn't explode into tiny Jason nuggets. "Missed!"

"Nope," Garth said, looking across the valley.

The smoke trails of six rocket-propelled grenades still floated on the air. Below, two more tanks burned. On the far ridge, a dozen soldiers brought their RPG launchers to their shoulders and let fly their rockets toward the motor pool.

"Like fish in a barrel," Chris said.

For the moment, no one shot at them, although terrifying sounds of battle boomed from all sides, stretching out into the distance. Lewis set Chunky down and punched something into his computer terminal. Trieu checked Rachel while Garth plugged her helmet into her backpack computer and got it up and running.

Jason took Rachel's face in his hands. She looked tired beyond belief. He felt his own insides somersaulting over getting her back safely. Words came to him in a jumble, all of them sounding ridiculous. So he just bent down and kissed her on the mouth.

She stumbled back, holding her helmet and looking surprised—and maybe a little wistful.

"Repeat after me," he said, pointing at her nose, "I cannot be Rambo."

A hint of a smile touched the sides of her mouth.

"Come on," Garth said, "we're not out of this yet."

The MiGs strafed the other hillside with their 30mm cannons. Decapitated trees rained leaves and woodchips on the beclouded ridge. If anything still lived over there, it would be ten minutes before anyone could find out about it.

"Which way, Kromer?" Chris said.

Jason went to one knee and envisioned where they were on his map. "We head south along this ridge. The rebels came up from that way, so maybe it's still clear. We punch through the fighting and find someplace secure to wait it out until nightfall. Then we use night vision gear to go anywhere we please."

"What about the four-wheelers?" Trieu asked.

Jason looked down at Rachel's ATV. Besides its flat tire, it had been scorched by the tank burning beside it. "That one's no good and our others have probably been discovered. Anyway, they're east and we're going south."

Rachel rose to her knees and pointed into the valley. "Look!"

Five heavily armed GOS soldiers rushed toward the only jeep left untouched in the valley floor. They were escorting two officers.

"You know them, Raych?" Chris asked.

"Yeah."

She waved until one of the officers looked her way.

"What are you doing?" Garth said. "Stay down."

The officer took out binoculars and trained them on Rachel and the team. Rachel blew him a kiss. He lowered his glasses and shouted to his men. But his orders were never carried out, because shells began to cook off inside the first tank that had been hit. The turret flew twenty feet into the air and smashed down beside the officer and his bodyguard. They ran for cover and were lost to view behind a column of smoke.

"Okay," Jason said, "let's go. Chris, take point. Garth, cover our tails. Patrol formation. Move out."

Rachel held up her MP5. "I'm out of ammo."

"Lewis," Jason said, "give Rachel some of your extra mags. Hey, where's that thing going?"

The PackBot was moving away at walking speed.

"South," Lewis said, pulling a few magazines of Versed darts from pockets in his load-bearing vest and handing them to Rachel. "You're right: I can't carry him. But I'm not going to just leave him, either. I gave him the GPS coordinates of a village near the border and told him to get there any old way he can." He nodded his chin toward the little robot. "He'll probably be the only one of us that makes it."

Garth looked back at the team from his position at the rear. "Jason. . .time to go now. Bad things coming."

"Right," Jason said, turning to Chris. "Take us there, skitch."

In combat, Jason had learned, all the normal rules of civilization are out the window. The soldier in a combat zone violates laws of ownership, property, borders, and civic behavior constantly and at will. The only rule is survival. It's a much simpler way to live, really. If you are in an urban combat zone and you get hungry, you kick open a door and raid someone's fridge. If you are on a shoreline battlefield and you must escape, you get on the nearest boat and motor away. Cars, guns, water, medicine—even shaving kits and toothbrushes—become the property of the soldier under fire.

The only problem is returning home and having to put that burden of societal propriety back on your shoulders. Some people couldn't do it.

Jason slipped back into combat mode as easily as into his favorite pair of jeans. There was only one truth now, one simple goal that lit his path like a headlamp: Get the team out alive. In this moment, the Dinka did not matter, did not even exist. Slaves and slavery did not matter. The causes of the civil war in Sudan did not matter. Even Eloise, Bigelow, Akron, Utah, America, and the world itself faded into insignificance. All that mattered was survival.

The universe shrunk around Jason like a deflating balloon. There were near threats, distant threats, and safety. The uniforms didn't matter—bullets from a friend would kill them just as quickly as bullets from an enemy. As the team moved south with cautious speed along the wooded ridge of a river long extinct, the world divided itself into these categories.

Near threats: Company-strength light infantry in the valley ahead; three armored platoons advancing on them from the north; twenty to thirty cavalrymen to the right, flanking the infantry or maneuvering against other opponents.

Distant threats: Sounds of mechanized units fighting to the east, west, and south; fighter/bombers above but currently elsewhere; heaviest fighting to the right and in the valley behind. No one was shooting at them just now.

"Hey, Lewis," Rachel said over the squad radio.

"Yeah?"

"When we get out of this, remind me to talk to you about putting some kind of password or something on these helmets."

"Why?"

"The soldiers had my gear. They couldn't figure out how to work it; but if they had, they would've seen where you guys were on the dot map."

Jason thought he heard his whole team take a gasp of air.

"O-okay, Raych," Lewis said. "I'll get right on it."

Chris stopped in front and went to a knee. "Problem."

Jason knelt beside him and looked ahead. "What?"

"We're out of trees."

The flattest, driest, most exposed prairie Jason had seen since Kazakhstan lay before him now. There was no thatch, no village, no elephant grass, no tukul, no airstrip, no rotting truck carcass, no tribe of helpful Dinka—not even a mama wildebeest—between their position and where the edge of the earth butted up against dark gray clouds just now swallowing the sun. A pair of Antonov AN-26 bombers moved along far to their left. Sounds of fighting were lost here, blown into submission by the steady wind.

Jason whistled. "Well, anybody got a better idea than just hightailing it across this flatland and not stopping for five miles?"

He heard sighs and saw belts being cinched tighter, but received no complaints.

"At least we ought to blend in well," Lewis said. "Whoever figured out desert camos was a genius."

"Okay," Jason said, standing, "let's do it. Safety or bust."

Chris strode out ten paces, his CAR-15 to his shoulder. He swept the horizon from left to right, just as Jason did with his binoculars and Trieu did with her scope. Chris swung back to the left. "Clear."

He took off forward in a crouched jog, his rifle at his shoulder. Jason came next, watching their right flank. Trieu followed, watching the left. Then came Lewis and Rachel. Garth brought up the rear, watching behind them.

The temperature dropped as the cloud wall thickened across the sun. The horizon on Jason's side was an unbroken navy blue band from the ground up. A distant fork of lightning stabbed downward like God spearfishing. The grass here was brittle and the earth was hard, but it made for excellent cross-country running and very little dust. The team made it a good three hundred yards from cover before their little field trip became the center of the battlefield.

# CHAPTER 26

## CHAOS THEORY

*NOT GOOD.*

Fifty Sudanese tanks raced south at the team's right. Behind Jason's team, mechanized units of SPLA troops rushed southeast. Even as they established a hasty line facing south, the southernmost tank platoons wheeled around and faced north.

The Firebrand team was right in the middle.

"Looks like the GOS broke through the encirclement," Jason said.

"Cut the Annapolis report, admiral," Chris said. "We're in deep poodoo."

"I'm just saying," Jason said, "that it looks like the tanks left over are trying to flank the rebels and come in from the side before the main force can reset their lines. That's what I would do."

Lewis shook his head. "I don't get it. Why send all these tanks and stuff just to get us six?"

"They're not just here for us, Lewis," Chris said. "They don't know for sure that it's just six of us. Besides, they come out here every year, remember? We're just their excuse this time."

"Okay, chief," Garth said to Jason, "what are we going to do to get out of this?"

Trieu motioned with a flat hand to the ground. "Can we just lay low and let them pass by?"

"And hope we don't get run over?" Lewis said.

Jason nodded. "I don't see any other—"

A descending scale whistle sounded above them.

"Incoming!"

The team flattened themselves. The ground pulsed beneath them, and a wide fountain of dirt and grass erupted fifty yards beyond them, between them and the tanks.

"The rebels have artillery," Garth said, almost in awe.

Jason looked back toward where the valley emptied out onto this plain and saw four puffs of smoke cough up from the eastern ridge. "More coming!"

The sound of the big guns firing reached them at the same moment the shells impacted the earth; but the sound of the explosions themselves followed almost instantly, giving a double-whammy that made Jason's innards feel loose.

"Here they come!" Chris shouted.

Jason looked south. Six platoons of tanks rushed toward them in a staggered line. They were still about a mile away, but closing at over forty miles an hour. An unemotional part of his brain noted that at least two platoons had broken off from the others and were headed northeast. They passed behind a low mound and then popped out the other side. In another ten seconds, the main body of tanks would be within the artillery's range.

"Everybody stay flat," he said. "They won't be expecting anyone to be out here, so they'll be coming in a straight line. You should have plenty of time to dodge them. I can't think you'd have to dodge more than once or twice."

"Oh, great," Lewis said. "I only have to dodge *two* battle tanks. He says it like it's a good thing."

Rachel moaned. "I hate just waiting here. What if they start aiming those big guns closer right when the tanks go by?"

"Nah," Garth said, "they're terrible shots. Won't be a problem."

Jason didn't answer. Why worry the girl any more than necessary? He hated sitting there, too. He felt like the Scots in *Braveheart*, standing in place while the English heavy cavalry thundered toward them. And it was certain that the gunners *would* adjust their aim and could quite easily drop their deadly shells right on top of their heads.

"Something's wrong," Chris said. "They should be closer now."

Jason looked. The tanks were still kicking up dust, but they weren't moving. Only the high-frequency creaking of their treads reached him across the distance. He reached for his binoculars, his nose detecting the scent of rain.

"They're stuck," he said, looking through the glasses. "It looks like mud or a swamp or something. They're spinning and sliding. At least one's in up to its turret."

"Oh, yeah!" Lewis said.

"Is that good for us or not?" Trieu asked.

"It's good," Jason said. "Come on, let's try to cut over to that low hill on our left. Maybe we can duck out from under the artillery and be out of the way before the tanks get unstuck."

Chris led them at a controlled run due east. Occasionally artillery rounds would fly overhead and the team would hit the dirt, but then they'd be up and running again. A raindrop struck Jason's cheek.

After thirty yards, Trieu and Rachel spoke in unison: "Uh, oh."

Jason looked to his left. The SPLA units were advancing—infantry, jeeps, dune buggies, and motorcycles. "Yeah," he said. "Seizing their advantage. I would charge, too. Let's be sure we're out of the middle before they—"

"Trouble!" Garth said from the rear. "Cavalry coming up fast."

A line of Baggara raiders charged toward the Firebrand team, on a path that would drive them into the SPLA's flank when they intersected.

"More trouble," Lewis said, pointing to the team's right. "The tanks have gotten loose."

The tanks rumbled deeply. Their treads squeaked like old joints. The diesel engines whirred and ramped up in pitch like a bulldozer stampede. Then the rumbling became articulated—a choppy sound like a car accelerating across a road of railroad ties. Jason couldn't pull his eyes from the rolling treads, conveyor belts of death.

"I've got the worst news yet," Chris said from point. "Some tanks swung around east and are now closing on us at full speed."

An image from the movie *The Four Feathers* sprang into Jason's mind: an outnumbered phalanx of British troops being charged upon from all directions at once.

He looked at his team. They were hunched down in the knee-high grass, but it was inevitable they'd be found. *O Lord, help.* The noise had shut their helmet speakers down, but it only continued to crescendo. He gathered his team in his gaze but stared mainly at Rachel and Trieu.

"Stay together!" he shouted. "Wait for them to pass, then make for the hill. Stay down!"

And then time stopped. In perfect clarity, like a paused DVD, Jason saw the moment the final battle began. Five tanks fired their main guns. The shells were silver gleams in the cloudy light, frozen in a bizarre *Matrix* still-frame that Jason could walk around inside. On the other side, three RPGs hung on smoke ropes tied to the launchers on men's shoulders. To the west, the first Baggara rider's sword was stuck as if bronzed into a man's shoulder. To the east, an orderly flight of bullets sprayed across the battlefield like a high-speed photo of a man watering his lawn with a hose. Overhead, a bomb rolled off an Antonov's cargo ramp. He could see the foot of the man who'd kicked it out. Two MiG-29s stood on their wings as if mounted there by a modeler. On the hillside to the north, three of the howitzers blew smoke from their muzzles.

Then time switched to fast-scan.

Two screaming men ran over Jason's head.

One tripped and fell, where he was crushed beneath a Baggara stallion.

Treads reared up before him, sucking everything into the crusher. He dove out of the way.

*Fire burning in the grass. Get away from it.*
*Shadow passing over me.*
*Shockwave throwing a horse and rider to the ground.*
*Shoot that one with pepper.*
*Two tanks colliding.*
*Rachel firing her gun. Looking deadly and beautiful.*
*A gap. Run for it.*
*Whump-whump-whump.*
*Men fighting hand-to-hand. Stay low.*
*Another tank coming. The size of it!*
*No, it's hit by a rocket.*
*Trieu and Lewis dodging horsemen.*
*Chris tossing a smoke grenade.*
*Screaming man lunging at me with bayonet.*
*Sweep point away.*
*Grip the rifle stock.*
*Punch in face. Kick in solar plexus. Stab with bayonet.*
*No, don't stab.*
*Throw gun down and move.*
*The earth rippling like water?*
*Men climbing on a muddy tank. Trying to get in.*
    *Opening the hatch. Grenade.*
*Tank swerves. Men falling off.*
*Grenade!*
*Am I hurt?*

*Where is my team?*
*Garth pulling a man off a horse. Good, go there.*
*A nice rain shower.*
*Pushed from behind. Roll over.*
*Baggara cutting down with his sword.*
*Arms up!*
*Baggara bayoneted. Pushed off me. His blood's on my face.*
*Trampled by my rescuer.*
*Roll up. Move toward the hill.*
*More tanks.*
*Who is that screaming?*
*Is that rocket turning to chase that MiG?*
*So many bodies.*
*Look, most of the tanks are past me now.*
*Chris in front of me, motioning me to him.*
*The others are there.*
*They're yelling at me, but I can only see their lips move.*
*Trieu is pulling Garth's boot off. There's no blood,*
  *but his leg is bending where he's not supposed to have a knee.*
*Is Lewis crying?*
*I need to go back to them now. They need me.*

"Okay," Jason heard himself saying. "Okay, okay, okay, okay. I'm here. I'm back. What's happening?"

"Garth is hurt!" Chris was yelling. "A tank clipped his leg. Wake up, Kromer!"

"No, I'm all right," Garth said, pulling his CAR-15 up and firing.

A Sudanese infantryman fell coughing to the ground at Jason's feet. Rachel shot him in the leg with her MP5, and Jason sat on him for thirteen seconds.

Trieu looked from Garth's leg to Jason. "His tibia and fibula are fractured. There is no pulse in his foot. I've got to straighten his leg or his foot will become ischemic and die."

"Straighten that?" Lewis said. "Oh, no."

"It can wait," Garth said through clenched teeth. "I feel fine."

"I doubt that. But you can't wait unless you want to lose the foot."

Jason looked around. The battle was moving north, but scores of men still fought hand-to-hand or scurried about close to the ground. A dozen tanks were fighting their way toward the SPLA artillery. Riderless horses galloped away from the noise, their tassels and bells bouncing merrily. Hundreds of wounded or dead soldiers lay around them. A sword stood upright in the dirt. Thunder rolled above them. The temperature had dropped. Rain fell gently. Thirty tanks lay burning or abandoned. A massive fire burned half a mile to the west, where part of Jason's mind remembered seeing a MiG go down in flames.

To Trieu, he said: "Can you do it fast?"

She answered by pointing at Chris and Lewis. "Hold him so he doesn't move." As they grabbed Garth's arms, Trieu sat at his feet. She picked up the injured leg. It wobbled obscenely in the wrong direction. She put one of her feet up against Garth's tailbone and steadied the wounded leg in her arms. She took a deep breath. "This is going to hurt." Without waiting for a reply, she yanked her body backward like a competition rower.

Garth cried out, and Jason heard a sickening crunch.

Trieu's hand was on Garth's foot. "I've got a pulse!"

"Hurry," Rachel said. "The grass is moving over there. Something's strange about it."

Trieu dug in her backpack and produced what looked like a giant rubber sleeve. "Help me get this on his leg." While Jason slid it over the leg, Trieu bent down and began inflating it by mouth. "It's a splint," she said between breaths. "He'll be able to walk."

In no time the splint was fully inflated and held Garth's leg snugly.

"How does it feel?" Trieu asked Garth.

"Terrible. But not as bad as before you straightened it."

Jason noticed Lewis holding his ribs. "What's wrong with him?"

"Horse fell on him," Garth said. "My fault."

"No," Lewis said, wheezing. "You did good. Accident."

"Fractured ribs," Trieu said, helping Garth to his feet. "He can travel."

Jason nodded, though he found his hands were shaking violently. He gripped his boots. "Is everybody else okay? Can we all walk?"

Suddenly twenty infantrymen rose up from the grass and charged the team, bayonets lowered.

Jason launched his tear gas canister at them. Beside him, he heard his team firing tranquilizer darts and pepperballs.

Then to his right, another dozen infantrymen put down the SPLA soldiers they were fighting and added themselves to the charge. The moment felt familiar somehow. Then he remembered: the ambush in Utah.

"Australian peel!" he shouted to his team. "Make for the hill. Fall back."

He pulled two smoke grenades off his vest and tossed them both between the team and the infantrymen, thirty yards away and closing. As his team moved away, he stood alone against the rush, firing both his CAR-15 and his pepperball pistol.

Ghostly figures writhed in the cloud of smoke and tear gas and pepper powder. He heard them shout and fall and cough.

His guns were empty. He hoped somebody was ready behind him, because he'd done all he could do. He turned and ran.

The Firebrand team was arrayed perfectly before him. Chris fired pepperballs to either side of Jason as he retreated. As Jason passed, he heard Chris fire the tear gas launcher. Again men cried out behind him. Except now they were firing their weapons—blindly, maybe, but in the right general direction. Jason went as low as he could while staying on his feet.

He passed Trieu next. She sat on the ground, elbows on knees, as her Dragunov spat cones of gas at the infantry. Jason was amazed at the sheer calmness on her face—a calmness reflected in her methodical actions. He saw a smoke grenade and her pepperball pistol on the grass beside her, ready for when she would be the point of their retreating spear.

Ahead was Lewis, just dropping down in his position. He gripped his side tightly, and his right arm was clamped against his ribcage; but when he turned around, his jaw was clenched and his MP5 was up and ready. Jason put a new tear gas canister in his launcher.

Rachel hurried on ahead, helping Garth limp. Jason relieved her of Garth. She pulled a smoke grenade off her vest and chambered a round of Versed into her submachine gun.

Behind them the gunfire increased. The tear gas had probably been blown off by the wind on the savannah. This would've been a bad situation even if they'd had real bullets and grenades and no compunctions about using them.

Before Jason had gotten Garth to his position twenty yards beyond Rachel, the big guy had a pepper powder claymore in his hands. Jason dropped him just as Chris arrived in retreat. They ran together twenty yards toward the hill, still a hundred yards away. Then Jason dropped, and Chris went on another twenty yards.

While he reloaded his rifle, Jason turned to see his team executing the Australian peel with expertise, if also brevity. Trieu was zigzagging back toward them on the damp ground. Lewis was firing on full auto, but the Sudanese were almost upon him, charging again with bayonets. Lewis got up and ran, tossing two smoke grenades at the pack but not waiting to see where they landed.

Some of the soldiers fell coughing. Others tried to wave the smoke away. But a few lowered their assault rifles and fired.

Trieu was twenty feet from Jason when she was hit. She spun awkwardly to the right, crying out in surprise and pain. She hit the ground hard, her sniper rifle falling from her hand and then reeling against her chest before she'd stopped rolling.

"Trieu!"

Jason ran for her, firing tear gas from the lower barrel and pepperballs from the upper. He and Lewis reached her at the same time. She was conscious, but a dark stain spread out from under her backpack.

"Oh, no!" Lewis shouted. "Not Trieu. She's our doctor! How can we—"

"Go, Lewis!" Jason shouted. "Take your place in the peel."

With a look of panic, Lewis turned and ran.

Rachel moved to a position between Jason and the attackers to cover their retreat.

Jason picked Trieu up like a child and pounded the earth toward the hill, now eighty yards away.

Rachel emptied her magazine and had to run. Chris took point and opened fire on full automatic.

The soldiers alternated from charging to shooting and back. But always they persisted, perhaps stuck on the realization that there were sixty-five wolves and only six sheep.

Jason passed Garth, who had set his claymore and was crawling away, and looked for Lewis.

Lewis was sixty yards too far. Almost at the hill.

"Lewis!" Jason shouted. *He's done it again. Trieu getting hit freaked him out, and he's left the team again.*

Twenty soldiers ran around to Jason's left, flanking their line faster than they could retreat. He lowered Trieu to the ground and fired his last tear gas canister at them. That slowed their advance, but already the wind was whisking the gas away.

His team was split up again. Just like in Utah. Lewis was way off on his own. Garth was half-lunging, half-falling forward. Ammunition had run low. Trieu was losing blood. And still the soldiers kept coming.

Should he hold his ground and finish the fight here, where there were at least four from the Firebrand team who could shoot? Or should he lift Trieu again and make a mad dash for the doubtful safety of the hill? Bad option A or bad option B?

He felt Chris's presence, felt the pressure to make a decision before Chris tried to take over. But a fast bad decision wouldn't help anybody.

There had to be fewer attackers here. Half of them at least should be sleeping forgetfully. But more could arrive at any moment. Could they fend off thirty? In hand-to-hand, possibly—his team were all adept at martial arts, with the exception of Lewis, who was off on his own safari anyway. But if the thirty just stood up and fired, it would be all over.

Jason's eyes went to one of the many rifles lying around nearby. If he had to, he could just pick up one of those and do what navy SEALs do. That would solve the problem in a hurry.

A helmet-rocking explosion went off behind him, and twenty-five attackers disappeared in a white cloud.

Garth's claymore.

The smell of the powder reached Jason almost instantly. He put Trieu down and handed her his reloaded pepperball pistol. Her eyes were sleepy, but she was conscious. "Here, honey," he said, touching her rain-wet cheek. "Do what you can."

He pulled two flashbang grenades from his belt. "Chris, what say we take 'em now while they're down?"

Chris stopped firing and shot a look at him. "Are you crazy? There's fifty guys in there!"

"If we're going down," Jason said, pulling the flashbang triggers, "let's at least do it on our own terms."

"Look!" Rachel shouted, pointing to their right.

Jason turned. Ten trucks and other military vehicles—but no tanks or armored personnel carriers, thankfully—were coming up fast. He even saw a couple of dune buggies.

"Wait a minute," he said, "those are SPLA!"

"Jason!" Chris shouted. "The grenades!"

Jason cast them toward the infantrymen like explosive hot potatoes. *POW-POWWW!*

Men dropped their guns and fell to the ground holding their ears.

The dune buggy brigade roared up and stopped. Rebel soldiers piled out and engaged the stunned GOS soldiers.

"Come on!" Jason said. "Let's get out of here."

"Look out!"

The voice came from behind Jason. It was a voice he knew. He spun left and saw a huge black soldier with a bayonet in his hand running at him, murder in his eyes.

Jason braced for contact.

Four steps away, the man raised his hand across his body to deliver a wicked backhand slash. But then he winced and grabbed at his side.

Jason didn't care why. He dodged left, away from the blade, grabbed the man's uniform, and propelled him across an extended leg.

He fell hard, but quickly rolled. Chris smashed at the man's hand with the butt of his rifle.

"It's all right."

It was the same voice that had warned him. Jason turned to look. *"Lewis!"*

"It's okay, Jason," Lewis said, looking at the soldier. "Just stay away from him for another eight seconds or so."

The three of them backed away from the soldier. He smiled, perhaps pleased to have three soldiers apparently cowed by his awesome presence.

That was probably his last thought before he collapsed unconscious.

"Lewis!" Jason said, slapping Lewis on the shoulder, an action that made the kid wince. "You came back."

Lewis pointed his thumb over his shoulder. "Yeah, I. . . Anyway, glad you're okay."

"Come on," Chris said, lifting Trieu in his arms. "Let's go."

Jason helped Garth to his feet. Rachel and Lewis covered their retreat from the brawl still going on behind them. But even as they turned to go, GOS soldiers at the edge of the melee dropped their guns and fled across the open prairie, lightning flashing above them.

The rain turned heavier. The yellow grass quivered with every drop. Chris held his fist over Trieu's shoulder. Jason ran beside Garth, helping him move.

The hill was farther away than it had appeared, but that also meant it was higher. If they could get behind it and out of sight, they might be all right. They were twenty yards away from it, and Jason was feeling home free.

That should've been his first clue.

"We've got company!" Lewis shouted from his rearguard position. "Cavalry coming up fast."

Jason looked. Two hundred yards away, scores of Baggara horses galloped toward them in a line. The riders weren't all in white, but they appeared heavily armed. It was obvious they'd seen the team. Perhaps they'd pillaged the SPLA bodies and were riding hard for one more easy kill.

*Oh, great. Give me a break!*

"We can make the hill!" Rachel shouted.

"No, we can't!"

"We have to try."

"Run for it!"

Garth pushed Jason away. "Get the others out. I'll hold them off."

"No," Jason said, feeling his body flood with adrenaline. "We're not running. It doesn't matter if we make it to the hill if they're still chasing us. Come on, people, we can take a few punk slavers or we're not the team I thought we were."

He dropped his helmet and backpack to the ground and went to one knee.

The others came online beside him, reloading weapons with their last magazines. Chris propped Trieu up against his helmet and handed her the Dragunov. It drooped in her grip, but she might be able to get a shot off if she had to

The wet ground rumbled beneath them. Jason could feel the hooves pounding up his legs as if he were standing too close to rock concert speakers. He brought his CAR-15 to his shoulder and saw the rest of Team Firebrand raise their guns, too. Now it really was *Braveheart*.

"Ladies and gentlemen," Jason said, "it has been my great pleasure serving with you. No matter what happens next, I have been honored to serve as your leader."

"Yeah," Chris said with a smile for Jason. "It's been good."

"It won't come to that," Garth said.

"Oh, come on," Lewis said, "it's the Kobayashi Maru." He looked at Jason. "It's unwinnable."

Jason smirked. "Too late to reprogram the simulation?"

"I think so."

"You guys," Rachel said, "I love you all."

Jason spared a glance at her. She was looking at him. He nodded.

"Hey," Garth said, "I just had a funny idea."

"He's delusional," Chris said. "He must be going into shock."

Garth chuckled. "How 'bout we put these guys to sleep and then ride all the way to Kenya on their horses."

Jason nodded. "Goodonya, mate."

Garth looked at him. "You like that idea?"

"Fair dinkum."

"Bob's your uncle."

The horsemen were thirty yards away and coming hard. Jason picked out the one he was going to shoot first. He squeezed back on the trigger.

Looks of terror appeared on the riders' faces. They reined up and tried to swerve. Had they thought the team would be unarmed?

Just then the *whump-whump-whump* Jason had heard in the melee enveloped his being and throttled him like a chew toy. Against his will, he spun around.

And beheld a nightmare.

Three Mi-24 Hind helicopter gunships rose over the hill like wraiths up from the grave. They were beautifully lethal, like sharks. Their sides were mottled green. Weapons wings stretched out, bearing an arsenal of mayhem like a farmer hauling water. Rocket launchers, missile clusters, and tank-busting machine guns pointed at Jason and his team. Twin cockpit globes bulged on the front like eyes stacked vertically. The Gatling gun on the chin of the lead gunship swiveled forward.

Awash with the wet wind of the blades, stunned by the sheer power and noise, Jason could only stand there and wait for death. He saw the pilot in the center gunship point at him. The minigun swiveled to aim right at Jason's head. The barrel began to spin.

*Oh, sweet Jesus.*

When the rocket struck the helicopter, Jason thought it was the first hundred bullets from the Gatling gun striking him. He flinched and stumbled backward.

But then his mind caught up with what his eyes had told him: Someone had shot the helicopter with a missile.

The explosion shook the ground like a towel, toppling man and horse to the turf.

The helicopter listed left. Its rotors chopped through the gunship next to it, sending it spinning counterclockwise. The tail of it slammed into the first one, and they struck the far side of the hill together. Jason felt the heat of the impact explosion even through the hill. Still he couldn't move.

A rocket seared the air above him, and the third helicopter crumpled like a Coke can.

It crashed down at the hill's summit and perched there while it burned, metal pieces spilling out. An internal explosion belched fire toward Jason and the team, but it passed over their heads. The force of it sent the gunship tumbling away down the other side, where rockets from the others began to cook off.

It was then, while the pyrotechnics continued and a continuous stream of fireballs curled into the sky, that Jason realized who had saved his life. He stared at the horsemen. They had all dismounted. Most of the horses had run off a good distance. Two of the men held US-made Stinger antiaircraft missile launchers.

Jason faintly recognized the tall black man in a strange helmet who stepped toward him. "Hello. Do you remember me? I am General Deng of the SPLA. We have won our battle. Would you care for a lift?"

# CHAPTER 27

## REAR AREA

"WILL she be all right?"

Jason looked down at Trieu, who was sleeping on a cot in a long white tent lit by kerosene lamps.

Rachel looked up at the doctor, a slight man with curly brown hair and a bushy brown beard. She spoke to him in French. The doctor tucked his stethoscope in the pocket of his white lab coat and answered.

Jason couldn't understand the man's words, but his voice sounded positive; and when he looked at him, there was a sparkle in his eye.

Rachel shook his hand. *"Merci beaucoup."*

Jason shook his hand, too. *"Merci,* Doctor."

With a wink at Rachel, the doctor turned around and began looking to one of the many other patients in the tent.

Rachel looked at Jason shyly, seemingly unable to hold his gaze. "He said she will be fine."

Jason sighed mightily.

"The bullet broke up when it hit her shoulder blade," Rachel said, staring at the edge of Trieu's cot, "but he's sure he got the main pieces. The shoulder blade will heal like any other broken bone. You don't even have to set it."

Jason brushed Trieu's black bangs off her forehead. "Thank You, Jesus!"

Rachel sniffled.

Jason saw she was weeping. "What is it?"

She wiped tears from her cheek, leaving clean semicircles on her otherwise grimy face. "No. It's just that it hurts when I see you touch her like that."

"Rachel, I'm just—"

"Let me finish, okay? It hurts because I know you love her."

Jason opened his mouth to explain. But then again, how *was* he going to explain?

"It's okay, though," Rachel said, "because I've learned. . .I've. . . because I've learned to. . ." Crying overtook her.

Jason brought her into his arms. Was this a ploy to move him away from Trieu? While she sobbed against his shoulder, Jason looked down the tent toward the cot where Garth was sitting, his foot in a hard cast. He played cards with Lewis, who sat in the next bunk, and a couple of other people.

Rachel collected herself. She looked up at him with her glossy brown eyes. Jason saw *that look* return to her gaze, the look that was more debilitating than a double shot of oleoresin capsicum and Versed combined.

"It's okay," she repeated, "because I've learned to let go of those I. . .those I love." Her eyes filled with tears again, but she didn't stop talking. "Something happened to me when I was captured. No, nothing physical." She brought both hands to her sternum. "Something in here. God showed me some things that. . .weren't very pretty. But somehow His Spirit broke through—or I finally let Him break through, maybe." She laid her hands against his chest. "Jason, I want you to grow your relationship with Trieu. I'm a big girl. I'll be okay. And I have a big God. He'll take care of me. He'll bring someone else to me who will like me for more than my looks." She looked at him quickly, almost cautiously, then turned to go.

Jason took her by the shoulders. He spotted an empty bench beside a medical supplies table and guided her to it.

"Rachel, one day I want you to tell me everything that happened to you on your. . .adventure. But right now I want you to listen to me as I try to figure out what I have to say. Okay?"

Her smile pumped him with confidence.

"Okay," he said. "First, I have to tell you that I do have feelings for Trieu."

He glanced at Trieu. She was serenely beautiful in sleep, just as she was when awake. Her slender arms lay on the blanket, and more than anything Jason wanted to stroke them gently.

"She's kind and smart and beautiful. She's skilled at what she does. She plays the cello like nobody's business. And I don't think I've ever known anyone as spiritually mature as Trieu. Plus there's something about her. It's this centeredness, you know? This depth. She's like that picture of the lighthouse with the waves smashing around it. No matter what the sea throws at her, she just keeps beaming that pure light like there's no storm at all. I need that peacefulness, that rock-solid stability in my own life."

Jason turned back to Rachel. "Oh. I guess it's not very polite to talk about how much you like one woman when you're sitting there with another, huh?"

"No, it's all right. She's someone you could pray with. I understand."

"Hmph. Well, I'm glad one of us does. Rachel, I needed to tell you how I feel about Trieu." He took her chin in his hand and lifted it until she looked at him. "But now I need to tell you how I feel about you. Rachel, you. . .you are amazing, girl. First of all, with these other studs around here—not to mention all the other men in the world who would marry you in a heartbeat—I'm stunned that you're even interested in me. I mean, who am I compared to what other guys can offer you? I'm about as romantic as a blow fly, and I haven't had a successful relationship with a woman since my mom."

She smiled.

"Rachel, you are really good at what you do. And you're so smart it hurts. You think on your feet like nobody I've ever seen. And your mouth works just as fast."

She giggled. "Or faster."

"Maybe. Makes me wonder if you've got a little Latin blood flowing in that big Hebrew heart of yours. But the Lord knows we needed that this time. You more than carried your weight on this mission, just like last time. And your passion. . ." Now it was his turn to tear up. "When you ran out after Anei, I was so mad at you. I even had Trieu try to shoot you with her rifle. I mean, *I'm* the only one who's supposed to break out and do stupid things in a rush of passion, okay?"

They laughed together then—an easier, more meshed laughter than they'd shared since before Australia.

"But even though I was fit to be tied when you went off like that, I sure couldn't fault your heart. Believe it or not, my respect for you went up about ten notches when you did that. Of course, if I'd caught you, I'd have had to give you what-for. But I'm kind of glad I didn't catch you." He leaned forward. "Still, it was a stupid thing to do. You're lucky to be alive. Don't ever do anything like that again."

She smiled. "I cannot be Rambo."

"Good."

Rachel tucked her hair over and behind both ears in an uncharacteristically unsure gesture. "Jason, don't you think I'm pretty anymore?"

"Excuse me?"

"Have my looks already lost their power on you? You said Trieu was beautiful, but you've only talked about my mouth being faster than my brain and all the stupid stunts I've pulled and, let's see, am

I leaving out any of your other praises? But you haven't said if you find me, you know, attractive at all anymore."

Jason chuckled softly. "Rachel, that's baloney. You are quite easily the most beautiful woman I have ever had the privilege of calling my friend. But you've got to quit caring about that, remember? I was just trying to talk about, you know, your inner qualities, the things that make you beautiful when my eyes are closed."

Her forehead was furrowed. Jason didn't know what he'd said wrong. But then she picked up his hand and rubbed it against her cheek, her lips.

"Jason, don't let anyone sell you short. I think you're way more romantic than a blow fly."

"Okay," he said, "so now you know how I feel about you, too. I have strong feelings for Trieu, and I have strong feelings for you. I have to say that having two such amazing women as you both showing some level of interest in me is a lot more than this poor slob deserves, that's for sure."

"Poor baby."

"If your fathers were here, they'd tell you to dump me." He scratched his cheek. "I'm so glad there's no rule that says I have to pick one of you for all time, because I don't think I could."

"Careful, there, hero," Rachel said. "Trieu and I are not cars on the showroom floor that you can just choose between and drive away in. Who says we're waiting for you to choose one of us? And who says we'd be interested if you *did* try to choose one of us? There are other fish in the sea, in case you haven't noticed."

He held up his hands in surrender. "Okay, okay, I'm sorry. I didn't mean it that way. I'm just saying that. . . Well, I actually don't know what I'm saying. Do you?"

"Yes," she said, her anger instantly gone, "you're saying that you're a sweet man who has a lot of love but isn't ready to get married yet. Because when you're ready, you'll know who the right woman is." She winked at him. "Even if it's neither one of us."

"Whew," he said. "Thanks for making me sound noble."

From the other end of the tent came Garth's voice, holding his hand of cards in the air and hooting.

"Come on," Jason said, standing and offering his arm, "let's pretend to be doctors without borders and go check out the other patients."

"Why, Jason," Rachel said, taking his arm, "are you asking me to go play doctor?"

He felt his face redden. He sputtered and stammered.

"Relax," she said, resting her head against his shoulder, "I'm only teasing."

They passed the twenty patients—SPLA soldiers in various degrees of injury and consciousness—in their cots and arrived where Garth and Lewis played cards with a pretty French nurse and a very tall black man with a white bandage over his left eye.

Garth leaned back from the others and held his hand close to his chest. Then he palmed his card—he had only one left—and leaned toward the nurse. "Mademoiselle Angelique, do you have any fives?" He held up five fingers to the rebel soldier while looking at the black-haired nurse through half-lowered eyes. "Un, deux, trois, quartre, *cinque*."

The nurse clucked and drew out three fives and laid them on the cot. She launched a string of perturbed French Garth's way.

He laughed like a cad and placed his last card down on the nurse's three fives. "I'm out."

The black man took a colorful bead necklace from around his neck and pooled it in Garth's big hand.

"Thank you," he said, with only a hint of gloating in his voice.

Lewis wrote something on a piece of paper and handed it to Garth.

"Thank you." He turned to the nurse and smiled like he'd just snitched a fudge brownie from the jar. "Angelique?"

She stood beside him and stroked her fingers across his bald head. She leaned down and looked into his eyes, speaking softly and lifting her eyebrows saucily. She trailed a red fingernail along his cheek and walked away.

Garth looked to Rachel feverishly. "What'd she say?"

"She said, you big hunka man, that you'd have to wait until she got off duty to collect your prize from her. What'd you ask for?"

He shrugged and watched the nurse exit the tent. "I just wanted her to show me how the girls in Paris are kissing these days."

"Yeah," Lewis said peevishly, "and I really wanted that prize, too."

Jason sat beside Garth. "I've never heard of betting on Go Fish."

Rachel sat on Lewis's cot. "What did you have to give him, Lewis?"

"It's an IOU."

"For what?"

Lewis smiled despite obvious effort not to. "He wants me to teach him how to use computers and the Internet."

Jason and Rachel looked at Garth. "You don't know how to use computers or the Internet?"

He shrugged again. "So sue me. I. . .I had a bad experience when I was a kid, okay? Can you leave it alone now?"

Jason patted him on the shoulder. "I'm proud of you, big guy. It takes courage to admit you don't know how do to something that everyone else on the planet knows how to do."

"Oh, you're funny."

"Instead of getting that guy's beads, you should've gotten his E-mail address."

"Real funny, squidhead."

"Garth?" Rachel said, amazed. "Are you blushing? I never thought I'd live to see the day."

"Yeah, well, now you can die a complete woman, all right?" Garth's ears were bright red. "So now you know my dirty little secret. But I'm going to learn, and then Lewis is going to show me those online dating services and I'm going to have some fun then."

Rachel laughed. "Oh, silly, you don't need that. A big ol' stud like you. But you might want to learn E-mail so you can keep up with Angelique."

The flush extended across the top of his scalp, but he acted like nothing was happening. "Oh, baby. Rachel, did you just call me a stud? Come over here and sit on a wounded veteran's lap. You can be the USO for me, honey."

"Forget it," Rachel said. "You've got a hot babe in a tight uniform waiting for you, remember?"

The tent flap nearest Lewis's cot flipped open and Chris stepped through. "There you guys are."

"Hey, Chris," Jason said. "Join us."

"In a minute. Right now you might want to come on out. General Deng's just back from checking out the battlefield. Dhor brought him in the Land Rover."

"Oh, okay," Jason said.

Rachel swept past Chris without waiting for the others.

Chris jutted his chin toward Trieu's bunk. "How is she?"

"She'll be okay," Jason said. "Shoulder blade's fractured, but they got the bullet. I was afraid the thing had shredded up her insides."

"Yeah," Chris said, his voice catching, "me, too."

Jason stood up and turned to Garth and Lewis. "You guys coming?"

"Nah," Garth said, lifting his cast back on the cot. "I'll wait for the movie."

Lewis leaned back gingerly. "Me, too."

Jason and Chris stepped out into the SPLA camp. The sun might've gone down a few minutes before or it might've still been up, they couldn't tell. The rain had continued off and on throughout the afternoon. Right now it was off. Torches and lanterns and cooking fires appeared across the fenced area, smelling of onions and ghee cheese.

Before today, this area had been just another stretch of savannah next to an airstrip. But Deng had turned it into his field headquarters. Razor wire stretched across the grass connecting the seven sandbag circles—machine gun and antiaircraft nests—that guarded the two vehicle entrances and kept watch for zebras and MiGs.

Twelve green canvas tents were clustered together in the open space. The long white tent where the *Médecins Sans Frontières* personnel had their mobile hospital stood across the way. Dune buggies, motorcycles, and the occasional GOS jeep or tank were parked in more or less straight lines in the back. The rest of the space was open grass, but appeared to be where the SPLA soldiers were going to cook, eat, and sleep.

Deng set out a large map on a table, his officers standing around. He still wore his tan helmet with the long basset hound earflaps. He held his elongated pipe clenched in his teeth. Jason and Chris headed that way.

Halfway there, Chris elbowed him and pointed.

Jason saw Rachel walking over to where the black Land Rover was pulling up next to the first vehicle on the lot. The brake lights went off and the driver got out. It was Dhor. Rachel stepped up to him. Jason was about to turn away to listen to General Deng when he saw Rachel rear back and land a slap on Dhor's face so hard that Jason flinched from thirty yards away.

"Uh-oh."

They broke into a run toward her. Other soldiers had seen the slap and began gravitating that way, too. The rain began again.

Jason was ten feet away when little Rachel put her forearm against Dhor's chest and drove him into the Land Rover.

The rebels grumbled, and Jason doubled his speed.

He got to Rachel in time to grab the backhand that was coming next. She elbowed him viciously and cuffed Dhor again.

This time Dhor grabbed her wrist and held it tight.

The soldiers' grumbling turned to shouting, and Jason was jostled from behind. He pulled Rachel toward him while Chris had his back. But Dhor wasn't letting go.

Things were just about to get seriously out of control when the crowd parted and Deng approached.

"What is happening?" the general asked.

Rachel struggled against Jason with her free hand. "Let me go. Jason, he's the one! Dhor's the one who told the north where we were. That whole ambush was because of him. He's the traitor!"

"What?" Chris said. "It was the middleman."

"No!" Rachel said. "I heard the GOS officers say it was him! They said it was the Dhor who drove a Land Rover who told them we were Americans and where they could find us."

Jason kept his grip on Rachel's arm, but he turned his eyes on Dhor. "Is it true? Did you betray us, Dhor? Your Christian brothers and sisters?"

Dhor's fist shook with the effort of holding Rachel's arm. But his jaw was tight, and he did not answer.

"Friends," General Deng said disarmingly, coming to stand between Dhor and Rachel. "Let us all calm down. What Dhor has done can be explained. Please, let us get out of this accursed rain and I will make everything clear."

\* \* \*

"Dhor did not betray you," Deng said with his British accent. "He served the south of Sudan. He is still your Christian brother and a hero of whom a story dance shall be made. And yet, technically, he did betray you."

There were no chairs in Deng's command tent, so everyone stood around the large square table in the center. Deng, looking barely twenty without his helmet, and two of his officers stood along two sides of the table next to Dhor. Jason, Chris, Rachel, Garth—on crutches—and Lewis stood across from them. Three kerosene lamps hung from the diagonal roof supports, moths fluttering around them hungrily. A map of the area around Akwer Nhom lay on the table. Rain pattered on the tent roof in a soothing drone. Jason could smell the sweet tang of Deng's pipe tobacco.

He brought his sleeve up to wipe the rain from his face. "You're going to have to go over that again, general."

Deng smiled. "You see, for years we have fought the GOS on their terms. Every dry season they come, and we go out to fight them.

They come to clear their oil fields, and we arise in response. They raid a village, and we race to protect our people, but quite often we arrive too late. We are continually reacting and defending. That is no way to win a war, gentlemen, as I'm sure you are aware.

"If only we could know when and where they were going to be, then we could crush them. Yes, they have superior equipment, but the difference is not paralyzing. For every one of their tanks, we have five RPGs. For every one of their jets, we have five thousand brave men. With what we have captured for ourselves and what we have purchased or. . .received. . .from other sources, we knew we had enough to strike a killing blow. All we lacked, you see, was the where and the when."

He spread his arms to them like a king in a generous mood. "And then, *you* came to us. From where? We do not know precisely. Why? We do not know. Not to dig wells, I am quite sure. On whose side? Ah, that became evident. Never in the history of Africa's longest-running civil war has the north suffered such defeat as you have given them these weeks you have been on our soil.

"I remember sitting in this tent in another place such as this looking at the map showing your attacks. I was astounded." He laughed brightly. " 'What courage these Westerners have!' I said. 'Can there be only six of them on three tiny vehicles? What cheek, what impudence! To strike the oil pipeline so that it does not pump for twelve days! To slash the tires of the bombers! To destroy the railroad bridge! Why have we not been so bold as this?' I asked myself. That is what you have given me, my friends: You have given me the vision that it can be done. You helped me see that the north could be beaten—if only one had the insolence to attack.

"A plan began to form in my mind. A plan of such daring and foolhardiness that I believed it could actually work. And so it has! But I get ahead of myself. I determined to set a snare for the north. If somehow I could gather them in one place, I could strike them with all my brigades and crush them! But of course I needed to bait the trap. I wondered what these audacious Westerners would use to bait such a trap.

And then," he said, his hands rolling forward as if displaying a velvet robe, "I knew."

Jason folded his arms. "Us. We were the bait."

"Of course!" Deng said. "It was the very thing. By then rumor of your presence had reached the ears of Khartoum. Though you were very careful, I'm sure, it would be clear to an infant that something had changed in the south of Sudan. Word that it was Westerners—American soldiers, to be precise—who had done this reached the desk of the military command in Khartoum just as it reached my own. If it were I, I would be furious at the humiliation done to me. I would be searching with all my energy to find these irksome American soldiers and crush them under my boot. And so," he said as if revealing the answer to an unsolvable riddle, "we used you as our bait."

"Oh, man," Lewis said. "Am I hearing this guy right? Jason, is he saying what I think he's saying?"

"Yes, Lewis," Jason said. "Let him finish." He looked over at Rachel, who was staring at the map emotionlessly.

"When word came to me that the north was offering cash for informants about these Americans, I knew my plan would work." Deng put his hand on Dhor's shoulder. "I ordered Dhor to go to the GOS officials, posing as a traitor to you and the SPLA, and tell them that the Americans could be found in Akwer Nhom."

Jason and his team looked at Dhor. His round face twitched, but otherwise he was still.

"He did not want to do it," Deng said, staring at Rachel. "Do you hear me, young lady? Dhor said, 'Send someone else.' But I could not, you see. Because Dhor has an honest face, does he not? He felt wrong to betray you, so there was real shame in his eyes when he did it. He was quite believable."

Jason saw Dhor's eyes meet Rachel's. When they did, a tear trickled down Dhor's cheek.

"When Dhor returned," Deng said, "he would not accept the reward I had promised him, and he would not speak to me."

Rachel went to Dhor and gave him a hug. "I'm so sorry," she said, stroking his face.

He held her as if she were his daughter. "Forgive me?"

"Yes, Dhor. Yes." She hugged him roughly. "I forgive you. I release you from your bondage. Be loosed, my brother, you are forgiven."

"Dhor will be a national hero," Deng said, "when the south is sovereign and free. It is true, and he knew it very well, that his action could cost you your lives. We were all saddened by this. Who else has helped us so much? Who else has shown us that our enemy can be cast down after all? And yet if by risking your lives we could win such a victory and save so many thousands, perhaps millions, of lives in the south, we felt it must be done, however regrettable it might be."

Jason looked at Garth, Chris, and Lewis. Garth was nodding slowly. Chris's jaw bunched and released. Lewis's eyebrows seemed to have gotten hung half an inch above their usual position.

"I can't believe it," Lewis said. "We come here to help them, we stay longer and risk our lives to do what *they* should've been doing, and they thank us by throwing us into the lions' den?" He glared at Deng. "You tried to kill us! Or you didn't care if we died—what's the difference?—so long as you got your trap baited. What is that, some kind of African thank-you?"

Jason put a hand on Lewis's back. "Okay, bro," he said softly. "Stand down."

Deng's face was stern. "It is unfortunate that the situation required such measures. But it appears that it is quite true what the Dinka of Akwer Nhom told me about you."

"What's that?" Jason asked.

"That the Christian God favors you. Whatever you touch improves. Wherever you go, people gain hope. And whatever danger you enter, you emerge from safely."

"Safely?" Chris said. "General, maybe you haven't noticed these crutches or our cuts and bandages—or our other teammate unconscious in the hospital over there."

Deng waved his hand in an arc. "You will all recover. Three months from now, you will be as good as new. Then you will return here. I already have splendid plans to send you to Khartoum on a special mission."

"Uh. . .no," Jason said. "Sorry, General, but we are leaving in the morning when the TrackMark plane arrives. We have no plans to return to Sudan."

"But I think you will like this plan. It is *impudent.*"

"No doubt. But you're going to have to send your own people. We're not part of your army, sir. We may all be well in three months, by the grace of God; but when we are, we'll be headed elsewhere."

Deng's shoulders sagged. "It is a pity."

Garth pointed at the map. "Show me what happened in the battle, General. We knew there were at least three brigades headed toward the village. Were you right behind them, then?"

"Ah, yes," Deng said, brightening. He took a pen from his pocket and used it to point on the map. "Akwer Nhom is here in this valley. The GOS came from here, here, and here. They took up positions on the east and west of the village—here and here—while tank, infantry, and cavalry elements flooded the valley. As soon as my scouts radioed that the GOS forces had passed their position, I ordered my forces to envelop."

Deng clicked his pen and smiled. "It was marvelous. They never suspected. They were so focused inward and so accustomed to moving without opposition that they paid no heed to anything else. My lead units attacking from the east reported that the GOS hadn't even put up pickets at the perimeter. We destroyed them in place, then swept over and poured our rockets into the valley where the tanks were sitting blind and still."

"You said there were no pickets on the east," Garth said. "Were there any on the west? Is that why you met resistance there?"

Deng grimaced. "Quite so. They were surprised by our assault, to be sure, but we were noticed. We hit them hard, but they were able to wheel and engage us. Our forces from the east came across the valley to engage, too; but by then the tanks had destroyed my fifty-seventh, third, and twenty-second companies and burst out of containment. They turned south, seeking to outflank us, and we rushed to move our line. That, I believe, is when you were caught in the middle."

They were silent in the command tent, staring at the map or into space. Moths *tinked* against the glass lantern cowlings and fluttered frantically around the light. Outside the rain continued to fall. They heard splatters and drips from a steady stream of runoff.

In his mind, Jason was back on the battlefield, lying on his back. He saw the soldier chopping down with his sword. Then he saw a tank's massive treads and gears rolling inches from his legs. He saw horses falling, their eyes wide with fear. He saw Trieu spinning and falling. His ears were full of the racket of war. He saw the helicopter gunships rising over the hillside—and the pilot pointing at Jason, like Death itself singling him out.

He shook his head quickly and looked up at Deng. "We didn't know it was you riding after us on the horses."

Deng chuckled. "Yes, my command jeep was struck by a tank shell. Fortunately I was not in it at the time. But the battle was moving quickly, and I needed to get around to see and give orders." He rubbed the side of his nose. "Many horses had become available, so we appropriated some for our use. My people are not known for being riders," he said, his lips twisting into a frown. "I believe I will not sit down for five days! However, I found it most useful at the time. The horse was far more mobile over that kind of terrain than my jeep. Perhaps I will be like your Civil War generals and command from the back of a horse from now on."

Jason nodded. "But why were you riding out to us? We almost shot you."

"How well I know it. We were only coming to give you assistance if you needed it and to tell you the battle had ended."

"Except it hadn't ended," Lewis said. "There were those big

attack helicopters."

"Yes," Deng said, "and for you I am glad we came so fast on those horses. Perhaps we would not be here having this talk if we had not."

Chris sighed. "No kidding."

"General," Jason said, "we do want to thank you again for arriving when you did. We're glad that we didn't have to shoot at you, we're glad you were friends instead of enemies, and we're especially glad for what you did to those gunships. Where did you get those surface-to-air missiles, anyway?"

"Ah," Deng said, one eyebrow rising, "we are not altogether without friends, you know. Three fewer Hind helicopters, two fewer Antonovs, and one fewer MiG-29 harass us from the skies today, thanks to Stinger missiles built by. . .by Americans, I believe."

Over the sounds of the deluge, they heard vehicles passing nearer, sloshing in the mud. Men spoke in greeting and instruction. A bedraggled soldier poked his head into the command tent and said something to Deng in Dinka.

"Ah," Deng said to the Firebrand team. "Come see what my men have found. I think you will be interested."

It was fully dark outside, made darker still by the overcast sky. Through rain-streaked beams of headlights, Jason could see that three troop transport trucks had pulled up and were idling in the muddy path in front of the tents. Soldiers hopped down and helped others, some wounded, off the trucks. Doctors and nurses from the hospital hurried out to help. It looked like a scene from *M\*A\*S\*H*. Two more sets of headlights, placed more closely together, came up from behind.

"Our ATVs!" Chris said, splashing out toward them.

Jason went with him, the rain soaking his hair and sliding down his scalp.

Each ATV had one rider and one passenger, and each passenger carried something heavy. Chris went to one four-wheeler and Jason went to the other. The riders got off reluctantly. Dhor came up and spoke to them.

"Look," Chris said, bringing something heavy into the light of his ATV.

It was the speaker and microphone assembly from the bridge.

"And lookee what I found," Jason said, bringing his load into the headlights.

"Sweet!" Chris said.

Dhor explained to them where the riders had found the stuff.

"Oh, Lewis," Jason called, walking toward the command tent, carrying something.

Lewis did a beautiful double take. "Chunky!"

Jason handed over the little wheeled robot. "They found it plugging along about ten miles south of the battlefield coming up out of a ravine dripping wet."

"That's my Chunky!" Lewis said, actually hugging the thing. "Totally autonomous. I told you he'd survive."

Jason heard a small voice call his name. He looked in the direction of the middle truck. "Anei?"

The girl sat in the back of the troop transport sharing a sopping blanket with Lual.

"Come on," Jason said, lifting her down and helping her father off the truck. "Let's get you guys inside. Are you hurt?"

Rachel ran up and grabbed Anei in a fierce hug. "Anei! Lual!"

They spoke together in Dinka and Arabic all the way to a vacant tent. Jason found a lamp and matches and set the lit lantern on the floor of the canvas tent. The four of them sat on the floor.

Rachel turned to him. "They came to find us! They got to the hideout just fine. Most of the villagers made it, and I think all the cattle and goats. They're going to survive another day." The lantern lit her face from underneath, her cheeks casting curved shadows over her eyes. "When they got the others to the hideout, Anei and Lual wanted to see about us. They went to the battlefield and came upon SPLA troops in dune buggies and motorcycles. Those men told them that they'd heard some reports of some Westerners out in the middle of it. They said they saw the helicopters explode. After we went off on the horses, they convinced these guys to bring them here to us."

Jason stared at Lual, looking stoic and ancient as he sat cross-legged beside the lantern. The scars across his scalp covered his head in a triangular shadow and yet lit the sides of his head perfectly. It was an eerie, powerful image.

"Did they come out to beat us up for destroying their village and bringing all this suffering upon them?"

"I don't think so," Rachel said, "but I'll ask."

Anei answered first. Rachel translated.

"We would never seek to harm you. We came to help you. And to thank you, if we could. On the day my village was attacked, I watched while my brother Mabior was thrown into a burning tukul and killed. I should have tried to save him, but I didn't. I promised myself that one day I would avenge him. Wa tells me that revenge is wrong. I will try to learn. And I do pray for my enemies. But when you came, hurting the Jellabah who hurt my people—who killed my brother, my sister, and my mother—I believed I was getting my revenge. The world was put right."

Anei smiled softly at Jason. "Thank you," she said in English.

Jason's chest shuddered. He nodded.

Then Lual answered gravely, in succinct phrases to allow Rachel to translate.

"Every year we suffer. The Dinka of south Sudan. When our people first were created by the gods—by Christian God, I mean—we were alone. We ruled all Dinkaland and beyond. All *was* Dinkaland. We were always at war with the Nuer. But we always made peace. Then came the Arab. The Baggara, the Masariyyah, the Rizayqat, the Zaghawah, the Egyptian. They came with guns and horses. They ended our freedom, ended our peace, and made us slaves. The elephant disappeared. The lion and impala and zebra. Then the British came, and things were better. But they left and war began and continues. Slavery has returned. Still, we remember what it is to be free.

You helped us remember. You helped the Dinka learn to survive and prevail. One day we will rule Dinkaland again."

Lual brought Anei into his lap, and his face disappeared in shadow. "I have lost my wife. I have lost all my children but Anei. Our village is ruined. Now, because of what you have done, the SPLA has become bold. And because of what *they* have done, the Dinka will suffer more. Our mothers and sisters and brothers and sons in slavery, many of them will be beaten and killed as revenge for today. And next dry season, the raiders will come back.

"And yet. . . ," Lual said, leaning forward so that just the dome of his head shone in the lantern. His eyes glinted like black moons. "And yet, I would not have it made different. The Dinka suffer every year. This is true. So, if it is to be the will of God that we are to suffer anyway, better to suffer because we have hurt them."

He clasped Jason's hand in both of his. "Thank you for coming, my friend. Thank you for giving me my daughter. Thank you for showing me that the Ahmeds of Sudan may be conquered. And thank you for bringing the light of Christ to our beloved and barren land."

# EPILOGUE

THE PIGEONS outnumbered the humans, but all of them were free.

The steps of the Lincoln Memorial were speckled with visitors, human and avian, gathered for a day in the sun and a chance to see the big guy. The lawn around the reflecting pool, too, was crowded. But here at least the Firebrand team had a little elbow room.

The six of them, along with Eloise Webster and Doug and Jamie Bigelow, sat on a blue gingham blanket finishing up a bucket of fried chicken. Butch, Garth's hound dog, hadn't been invited to DC this time. Jason sat next to Trieu, who was sitting up carefully.

A column of metal scaffolding called an external fixator enclosed Garth's leg. It looked like he'd gotten his leg stuck in a Gatling gun and managed to rip himself free, but the barrel had come with him. His surgery had gone well; and, with the help of the ex-fix, the doctors were predicting 100 percent recovery in about eight weeks. Trieu's scapula fracture, too, wasn't expected to keep her out of action any longer than that.

"You know," Lewis said, wiping mashed potatoes from his mouth and looking at the white monument, "I still think it looks like a penny. Look, there's even the hint of the statue in the shade there in the middle."

"Uh, Lewis. . . ," Chris said, looking up from his chicken.

"I know," Lewis said, "it *is* from the penny. But still, it just, I don't know, really looks like the penny. Except it's white and not bronze."

Eloise put her Diet Coke down. "Son, you do know they made this first and they imprinted the pennies later?"

Lewis's eyes widened briefly, but then he shrugged. "Duh."

Garth leaned on his elbow. "Hey, who'll be kind to a man wearing a birdcage on his leg and give him another piece of white meat?"

"I will," Bigelow said, rolling his wheelchair to the red and white bucket. "But you gotta work for it, dogface." He set the chicken on a napkin a good five feet from Garth.

"What?" Garth said.

"It's called physical therapy. Right, hon?" Bigelow said to Jamie, sitting beside him.

"The trick to PT," Jamie said, shooing her blond bangs from her eyes, "is knowing where the line is between challenge and cruelty."

"Well," Rachel said, lying on her stomach on the blanket, "which is this?"

"Is it possible," Garth said, grabbing a fistful of blanket and drawing the bucket toward him, "for something to be a challenge to some. . ." He grabbed a drumstick. "And at the same time cruelty to others?" He pegged Bigelow in the head with a packet of ketchup.

"I'd go easy on the fried chicken, Garth," Jason said.

"Yeah, why?"

"Well, just because I've never seen so much throwing up as we've seen and done and caused in Sudan. Might want to be careful what you eat."

Garth answered by taking a huge bite out of his chicken leg. "Mmm-mmm!"

"Come on," Chris said, standing and picking up a football, "who's up for catch?"

"You got it!" Lewis said, standing.

"Watch your ribs now," Chris said.

"Hey, jarhead, I know what I'm doing."

Chris beaned Lewis with the ball. "You have to be in the service to call me *jarhead*, fanboy."

"Hey," Lewis said, smoothing his newly gelled coiffure, "watch the hair."

Rachel jumped to her feet. "I'm in. Come on, Jamie, let's take 'em."

"Really, Rachel?" Chris said. "You're going to leave Jason alone with Trieu? Aren't you afraid they're going to start going after each other on the blanket as soon as you leave?"

Rachel closed her eyes and lifted her chin. "I'm above all that now, Christopher." Then she opened her eyes and ran toward him. "But I'm not above kicking a white boy's behind."

Chris ran, his tail end just vacating the spot Rachel's foot now occupied.

"Hey," Bigelow said, "I wanna play, too."

"Tough," Garth said, clanging his ex-fix into the wheelchair as he rose. "It's too much of a *challenge* for you, squiddy."

"Oh, yeah?" Bigelow said. "Come on, baldy, let's you and me show 'em what a couple of old cripples can do on the gridiron."

Chris tossed the football to Jason. "Come on, chief," he said. "Throw me one long."

Jason tossed him the ball. "In a minute."

The six of them ran, rolled, or hobbled across the lawn and began tossing the football. Chris was a superstud, looking like a collegiate quarterback, while Lewis played his young protégé, superdud.

"Go on, young man," Eloise said to Jason. She was wearing a pale blue sundress and a yellow tennis visor. "Me and Trieu'll keep each other company."

"I will in a minute, ma'am."

Jason looked at Trieu. She was wearing a blue tank top and matching shorts. He could just see the clear tape of her bandage beneath the armhole on her right shoulder.

"How are you feeling?" he asked.

She smiled evenly. "I feel fine, though I fear I am a better doctor than patient."

"Girl," Eloise said, "I told you to make somebody else carry that stuff. You better start taking care of yourself, or I'll have you tied up so you don't move it, you hear me?"

Trieu smiled. "I hear you."

"Now there you go, Eloise," Jason said, "talking about putting a woman of color in bondage right here on the steps of the Lincoln Memorial. I thought you brought us here to celebrate the end of slavery."

"Oh," Eloise said, smiling, "you know I'm only teasing." She sighed deeply. "You do not know how happy I am that you all made it home. I know our girl here got hurt and Garth's got a hitch in his getalong, but you'll all be all right. I don't believe my widow's prayer group and I have *ever* prayed this hard about anything. Praise God, you people are all right." She wagged a finger at Jason. "Next time you want to stay longer than we planned, and the next time I think it's a good idea, the answer to both of us is *No!* Got it?"

"Got it."

"And I want you wearing body armor next time."

Jason shook his head. "It's so heavy. You don't want us loaded down with all that plus everything else—especially since it won't actually stop a rifle bullet unless you've got the ceramic plates in, and those only work once, since they break on impact."

Eloise held up a finger. "We're going to look at it for next time. End of discussion. If Trieu had been wearing it, she wouldn't have been injured. Besides," she said, wagging her head, "I know a few folks, if you haven't noticed. We'll get the best and the lightest for you."

Jason sighed. "Okay, we'll look at it." He took a drink of Coke. "Well, what about it, Eloise? Did you get your money's worth out of our trip? Did we do everything in Sudan you wanted to have done?"

"Did you do everything? Sugar, did you ever. You did it all and then some, my brother. You know, when I formed this team, I told myself that it would be a failure if I ever read in the newspaper about something they did. So you can imagine my consternation, child, when I heard about it on CNN." She shook her head and her short black hair glistened in the sun. "No, sir, that was too much. Too much, too long, and too close. But I will say," she said, leaning toward them, "that it did give me great satisfaction knowing that something you and I did hurt slavers that much. Yes, sir. That was fun indeed."

Trieu began picking up the trash she could reach. "You told us when we signed on to this team that we would be far away from the front lines, that we would be going after targets that would not require us to use our weapons even once. Do you remember?"

"I know it, Trieu," Eloise said, holding a garbage bag open for the trash. "And I do apologize. Again, this mission was more than I ever planned. No more like that, deal?"

"Deal."

"Now, Jason," Eloise said, "I want to ask you something."

"Go ahead."

"When you were beating the tar out of that fool slave owner. . ." Eloise paused and her eyes grew distant. "What was it like? Did it feel as good to you as I think it would feel to me?"

A lump formed in Jason's gut. It had been there off and on since that night. He'd been too busy—first carrying out his crusade and then trying to stay alive—to give it any attention. But now it had no competition. His stomach was suddenly more sour than the fried chicken grease alone could account for.

"When I was doing it, ma'am," he said, staring down the National Mall, "it felt wonderful. It was as if all the fury I've felt since I ever heard about child predators—not just those in Sudan, either, not by a long shot—got balled up into one giant bomb that just exploded when I came face-to-face with Ahmed. Garth and Chris say they're going to quit following me as team leader if I keep being a loose cannon like that on every mission, and I can't blame them. But I don't know if anything but God could've kept me off of that guy. I was. . ." He took a long breath and blew it out carefully. "I was out of control."

Trieu touched his shoulder soothingly.

"Every punch or kick or elbow was like a blow for freedom and for justice and for. . .well, for revenge, I guess," he said. "But doesn't the Bible say something about not taking our own revenge but leaving room for God to do it up right?"

Eloise tilted her head, as if to say, *Yeah, but. . .*

"So, in the middle of it," Jason said, "it felt awesome, like this huge release of years of anger that finally found a way out. You always hear about little children getting taken and hurt, and it's always somewhere else, you know? No matter how much I hurt or pray or search, I'm never within reach of it. It's on TV or in another state or in the hands of the police. But here, right there in front of me, was one of those guys. It's like in that moment he became *the guy*, the representative of all the pedophiles and slavers and predators that have ever lived. And he was right in front of me. So, yeah, when I got the chance to beat the crud out of him, I took it. And ooh, baby, it felt good."

"I knew it," Eloise said. "I knew it."

"But afterwards, Eloise. . .afterwards, I started thinking about it. I started seeing this poor slob on the ground having been beaten to a pulp by me, and I started wondering, 'What am I doing?' When I was in it, it didn't slow me down one bit. But afterward it hit me: I'm using superior strength to beat down another human being. It didn't matter to me that he was defenseless. The rage in me burned no matter what. My hatred was so strong that I. . .I would've killed that man if they'd hadn't stopped me.

"So how was I any better than him, Eloise? I was mad at him for using his superior strength to crush someone weaker, but that's exactly what I was doing to him! In that moment, I had become him. I had stooped to his level. Sure it felt good to give him a taste of his own medicine, but. . ." He sighed. "I don't know. Maybe everything we did over there was nothing but revenge, pure and simple. Maybe we said we were there in the name of Christ, but I wonder if we really were there in the name of pure human retribution."

He folded his legs under him. "The worst part is that I don't feel any better. It didn't last, you know? When I think of those poor babies. . .nothing's changed. They're still gone. What was done to them was still done. Their families still have gaping holes in their chests. And I'm still angry. In the end, even though I did what I did and even though all of us did our little crusade, nothing can ever bring those little girls back. And tomorrow or next week or next month, someone else will prey on another little girl, and nothing I did will have made one bit of difference."

The three of them sat there silently, watching the team throw the football and tourists strolling around the reflecting pool. Sparrows landed and pecked at bread crumbs. Bees buzzed over the remains of the chicken. The day was turning hot.

"I think you're wrong, Jason," Trieu said. "I can't believe that everything we did there was about hatred and vengeance. I can't believe that what we did made no difference. Look at the people who were saved—in both senses of the word—because we were there. Look at the light we shared in a dark place. Look at the families restored and the faith built. I think God began something wonderful there because we went." She shrugged. "Did we cross the line a few times? Perhaps. But I will not believe that all of it was the result of human anger."

"I'll add one more thing to Trieu's list," Eloise said. "That poor boy, Jok, who lost his nose. If you hadn't been there, that baby would probably have died. I hadn't told you yet, but I'm having that boy flown to a specialist here in the States for reconstructive surgery. And if we can't find his family after that, I'm gonna make sure he gets adopted here." She pointed at Jason's face. "Don't tell me you going there was a waste of time or all about man's goals and none of God's. Hear?"

One side of Jason's face smiled. Then the other side caught up. "Yes, ma'am."

Eloise gathered them both in a maternal squeeze. "I love y'all, you know that? Your whole crazy bunch. I'm so glad you're safe and I'm so, so, *so* proud of what you've done." She got to her feet. "Next time I'll send you someplace safer."

"Ha," Jason said. "I don't believe it for a minute."

"Well," she said, picking up the rest of the trash, "it sounds good, doesn't it? Now, you two hold the blanket down while I go throw this food away in that barrel."

Jason watched her walk away. He turned to Trieu. It felt right, somehow, being alone with Trieu. He had a brief flash of sitting out here not with a bunch of adult friends but with his and Trieu's children running on the grass playing. He shook his head abruptly. Where had that come from?

"What?" Trieu said, looking at him with those soft eyes.

He licked his lips. "Oh, nothing. Trieu, I. . .I'm so glad you're okay. I don't think I'll ever forget seeing you get shot. It was horrible. Your body spun around and you fell. I wanted to be right there to catch you and get you somewhere safe. I didn't even want you to hit the ground. I wanted the bullet to have hit me instead."

She reached toward his face, then stopped, glancing toward the others. Jason saw Rachel observe the moment. *Oh, great.* But then Rachel smiled and waved to them and went back to football.

Trieu tilted her head back and parted her lips. "You are like our Father, Jason. You don't want any of your children to be harmed."

He shook his head. "No, Trieu, it's not only that. Not with you." His chest felt constricted. "I don't. . .I never know how to talk about this. I mean, you know that I have feelings for Rachel."

"I know." Her hand was back at her side.

He picked it up. "But I have strong feelings for you, too. It's. . .I was. . .I was so worried about you." He winced. "I know you probably have no sympathy for a guy like me sharing my affections for two women. But—"

Trieu put her fingers to his mouth. "Do not speak of it." She smiled sadly. "Jason, I learned a long time ago what it sounds like Rachel learned on this trip: to let go. If God has a future for you and Rachel, it will become clear, it will come to you. And if," she said, her eyes clicking on to his, "there is a future for you and me, that will come to us, too."

Jason nodded, feeling his stomach relax.

"You are a loving and passionate man, Jason. It is as if all of us are propelled by your passion. God has placed you here as His man, His choice, to lead us with that passion. Now," she said, leaning away, "Eloise is coming. Get out there and play football."

He kissed her on the cheek. "Thank you, Trieu. I'm so glad we are friends."

Then he ran down and played some football.

High overhead the sun shone down on them, giving light and heat. Too much to some, too little to others. On the evil and the good, the slave and the free. Because the sun does not rise differently when it is to be a day of death. But it does always rise.

Would you like to offer feedback on this novel?

Interested in starting a book discussion group?

# AUTHOR BIO

Jefferson Scott has written several thriller novels, including *Operation: Firebrand, Fatal Defect,* and *Terminal Logic.* A graduate of both seminary and film school, he currently lives in the Pacific Northwest, where he writes full-time. Visit the author's website at www.jeffersonscott.com.

# ALSO FROM
# BARBOUR PUBLISHING

*Operation: Firebrand* by Jefferson Scott
ISBN 1-58660-586-0

Former navy SEAL Jason Kromer is appointed leader
of Operation: Firebrand, a covert operations team
specializing in nonlethal missions of mercy. Its first
challenge: a winter rescue of orphaned children
made homeless by Russian rebels.

*Time Lottery* by Nancy Moser
ISBN 1-58660-587-9

After twenty-two years of scientific research, three
lucky individuals will receive the opportunity of a
lifetime with the Time Lottery—to relive one decisive
moment that could change the course of their lives.

*Face Value* by Andrew Snaden and Rosey Dow
ISBN 1-58660-589-5

Just days after Beth Martin's long-awaited facelift
operation, she is found dead—and her cosmetic
surgeon, Dr. Dan Foster, finds himself playing
amateur detective after being framed for the killing.

*Interview with the Devil* by Clay Jacobsen
ISBN 1-58660-588-7

Journalist Mark Taylor has landed the story of his career—
an interview with the coldhearted leader of a new terrorist
network. Mark is taken hostage, tortured, and beaten.
Now this Christian's only hope lies in God's sovereign
hands—and in the heart of the terrorist's nephew, a
devout Muslim man Mark befriended during the Gulf War.

## Available wherever books are sold.